Hardhearted:

It's Better to Be Feared Than Loved

Beating the Odds 2

Hardhearted:

It's Better to Be Feared Than Loved

Beating the Odds 2

Sherrod Tunstall

www.urbanbooks.net

Urban Books, LLC
300 Farmingdale Road, NY-Route 109
Farmingdale, NY 11735

ISBN 13: 978-1-64556-107-1
ISBN 10: 1-64556-107-0

First Trade Paperback Printing September 2020
Printed in the United States of America

10 9 8 7 6 5 4 3 2 1

This is a work of fiction. Any references or similarities to actual events, real people, living or dead, or to real locales are intended to give the novel a sense of reality. Any similarity in other names, characters, places, and incidents is entirely coincidental.

Distributed by Kensington Publishing Corp.
Submit Orders to:
Customer Service
400 Hahn Road
Westminster, MD 21157-4627
Phone: 1-800-733-3000
Fax: 1-800-659-2436

Hardhearted:

It's Better to Be Feared Than Loved

Beating the Odds 2

by

Sherrod Tunstall

Dedication

This book is dedicated to the memory of my former label mate and author of *What the Streets Made Me*, Jada Dior. Sis, you were the true meaning of a hustler. You were not only an inspiration to me but also to the entire book industry. I'm so sorry that your time on this earth was cut short. You had so much to offer the world. Even though we never physically met, I loved the fire you had and your passion for being great. That made me want to push even harder in my career. I'm praying for your children and your family. Rest in paradise, Jada. Love you, sis.

Acknowledgments

First off, I have to thank my Lord and Savior, Jesus Christ. Lord, this is the hardest and longest book I've written to date. It took me two and a half years to write this novel. I went through so much depression, happiness, laziness, sad times, and so on while writing this book. But you got me through it. Thank you for still giving me great ideas to write these stories.

Lola, Mama, my true ride or die. Thank you for believing in me and having my back, no matter what.
Love you,
Your Baby

Brenda Hampton,
My literary angel/agent. Thank you for always giving me literary advice and breaking down the industry for me. Thank you, and I love you. May God bless you.

I have to say thank you to the entire Tunstall, Isabelle, Wilson, Johnson, Manuel, and Lowe families.

And to Carl and Martha Weber, and the entire Urban Family Staff, thank you for taking another chance on me.
For all my readers out there, I thank you all for rocking with me, and I won't stop writing!
If you want to contact me with any questions or feedback, email me at sherrodt05@yahoo.com,

Acknowledgments

Twitter: Sherroddaauthor,

FB: Sherrod The Author,

IG: Sherroddaauthor.

My website is coming soon.

Also By Sherrod Tunstall

Beating the Odds (Book 1)

You Now Have Entered the World of . . .

Living for the City (Chapters 1–6)

Previously on *Beating the Odds*

Paco, his boys, Brad, Swag, Tyler, and Travis, were in the private prison dining area, enjoying the perks of being in Paco's crew. They were having a good meal of fried chicken wings, collard greens, T-bone steaks, fried rice, baked potatoes, cupcakes from Diamond's Bakery, and all of the beer they wanted.

As the fellas were eating like kings, they noticed Brad slowly licking a chocolate cupcake with pink frosting and sprinkles. Brad knew that those delicious cupcakes were from the bakery where Diamond worked, or in Brad's mind, where she was *forced* to work. He imagined Diamond's beautifully manicured hands making cupcakes and mixing up the batter. In his mind, he was having a freaky vision of her in a Victoria's Secret bra and panty set. Her body was shaped like model Chanel Iman with a Nicki Minaj booty. He could picture her working in a hot, steamy kitchen with sweat dripping all down her sexy body as she was taking cupcakes out of the hot oven. He could imagine watching her frost every cupcake. Brad pretended that his fingers were hers as he licked them passionately.

The fellas were laughing at him because they knew what was wrong with Brad. Being in prison for weeks without any women around was hard on any man, and they jacked off at night. But Brad had gone too far, and he was looking like a desperate fool. Tyler threw a chicken wing at him, knocking him out of his daydream. He looked over at his boys, who were laughing up a storm.

"Damn, playa," Swag said, laughing.

"He workin' 'em fingers," said Paco. "Who's clit you imaginin' you eatin' out?"

They continued to laugh, and Brad gave them all the finger.

As they continued eating like kings, Paco cleared his throat. His crew knew when he did that, it was time to get down to business.

"Well, everyone, I have some bad news and good news," Paco said.

Everyone was silent.

"The bad news is we ain't getting out of here because my father only wanted me released, but I said, hell naw. I'm loyal to the damn end. So, I'm officially cut off from the Hernandez Cartel."

The fellas didn't say a word. They were stunned that their boy had risked his freedom, wealth, and family to be in a shit hole with them. To them, that was true friendship.

"The good news is I've been making contacts, and I'm now hooked up with a very powerful Costa Rican mob boss. We been talking business for years, and I'm thinking of joining that squad. The plan is to bring my father's piece-of-shit organization down and make the streets of Houston and Mexico mine, with you all as equal partners."

All the fellas clapped, including Swag, Tyler, and Travis, who really didn't give a shit about anything anymore except getting the hell out of Brazil by any means necessary. Brad felt the same way, but he had to find out what was up with Diamond.

"Shh!" Paco said. "Calm that shit down 'fore y'all wake up the whole damn prison."

The fellas silenced themselves again.

"But, Paco, if they gon' make us full partners, how we gon' do it from in here and they in Costa Rica?" Brad asked.

"Homies, if you just shut the hell up, I can tell you the rest of the story," Paco said sarcastically.

"Yeah, I know this cat in Costa Rica, and the boss is going to take real good care of us. We all gon' make more money than we ever dreamed of. We can kick it in Costa Rica for a few years until I can build my own dynasty and bring my father's down. Then, Houston can be ours for the taking."

Swag, Tyler, Travis, and Paco's boys were saying, "Hell yeah! Anything to get out of this hellhole."

Brad couldn't believe how his cousin and his boys were acting. He was greatly disappointed. They kept making the same mistake over and over again. And even though Brad had agreed to go along with the plan, he didn't want to. There was nothing to be happy about. He just wanted out, and he didn't give a damn about running the streets with men like Paco. And shame on the others for wanting to be down with him.

"Yo, B, you wit' us or what, bro?" Paco asked.

Brad pretended as if he didn't hear him. "What you say, man?"

"You down wit' us or what?" Paco smiled.

"Yeah, I'm down for whatever."

"Cool, gentlemen. In a few short days, we will be free and very rich men." Paco raised his cup. "To the future."

"To the future," everyone toasted, raising their cups.

Goodbye, fellas, Brad thought while taking a sip of his drink. *I'm so glad this is almost over.*

In prison that night, Paco held a little party for all of the inmates in the cell with jerk chicken, barbeque ribs, corn on the cob, white rice, and cake. No one, not even the faculty at the prison, questioned Paco about having the party. Since he was an ex-member of the Hernandez Cartel, he still had money everywhere, and with money, people always respected him. He had the power, no doubt. All of the prisoners ate like they never had food before. Hell, they hadn't had good food like that in a minute. One prisoner said, "This feast is even better than sex and Christmas combined."

All of the inmates laughed.

Paco watched as everyone was enjoying the food. *Eat up, 'cause it will be your last meal.*

As everyone was enjoying their meal, the officer brought a big orange water dispenser, which contained red Kool-Aid. Each prisoner grabbed a cup, but Paco warned his crew, Brad, Swag, Tyler, and Travis, not to drink it unless they wanted to meet their maker sooner than later. Paco proposed a toast to life and blessings, but in his mind, the real toast he wanted to say was, *Fuck you all and good luck in hell.*

All the prisoners ate and drank until it got quiet . . . and quieter. The cell went to a deathful silence. Brad and the fellas were scared shitless. Brad looked over and saw his boy Stan, who was now dead to the world. His eyes were wide open and without a blink.

Good luck in the afterlife, my friend. He tried to hold in his tears. Brad knew that he did wrong by his friend, abandoned Stan when he needed Brad the most. He knew he had to reap it later, but for now, all he wanted to do was get the hell out of prison, check up on Diamond, and get out of Brazil with her by his side.

There was a clicking sound, and then the cell door opened.

"Come on," Paco said.

Everyone followed his lead out of the cell. Brad stopped one moment to look back at Stan. "Deuces, my friend," he said in a whisper.

When he was heading out to meet his boys, out of nowhere, someone jumped on Brad's back, pulling him down.

The crew pivoted to see what was going on. They saw that it was Brad and Stan, fighting after they thought everyone in the cell was dead.

"You ain't going no-damn-where," Stan hissed like a demon. "You gon' stay in here with me and be the new bitch!"

"Get off me," Brad said, pushing him back and then putting him into a headlock. Stan was no longer the nice, funny guy Brad used to work and hang out with anymore. Stan had turned into a wild beast thirsty for blood, but Brad couldn't blame him. Brad had sacrificed his friend to the wolves, seeing and hearing his friend being beaten, raped, and the Nigerian warlords selling him for cigarettes or soap. That would make anyone go crazy.

"All I can say is I'm sorry," Brad said in a low voice while trying to calm Stan.

"Fuck you and your 'sorry.' I'ma—"

The sound of firecrackers went off. Brad was in a state of shock as blood splattered all over him from his friend's brains being blown out. Stan's lifeless body fell to the ground, and when Brad looked up, he saw the person who shot him. It was one of the officers that worked for Paco.

"Move it, fat ass, and catch up with your friends if you want your freedom. I'll take care of this piece of shit. Go!"

Brad stepped over Stan's body and hurried to make his way to his crew so they could get the hell out of prison.

Once the guys were outside, one of the other guards had a black van waiting for them. Brad smelled the air. It was so sweet. Now that he breathed the sweet victory of freedom, he thought about how he was going to get away from everyone. He didn't know his way around, and even if he got to the airport again, how would he be able to board one of those planes and get the hell out of there? He was sure that Diamond could help him, and he could help her too. She appeared to be a trustworthy person, and there weren't too many other people that Brad trusted right now.

As the van drove off, they all lifted their hands, waving goodbye.

While the van drove down the streets of downtown Rio, the fellas, Paco, and his crew were shouting, laughing, and drinking beer while saying, "Thank God. Free at last." "Costa Rica, here we come." That was, except for Brad, who was looking out the window and smelling the fresh night air. He glanced at all of the buildings and at the ocean that reflected the moon in the night waters. The scent reminded him of his arrival in Brazil, but then the flashbacks of his best friend shot in the head came back to haunt him. It wasn't the first time Brad had seen someone killed, but that was his boy. He soon snapped out of the flashback and gazed at his friends and cousin, not knowing who they were anymore. Paco had really filled their heads up with bullshit, and Brad refused to be one of Paco's puppets. He took a deep breath as he was preparing to make one of the biggest decisions of his life.

"Midnight, pull over," Brad said in a soft tone.

Everyone shifted their heads to look at him.

"Bruh, what did you just say?" Swag said, frowning. "We gotta get outta here ASAP."

Brad ignored Swag. To him, Swag was a perfect stranger instead of the cousin who'd had his back growing up. All Brad had now was himself.

"Midnight, let me out now!" This time, he put a little more bass in his voice.

Paco sighed and shook his head. "You stupid fool. I figured you would change your mind, but go ahead and be an idiot. You won't get far. You'll be killed by morning. I'm not going to stop you from getting out, and with one down, there will be more freaking money for us." Paco looked at

Midnight. "Pull over and let this dumb-ass piece of shit out 'fore he get us all caught up."

Midnight waited until he found a dark alley; then, he parked.

"Cuz, are you crazy? What're you doin'? You tryin' to get caught?"

"Nah, man. I just don't think this is the way forward. I'm gon' take my own route and see where it leads me."

"There is no other way," Travis said. "And I believe this is more about you trying to go back to that girl than anything else."

"Right. It's a bad time for yo' big ass to be thinking about some punany," Tyler said. "There's goin' to be plenty of Costa Rican ass for you to bone."

"Man, to hell with all that!" Brad shouted. "I just need to get out of here!"

"All y'all shut the hell up!" Paco yelled as he looked at Brad. "Go, you fool. I can't afford for you to slow us down. None of you will slow us down!"

Brad didn't wait another minute. He got out of the van, barely having time to look at his crew and give his final goodbye. They all shook their heads, thinking that Brad had made a horrible mistake by not staying with them. Then Midnight sped off.

And Now . . .

Chapter 1

The New Beginning

When Brad got out of the car without as much as a goodbye, Midnight sped off in the van like a bat out of hell. Swag looked back at his cousin for the last time before he saw smoke and nightfall cover Brad. *Much love, cuz.*

Swag turned back around and looked at Paco and his crew, plus Tyler and Travis, who continued their little party in the van. Swag couldn't believe Tyler and Travis continued partying with Paco after losing their friend since junior high. He shook his head and felt disgusted that he had just lost the only trustworthy and loyal person that had his back, no matter what. He and Brad had been through a lot together growing up in St. Louis and coming from a fucked-up family. Brad, however, got to know his father, who turned out to be an asshole. Swag had never met his dad. He ran out before he was born. That had always bothered him, and after what had just happened, Swag sat back on the seat with a pounding headache.

He'd been through a lot these last few weeks, particularly from getting locked up in one of Brazil's notorious prisons for trying to traffic drugs back to the United States. He was thankful that Paco Hernandez, the former head of the Hernandez Cartel of Texas and Mexico, saw potential in him and the fellas. If it weren't for Paco, he and the fellas would've been someone's bitch in that cell. The whole ordeal was scary, and Swag regretted what had happened to his friend, Stan, in prison. His conscience started to kick in, and Swag knew he was dead wrong for feeding Stan to the wolves. He should have known Stan wasn't built for, or about, that life, and he had betrayed him.

Back in the day, he viewed Stan as one of the lucky ones who grew up in a two-parent home with a father, who was the chief of police of Creve Coeur, and his mother was a nurse-turned-homemaker and president of Creve Coeur Police Wives Club. She spent most of her days taking care of her home, family, and planning/organizing events for the club. Stan was living the dream that every little black boy in the hood wished they had. He grew up not wanting for anything, but then Swag remembered that Stan's parents cut him off when they found out he flunked out at Lincoln University. After that, they made him get a job at the restaurant. It wasn't enough to pay his bills, so when their friend Armand mentioned the 50K deal to the boys, Stan saw a way out of his financial state and a chance to get out of his parents' home. Swag knew Stan was too much of a sheltered suburban type to take on this type of work, and in the end, it cost Stan his sanity, pride, and his life.

Swag knew Karma would come back to him, and even though he didn't want to be in the van with the other fools, he was glad to be free thanks to his new connections and poisoning others. His job title had changed from drug dealer to stickup kid, thief, trafficker, and now, fugitive from justice. He was on the run and had to play low key for a minute. He missed his kids, Solomon Jr., aka Li'l Swag, and Namond. He really missed his down chick, Zaria, too. She'd held him down in the past, even though he'd lied and cheated on her with many of the thots in St. Louis. All they wanted was his money and jock. No one ever gave him unconditional love like Zaria. It was like what his late grandma used to tell him when he was little, *"You don't know what you got 'til it's gone."* She was right, and so was

Brad. He'd also told Swag what a good woman Zaria was, and all he could think about was why he hadn't listened. He lowered his head, and with eyes full of sorrow and pain, all he could whisper was, "Damn."

"Yo, Swag, yo, Swag, Swag!" Tyler shouted and interrupted his thoughts.

Swag lifted his head and looked at him. "What, dude?"

"Man, you wanna hit this?" Tyler placed a fat, twisted joint close to Swag's nose so he could sniff it. He smelled it for a moment—it was a smell he missed while he was in prison. Since he was in desperate need to erase the bullshit that was happening in his life, he gave in.

"Pass that shit here, man."

Tyler smiled and watched Swag take a hit. It took a second for the weed to affect him, but soon, Swag was fucked up and started to think happy thoughts. His head fell back, and with a broad smile on his face, the horrific memories of that day washed away.

Chapter 2

Bow Down to the King

Finally, after several hours of driving, Midnight arrived at the Port of Santos in the city of São Paulo. He nudged Paco, who was knocked out in the passenger's seat.

"Boss, wake up. We here."

Paco slowly opened his eyes, still a little tipsy from the beer and blinded by the bright lights from the boats. But once he realized he was at the port, his eyes grew wide. *Yes, yes, yes,* he thought. *We made it with no distractions, except for that fat-ass fool Brad.* Paco looked in the backseat to see his boys Swag, Tyler, and Travis were all out like lights from celebrating their escape from prison. Paco quickly got into boss mode.

"Wake up!" He clapped his hands. "Hurry up. We here now, and we need to go."

Everyone started to wake up from their slumber.

Swag woke up, wiping his nose and the corner of his mouth. He gazed out the window, seeing all kinds of boats from fishing boats, light boats, and this huge, brightly lit cruise ship with weird foreign writing on it.

"Paco, what's going on? I thought we were getting out of Brazil," Swag asked.

"What are you talking about, fool? We *are* getting out of Brazil." He was irritated. All he wanted was some coffee and weed.

"But what's up with the boats?" Travis asked.

"Yeah, where's a getaway plane that'll get us outta here a little faster?" Tyler questioned.

"You fellas are some damn idiots. I can't afford for all of us to get on a plane. Y'all watch too many movies. The best way to get out of this country is by a ship, the last thing the authorities will expect."

Paco removed a cigar from the glove compartment. He lit it and took a puff before whistling the thick smoke into the air. The fellas waved their hands in front of their faces to clear the air. With Paco's nasty tone, they were now starting to see the asshole he truly was. Not to mention how he had spoken to Brad. But the fellas had to remain cool. They owed him a lot for getting them out of prison.

"A ship is less conspicuous, and before long, the FBI and Feds will be looking for us. We all can't look like targets. As I said earlier, my friend in Costa Rica got us. And once we get there, we'll be living like kings." *And I will bring down my father's operation and kill that bastard for what he did to the business and his infidelity causing my mother's nervous breakdown,* Paco thought, hating that his father had his mother committed to an asylum.

"P, is that the boat that says, *Malo La Perra El Rey?*" Midnight asked.

Paco looked at it. It was a big, beautiful cruise ship. It had numerous levels and a top deck that people could live on for the rest of their lives, sailing the ocean. Paco smiled. "Yes, that's the one. Park this van out of sight, and let's go."

Once the coast was clear, they got out of the van and headed toward the ship. Paco reminded everyone to stay cool and not look suspicious. By making conversation with each other and laughing, they seemed to be friends who were about to go on vacation. Once they got closer to the ships, a husky man wearing a black suit stopped them. His face was full of potholes, and his devilish eyes made him look wicked.

Paco and the man spoke in Spanish for a moment, and then he spoke into his headset. Once the conversion ended, he looked at Paco and the guys with him. "Go up. The boss is waiting for you all."

Paco grinned as he and his men made their way up to the ship with smiles on their faces.

"Thank God," Swag said, taking a deep breath. "It's finally on."

The others agreed, and they stood for a moment in disbelief. They were grateful for their newfound freedom. But they knew once they got on that ship, there was no turning back. They had to say goodbye to their families, St. Louis, their dreams, and goals. But as Paco said, they would live like kings. And to them, losing some to gain a lot seemed like the right plan.

Paco shouted as they stood in thought, "Y'all coming or what?"

Tyler and Travis rushed on the ship like there was no tomorrow. Swag slowly walked up the ship. He was thinking of the wise words of his cousin, Brad, who he was sure he would never see again.

"Man, you gon' get yo' ass caught up one of these days. You got your girl and your boys to think about."

While that may have been true for Swag, he also had to think about himself. Still, Brad's words wouldn't depart from his head. He thought about his sons and what life would have been like with Zaria had he done right by her. He thought about his life, mainly being a high school dropout. Swag was thinking about how he should have been in college by now or in the NBA. Back in Swag's teen years, he was a great basketball player on the courts. But one of his regrets was not telling Brad about his surprise. He wanted to let Brad know that after this drop, he was going to stop working for Armand and being a stickup guy. He was going to return to St. Louis, study for his GED, and open up a business with the money he had been saving. But now, it was all too late to make things right. Now, he was a fugitive, and whatever Paco and this new partner wanted him to be in Costa Rica.

Once on the ship, all the guys saw how amazing it was. The main thing was the numerous, sexy, topless women walking around and conversing with other men on board. Swag, Tyler, and Travis wanted to forget about their dealings with Paco. They stood with lust in their eyes, hoping that they would be allowed to entertain the women soon.

In the meantime, one of the security guards led the guys to the ship's dining room. It was so large that it could fit, at least, 10,000 people. Gold and diamond chandeliers hung from the ceiling. White silk tablecloths, solid gold plates, solid gold silverware, and crystal champagne flutes covered the tables.

Swag couldn't believe his eyes. Money always excited him, and he loved this type of atmosphere. The men sat down. Once everyone was seated, a loud horn blew, and the ship started to sail. Relief came over the fellas, and they were eager to make it to their final destination.

As the ship sailed, the guys were served a breakfast feast fit for kings, thanks to their new boss. They ate French toast, bacon, eggs, and biscuits with gravy. Also, there were Costa Rican dishes such as gallo pinto (red beans and rice) and fried plantains. Champagne was available as well, from Cristal to Dom Pérignon, and Chardonnay. They were served it all. That included shoulder and dick rubs from the topless ladies, as well. They felt as if they were in heaven, and compared to where they had come from, it *was* heaven to them.

As they were eating, a bell rang. The guys looked up and saw the large guy from earlier who blocked them from entering the ship.

"Ladies and Gentlemen, may I have your attention, please," he said. All eyes were on him. "It gives me great pleasure to introduce you to my boss and the king of all bosses. Give it up for King!"

The man stepped aside, and everyone's eyes shifted to the grand staircase. Swag, Tyler, and Travis were expecting a Marlon Brando *Godfather* mob boss to come down. But all the guys were amazed by a five-foot-seven Costa Rican chick who looked to be no more than 21 years old. She appeared to be mixed with Italian ancestry, and she cascaded down the stairs with the vision of billions of dollars blowing around her. She had long, curly, honey-blond hair that went past her shoulders. Her makeup was flawless, but her natural beauty didn't require her to need much at all. She had a body that would put many video girls out of work. It showed well in a black lace teddy that left nothing to the imagination. Her black heels were at least seven inches, and her arms and legs were toned. A tattoo of a leopard was on her left arm. And on the right of her 32DDDs was a tattoo that read *Femme Fatale* with a crown on top.

After her feet touched the dining room floor, she sauntered over to the table where Paco, Midnight, Swag, Tyler, and Travis were sitting. Going over to Paco first, she passionately kissed him while rubbing his face. "Hello, Paco." She sat on his lap, then snapped her fingers. One of the topless girls gave her a glass of champagne.

Paco smiled. "Fellas, this is our new business partner who is going to make us all wealthy men. Meet King Kia Costello."

She smiled. King had the most beautiful pearly white teeth, and her green eyes sparkled with excitement.

Swag was in total shock and disbelief, but he sensed something very wrong. He didn't like doing business with women. *Oh shit! Now, me and my boys are doing business with an even deadlier mofo.*

He remembered seeing something about her. It was on Gangland, on the History Channel. The show was titled, *The Green-Eyed Beauty King, Not Beauty Queen: The Rise of a Costa Rican Gangstress.*

According to the program, King Kia Costello, aka King K, aka K.K., aka K.C., is an international female don of the Leopard Clit. The Leopard Clit was a criminal organization that specialized in smuggling diamonds, gold, and military machine guns across the globe. She was also a madam running a powerful prostitution ring that ran from Costa Rica, Japan, and Puerto Rico. Also, King was a deadly female assassin who would kill you without even blinking twice. She was even offered $2 million from the Ku Klux Klan to assassinate President Barack Obama when he first got into the Oval Office. But two million was chump change to a femme fatale who was worth $150 billion.

King was born to an Afro-Costa Rican prostitute, Ivy, and her father was believed to be the notorious Italian mobster, Bruno Bello, head of the Bello Family, an American Mafia crime organization. In interviews, Bruno denied King being his child and said that Ivy was a liar. But Ivy knew the truth. That family didn't want any Negro or Hispanic biracial bastard child's blood messing up their perfect Italian, pasta-eating bloodline. And that all women of color like her were only useful for a good time. Ivy told King when she'd first met King's father, he was charming and made all kinds of promises to get her out of the whorehouse where she lived and worked. He promised to take her back to America, marry her, and make her a proper lady. But like all the men she'd slept with, he left, and she was stuck with his seed.

When King was born, her mother wanted to name her something special, so "King" fit perfectly. It was a way of letting her know that she came from royalty, and she was the child of Bruno, who her mother once believed was her king. Eventually, King and her mother were kicked out of the whorehouse to fend for themselves. King grew up on the hardcore streets of La Carpio, one of Costa Rica's dangerous ghettos, where crime, drugs, and prostitution flourished everywhere. Ivy got a small apartment in the area. To support herself and King, she became the one thing she knew how to do. That was becoming a whore once again. But Ivy soon became a drug addict as well, addicted to cocaine.

King hated the way her father just played her mother like a doll and then threw her away. She made a promise to herself not to end up like her mother and to get revenge on the Bello Family, who she knew would never claim her. Through her youthful years, without any proper education, she taught herself to read, learned about art, different cultures, and fashion. She began her life of crime by seducing men, just as her mother had done. She learned the art of killing from one of her mother's clients. She would seduce some of the wealthiest men in Costa Rica, then rob them blind and send them to meet their maker. The art of smuggling came from a drug powerhouse in her neighborhood. At the young age of 14, she smuggled drugs from Costa Rica to Miami successfully, but the drug thing wasn't for her. She wanted to smuggle items of extreme value, and that's when she learned the art of stealing jewelry.

At the age of 16, King was the diva of crime, commanding over a hundred soldiers who would lie, kill, and steal for her. King was brought to trial seven times in places away from her home, like Miami, Germany, and Korea, for stealing, smuggling, and possibly assassinating many political leaders. Seven juries saw her beautiful face, and with her sweet, well-cultured voice and her enchanting smile, no one believed she could've done those things. And the evidence always just seemed to disappear anyway.

Now, at 21, she was loved—and feared—by many in Costa Rica as boss. She owned one of the most beautiful properties she shared with her now-sober mother. All she wanted was to get revenge against her father, who left her and her mother in poverty while he lived a life of luxury in America. And the only way to do that was to team up with Paco, wanting to get over her fears of the effects of drugs and get some of the drug trafficking money she was missing out on. Once she got rid of her father and the Bello Family, she would be the number one kingpin.

Even though Swag knew she was a dangerous chick, he couldn't see how someone so beautiful could be so deadly. He also remembered in the documentary that she was well known for her many sexual vices and that King was openly bisexual. She had said, "The one type of people I love to have sex with is a transgender because you get the best of both worlds."

Remembering all this about her, Swag knew he had to stay in her good graces. She was definitely *not* one to be messed with.

"King? What kind of name is that for a chick?" Travis shouted. He was slightly tipsy from all the wine.

Everyone, including his boys, glared at him as if he had just lost his mind.

"You a chick. You supposed to be a queen," Travis laughed.

Man, would this dude just please shut the hell up, thought Swag, who was no longer calling the shots. *This dude doesn't know who he fucking wit'. This chick is a monster.*

King looked at him like a lioness hunting for her prey. She got off of Paco's lap and went over to Travis, where she leaned forward to kiss his bottom lip. He could feel his dick rising and seriously thought she was interested in him. She licked his cheek. Then her lips traveled to his left earlobe. She sucked on it for a second—but then she chomped down hard on it with her teeth.

Travis screamed like a bitch. "Aaaaah, shit shit shit!"

King bit off a small piece of his earlobe, spitting it out on the floor. As blood rushed from Travis's earlobe, he tearfully held it with his hand.

"Only a King can do that," she said, reaching for a napkin to wipe her bloody mouth. As she walked away, she put her long manicured, black fingernail in her mouth, licking more blood before returning to Paco's lap. The smile returned to her face as everyone stared in silence.

The other thing that Swag remembered from the documentary was that, for some sick reason, she loved to lick the blood of her many victims and enemies. Travis looked at her, still holding his wounded ear. She kept smiling at him, admiring her handiwork. Paco and his men began to laugh at Travis.

"You punk little pussy," Paco said. "How can you let a female punk you like that?"

Travis was embarrassed, and he wanted to get her back. But he ventured in the wrong direction. "You bitch!"

He got up, but almost immediately, he noticed that something didn't feel right with his right hand. He looked and saw that his right pinky finger was missing, and he was bleeding profusely from that spot. He glared at King, but now she had his pinky finger in one hand and a pair of pliers in the other.

"Looking for this?" she said, taking his pinky finger and stirring it in her glass of wine. She removed the finger, then licked the tip.

"Damn, Paco," Midnight said. "This woman is a straight-up beast and a G for real."

Paco laughed. "I know. That's why I wanted to do business with her. You always want someone this coldhearted and ruthless on your team."

"Fuck that, Paco! That bitch got my pinky finger!" Travis tried to charge at her—only to be stopped by guns pointed at him by her security team. Many of the topless women aimed everything at him from 9 mm Magnums to machine guns.

Oh shit, I'm fucked, thought Travis, who might be meeting his maker much sooner than later.

Swag and Tyler rushed over to pull him back to the chair. "Be cool, man," Swag said.

Guns were still pointed at Travis, and he figured they would blast him in a second. Swag went over to King, got on his knees, and held her hand. "King, please don't kill my friend. He's drunk and stupid. He don't know any better. If you spare his life, I'll do anything you ask me to."

King smiled at Swag. She admired his courage. She would usually cut out an eyeball of someone who invaded her space and eat it like a Swedish meatball. But something about him just mesmerized her. "All right." She raised her hand, and everyone lowered their guns.

Swag took a deep breath. "Thank you, King. I promise he will be no more trouble."

Swag got up and headed to his seat. He watched as Tyler wrapped his brother's hand with a napkin. King, however, stood with her wineglass, but she threw the pinky finger aside.

"Let that be a lesson to you all. I am a king, *not* a queen. And if any of you fuck me over, you will be sleeping with the fishes—or worse."

They all nodded at their new leader as she lifted her glass. "To a new future of making money, being rich, and bringing down the Bello Family and Hernandez Cartel so that we can be on top of the food chain. To a new future!"

"To a new future!" all the guys said, even Travis, who didn't want to lose any more fingers.

Swag looked around for a moment. He still couldn't believe how elegant the ship was, but deep down, he felt as if it were leading him straight to hell. He had finally gotten his wake-up call, and he wished he could turn back the hands of time. He wished he had never gotten involved with Armand and was back in St. Louis, smoking a blunt or two with his boys, but he could only wish. He looked at the food on his plate in a daze. And for the first time in a long time, he prayed. *Lord, protect my boys and me, including my cousin Brad. I hope he's okay. And, Lord, I ask for one more request. If you can, one day, I would love to see my sons again. I love them, and I need you to protect me on this unfortunate journey so that I can get back to them. Amen.*

Swag looked up and saw King undressing him with her lustful eyes. She was known for getting whatever she wanted, even if it were him. Swag put on a fake smile, trying to stay in her good favor. *And, Lord, please give me strength.*

Chapter 3

Mz. Chocolate

After King took a sip of her drink and gave Swag the "I wanna fuck you" eyes, she put her glass down. Then she clapped her hands with a smile on her face. "Come on, everyone. Enough of the drama and sad love song shit." She waved for her topless girls to go over to the guys. The fellas were in paradise with tits and ass in their faces—something they had missed for the last several weeks.

One thing about King, she had some of the baddest chicks from black, Asian, exotic—all shapes and sizes. She did an excellent job of selecting girls because the guys' jocks were getting hard like bricks. She knew these men didn't judge, especially since it was the first group of women they'd seen in a while. Sexual frustration was heating up the room.

King looked over at Swag, who was having a good time with a five-foot-two chocolate chick with a booty that Swag was having the best time smacking the shit out of while his face was between her big breasts. King couldn't lie. She was getting a little bit jealous. She had no idea why Swag was making her feel things that she hadn't felt in years. In her eyes, the trick that was dancing all on Swag was doing her thing like back when she was a stripper in a Las Vegas strip club scene where King had found her. She was popping that punany and grinding her ass while going to work on Swag.

Damn, she on him like he was one of them old big spenders she fucked with back in Vegas. Get it, ma, thought King.

The expression on Swag's face showed he was aroused and ready to bang the shit out of the chick.

God, I wish that were me, thought King, whose hormones were raging.

She seductively played with the strap of her teddy while avoiding her breasts. But watching this chick dance and grind on his wood was making her nipples hard. And when the chick ripped up Swag's shirt, King was in shock. His body was like a sexy Adonis—muscular and tatted. One glimpse got her pussy dripping wet.

In her mind, if the next man or woman asked her if she wanted to fuck, she'd do them right there on the table. King was just so damn horny that she started to sweat.

Paco sat back while looking down at her long legs. He could see her sweet juices running down them. He grinned, knowing that this was his time to put it on her. Hell, his goal was to be the *real* right-hand man in all things. He side-eyed Swag. *There is no way in hell I'm going to let this pretty boy nigger fuck up my plans with King.*

He got up and wrapped his arms around King's waist while rubbing his hard manhood up against her big ass.

"Aah," King moaned while guiding Paco's arms toward her titties. She leaned against him with her head on his shoulder and started groaning while grinding on his wood.

Her aggressiveness turned Paco on as he pushed her titties together and massaged them. He whispered in her ear, "How about we take this upstairs?" Before she could answer, he lowered his hand into her panties to feel her wetness. His index and middle fingers pushed into her folds and made her even wetter. Closing her eyes, King quivered and coated his fingers with her come. "Aah . . . Ooh . . ."

I got her where I want her, thought Paco as he licked her earlobe. "How about it, King? Let a *real* man beat that shit up real good."

She opened her eyes and smiled. "You think you can handle this sweet punany, papi?"

"Hell yeah, mami. This dick is like Nyquil. It'll put you to sleep."

"Okay, here's your chance." She reached for his hand and led him upstairs. But before they reached their destination, King looked back to glance at Swag. *While Paco is screwing me, I'll see your face and pretend Paco's shaft is yours.* Just thinking about Swag pounding her over and over again made her even moister. She couldn't believe, nor could she understand her immediate attraction to Swag. There was something about him that made her clit throb. She needed a stiff tongue or dick inside of her before she killed every last person on the ship. She looked at Paco.

"What are you waiting for, papi? You said you could handle my honeypot. Come on, show me what you're workin' with."

To Paco, she'd said nothing but a word. He picked her up and carried her up the stairs. He damn sure didn't want her to look back at Swag's ass again, and after he handled his business with King, he truly thought she'd forget all about Swag.

Swag, the fellas, and Paco's men were having the best time of their lives with the girls. King knew how to treat a man like a prince. The chick dancing on Swag was working what she had. And she had plenty of ass and titties but in a good way. Swag looked up at her. She was the sexiest chocolate woman he'd ever seen. He didn't know her name, so in his mind, he was going to call her Mz. Chocolate.

She had slanted hazel eyes, a bunny nose, heart-shaped lips, and high cheekbones like an Indian. Her hair was in long, black microbraids. Plus, baby was wearing a pink bikini showing off her well put together Jessica Rabbit shape. She had thick, toned-up thighs and a big ass for days that he loved smacking. Like LL Cool J used the say, "You juggling, baby." Swag could tell this chick worked at a strip club wherever she was from, 'cause the way she was throwing them hips and ass back and forth, she must have been the club's headliner. But her best feature that Swag loved was her 34DDs that he couldn't keep his face out of. Mz. Chocolate was doing a damn good job, and she'd made his dick hard as a rock. Swag was ready to put it on her once he felt the precome rising to his head. Mz. Chocolate was ready too. She reached for his hand so they could go elsewhere.

"Cum pon, love, let mi tek yuh to yuh room," Mz. Chocolate said in her thick Jamaican accent. She led him upstairs and into a bedroom that looked like a high-class studio apartment. The room had an urban vibe to it with black and gray furniture.

Swag closed the door behind them, and they proceeded to the bed, where Mz. Chocolate pushed him down and leaped on top of him like a leopard attacking her prey. They kissed lustfully, and their tongues wrestled vigorously. For Swag, it felt good to feel a woman's body next to his. He rubbed his hands on her back until he gripped her thick peach ass and caressed it tenderly.

Mz. Chocolate could feel his hard penis pressing against her, and she wanted to give him something he could feel. She lowered herself and held his manhood in her hands. "Damn, baby, yuh shit looks gud. Plus, yuh get one of dem mushroom heads mi like. Damn, mi hope yuh hood taste as gud as it looks," she giggled.

"Ha ha ha," said Swag sarcastically. "I hope you can suck a dude off as good as you kiss."

Mz. Chocolate smiled . . . and delivered. She wasn't King's best girl for nothing, but even she knew the boss had a thing for Swag that would cause all hell to break loose sooner rather than later. That night, however, Swag was all hers.

Chapter 4

Relief

If only Swag and Mz. Chocolate knew that King herself was watching their first fuck fest and now their second. She sat in her private security office, looking at the surveillance footage. Hell, she was a king, and for now, this ship was her temporary palace until she reached Costa Rica. She deserved to know every waking move on her ship. The security room and her room were in the same area. It was painted in a sparkly gold and white color. It had a touch of eighteenth-century vibe to it with a white and gold Victorian bed. Sheets were scattered all over the bed, where Paco slept in dreamland. King put the punany on him, and it put his ass to sleep.

She took her eyes off the screen for a moment to look at Paco. He was surely calling some hogs. King shook her head. *Did he really think he did something to my gold-plated vagina and pierced clit?* She was pissed at him, and he had the nerve to have a smirk on his face while sleeping! Plus, he'd kicked her expensive Egyptian cotton sheets on the floor and scratched his hairy balls. King was disgusted. She couldn't believe how a man this fine had a weak dick game. He only knew one position and came after eight short strokes. All that mad game he'd talked at the table while King was getting turned on to Swag meant nothing. If it weren't for the image of Swag and Mz. Chocolate in her mind while Paco was somewhat dicking her down, she would've never come.

King rolled her eyes and looked back at her screens. She was turned on by how Mz. Chocolate was turning out Swag. She could feel more wetness between her legs. She sat back on the chair, completely naked. King loved her body. Shit, she worked hard with some of the best fitness trainers in the world to get her body cut to perfection. In her opinion, she couldn't run her kingdom with her body looking whack. She had to be polished from head to toe, and she put forth every effort to look her best. Her best never went unnoticed, and she was sure Swag had taken notice too. She had never been this infatuated with a man in a long time. Not since she was 16. Her first lover broke her heart. Swag reminded her so much of him. From his boldness from standing up to her earlier to Swag's pretty-boy face to his tone of voice, it told her that Swag used to run shit where he was from. Something about Swag triggered her and made her hot all over. In fact, she thought she was catching a fever, but deep down, she knew it was lust eating her whole body like a virus. After taking a deep breath, she touched the screen and pretended she was touching his face.

"Don't worry, baby," she whispered. "We'll have our time real soon." She blew a kiss to the screen and went to her master bathroom to give her a sexual fix.

Chapter 5

Reminiscing

Swag was in bliss after going four rounds with Mz. Chocolate. Being with her was so addictive. He knew he was addicted to her chocolate and needed more. But after four rounds of pure sexing, it was time for a little rest. He gazed up at the ceiling while taking a few puffs of the Cuban cigar. He then looked at Mz. Chocolate, whose arm was wrapped around his sweaty, tatted chest. Even though her hair was all over the place, she was even sexier when she was sleeping. Swag smiled at the Jamaican beauty. At that moment, he felt like "Tony" Montana in *Scarface*. He took another puff of the cigar and blew out the smoke. Then he snapped back to reality when he looked at the view out of his window and saw nothing but ocean. He shook his head and said, "Damn." Everything about this felt right, but he knew it wasn't going to be all good.

He eased out of bed and put on his boxers that were on the floor. After entering the bathroom, he closed the door and looked at his reflection in the mirror. His eyes looked tired, and his chest had scratches, compliments of Mz. Chocolate, who had obviously had a good time. Swag examined the luxurious bathroom that had a gold toilet, sink, and shower. The one thing he could say about King was the woman had some excellent taste to be so crazy. He turned on the faucet and splashed cold water on his face.

As he looked at his wet face in the mirror, many questions flooded his mind, and he repeated, *How the fuck did I get here? Where did the fellas and I go wrong with this operation? I went from a thief, a stickup kid, a dope boy, a drug trafficker, and now, an international fugitive. Shit, I have one hell of a résumé.* He laughed, even though he knew the shit he was in wasn't funny. He didn't know what his future was going to look like now, and he never thought in a million years that his life would be like this.

Swag had bigger dreams besides this. He knew that his nana was turning in her grave right now, wondering where she went wrong with her grandson, who had so much potential. Thinking about his nana made him smile. He missed her so much, along with his sons. He looked at his reflection even harder in the mirror and didn't even recognize the person who was staring back at him anymore. He knew he'd lost someone. It was Solomon Carter. *Whatever happened to Solomon Carter?*

Swag couldn't help but think about how he'd been on his own since he was a teenager. His mother, Juanita Carter, only cared about partying, looking good, drinking, men, and sex. Two years after having Swag, she had triplets—two girls, Tamika, Tamara, and a boy named Mickey Carter. Swag's father was serving life in prison for a crime he claimed he didn't commit. Swag and his siblings were mainly raised by his grandma, Nina, whom he called Nana. Nina was more of a mother to him than his mother was.

When Swag was young, Juanita lost custody of her children, and Nana had full custody of all of them. Swag loved how hardworking his nana was. She worked as a teacher's aide and told her grandchildren they were all special.

Remembering his nana brought a big smile to his face, thinking of all the wonderful memories he had of her. He turned on the sink again, using his hand to cup some water to drink and looked up at his reflection once more, and more memories came back.

Swag remembered he used to love playing basketball, and everyone supported him when he was 13. Things were good for Swag and his siblings until he was 15, and Nana died suddenly of a massive heart attack. Then Juanita came back in the picture, now claiming she was a changed woman. Juanita was dressed to the nines in designer clothes, hair done, nails done, and she drove a new Mercedes-Benz. She was living high in a fly-ass crib in East St. Louis and had a job as a paralegal. And she also splurged on her children with expensive gifts. After a judge and social worker looked over everything, the courts placed the children back with Juanita.

But life in East St. Louis was hell for Swag and his siblings. The picture that Juanita and her attorney painted for the judge was fake. She didn't live in a luxurious home. She lived in a run-down apartment building in the ghetto. And Juanita's so-called job as a paralegal was really as a drug dealer and runner. Along with her drug money, she received a government check for the kids and went shopping almost every day.

There was also a new man in her life. His name was Mitch. He was a low-life drug dealer and stickup guy that would rob a 2-year-old if he could. They treated the kids like slaves, and for entertainment, they would beat them. These actions caused the kids to do poorly at their new schools.

Swag gave up his dreams of being a pro basketball player in the NBA. It wasn't long before he dropped out of high school and furthered his education in the streets. Robbing, stealing, selling drugs . . . He did it all. By the time he was 17, he'd saved up about $10,000, which he never brought home.

The thought of his mother pissed him off. He remembered his mother and Mitch telling him and his siblings they would never amount to anything, how his life was never supposed to be that way. He was so pissed he had to take a shit and pissed. He lifted the toilet seat and sat. As he was taking care of business, he remembered a moment that would change his life forever.

He remembered the night Juanita and Mitch were fighting in their apartment. They fought because Juanita caught him having sex with her 15-year-old daughter, Tamara. As Juanita and Mitch fought, Swag intervened to help his mother. Then Mitch and he started to fight, and a frightened Juanita went into her bedroom and returned with a 9 mm. Unfortunately, she shot Swag by accident. He was bleeding profusely on the floor and in unbearable pain. While Swag was in a coma for a week and a half at the hospital, Juanita threatened to kill anyone who revealed the truth. While lying in the hospital bed, Swag told himself, fuck her! Fuck everything! Fuck his family, and he was thankful that he didn't leave his stash at the crib.

Once he was out of the hospital, the first place he went was to an old abandoned warehouse near railroad tracks. He cleared the dusty trash cans and pulled out a huge green bean can. Once he opened it and saw his stash of $10,000, plus a few dime bags, he couldn't wait to get back to St. Louis to sell them and get a connect.

Once Swag was done pushing out the last piece of shit from his system, he wiped himself real good. He flushed the toilet and went back to the sink to wash his hands and look at his reflection. "Damn." He thought about how disappointed he was in himself, but mainly how he disappointed Nana with the dumb decisions he made in his life.

"Swag, Swag!" shouted Mz. Chocolate as she tapped him on his shoulder.

Swag had stopped reminiscing over his past as he looked at Mz. Chocolate's naked reflection in the big mirror, not noticing she came into the bathroom. He could feel his manhood getting hard again. "What, ma?"

"Damn, daddy, mi wake up wanting to feel sum more of dat yello banana beefcake inna mi, but yuh did gaan," Mz. Chocolate said, wrapping her arms around his waist. She licked his back like it were her favorite butter pecan ice cream. "Yuh tire of mi already, daddy?"

She reached inside his boxers and jerked his snake. He was turned on as he leaned back on her. "Shit!" he laughed.

Yet again, Swag started to forget about his problems. All he wanted was some of that Jamaican sweetness. He turned around and picked her up. She laughed.

"Come on, baby. You ready for some more of this long banana beefcake in your pudding, ma?"

"Yuh kno it, daddy. Dis pussy dripping fi dat hood," Mz. Chocolate replied while licking Swag's ear.

They moved to the bed and got ready for round five.

Oh, Lord, give me strength, Swag thought with a smile on his face.

Chapter 6

The Journey Begins

After a few days in the ship, the fellas, Paco, and his gang were having the best time of their lives, partying every day and night with King's girls turning them out with moves they had never seen in America. But Swag, unlike Tyler and Travis, knew once they arrived in Costa Rica, playtime would be over. Swag knew the underworld lifestyle too well. Hell, he lived it most of his life. One minute, it was caviar and champagne. Next, it would be bloodshed and bodies popping up.

The ship's horn blew and woke up everyone who was still drunk or high from the night before. But Swag and Mz. Chocolate were still knocked out. Mz. Chocolate had put her chocolate heroin on Swag, and that'll knock anyone out. But the horn got even louder and finally got their attention.

"Damn, what is it now?" shouted a sleepy Swag while rubbing his eyes.

Mz. Chocolate shook her head. She was still a little tipsy. Before she said anything, the door to their suite flew wide open. One of King's muscular bodyguards stood in the doorway in a three-piece black suit. Swag and Mz. Chocolate reached for the sheets to cover their naked bodies.

"Damn, bruh, what's up?" Swag yelled, horrified.

"Yeah, Blood, yaah crazy man. Yuh nuh kno there's a uhman present inna di room?"

Blood, the henchman, laughed while looking at Mz. Chocolate with his brown puppy dog eyes. "Damn, Desiree, chill with that shit. I know every part of yo' sexy ass. You ain't got nothing to hide." Blood licked his lips. He glanced over at Swag with a smirk on his face.

At first, Swag let Blood's words get him. Mz. Chocolate, or Desiree, was treating Swag like he was hers. In Swag's mind, she was. But he had to remember it was her job to make him feel that way. She was just a high-priced whore that was a drug used to drain his system slowly.

Blood focused on Swag. "Dude, get your ass dressed. King wants you and the guys on the lower level in fifteen minutes. You hear me?"

"Yeah, Bigfoot. I mean, Blood," Swag said sarcastically.

Swag knew that Blood was a big dude and didn't want to tango with him, not yet anyway.

Blood twisted his lips at Swag and looked back at Desiree. "And you, sexy, you stay here. The crew is going to be in here to fix you up. You have an appointment with one of your regulars in L.A., and you know how demanding this dude is."

"Yeah, I know," Desiree said, getting out of bed.

Swag looked at her curves, and her sexiness started to make his jock hard again. He needed some more of that chocolate heroin in him, but Blood snapped his fingers in Swag's face to interrupt his thoughts.

"What, dude?"

"Ten minutes. And if I were you, I'd hurry. The king don't like waiting."

Blood and Swag stared at each other for a moment, until Blood left and closed the door behind him. Swag got out of bed to stretch. He scratched his stomach before looking for his clothes. After he put his dirty clothes back on, he glanced over at Desiree. She was sitting on the recliner with her legs wide open as a cigarette dangled from her mouth. She lit the cigarette and took a long drag. While looking at Swag, she whistled smoke in his direction.

"Bowy, yuh betta hurry up an' get ready before Blood comes back up inna here again."

"Man, fuck Blood." He laughed as he walked over to her. He dropped to his knees in front of her. "So, when can we hook up again?"

Desiree laughed. "Bowy, yah couldn't afford dis gud pussy. Wah mi been giving yuh di laas few days a dosage of mi gud shit. Mi ongle gi my shit up to real bosses."

Swag smirked. "Oh, really? And wah boss yah talk 'bout, man?" Swag imitated her Jamaican accent.

Desiree took another puff of her cigarette and blew the smoke out. She waved her hand at Swag. "Bowy, nuh get smart or mi wi ave Blood inna here suh fast, it'll mek yuh head speed." She lightly smacked him on his cheek and then sauntered over to the messy bed. "Now, one of mi biggest bosses tis here. He cum from Los Angeles. Just sey him a hip-hop icon. Him rapped inna one of di notorious rap groups inna history. Him a Grammy award–winning produca. Him owns one of di biggest labels inna di music game, an di biggie him a billionaire," Desiree said, smiling. "Now, yuh cyn beat dat?"

"Damn," said Swag knowing exactly who Desiree was talking about. It was one of his all-time favorite rappers. Swag must have played his solo debut album over and over again as a kid. He just couldn't believe celebrities like that still paid for some ass, and they were married pricks at that. He wanted to know more about the celebs Desiree had in her chocolate web. But before he could get more info, he heard a loud voice yell, "Swag! Bring yo' high yellow ass on!"

Swag was annoyed as he looked at Desiree. "Well, thanks for a great few days. You really relaxed me and helped me take my mind off things."

Desiree planted a soft kiss on his lips. "Get yuh ass outta here before Blood kills yuh."

Swag left the room, knowing that what she'd said was a possibility.

Nearly everyone made their way off the ship. It was indeed a beautiful and sunny day in San José, Costa Rica. Limousines awaited some people, and as Swag was about to get into the limo with the twins, Blood tapped his shoulder.

"What's up, bruh?" Swag asked.

"Come with me now." Blood walked off, and Swag followed.

They passed by Paco, who gave Swag a dirty look and mumbled underneath his breath, "Puta nigger." Then Blood opened the door to a white limo. Swag stood for a moment, not knowing what was going to happen. He thought maybe some dudes were in there waiting to beat the shit out of him. Or even worse, the FBI was waiting for him. After all, he *was* a fugitive on the run from the law.

"Get yo' ass in there, bruh," Blood said, shoving him inside.

Swag's face twisted, and his voice went up a notch. "I'm moving, but you don't have to put your fucking hands on me."

Without saying another word, Blood grunted and slammed the door shut. Swag looked at King, who sat across from him. She looked just as sexy as he remembered. Her long hair was pulled back into a sleek ponytail, and her makeup was on like artwork. Baby was showing all body in a pink, one-shoulder, side-spliced short dress with her legs crossed and showcasing her black spiked pumps. She wore diamonds on her neck, ears, wrists, and ankles. Her perfectly manicured nails were painted gold, and a broad smile graced on her face.

Swag cleared his throat. Beads of sweat started to form on his forehead. The limousine took off, and Swag could see Blood on the passenger's side.

As the limo drove down the street, Swag couldn't get over how breathtaking King was. He was nervous in her presence. He knew this chick was deadly, but at the same time, it was a turn-on for him.

King, on the other hand, noticed the woody in his pants. It made her nipples hard. She uncrossed her legs and crossed them again as her goodies started to throb. She looked at Swag, who was still sweating bullets. It was hot in San José, but King knew Swag's heatwave was coming from *inside* the limo.

Swag stared at her for a moment before looking out the window and admiring the beauty of San José. He saw the Plaza de la Cultura and the beautiful San José skyline with the mountains in the background.

King cleared her throat. She could sense that Swag was trying to ignore her. "Swag, sweetie, come sit next to me." She patted the empty seat.

Swag shifted his head toward her. "What, ma'am?"

She laughed and held her chest. "None of that 'ma'am' stuff. You American men with this 'ma'am' stuff." She patted the empty seat again. "Come sit next to me."

Swag took a deep breath as he glanced at Blood, who kept turning around to look at him.

"What the hell are you looking at me for? Boss lady wants you, not me. Now get your ass over there 'cause she don't like to wait." He opened up his suit jacket to show off his gun.

Swag ignored Blood and looked over at King, who motioned for him to come her way. He eased over to the seat next to her. His heart started beating faster. He didn't know what to expect.

King lightly touched Swag's shoulder. He jumped like she put a bullet in him. Both of them laughed.

"Do I make you nervous?" King asked as she rubbed his thigh.

Swag cleared his throat and attempted to get into his macho mode. His inner "I fear no man but God" dope dealer self came into play. He relaxed and popped his collar.

"Nah, ma, nothing scares me."

King continued to rub his shaky thigh. "Relax, baby. How about some champagne to calm your nerves?"

Before he could answer, she moved over to the minibar, poured two glasses of 1990 Dom Pérignon, and topped them off with a strawberry. She gave Swag a glass and raised the other in her hand. "To us and our business."

Swag didn't want any drama, so he lifted his glass too. "To us and our business."

They took a sip.

"Mm," Swag said, admiring the taste of the champagne. "Damn, this shit taste good."

King removed the strawberry and sucked on the tip like she was sucking on a nipple. She then took a bite of it before putting it back in the glass. Her little gesture made Swag erect. He quickly downed most of the champagne before setting the glass aside. He could feel the champagne taking full effect.

"What's your real name?" King asked with a serious look in her eyes. His name was rarely something anyone had asked him, and he was caught completely off guard.

"What did you say?"

King twisted her lips but laughed it off. "Usually, I get pissed off for having to repeat myself. If you didn't hear me the first time, this limousine would be full of blood. But since you're so cute, I'll let it slide . . . this time. Just remember that for future references, I don't like to repeat myself." She placed her hand back on his thigh. "Now, what's your government name?"

Swag remembered from the documentary she meant business, and when she asked a question, it was wise to answer quickly.

"Solomon."

"Solomon. I like it."

Swag chuckled. "I guess."

They both reached for their glasses to take another sip of the champagne.

"Solomon is such a dignified name. Why screw it up by giving yourself a stupid American tag name? You know that in the Bible, Solomon was a king and a very wise man. I see so much potential in you as Solomon rather than . . . Swag. I only surround myself with bosses, not wannabe thugs."

Swag couldn't believe what he was hearing. He never ever let anyone disrespect his tag name or his street cred back at home.

"From now on, I'll be calling you Solomon," King said. "My Solomon. Now that you are with me, I need a real man to help me grow my kingdom. Not some fake-ass dude thinking he's the godfather or a John Gotti wannabe." King touched his hand.

Swag stayed focused on her beautiful green eyes that looked like a field of green grass you could run through. It wasn't long before he felt unbearable pain in his hand. At first, he thought she'd cut something off like she did Travis's finger. He quickly yanked his hand from her grasp. He looked at his hand, thanking God he still had it. Blood, however, was seeping from a cut. With tightened fists, he angrily looked at King, who smiled. There were no signs of remorse as she showed off the switchblade that she used to slice Swag's hand.

"Damn, King. Shit! What was that for?" Swag had so much fire in his eyes. He was ready to charge at her. Deep down, he wanted to take his bloody fist and punch her in the face. His thoughts, however, went nowhere, especially since Blood was now aiming a gun at him.

"Homeboy," Blood said, imitating Swag's voice, "I'd put that fist down real quick if I were you."

King addressed Blood. "Baby, put that gun away. He'll be just fine."

Blood was hesitant while still holding the gun. He didn't want anyone or anything to hurt his king. He had been her loyal right hand from day one. Blood never took his eyes off Swag. His intuition was telling him not to trust Swag—not one bit. To him, Swag just rubbed him the wrong way since seeing him on that ship. He didn't like him, and he felt that King was becoming very reckless lately by picking her play toys.

"Now!" King shouted while looking at Blood with daggers in her eyes. She was ready to cut him open like a fish.

Blood sighed. He was ready to taste Swag's blood.

Swag didn't care about their little beef. He was concerned about his hand.

"Just in case you haven't noticed, my hand is still bleeding. What was this shit for?"

King laughed while looking at the switchblade. She looked like a vampire waiting for her next feeding. She took the tip of her manicured index fingernail and ran it across the blade. Afterward, she put her finger on the tip of her tongue to taste the blood. She smiled as if she were tasting honey.

Swag kept a straight face, trying to show that he wasn't pissed. However, he wanted to show his real look of disgust, but his stomach started to hurt.

"Mm, your blood tastes divine, Solomon. My Solomon," King smiled wickedly. She looked down at his bleeding hand. "Oh, I'm sorry about that." King took his hand and kissed it. She even licked off some of the blood and kissed it at the same time. "Damn, your blood is good."

To Swag's surprise, she didn't have a spot of blood on her perfectly made-up face.

"Oh, don't worry," she said. "Once we get to my location, I'll take care of that for you. But in the meantime," King snapped her fingers.

That was Blood's signal to get out his handkerchief and give it to Swag.

"Thanks," Swag said, then nodded.

He wrapped his hand with the handkerchief and applied pressure.

"I cleansed you," King said. "I just took the blood of Swag out, and you're soon going to be reborn, Solomon. It's just one more thing to make your cleansing complete."

Swag looked at his wrapped hand, then at King. "And what does that mean?"

She took the tip of the switchblade on her middle finger and pricked it. A little blood was on her finger. She put her middle finger by his lips and looked at him with lust in her eyes. "Drink, baby."

Swag examined the blood drop on her finger. "Seriously? You can't be serious."

King laughed. "Drink, baby. Don't worry. I don't have any diseases or anything. I get a checkup every three months, so I'm clean. How else am I supposed to run an empire?" She lowered her other hand to rub his thigh and touch his manhood. "Now, drink."

"Eww," he groaned. Unable to deny her request, he put her bloody finger in his mouth and sucked it.

King continued to massage Swag's manhood and enjoyed her finger in his mouth. Swag imagined that her fingers were her diamond vagina, the documentary said she was known for.

"Shit, ma, I'm 'bout to come," Swag moaned with his mouth wide. "Aah . . ." He ejaculated in his pants. "Shit, girl." He sucked her finger one more time until she removed it from his mouth. "Damn, girl, you wild. Yo' hand game is out of this world."

King smiled. "I know, and by drinking my blood, you are all mine."

Her comment totally fucked up Swag's natural high. He just realized he'd sucked King's bloody finger. He wanted to spit it up and vomit, but after that bomb-ass hand game, he was confused. He didn't want to say the wrong thing to her, so all he said was, "Yeah, baby. I'm all yours." Swag knew that was what she wanted to hear.

King patted his thigh. "Good boy."

Blood looked at Swag like he was shit on the back of his shoe. He hated him for sure, and all he could think about were his plans to get rid of him for good.

Chapter 7

The Kingdom

Everyone finally arrived at King's Palace, which was in the middle of downtown San José. From the outside, it looked like a twelve-story, five-star hotel where only the rich and famous stayed. Everyone got out of their limousines, looking around. Paco stretched his arms and legs. He was relieved to be out of such discomfort. But nothing pissed him off more than when he glanced over and saw Swag and King getting out of their limo. His eyes went straight to Swag's. If his eyes were bullets, Swag would be lying down on the ground, drenched in blood.

"Boss, you good?" Midnight asked, tapping Paco on his shoulder.

Paco snapped out of his murderous thoughts. He looked at his main dude. "What you say, big homie?"

"You good, Boss?" Midnight nodded. "I know that look in your eyes."

Midnight knew his boy to the tee, ever since they were kids. When Paco had that "look" in his eyes, it was time for someone to be taken off the scene. But Midnight had to keep in mind that they weren't in Texas anymore. Now, he was in the King's domain. And from what he saw on the cruise ship, this chick was no one to fuck with.

"Nah, big homie, I'm good," Paco said. His eyes shifted to King, and his thoughts returned. *Now, I have to get up with this crazy bitch so I can reclaim the position that is rightly mine. Shit, I didn't break out of that Brazilian shithole for nothing. The Hernandez Cartel will be mine.* "Excuse me, homie." Paco hurried to get next to King. He wrapped his arm around her shoulders like she was his woman, forgetting he had a wife back in Texas.

King hissed and gave him a look of "Bitch, what?" To her, his touch was like a hairy ape to her jasmine-scented skin. She wanted to use her switchblade that she used to cut Swag's hand with and slice Paco's throat. But she was too close, and she needed Paco at that moment.

"How was the ride?" she asked with a fake smile. "Were your expectations met?"

Paco laughed as he kissed her petal-soft lips. "Ma, you did that shit. You really know how to welcome someone to Costa Rica."

King laughed, but deep down, to her, his kiss was like poison. It was worse than his dick. "I aim to please."

Paco then looked at Swag with a slick smile. He glanced at Swag's hand that was covered by a handkerchief with blood seeping out. "Damn, playboy, what happened to you?" Paco pretended to be concerned, but inside, he was dancing with joy.

Swag didn't respond because he saw the twins coming their way.

"What's up, bruh?" Tyler asked, patting Swag on his shoulder.

"Yeah, man, what's up?" Travis said as he looked at Swag's hand. "Damn, man, you okay? What happened to you?"

Travis looked at King with cold eyes. He wanted to slice her throat open like a piece of fruit. His blood was boiling at the sight of this woman. To him, King was like Satan in a nightie. He balled his fist up and thought about what she'd done to his finger. Luckily, his wound had been tended to. He still wanted revenge, though, but he snapped back into reality when Blood showed his gun, and King played with her switchblade.

"You better put a smile on that face when you around the King and on her property," Blood said, waving his gun around.

Travis knew not to challenge Blood. He just put his head down, knowing he was defeated. Whomever King hired as an undercover sniper, they were ready to blow anyone's brains out at her command. The only thing Travis had on his mind was sweet revenge for King. *An eye for an eye,* he thought. *But in my case, a finger for a finger.*

"Gentlemen, let's not stand outside. Let's go inside my home," King suggested.

She, along with Paco, walked side by side to the front door of her palace. Then King looked at Paco and cleared her throat.

"Are you okay?" Paco asked, concerned with his future queen looking at him like he was one of her victims.

"First off, Paco, this is *my* palace, and *you're* a guest. The King will make the grand entrance into her palace alone. Your job is to be eight steps away from me until I send for you." King rubbed the switchblade on Paco's hand, covering it with Swag's blood.

No one knew what to expect from King at that moment. Was Paco her next victim or not? Swag remembered in the documentary that when King rubbed her switchblade on you, it meant she didn't want whoever touching her. He also recalled from the documentary that the last man that touched her didn't stop after the switchblade warning. When he stuck his tongue out to lick her cheek, she used scissors to clip the tip of his tongue off. The man was in unbearable pain with blood spurting everywhere. But she wasn't done with him. She used her switchblade to cut the man's whole tongue out and fed it to her Doberman pinscher.

Paco looked at his hand and saw that King had covered it with Swag's blood. "Eww, what the hell?" He removed his arm from King's shoulder. Deep down, he was scared shitless. Not because of King's psycho ass, but because some of Swag's DNA was on his hand. Paco wanted to vomit right then and there but managed to keep it together. It was bad enough he was business partners with Swag. That was something he already regretted. But in the end, Paco believed he was going to be the captain of this ship—or die trying, as long as he kept his cool. He wiped the blood on his pants.

Once King was by herself, her doorman, Cleo, an older, dark-skinned man, was at the door. Cleo had been the doorman for years at the building, way before it was King's Palace. The stories he could tell about that building weren't pretty. He smiled at King and her guests and opened the golden doors.

King walked into her palace but not before saying, "Thank you, Cleo."

"You're very welcome, Your Highness," Cleo smiled and bowed down to her.

Inside her home, King looked around. It was absolutely stunning with a seventeenth-century Victorian-style vibe to it that made it look like a touch of royalty. The colors were white and gold with touches of diamonds everywhere, including the grand hall. Floor-to-ceiling white columns separated several rooms, and a double-circular staircase led to the upper loft level. The fellas were in awe. Their eyes were as big as saucers. They thought they'd died and gone to heaven.

Swag knew that King ran an elegant business as far as whorehouses, but, damn. It wasn't just the décor of King's Palace. More beautiful women stood around that made the men's jaws drop. They knew the women were escorts, but they weren't the typical hookers they would see back at home. It was evident that King had trainers coming to her palace to keep her ladies right because the girls' bodies were snatched to the gods.

Swag remembered in the documentary how King would turn her girls out. Some of them were working for low-life pimps in other countries, showgirls/strippers in local clubs around the world, and some were local college girls trying to pay off their tuition. King would pick a part of the world and scout for girls or guys. Some of the people she would meet were either gay, bisexual, or straight. It didn't matter to her because money was money. She would talk realistic shit by telling them they could live a life of luxury, comfort, be wined and dined for doing almost absolutely nothing. Eventually, they got hooked. They enjoyed the lavish lifestyle, as well as catering to some of the wealthiest people in the world from A-list Hollywood celebrities to political leaders all over, and royalty, including men from Saudi Arabia.

King was amazed at what some of the influential people liked. One of her clients was one of the famous religious leaders in the world, especially in the Roman Catholic faith. King had evidence that the leader dressed in full-blown drag and loved to be pimped out like a trashy hooker. She knew the tapes she had in her possession would create a massive scandal throughout the world. The money she could get for the recordings would be enough money to take care of a small foreign company for thirty-plus years. But King would save those tapes for another time.

King looked at the guys and shook her head. "Uh, gentlemen, put your tongues back in your mouths. Flies will enter."

All eyes were on King.

"Now, you, you, and you come with me." She pointed at Tyler, Midnight, and Swag. She looked over at Blood. "Blood, dear, show our other guests out, please."

Paco don't know what the hell was going on while standing there looking dumbfounded. He couldn't believe he wasn't staying in her palace. He was heated and pissed off on another level. "What? What about the rest of us? Why are these three the only ones staying in your place? I thought we"—he pointed to himself and King—"were partners? Why is my boy and these puta niggers staying and not me? Bitch, we had a deal! Why you—"

Before Paco could say another word, Swag punched the shit out of him.

"Who the hell you callin' a bitch, nigga? Bitch!" Swag yelled.

Tyler kicked him in his stomach. "Yeah, you wetback!"

Usually, Midnight would go to his man's defense, but not knowing what King's next move was, he didn't move. In Midnight's mind, it was every man for himself.

King enjoyed watching Swag and Tyler whip Paco's ass, but she needed them both to save their strength. She had other plans for them. King didn't like Paco's ass in the beginning, and after he called her a bitch, well, that was total disrespect to her. She's killed someone for disrespecting her, especially in her home and place of business. The fire in her was flaming hot in her mind. She looked at her switchblade. She imagined herself stabbing Paco many times, starting with his eyeballs. She wanted to cut them out and eat them like Swedish meatballs. She badly wanted to taste his blood, but she needed his power. Her hunger would have to wait. She motioned over to Blood.

Blood nodded. He reached into his coat pocket, pulled out his gun, and fired into the ceiling.

Everyone paused, frightened. Immediately, Swag and Tyler stopped beating Paco's ass and looked over at Blood.

"Now that I have your attention!" Blood shouted as he put his gun back in his coat pocket. He looked at King for her next plan of action.

King looked down at Paco, bleeding on the floor. He wiped his bloody lip and could barely talk because several teeth were missing.

"Do you see what they did to me? Aren't you going to do something? I didn't mean to call you a bitch."

King bent over and held his face up with her hand. Paco didn't know what to expect from her, but he knew it wouldn't be good. King saw Paco's blood on his lips, so she stuck her tongue out to lick it off.

"Umm, delicious . . ." She sinisterly smiled at him before standing straight up. Afterward, she lifted her foot and kicked him right in the balls.

"Aah . . ." Paco hollered in agony while holding his aching manhood and rocking side to side.

Everyone laughed at him.

"Blood, have security throw out this piece of shit and the rest of these fools before there's a blood feast in here." King looked at Swag, Tyler, and Midnight. "You three come with me."

She led the way as the three young men followed. Tyler looked back at Travis, and like always, Travis's hands shook from being nervous. Deep down, he wanted Tyler to speak up for him, but he knew this was all about survival. He just hoped that he and Tyler wouldn't be separated. They were all they had in this crazy life of crime.

No one knew what was going on, but they could hear chaos erupting.

"Release me, you idiots!" Paco yelled.

"Silence yourself before we break your fucking neck!" a guard ordered.

Two security guards picked up Paco, who was downright humiliated. No one had his back anymore, not even his main man, Midnight. *Bitch-ass gorilla African!*

As security dragged him out of the Palace, he remembered one rule his grandpa had told him: "*In this life of crime, as soon as you fall, they will all leave you. Trust no one."* Security placed him in the limousine, and Paco thought about Brazil and his asshole of a father. *Maybe I should've taken the lawyer's offer and left these sheisty muthafuckas in that shithole in Brazil. Hell, I could've been at home with my wife and child. I would've killed my father by now, and the Hernandez Cartel would've been mine. Fuck, I had the chance and didn't take it. Now, I'm in Costa Rica being disrespected by one of the most dangerous women in the world. But I'm going to get my respect—one way or another.*

Inside the Palace, once all the drama was gone, Blood barked at everyone. "What, people? The show is over! Ladies and gents, do what you know how to do."

Blood walked off and could tell a storm was brewing.

Chapter 8

Meet the Family

King escorted both Tyler and Midnight to their rooms on the tenth floor. She told them to get settled in, but not to get too comfortable yet.

She and Swag were about to head up in the elevator to the twelfth floor until an older woman shouted, "King! King, sweetie!"

Both King and Swag turned around and saw two women coming their way. One of the women appeared to be King's older sister. She looked about 37 and had green eyes, just like King. Swag wondered where King and the woman had gotten those beautiful green eyes from. Even though she was a little heavier, she still had a lovely figure that showed well in a black blouse, denim ripped jeans, and Gucci sandals. Her makeup was beat to the gods, but she didn't need it because of her perfect olive complexion. She also rocked the famous Halle Berry short cut. The other woman beside her looked to be in her 60s but was still attractive for her age. Even though she was a little older, she had an hourglass frame that showed well in a long, blue, velvet gown. Her caramel complexion was wrinkle-free and smooth like honey. She set it off with diamonds on her earlobes, neck, fingers, and wrists.

"Mama! Grandma!" King shouted with a big smile on her face.

Swag admired King's smile when seeing her mother and her grandmother. She looked genuine and angelic. King and the women embraced each other in a group hug.

When King was around her mother and grandma, she felt so safe. She could put her boss mode guard down and just be a woman. There was nothing like the family in her mind. King didn't know what she would do if anything were to happen to her mother and grandmother. The women stopped hugging and looked at one another.

"God, Mommy and Grandmother, I missed you both so much." King's voice cracked. She sounded as if she hadn't seen her mother and grandmother in years.

Swag couldn't believe what he was looking at right now. The King he'd first met or seen in the documentary, or on the ship, in the limousine, and the grand hallway was nothing like the girl he saw now. She was now this vulnerable, caring, and loving person. To Swag, it was like he was looking at two different people. It was like a Dr.-Jekyll-and-Mr.-Hyde-type moment.

The older woman said something in her Creole language, and Swag was totally lost at this point.

"Don't worry, sweetheart. Mommy missed you so much." Her mother kissed King on her forehead.

King melted like butter when her mother kissed her. She loved her mother so much despite their earlier years of conflict and neglect. But with lots of healing, talking, and, of course, Grandmother King, their relationships got better.

King's mother smiled at her, but her eyes traveled to Swag. She looked him up and down like he was something to eat. She walked around her daughter and sauntered up to him. There was a hunger for him in her eyes. She wanted to devour every last drop of him. He was that delicious to her. She wanted to sex him right then and there in the hallway and fanned herself with her hand.

"God, it's hot in here."

One thing she could say about her daughter was that she had good taste when it came to men. She just hoped that one day, King would find the right one and make better choices in them than she ever did. She looked Swag up and down again. His clothes were a little wrinkled, but she knew once King cleaned him up and put him in a nice suit, he'd be just fine. She figured Swag was going to make her daughter a lot of money and be number one for female clients.

"Well, hello, there, big fella," she said, then looked at King. "Darling, who is this sexy man?"

Swag had a lump in his throat. It was bad enough King was on his jock. The last thing he wanted to be was cougar candy, even though in the back of his mind, he was flattered.

King just smiled at the fact her mother was flirting with Swag. One thing she knew about her mother ever since she'd been sober was that she had a thing for younger men from the ages of 18 to 25. She would have her time with them and then send them on their way. But King felt the only reason her mother liked messing with younger men was that she was trying to relive the last few years she'd missed out on. She went from going drug crazy, after major humiliation from being the hottest escort of all of Costa Rica, to a local crack whore. But King was happy that her mother was back on the right track, and that she stayed that way.

King's mother went over to Swag and rubbed his chest. "What's your name, Boss?"

Swag cleared his throat and grinned at King's mother. "Ma'am, I'm—"

"This is Solomon. *My* Solomon, Mother," King said, cutting Swag off and standing next to him. "Solomon, this is my mother, Ivy Costello." She pointed to her mother.

Swag nodded.

Ivy blew him a kiss, but she also knew when King said, "My Solomon" that he was in the house for a purpose. And that any man or woman like that was off-limits. As fine as Swag was, Ivy knew she and King were going to bump heads. For now, things were going to remain neutral.

King shook her head as she looked over at the much-older lady. "And, Solomon, this is Sophia Lourd, my grandmother."

Sophia smiled and held her hand in Swag's face. She wanted him to kiss it. "My hand. Kiss it."

Without hesitation, Swag obeyed.

"Nice, soft lips," Sophia said. She looked at his wrapped hand. "What happened to your hand, young man?"

Before Swag could answer, King interjected. "Oh, baby, uh, go up to the next floor. There's a bathroom up there on the far right with a medicine kit. You should find something in there to heal that wound."

He looked at King and smiled. "All right, then." He looked back at Ivy and Sophia. "It was nice meeting you, ladies."

Ivy struck another sexy pose and put her perfectly mani-cured hand back on his chest. "Nice meeting you too, baby. I hope to do lunch, dinner, or just skip to dessert with you real soon." She examined his manhood and licked her lips. "Mmm . . ."

Swag turned around, but before he walked over to the elevator, he felt a tap on his butt. He turned around and saw Ivy smiling seductively.

"Damn, baby, you got a nice, firm, phat ass," she said, grinning lustfully.

Both King and Sophia giggled.

Swag shook his head and speed-walked to the elevator.

Chapter 9

Twinkle Toes

Once Swag got on the eleventh floor, he followed the directions King told him to find the bathroom where the first aid kit was. Once in the bathroom, he closed the door and locked it. The last thing he wanted was King's crazy ass popping up. And he especially didn't want Ivy's horny, schoolgirl ass in his business too.

Swag took the handkerchief off his wounded hand. He couldn't believe what he saw. Facing him was a huge, ugly cut—the kind you saw in horror movies. Looking at the wound, he knew he needed stitches before his hand got infected. He started to wonder why he'd even left the prison to come to the Palace. Then he thought if he stayed in the rat-hole prison, he and the fellas would've gotten a three-to-five-year sentence. Plus, Swag considered himself to be too fine to be in anyone's prison. His freedom was way too valuable to him.

As he opened the door to the medicine cabinet, he saw it was like a mini pharmacy. It had everything you might need from condoms, medicines, to Xanax, and painkillers. Swag also saw something he hadn't seen since he was a kid. Iodine. He grabbed the bottle of alcohol, cotton balls, iodine, and a few painkillers. Then he doctored his hand with the alcohol. "Aah . . ." he shouted in agony from the burning feeling. "Shit!"

Once the alcohol finished working its magic, Swag put some iodine on his hand. It burned a little, but not as bad as the alcohol. When the iodine dried, he wrapped his hand with the bandage. After it was tightly wrapped, he looked at himself in the mirror. He no longer saw that hardcore pretty boy who was running the streets of the Lou that everyone feared and loved. All he saw now was a scared little boy who didn't know if he was going to live or die. He lowered his head, trying to hold back his tears. One thing all the hustlers taught him was not to show any fear. If you did, you were considered weak. Swag took deep breaths. He was determined to win this battle and get himself out of the shit he'd gotten him into, along with his boys.

He then thought about his cousin, Brad. He wondered if Brad was still alive, if he ever got out of Brazil in one piece . . . even if he got his lady, Diamond, and that if he would ever see his cousin again. Swag lifted his head, shaking it for a moment, not knowing the answers to his own questions. He turned on the water and splashed it in his face. He also took a sip to wet his dry throat. While gazing at the mirror again, he made promises to himself that he wasn't sure he could keep. Those promises, along with prayers, revolved around his boys, keeping them safe, and finding Brad. Swag crossed his fingers, pounded his chest, kissed his balled-up hand, and pointed his index finger to the most high. "Amen."

He left the bathroom and paused when he heard music coming from down the long hall. At first, he thought about heading back down to where King was, but then he thought of Ivy's horny ass. He decided to be like a nosy white person from a horror film and investigate the noise.

Swag moved closer to the classical music, which, in his mind, was very weird to him to hear coming from King's place. When he got close to the door, he tried to remember where he'd heard that music before. A lightbulb came on in his head. Swag remembered the music to Pyotr Ilyich Tchaikovsky's famous ballet, *Swan Lake*. His little sister, Tamara, was the lead as Odette for one of her many boring dance recitals his nana used to drag him to along with his siblings.

Tamara was a talented dancer who danced hip-hop, tap, but her love was ballet. She was a mixture of the late, great Janet Collins and Janet Jackson. Swag remembered his baby sister being beautiful as a child, even though he would make fun of her. And he remembered her telling him and Nana, "When I grow up. I'm going to New York to attend Julliard to study how to be a famous prima ballerina, travel the world, be an actress and singer, live in Rome or England, marry a Russian billionaire, and have thirteen children when I retire from dancing at 55." Swag remembered Nana just laughing, especially about the parts of marrying a Russian billionaire and once she retired at 55 to have thirteen children. But the part that made Nana melt was when Tamara told her she was going to take care of her, and Nana was going to live with her in a mansion in either Rome or England.

Swag smiled at the memory, but then his face fell flat as he looked at the floor, and evil memories came into play . . . memories that related to Juanita and Mitch. They'd said negative things to Tamara like, *"You too black," "You too ugly," "You can't dance," "You a ho bitch."* Swag tried to do his best to encourage her, but he was too busy in the streets saving up to get the hell as far away from his mother and Mitch as possible. Years later, Swag was glad to find out Mitch was gunned down and killed from a drug deal gone bad.

Unfortunately, the last update he'd heard about Tamara was that she was nothing but a petty-ass thot with a coke problem. Also, before the age of 18, she'd had three kids:

two boys and a girl who were all taken from her and put into the system.

The music behind the closed door began to get even more intense. He was curious to know what was behind that door. He turned the knob and poked his head inside.

On the other side of the door was the ultimate shock surpassing all that he'd seen the last few days. It was as if he'd seen an angel that God brought to him. It was like a breath of fresh air, and he opened the door wider, realizing the room was a huge dance studio. The floor was so shiny that he could see his reflection. The walls were painted white and Tiffany green, and all the furniture pieces were from Tiffany's. What really caught Swag's eyes were the numerous photographs on the walls of the legendary dancer/singer, and St. Louis's own, Ms. Josephine Baker.

Swag took his eyes off the late Josephine Baker's photos and saw a vision of loveliness. There she was . . . a sexy, flawless, cinnamon-colored bombshell dancer in the center of the room in her own world. She was gorgeous, and she made Zaria look like a common stripper, and Milena, who he'd met back in Brazil, the ultimate gold digger she was. Swag smiled and decided to nickname the dancer "Twinkle Toes." She was petite, had soft, almond-shaped brown eyes, a cute bunny nose, kissable full lips, and her face was adorable like an expensive china doll.

Even though baby girl was petite, her body looked good in the light blue, sequin tutu with matching ballet slippers. She also had a blue headwrap on, making her even more mysterious looking. Twinkle Toes looked like she had been dancing all her life. She was making every move from a croisé, pirouette, and a plié.

Swag remembered some of the terminology Tamara had to use when she was in ballet school. He couldn't stop thinking about her as he kept watching the dancer with fascination and amazement. As the *Swan Lake* music started to die down, Twinkle Toes went behind a four-panel divider. Within seconds, African tribal music started playing. Twinkle Toes came back, but this time in a whole different outfit. She was now wearing a vintage cocktail retro with an African print Ankara dashiki dress. She still wore her head wrap, but she didn't have her ballet slippers on. She did an African traditional dance as she worked her hips and butt like she was working for tips. Swag was so impressed with this chick. He wondered how she could go from a beautiful swan to a gorgeous African goddess so quickly. He could tell she didn't belong in this brothel, and once the music was over, she bowed and sat on the floor while lowering her head.

Swag clapped his hands. "Bravo! Bravo!"

Startled, Twinkle Toes snapped her head to the side. She looked Swag's way and got off the floor. As she walked in his direction, he continued to clap.

"Hold up! What do you want? If it's what I think you want," Twinkle Toes hissed as she marched toward him with a dagger in her hand, "then you have another think coming, sir."

Swag lifted his hands and laughed. "Hey, hey, ma, it's okay. I was coming out of the bathroom when I heard your *Swan Lake* music down the hallway. I had to see what was up. I watched your routine, and I loved it. I liked how you took a classic and mixed it with African culture. It was beautiful."

Twinkle Toes had a change of heart and put the dagger behind her. She smirked at him. "Thank you, sir. But what you thought was African is a Haitian dance."

"Oh, my bad. I didn't know you were Haitian."

"Yes, sir, I'm Haitian Creole."

Swag smiled. "Damn, that's sexy. Say something in Creole for me."

She playfully rolled her eyes. She didn't want to admit it, but she knew Swag could most definitely get it. She couldn't get over how fine he was, and to her, he resembled model Don Benjamin. So, she said in Creole, "What the hell you want from me?"

"Nothing, I think you kind of fly, especially the way you dance, baby girl," he replied, remembering some of the Creole he learned while messing around with a chick in Miami.

Twinkle Toes was so impressed. "Damn, you speak Creole beautifully. Are you Haitian as well, sir?"

Swag laughed as he seemed to have her undivided attention. "Oh, nah, ma. I'm black mixed with Puerto Rican." He pointed at her with a smile on his face. "And don't ask me to speak Spanish."

They both laughed.

"I won't, sir."

"None of that 'sir' stuff." Swag held out his hand to shake hers. "I'm—"

Before he could introduce himself, they were interrupted by King's voice. "Oh, there you are."

They turned around to look at King, who was walking their way. When Swag walked into the room, the essence was so warm, vibrant, and peaceful. Now, the atmosphere felt below zero degrees. She was undoubtedly the Snow Queen or "The Snow King" of her palace.

King looked at Twinkle Toes, then at Swag. She smiled. "I see you two have met."

"Oh, not officially," Twinkle Toes said with a chuckle.

"Really?" King said. "Well, Solomon, this is my daughter, Josephine Batiste." King pointed to Twinkle Toes. Josephine and Swag shook hands.

"You can call me Josie," Josephine said.

"No, he will not. You are strictly Josephine after your idol, Josephine Baker. Josephine, this is our houseguest, Solomon Carter."

Josie ignored King and continued to smile at Swag. "Nice meeting you, sir. I mean, Solomon."

"You too, ma," Swag said.

He stood in amazement because he didn't know King had a child. "Your daughter? How? King, was you six years old when you had Josie or something?"

King shook her head and laughed. "Oh, no, baby. Josie isn't my blood child. There is no way in hell I'm fucking up this body for nine months of pure hell. I have a world to rule." She walked over to Josie. "For now, I have an adopted child and protégé." She put both her hands on Josie's face. Then she walked in circles, admiring her child. She'd cared for Josie ever since she was 12½ years old. At first, she nurtured her like she were her flesh and blood child, but now that Josie was getting older and sexier, King had so many plans for her. Sometimes, after sex with one of her guys or girls, King would often masturbate herself to sleep just thinking about Josie. And the best part about Josie that turned King on was that baby girl was still a virgin. If there were one thing King loved, it was a good ol' virgin, especially a female. Her passion for Josie, however, could wait. She noticed a few things with Josie were out of place, so she frowned.

"Sweetie, what did I tell you about dancing to that god-awful African jungle music? This won't take you places like ballet will. And what's up with the getup?" King pointed to the African attire and head wrap. "I make sure you have plenty of prima ballerina outfits and materials to help you make your own. Not this mess."

Swag couldn't believe King was insulting Josie's attire and Haitian culture. But what got him was how Josie was taking King's insults with a simple sweet smile on her face.

"Please dispose of the garment, ASAP," King said.

"Sure, Mother, no problem," Josie replied softly, knowing damn well she wasn't throwing away an outfit she'd made—

especially one she considered the best outfit she made
yet. For now, she was going to put it in her secret place
where she kept outfits King didn't approve of.

King smiled and looked up at the head wrap on Josie's
head. "For God's sake, Josephine." Without asking, she
took the headwrap off Josie's head.

Swag had a look in his eyes like, "Oh no, this trick didn't."
Now that was mad disrespectful what this bitch just did.
This chick! But then Swag noticed why King wasn't feeling
the head wrap on Josie. It was covering her long, black girl
hair, which, in America, would be considered good hair.
Josie's hair flowed down her back. It was the icing on the
cake that brought out her beauty.

King threw the head wrap to the side and stroked Josie's
hair. "You know how I feel about these rugs on your head.
No child of mine wears those. Hair this good should never
ever be covered or even cut. I don't want you ever to wear
this shit in my presence. The only towel I want to see on
your head is the one you come out of the shower wearing.
Understand?" King placed her hand on Josie's shoulder.

Josie thought her mother's hand on her shoulder was
like venom from a snake, but she didn't want to make her
mad. She put a smile on her face and told King what she
wanted to hear. "Sure, Mother, not a problem."

King smiled. "Thank you, my child. Now, go to your
room and get out of that outfit. Dinner will be served in a
few hours."

Josie nodded.

King narrowed her eyes and looked seductively at Swag.
"Come, Solomon." She walked toward the door to exit.

After King left the room, the chill from her negative vibes
evaporated.

Swag addressed Josie again. "Nice meeting you, Josie.
And don't worry about what King said. You look beautiful
in that outfit, with or without the head wrap."

Josie was flattered. "Thank you. It was nice meeting you too, Solomon."

"Swag."

"What?" Josie asked with a confused look on her face. "Swag?"

"Yeah, that was my tag name back home. If I call you Josie, then you can call me Swag. Just not when King's around. Between us."

Josie giggled and nodded. She was about to open her mouth when she heard King from outside the room, yelling, "Solomon! Come! Now!"

Swag walked to the door, and in moments, Blood entered the room with a twisted face.

"Hurry up. The King doesn't like to wait," Blood said. "Let's go."

"Nice meeting you, Ms. Josephine," Swag said.

Josie nodded and mouthed, "You too, Swag."

That bought a smile to Swag's face. He felt all warm and fuzzy around Josie. He hadn't had this feeling inside him for years. He didn't know what kind of Haitian voodoo Josie had put on him, but it was working. The feeling he had wasn't sexual—it was like something he hadn't felt since Zaria. He wanted to get to know Josie on a physical level. She seemed so pure, innocent, and like a diamond in the rough. Being around her made him feel like he was a teenager again. But Swag's mood changed when he felt a hard blow to his head.

"Ow!" Swag fell to his knees. "Shit! Shit, man!" He rubbed the back of his head. It felt like his head was on fire from that hit. "That shit hurt!" He looked up at Blood, who was in his space. Blood chuckled as he cracked his knuckles.

"Young buck, what I gave you was just an appetizer out of respect for the King, *my* King. If you fail to follow the

King's orders again, trust and believe, the repercussions will be a whole lot worse."

Swag rolled his eyes and rubbed his throbbing head.

"You hear me?" Blood said, pulling Swag up by his neck.

Swag was in utter shock. He didn't know if Blood planned on snapping his neck.

Blood shouted in his ear. "Do. You. Hear. Me?"

Josie moved in another direction because she didn't want to be in the middle of this bullshit. Her heart went out to Swag. *Please don't hurt him,* she thought.

Swag was in so much pain that all he could do was cooperate. "Yeah, yeah! I hear you, man. Shit!"

Blood smiled and patted him on his head. "Good boy." Then he pushed him down to the ground. "Now, move your ass!"

Swag struggled to get up, and Josie rushed over to help him. He waved her off. "Back up. I got this! Shit!"

Josie stepped back. "Fine!"

Swag regained his balance and walked out of Josie's dance room. She walked around for a moment, trying to process what had just happened. "Damn," she whispered.

She was at a total loss. She had no idea what her mother was going to do with Swag. She knew it wasn't going to be good, so she lost her enthusiasm to dance and went to shower.

Swag and Blood walked down the long hallway and headed toward the elevator. Swag looked back at Josie's door. He didn't mean to raise his voice at her, but he'd be damned if he was going to look like a punk in front of any female. Hell, in his mind, he was still fearless and savage at heart. The only thing on his mind, at the moment, however, was to crack Blood's skull in half and get that ass when he was off guard.

Blood turned his head back around and made himself clear. "No, not for you. Josephine is off-limits."

"What you mean about off-limits, playa?"

Blood grabbed Swag's arm and twisted it before pushing the up button on the elevator. "Listen, I'm only going to say this once. Don't look, say, or do anything to Josephine. She's King's child, and no man is to touch her. So, as a fair warning, don't touch her. Understand?"

The elevator door opened, and Blood pushed Swag inside and made him hit the stainless steel wall hard, causing Swag to fall to the ground. Blood joined him inside and pulled Swag up by his collar. "I said, do you understand? Don't touch Josephine!"

"I heard you, man. Do you have to keep saying it?" Swag said, giving Blood cold eyes and twisting his lips.

"You better put a smile on that face, pretty boy."

Swag ignored him.

"Trust and believe, playboy, we goin' have our time," Blood pointed in Swag's face.

I'm looking forward to it, Swag thought and smiled at him wickedly.

Chapter 10

Home Sweet Home

Swag and Blood arrived on the twelfth floor and kept going back and forth with each other. That was, until they saw King leaning against one of the three golden doors with a frown on her face.

"Stop all the nonsense," she said. "We have work to do."

"You lucky I listen to the boss," Blood said as he backed out of Swag's space.

After Swag moved away from him, he looked at King, who had changed her look a little. She was now only wearing a bra and a white lace skirt. She took off her heels, and her long hair flowed down her back. Swag thought she could be a Victoria Secret's model the way she looked.

"Solomon, come to me." She held out her hands.

Swag was skeptical about King's unpredictable ass. First, the girl cuts Travis's finger off, sliced his hand open, and even drank his blood. He still couldn't get that sick shit out of his mind, and he wondered where Travis and Tyler were. Like Brad, he didn't know if he would see them again.

As Swag approached King, she put her arms around him and licked his neck as if it were ice cream and bit his earlobe.

In a weird way, what King did to him turned him on. She stopped hugging him and looked at his rough face and hand. She also looked at a bruise on his face where Blood had hit him. "My, my, my poor boy. I'ma get my peoples up here to take better care of that hand. The last thing you need is to get your hand infected." She took his hand and sucked on every finger. Mainly, his middle finger that she eased in and out of her mouth. She also pecked the bruise on his face. "I'm sorry Blood played rough with you."

Swag didn't believe her.

"But when I say come, you need to come. Got it?" King ordered.

"Got it," Swag said dryly.

King laughed, knowing she was now dealing with a hardheaded dude. But for now, she was going to let his dry-ass remark slide. In her mind, he was going to learn that she was nothing to fuck with. She ran Costa Rica, and what she said goes.

"Now, this is your room." She turned around and opened the door wide.

They walked into the room, and Swag looked around at how nice it was. It was spacious and had a black and gold Victorian bed with white, Egyptian cotton sheets, and beautiful throw pillows on top. The walls were painted an eggshell color, and the carpet was a plush white. All of the furniture in the room, from the nightstands, lamps, and chairs, were black and gold—Versace inspired.

"Solomon!" King shouted to get his attention. She then snapped her fingers. "Swag!"

Swag responded, knowing she didn't like to wait to be answered. After what he had been through today, he knew he was dealing with an even crazier motherfucker than he was used to. Swag was willing to do anything to stay in her good graces.

"I'm sorry, King. I was just lost in the dopeness of this room."

"I'm glad that it meets your approval." She stood behind him and wrapped her arms around his waist, then started to rub his back.

Again, Swag was both scared and turned on at the same time. He even started to get another woody in his pants, but unfortunately, he didn't know if she intended to hurt him or use him for sexual pleasure.

King loved the way Swag's body felt next to hers, even though he was wearing his clothes. But the one thing she hated was he smelled like the ship they'd been on. King was so tired of seeing him in the same clothes. If it were up to her, Swag would be walking around butt-ass naked. She smiled at that thought, but she thought about her horny younger-men-loving mother. King loved her mother to death, but she would be damned if her mother messed with this gem. King didn't know what between Swag and Josie was driving her crazy inside, but she wanted them both. Yes, she wanted her *child* sexually, but she was now focused on Swag, as well.

"I love my men in nothing but the best." She pointed to a golden closet. "There are clothes in there. I suggest you bathe because you smell. Also, I'll have someone come in and take a look at your hand and face. Dinner is in two-and-a-half hours in the great room, and your attendance is required." She kissed him on his cheek and then whispered in his ear. "Two-and-a-half hours. Not a minute later." She smacked him on his butt, but before she headed to the door, Swag asked her a question.

"Will my friends be joining us for dinner too? I've been wondering if they're okay, and where they're at."

"No worries," King said. "They're fine. As for you, I'll see you later, sweet cheeks." She blew him a kiss before leaving the room. Then she walked out, closing the door behind her.

Swag didn't like her answer, but he went over to the door and locked it. He took off his shirt and smelled it. It *was* sweaty and stinky. He tossed it on a chair, and needing to relax, he wished he'd had a blunt or some of that good old

Brazilian cocaine. For now, his best bet was the Xanax in his pocket and a nap. He reached into his pocket to get a pill. After that, he sighed and flopped down on the bed. It felt so good, and the sheets were soft as clouds. He pulled one over his head, grabbed a pillow, and let the Xanax take effect.

Chapter 11

Paco's New Plot

When arriving at Escazú, a second canton in the province in San José, to a beautiful white mansion in an Exquisite Escazu Residence, everyone except for Paco was in awe. They'd never seen fly shit like this except in rap videos with a lot of video girls dancing around. Once the limousine was parked, Paco, Travis, Ike, Rock, Landon, Miguel, and Nash got out of the limo. The estate on the outside had a well-manicured lawn and beautiful white roses everywhere. The butler, a big dude looking like Lurch from the Addams Family, stood in the doorway and waved for everyone to come inside. It was almost identical to King's Palace but on a much smaller scale. Paco was the only one who didn't seem impressed. He was still bitter about what had happened to him.

He remembered having his first meeting with King and their possible partnership to take down his father and the Hernandez Cartel. He also remembered the steamy sexy nights he and King had in the mansion. Those were the good days, but now, he had nothing to smile about.

The butler invited everyone to find a room and get settled. As Paco headed to the main room, he remembered being in, on the way there, he couldn't stop thinking about King's and Midnight's betrayal. None of the men he'd known for years had done a damn thing to help him, but the main person he thought for sure would have his back was Midnight.

At that moment, Paco knew the glory days of being the Prince of Texas were officially over. He opened the door to the suite, and with so much confusion on his face, he sat on the edge of the bed. He kept thinking of who to blame for this mess. There was enough blame to go around, but all Paco could do was turn his anger to Swag. "Son of a bitch," he mumbled.

Feeling angry, he grunted, paced the room, and ripped his shirt. After tossing it aside, he examined his Adonis physique. He checked to see if he had some broken ribs, but luckily for Paco, nothing seemed broken, just swollen. He turned on the water in the sink and let it get warm. Once it was the right temperature, he took a bar of soap and rubbed it on his face. If he could somehow wash away all the dirt he'd done and go back to the person he used to be, he would have. But crime money was flowing within his family, and within one year of being in the family business, he made the Hernandez Cartel the top of the food chain—even more than his father or grandfather ever had. With that significant accomplishment and drive, Paco Hernandez was going to be the Mexican version of John Gotti.

He looked in the mirror and mouthed, "I fucked up." He remembered the conversation he and his grandfather had when he decided to drop out of college and build the family business.

"Little Paco, you need to go back to school. Fuck that basketball and cartel shit. Make something better out of yourself. Become a sports doctor, a lawyer, or even a sports agent."

"Naw, Papa, I'ma focus on my bread and making the family business number one."

As he wiped his face with a towel, Paco thought of how stupid he was for not taking his grandfather's advice. He took a breath as he looked at himself again in the mirror. He still looked rough, but he was glad to be all alone and at peace for the time being.

"Aah," he moaned as he lay on the bed.

He closed his eyes for a moment and tried to clear his mind. Just as he was about to relax, he heard the door crack open. He quickly opened his eyes, and when he reached into his pants pocket, he realized he didn't have his gun or a knife.

"Shit! I don't need any more surprises today," he whispered.

He lifted his head, only to see his friend Landon. He was the pretty boy of Paco's crew, a mixture of Mexican, African American, and Chinese. With a smooth butter complexion, slanted, dark brown eyes, and a lean muscular body, Landon had all the chicks back in Texas going crazy over him. Paco sighed from relief that it was only him.

"Shit, man, don't ever sneak in on me like that," Paco said.

Landon cocked his head back. "Damn, man. Chill out with that shit." Landon came into the room wearing cargo shorts and a wife-beater. His left arm was covered with a Chinese dragon and a naked Mexican woman, showing honor to his Mexican and Chinese heritage. On his right arm were tattoos of his family. He sat beside Paco. "Just checking to see if you was cool, that's all. You okay?"

"Now, I know you ain't ask me that question. I didn't see you help me after getting my ass kicked by both Swag and Tyler or Travis, whichever twin lost a finger. And you have the nerve to ask if I'm okay? Hell no, I'm not okay! I'm pissed off with that bitch, King, but mainly that nigger, Swag. I want his blood so badly I can taste it."

Paco was so fired up that he balled up his fist. And without warning, he punched Landon right in his eye. Landon fell to the ground and covered his eye.

"Damn, man." He looked up at Paco. "What was that for? What in the hell is wrong with you?"

Paco laughed and felt somewhat better. He didn't mean to punch Landon, but he had to let out his frustrations. In his mind, he was pretending to hit Swag's ass. Paco knew he needed some control back on his ship. He was only in Costa Rica for one reason, and that was to bring down his father so he could rule the Hernandez Cartel. But the first thing he had to do was put his boys back in check. Meaning that *he* should be the one thing they feared day and night. Paco got off the bed and stepped up to Landon.

"That was for not having my back earlier. That punch was just an appetizer, but next time, you'll get the main course if you betray me." Paco pretended to slice his own throat. "Do you understand me?"

Landon didn't respond.

"I *said,* do you hear me?" Paco shouted and slapped Landon's face.

He winced and hurried off the floor. "Yeah, I hear you."

"Good." Paco walked away and sat back on the bed.

With a mean mug on his face, Landon stood at a distance. He felt kind of bad for not helping Paco, and he also knew there would be consequences, sooner or later.

"I apologize for not having your back, and it will never happen again. But what do we do now, P?"

Paco looked at Landon with a devilish smile. "Bro, the first thing is to get back on King's good side. Work out a plan to murder that bitch-ass father of mine, along with everyone associated with the Hernandez Cartel. Then I can finally collect what is mine. We need to figure out a way to get that bitch, King, alone, without that clown-ass Blood so I can snap that pretty little neck of hers. And other heads I want on silver platters are Travis, Tyler, and the big prizes, Swag and Midnight."

Landon curiously looked at him. "But why Midnight? He's our boy. And why kill King? If it weren't for her, we'd still be in that shithole back in Brazil."

Paco shook his head and laughed at Landon.

"Landon, you're so young and naïve, my homeboy. Of course, I know Midnight is my boy, but today, he showed his disloyalty to the future Hernandez Cartel and me. You see, just like you, he didn't come to my defense. I would expect a young buck like you not to come to my defense, but Midnight? I knew that dude since we were kids, ever since his family came from Ghana with only three dollars to their name and no place to stay until my grandfather made Midnight's father an employee and life member of the Hernandez Cartel. Midnight and his father signed their signatures in blood to this organization. They serve *me*, not that King bitch. So he has to die. And King! That bitch must die, even though the sex was damn good."

Landon laughed. "Damn, man, that crazy girl's punany is that good?"

Paco nodded. "Homes, that shit is better than a virgin's and so tight. The taste was delicious, like butter pecan ice cream."

Landon laughed again. "You lucky bastard."

Landon couldn't remember the last time he had a chick's good-good like that, especially from those messy hoodrats back in Texas. "Why is it that all the psycho chicks are all beautiful and have that bomb-ass pussy?"

Paco laughed, losing thought of his plans. To him, the answer to that question would always be a mystery. In his playboy days, he loved to mess with the crazy chicks or the ones with low self-esteem. He loved those days . . . until he'd met the love of his life, Raven. Thinking of her, he reached into his pocket and pulled out a photo. It was a photo of him, his wifey, and their daughter. He smiled while looking at his family. He missed them so much. He'd thought about all the times he cheated on her, and Raven gave so much to him. Kind of how his father did his mother in the past.

Paco's smile turned into a frown. His thoughts went back to the reason why he was in Costa Rica.

"Look," he said to Landon, "fuck King, Midnight, and that bastard Swag. I'm going to get my revenge, and more blood than ever is going to be flowing in the waters of Costa Rica. It's time to show the world who the *real* king is."

Landon nodded and agreed with his true boss.

"Now, get outta here until I need you, my new lieutenant."

Landon was amazed. "Lieutenant?"

"Yeah, like I told you, fuck Midnight! Now, get the fuck outta my room."

Landon left, excited about his new status. Paco relaxed and looked at the beautiful view of the sunset on the waters. He smiled. *This shit will all be mine. First, the Hernandez Cartel, then the Bello Crime Family, and then the Leopard Clit. Like Julius Caesar once said, "I came, I saw, I conquered."*

Paco laughed hysterically about being the god of all the crime world with mofos bowing at his feet. "It's game time, bitches."

Chapter 12

Royal Treatment

Deep into his nap, Swag started to feel peaceful, especially after the eventful day he'd had. He dreamt of being with his sons.

They were in another country, in a big white house. They ran around the spacious backyard, and Li'l Swag giggled as he fell on the manicured green grass. Swag was holding Namond in his arms. All three of them looked dapper from head to toe. A woman exited the white house in a beautiful white wedding dress with a veil covering her face. Swag looked at the mystery bride with a curious look on his face. She was a little round in the stomach. He could tell she was expecting. She pointed to Swag and motioned for him to come to her. Swag smiled as he put Namond down and walked up to the lady in the wedding dress. She looked beautiful in her bridal gown, but he had to see who was behind the veil.

Maybe it's Zaria, he thought.

Swag lifted the veil . . . only to see it was King. She was the last person he wanted to see, and a few seconds later, blood started to stream down her face.

King laughed sinisterly. "Surprise!" She continued to laugh evilly.

Soon, blood covered her entire wedding gown. Swag stepped back.

He was so disgusted by this ordeal that he continued to back away from her. He looked at his boys, who were now bloody with cuts all over their faces.

"Eww," Swag said, frightened as he moved away from them.

Li'l Swag began to laugh sinisterly as well.

"Oh my God," Swag replied with tears streaming down his face. He turned around to run away from everything but was cut off by high flames of fire. He looked back at King and his children, who continued to laugh at him.

"Come join us," King said in an evil voice, still laughing. "Welcome to my world."

Swag's heart beat rapidly. He thought he had died and gone to hell.

"Oh God," Swag cried out and panicked. "Please, God. Please! Please!"

A hand touched his shoulder.

Swag shot up from his nightmare. He took a deep breath and noticed his body was soaked with sweat.

Thank God that shit was all just a dream, he thought.

He felt another tap on his shoulder, and when he turned around, he saw King standing there.

"Aah!" He was still a little startled by her, especially after that dream.

"Easy, easy, Solomon, darling. You just had a bad dream." King went over to the nightstand to get him some whiskey and two aspirins.

"What's that?" he asked with a tight face.

"Just take it. It'll calm your nerves." King gave him the pills.

Swag took the pills and tossed back the whiskey. He cleared his throat and gave the glass back to King.

"Good boy," she said, then put the whiskey and glass back on the nightstand. She stared at Swag and admired how he looked with sweat raining on his body. Her freaky thoughts made her laugh.

"What's so funny, ma?" Swag raised a brow.

"Nothing. I just came to remind you that dinner will be served shortly. I need you to get cleaned up because I will not have an unkempt caveman at my table."

Swag sucked on his lip. "No problem. I'll take a quick shower. I had intended to, but I fell asleep."

He began to get out of bed, but King shouted, "Sit!"

Swag followed her command and remained on the bed. She sauntered over to the door and opened it.

"Come in, ladies."

King was full of surprises. Entering the room were some of the most beautiful Japanese women he'd ever seen in his life. All three women stood in the middle of the room with matching lavender satin robes on. To Swag, these Asian beauties were so gorgeous that they didn't look real at all. King looked at her girls and snapped her fingers.

The women disrobed and let them fall to the ground. Their bodies were sickening, and for Japanese chicks, they were slim with thick curves, thick thighs, nice asses, flat stomachs, and tits for days. Swag had drool coming out of his mouth.

King could tell Swag was pleased, primarily through the lining of his pants. But to her, this wasn't *that* type of party. To King, Desiree and these three were just appetizers for greater things to come. *She* would be the main course, and those other girls had nothing on her platinum punany.

"Solomon, close your mouth before flies make a home in it."

Swag closed his mouth but licked his lips.

King stood front and center to let everyone know she was still captain of this ship. She walked back and forth, looking at her girls. Even though the ladies were naked, they were obedient and stood like soldiers in an army.

"Solomon, these are my girls." She pointed at the first one. "That's Mina."

Mina had a beautiful smile. She bowed down.

King pointed to the one in the middle. "She's called Blacknese."

Blacknese smiled and nodded.

Swag smiled, looking her up and down. *Damn, baby girl is thick.*

King pointed to the last one, "And that is Ms. Mami."

Ms. Mami was a little older than the other girls. She looked about in her mid or late 40s but was still attractive. She didn't smile at Swag.

"My girls are going to take care of you from head to toe." She looked back at her girls. "Ladies, take care of my special houseguest. He's all yours."

King moved closer to Swag. "Have fun, and see you at dinner." She left the room and closed the door behind her.

Swag was officially alone with the sexy Asian women. Mina and Blacknese pulled him off the bed. They started to speak in their own language as they took off the remainder of his clothes. Mina took off his socks. To her, his feet stank but were still pretty looking. Blacknese had the honor of pulling off his pants, along with his underwear. She admired his Adonis muscular body and his semierect penis. Then she glanced at his nice ass and smacked it. Swag enjoyed every bit of the attention. He couldn't wait to see what was next, and as they led him to the bathroom, they began to rub his back and giggled as they played with his ass cheeks.

The Jacuzzi tub was filled with warm water and bubbles. Blacknese was washing Swag's back, arms, chest, and stomach. She even shampooed and deep conditioned his hair. She used a razor to shave his face and line his beard. Swag was on cloud nine. This experience made him think of his favorite movie, *Coming to America,* starring Eddie Murphy. He felt a twitch between his legs that made him almost roll his eyes back.

"Aah," he groaned in so much pleasure. This whole time he was erect.

Blacknese patted the soapy sponge on Swag's back to calm the erection down. She smiled, knowing he was pleased with their performance. If they were doing their deluxe special service, Swag wouldn't be able to control himself. His eyes were half-closed, and he felt a little natural as he did with Desiree. Mina was in the water looking like Ariel from *The Little Mermaid.* She flashed her sexy smile. Swag's attention was on her wet hourglass frame and suckable, pierced nipples that were hard as black diamonds. Swag wanted to suck on them like a starving newborn.

In Japanese, they said, "Your beautiful penis and asshole are clean now, sir," she said.

Swag didn't understand a lick of what Mina had spoken. All he knew was that he felt good, and he was squeaky clean. He took a deep, relaxing breath.

Once the bath of pleasure was over, Swag came out of the bathroom wearing only a black and gold Versace bathrobe with Versace flip-flops. Ms. Mami led him to a manicure and pedicure station and placed his feet in a steaming hot foot bath.

"Ah! Hot, hot!" Swag yelled as he quickly lifted his feet from the water.

Ms. Mami turned off the water and rubbed his feet. "Sorry, sir. I hope I didn't hurt you."

She turned on the cold water, and once the bath was filled, Ms. Mami checked the temperature, knowing Swag would be pleased. He was.

"Aah, much better." Swag let the warm water soothe his feet while Ms. Mami massaged them. She also worked on his hand. While in the process, she looked at Blacknese and Mina, and spoke in Japanese, "All right, you two know what to do. And do it good to keep this black American entertained."

Blacknese and Mina faced Swag, but Mina was behind Blacknese.

Swag was tuned in and wondered what they were about to do. At first, they started caressing each other. Mina massaged Blacknese's breasts while she rubbed Mina's long legs.

"Mmm," Mina groaned as she bit into her lip. "Yes! Right there!"

Mina looked between Blacknese's legs, and baby girl was dripping really good. She licked her lips while zoning in on her wetness. Feeling thirsty, she sucked on Blacknese's neck like a vampire and tried to drain all the blood out of her.

Blacknese breathed heavily. She was lost in total ecstasy as she rubbed on her stomach. All Mina wanted to do was feel Blacknese take her all in. Sometimes, Mina wished she had a dick to do the work, but she knew she had the next best thing. She slowly rubbed on Blacknese's hard nipples. Then she lowered her hand to her wet pussy. Mina started to tease Blacknese's stiffened clit. They both were aroused, and when Blacknese began to shake, more juices oozed down her thick thighs. Unable to contain herself, she took two fingers inside of her goodness and used her other hand to tackle Blacknese's right breast.

Aahs and oohs filled the room, but Swag was locked in a trance as he watched.

"You like that shit, don't you?" Mina asked while pumping her fingers in and out of Blacknese.

"Yes!" Blacknese moaned and came uncontrollably. She was barely able to stand up anymore.

Mina whispered into Blacknese's ear, "Let's give this black American something that'll have him running back to tell his friends."

The ladies started to kiss each other hard, with so much passion and lust.

By then, Swag had a full woody and could feel the pre-come leaking out of the tip of his penis. But his focus was broken when he felt a needle going into his hand.

"Shit," he yelled as he looked at Ms. Mami, injecting him with a needle and putting some weird medicine inside of him. "Damn, lady, what are you doing? What are you putting in me? Stop!"

Swag tried to get up, but by then, Ms. Mami had put her potion in him—and she wasn't done. Next, she put the needle into his neck. Swag was weakened from the first needle and had no weapons to defend himself.

"Calm down," Ms. Mami said while holding the needle at his neck. "Continue to watch the show."

Feeling drowsy, he continued to look at Blacknese and Mina through narrowed eyes. Ms. Mami slowly removed the needle from his neck and began to do what she did best. She stitched his numb hand and kept massaging it. Swag, however, watched Blacknese and Mina go over to the bed. Blacknese lay on the bed with her legs wide open while Mina went in on her pretty pink walls. They were on a sexual roller-coaster ride.

Swag wasn't even thinking about his hand or whatever Ms. Mami had injected in him. If he were going to die, at least he was going to die a happy man.

He watched as the ladies started to bump pussies. The moaning and groaning took things to a new level. Swag wanted in. He couldn't wait much longer.

Ms. Mami looked at Swag's hard-on. "Oh my." She smiled and finished wrapping his hand. She was determined to get in on the action too.

As he watched the festivities, Ms. Mami dropped to her knees and put his manhood in her warm mouth. He was having the best of both worlds—engrossed in the best show ever with the chicks on the bed and getting sucked off in the process by Ms. Mami at the same time. He rolled his eyes back in total sexual bliss and enjoyed how Ms. Mami was treating his steel like royalty.

"Shit, Mami, suck that shit."

Swag was not paying attention to the microcamera in his room. King was in her room, looking at this sex orgy on her laptop and getting turned on. She zoomed in on Swag, whose mouth was open like he was praising God. King moved the camera over to her girls on the bed, getting it in.

"Damn," King said while licking her lips. Like the others, she wanted in too.

Swag was about to come. "Shit, aah, daaamn!"

He released all his babies in Ms. Mami's warm mouth and felt relieved. There were no more signs of stress on his face, only beads of sweat. He fell back on the chair and looked at Mina, who had passed out on Blacknese's juicy breast.

Everyone was on a high in the room that now smelled like sweaty sex. King walked in, clapping her hands.

"Bravo!" She walked over to where Swag was, eye-fucking him like he was the only person in the room.

Ms. Mami wiped across her wet mouth and stood up. Blacknese and Mina got off the bed. Swag tucked his penis back inside his bathrobe, and they all gave King their attention.

King laughed. "Relax, baby. You ain't got nothing I haven't seen."

The ladies put their robes back on and waited for King's directions.

"You all can go now, ladies. Thank you for taking care of Solomon for me." She waved them off.

Once the ladies left the room, King closed the door and turned to Swag. She no longer had a scarf on her head. Her hair was slicked back, and she was still wearing her kimono with bare feet. Her makeup was beat to the gods as she walked over to the bed and placed dry clean sheets on it.

"Hmm, I see you're relaxed."

Swag cleared his throat with a slight smile on his face. "*Very* relaxed."

King looked at his hand. "It seems that Ms. Mami did a great job stitching and cleaning up your hand."

Swag was pleased by the work Ms. Mami had done sewing his hand. "Wow, this is—"

"I know. Ms. Mami is a miracle worker. You'd better keep it covered for a while, and air it out when you go to bed. Don't worry; the stitches will dissolve in a few weeks."

Swag wasn't sure if he should thank her or not. After all, she was the one who had sliced his hand. King, however, planted a soft kiss on his lips. Swag hesitated to kiss her back, so she backed away.

"So, did you enjoy your time with the ladies?"

"What, King?"

She laughed, still knowing Swag was a bit dizzy from the injection and high from the festivities. But even though he was in his *Drunk in Love* moment, she still demanded her respect. She went back into her boss bitch mode.

"Don't play dumb. I asked you a question. With my girls . . . Did you enjoy yourself? Did they take care of you?"

Swag shrugged to avoid showing her his enthusiasm. "It was different. Something I know I won't get back at home."

King nodded. "Glad, you liked it, but don't get used to it. You can't afford the price for that show." She reached down and put her hand around his dick.

Swag jerked back and was caught off guard. "Ooh," he moaned.

"Down, boy," King whispered and licked the side of his neck. She let go of his meat and got off his lap. "Now, get ready for dinner. It's in thirty minutes, so don't be late."

King walked toward the door but turned to say one more thing to Swag. "You'd better save some of that for me."

Swag nodded and didn't say a word. He intended to stay on King's good side because he knew he had to come up with a master plan to get out of this beautiful nightmare he considered hell.

Chapter 13

Eat Me Out

Swag was in the bathroom, getting dressed for dinner. He looked at himself in the full-length mirror. He was starting to feel like himself again—the pretty dude that had all the money and every chick on his jock, especially since he looked so sexy in a red Dolce & Gabbana suit with a red dress shirt and matching red Ferragamo dress shoes. He topped off the look with diamond and gold jewelry King had left for him. With all the diamonds in his ears, a gold chain on his neck, a gold bracelet on his left wrist, and a gold and diamond Rolex on his right wrist, he felt like a mixture of Lucifer and a big-time pimp wearing all the red. Nonetheless, Swag looked at his reflection one last time before exiting the bathroom.

He looked at the messy bed and reminisced about Blacknese and Mina's wild lesbian sexcapade. *That was some wild shit,* he thought and laughed as he left the room to head to dinner. He looked across the grand hallway at the door that led to Blood's room. Swag lifted his middle finger and then headed to the elevator. When he heard a weird sound, he turned, and Blood's door opened. The last thing Swag wanted was to share the elevator with him. He hurried to push the first-floor button, and lucky for him, the doors closed before Blood got there.

"Yes, thank you, Jesus," Swag whispered.

As the elevator was descending, it stopped on the tenth floor. The doors opened, and Tyler stepped on, looking like a million bucks. His Afro was nicely sponged, mustache and goatee were trimmed, and he wore Versace dressed to the nines. From the sunglasses covering his eyes to a gold and black long-sleeve, button-down shirt and white slacks, Tyler was hooked up. And just like Swag, he was dripping in jewelry. As the elevator closed, they looked at each other with smiles on their faces.

"What's up, bruh?" Tyler asked. "I didn't know where you was at. I haven't seen my brother, either, and I just want to make sure he's okay."

"Me too. How you holding up, man?" Swag asked.

"As good as can be expected."

"That's cool, but you do know that Travis can handle himself, right? Deep down, I believe he's okay."

"I don't know, bruh. You know as well as I do that Travis has always been the laid-back twin. It's always been him and me or all of us. He's never ever fought his own battles, and I was always there to make sure he was good." He paused and swallowed hard. "You know what my brother told me, man?"

"What was that?" Swag asked, feeling somewhat guilty.

"He told me that when we were in Brazil and when he got that fifty K, he was going to get his life together and go back to school."

"Damn," Swag replied, shaking his head. "That's still a possibility, man. Don't worry. Travis will be all right. Maybe some of that semi street mentality we all have will rub off on him."

Tyler lowered his shades to look at Swag. "I hope you right. I just feel bad about his finger, and only God knows where he's at. Plus, there's no telling what that fake-ass Mexican version of Michael Corleone will do."

They both laughed at Swag mentioning Tyler's street mentality.

"I do have street mentality," Tyler said.

Swag giggled. "Bruh, a year in juvie doesn't count as street cred."

They continued to laugh until Tyler cleared his throat.

"But for real, man, that's my twin. He's the only family I have left to keep me sane, especially after all the bullshit we've been through. Let's not forget we threw Stan to the wolves. Plus, the heart of The Fellas, Brad, is out there somewhere with his lady. This is all fucked up." Deep in Tyler's soul, he wanted to scream that this was all on Swag. But he knew at the same time he was a grown-ass man that made up his own mind. So the only person he could blame was himself.

Swag looked over at Tyler. "I know, man. I'ma figure something out. We goin' get outta this shit I put us in." Swag wanted to break at that very moment, but he couldn't right now. He wasn't going to give up until he made shit right.

"How do you intend to do that?"

Swag took a deep breath. "I don't know yet, but in the meantime, do what you can to cooperate. Just go with the flow and pretend that everything is good. Can you do that for me?"

Tyler nodded because he knew the key to all of them staying alive was cooperation.

The elevator doors opened.

"Here we go," Swag said and stepped off the elevator. Tyler followed.

An Asian dude in a waiter's uniform who looked to be in his twenties greeted them. "Good evening, gentlemen. Welcome," he said in Japanese.

Both Swag and Tyler looked at each other clueless, then looked back at the Japanese waiter.

"What's up, man?" they said in unison.

The waiter put a fake smile on his face and snapped his fingers. Immediately, two Asian women came out dressed in traditional geisha attire.

One had almond-shaped brown eyes, and her face was covered with a white mask with ruby-red lipstick. She wore a pink floral traditional kimono with matching zoris on her feet. The one standing next to Tyler had slanted eyes, as well, and she wore the same white mask with ruby-red lipstick, but she wore a black and gold traditional kimono with black zoris.

"Greetings, gentlemen, shall we?"

Tyler and Swag didn't understand them because they spoke in Japanese, but they still responded.

"Good evening, ladies," they said.

The waiter cleared his throat, and everyone looked at him.

"Follow me," he said, leading them to the dining area.

As the waiter escorted them to the dining room, Swag and Tyler saw ladies and some men walking in and out with clients. Swag couldn't believe how beautiful some of these girls were. And some of the clients they had looked very familiar to him. They passed the great room, which was decked out with seventeenth-century white and gold furniture, a floor-to-ceiling stone fireplace, and numerous expensive chandeliers.

The room made Swag and Tyler halt their steps to see if they saw anyone familiar there. They did see an old white man who was in his early 70s, with white hair and a white beard. He was slightly on the pudgy side that showed well in a sky-blue shirt, a black blazer, denim jeans, and loafers. He looked decent for an older man, and with glasses on the tip of his nose, he looked like a college professor—which he wasn't at all. He was one of the world's most well-known filmmakers and businessmen in Hollywood. His net worth as of 2013 was $7.3 trillion. He was known for his futuristic films and creating creatures from other universes since the late 1970s. He most recently sold his movies to another well-known movie studio for $10 billion.

Swag and Tyler couldn't believe they were in the same vicinity as a man whose films they grew up watching. The man was sitting on the sofa drinking a glass of scotch, smoking a Cuban cigar, and eating some macadamia nuts. He didn't even acknowledge Swag and Tyler, because he was too busy looking at the expensive artwork on the walls.

Swag was in deep thought, thinking the man must've been there for entertainment just like many other people were.

The geisha girls pulled the two men toward the dining room. "Come on, sir," said the one next to Tyler.

The Asian waiter opened the French doors, and they all went into the all-red-and-black gothic-inspired dining room. The only thing that balanced the colors in the room were the gold plates and utensils, the crystal champagne flutes, and famous paintings hanging on the walls.

Swag thought the room was unique, but at the same time, it looked satanic, like he was going to eat dinner with the devil.

The geisha girls led the men to their seats, and after they were seated, the girls exited the room. It was dead silent. Tyler and Swag nervously looked at each other. They started to leave until they saw Midnight come into the room. Midnight looked like sexy chocolate, rocking an all-white Armani suit with matching shoes. Another beautiful geisha girl escorted him inside and led him to his chair. He took a seat next to Tyler. Midnight looked at both Swag and Tyler before checking out the dining room.

"This some fly-ass shit in this place," he said.

"Yeah, tell me about it," Tyler said, trying to make small talk.

Midnight cleared his throat and looked at Swag. "So, aye, did you hear anything from your boy, Travis, aka chicken fingers?" Midnight giggled.

Tyler mean-mugged him. "Watch it, Blackie. That's my brother you talkin' 'bout, man."

"Blackie!" Midnight barked with a twisted face.

Midnight was insecure about his dark complexion and African features. He hated it when someone called him Blackie or Darkie because it reminded him of when his classmates used to tease him.

"Watch the name-calling, asshole!" Midnight said and pounded his fist on the table. "Words like that will get you killed."

"Yo, both of you chill out with that shit!" Swag shouted. "We don't have time for this, especially not in the predicament we're all in."

The two men silenced themselves—but only for a few minutes. Swag felt terrible for not saying anything to defend Travis at the moment, but right now, it was every man for himself. That was . . . until Swag could get a plan together to get them all out of Costa Rica in one piece. He did, however, have a question for Midnight.

"Have you heard anything from dickhead? Oh, I mean, Paco?"

"Don't be talking about my boy like that!" Midnight yelled and pointed his finger at Swag.

Swag laughed and looked at Midnight in disbelief. "Oh, he wasn't your boy when me and my friend," he pointed at Tyler, "was beating that wetback's ass down to the ground."

Midnight had a dumbfounded look on his face.

"Yeah, if that was your man, where was your ass at to help him? Huh?"

"Shit! Do you see where we at? King or Blood probably would've fucked me up too," Midnight said, knowing he'd screwed up as far as the bro code.

Tyler shook his head. "Punk ass." He laughed. "You disloyal as hell. And you scary as hell with all those muscles in a cheap-looking suit, looking like an ugly ape. I guess being bigger don't mean shit. All bark and no bite—weak-ass bitch."

Swag knew his boy was laying it on thick with Midnight. And don't get it twisted, if Midnight touched one hair on Tyler's head, Swag was ready. Swag thought Midnight, without Paco or his crew, was just a sheep without his shepherd. The Midnight that Swag and Tyler met back in prison in Brazil was now a cowardly lion like in *The Wizard of Oz*.

Midnight still kept the dumbfounded look on his face. He knew what he did by not helping Paco was fucked up. Paco or the rest of the crew would've done the same for him. But it was too late to turn back the hands of time. He had no way to get in contact with Paco to explain his actions. He knew Karma was going to catch up with him sooner or later. But in the meantime, there was no way in hell he was going to let Swag and Tyler punk him. So he brushed off Swag's comments. He began to laugh.

"Oh, I know you two are not talking about me being a disloyal asshole. What about that big dude, Stan? You all literally threw him to wolves back in Brazil."

Swag and Tyler looked at each other with stupid looks on their faces. They both knew Midnight was spitting the truth about their late friend, Stan. Even thinking about selling their boy to Satan's minions scared them shitless to the core. They knew one day Karma would catch up with them also.

"Yeah, you didn't know Paco, and I knew that goofy-lookin' scary dude was with y'all. I can smell an American black godfather wannabe anywhere."

Swag and Tyler were mortified by every last word Midnight was saying to them. And as ugly as it sounded, they knew Midnight was preaching the gospel truth.

"Yeah, selling yo' boy out for a taste of the good life sponsored by the Hernandez Cartel. Selfish American niggas." Midnight then looked at Tyler face-to-face. "And you . . ."

Tyler's eyes never left Midnight's. "What the hell about me, Mighty Joe Young?" He glared over at the gold and diamond steak knife. Deep down inside, Tyler could see himself slicing up Midnight's body in rage. But he kept his cool and took a deep breath.

"Oh, good comeback, you fake-ass-lookin' Trey Songz. You ain't no better because even though you fucked over your goofy friend, you sold out your flesh and blood."

Tyler and Swag looked confused about that comment.

"What the fuck are you talking about, Tar Baby?" Tyler asked, then took a sip of water.

Midnight laughed. "This fool really think he's hurting my feelings with these stereotypical names." Midnight shook his head with a big smile on his face, showcasing his perfect, pearly white teeth. "Bitch, you let your own brother get his lip bitten. Plus, you let him get his finger cut off by King's ass. And last, you let him get exiled from King's Palace. All yo' ass did was sit back and let her do it." He looked at Swag for a moment, then back at Tyler. "And you two niggas calling *me* weak and scary. As I look at you two, I'm *ten* times the man you'll ever be. Punk asses. In this house, you're selling out friends and being deceitful."

Swag couldn't take any more of Midnight's smart-ass comments. He picked up his steak knife and pointed it at Midnight.

On the inside, Midnight was scared shitless. He didn't know if he had pushed the wrong button when it came to Swag, but he just kept his tough-guy exterior on his face and didn't flinch.

"Listen, you fresh-off-the-*Amistad*-'Set-us-free'-looking bitch! Don't you *ever* disrespect my boys or me. And for your information, I did stick up for Travis. That's why I'm in this bitch now! Shit, King saw I had more balls than Paco's ass. And—"

"Shut the fuck up, both of you!" a loud male voice interrupted Swag.

They all looked toward the doorway where Blood stood, looking like a million bucks in a midnight blue pin-striped suit and black velvet Versace Medusa loafers. He rocked a nicely shaved bald head and trimmed beard. The only jewelry he had on was a gold chain around his neck and a diamond Rolex. To top off his look, he had Blacknese on one arm and Mina on the other. Both were wearing couture ball gowns. To Swag, they looked like totally different people in clothing than what he saw earlier.

Blood looked at the ladies. "Thank you both." He turned to Blacknese. "Be in my chambers at ten." He then turned to Mina. "And you be in my chambers at midnight."

"Yes, sir," they said. They both kissed him and then walked away.

Blood slithered into the dining room, looking at Tyler and Midnight, who both looked lost as hell. A chill entered the room with Blood. He focused on the knife in Swag's hand.

Swag wanted to turn the knife away from Midnight for a brief moment and point it at Blood. The timing was perfect . . . then again, maybe not.

"I'ma need you bastards to sit down and chill because royalty is about to make its way up in here," Blood said.

Both Tyler and Midnight stayed calm. The beef was now between Swag and Blood.

"Pretty boy, I suggest you sit your ass down and put that knife away real quick." Blood straightened his suit jacket.

Swag gave Blood a "fuck you" look as he slowly placed the knife back on the table. Blood shook his head and started laughing. His thoughts about Swag were surprising. *I like this dude. He got a lot of heart. But as long as I'm around holding King down, I'm going to show him who the real commander and chief in this bitch is.* Blood pulled out his 9 mm and aimed it at Swag's face.

He didn't budge and was rather tired of Blood waving his gun around and threatening him.

"I'ma need you to put that knife down a little quicker next time, and how about doing it with a smile."

All Swag did was smile.

Blood snarled at him and addressed the others. "Please, sit down before King comes in here. And believe me, she'll *really* bring the pain."

It had been a long time since Swag let another dude get under his skin . . . since Mitch back in Illinois. He swore that after Mitch, he wasn't going to let that shit ever happen again. Swag knew he and Blood would have their time soon, but until then, he chilled.

Blood sat in the chair across from Swag with a sly smile, knowing he was irritating the shit out of Swag's ass.

Damn! This dude is like an STD I can't get rid of, he thought.

As things settled down, a few men dressed in tuxedoes came in the dining room with trumpets. Once the musicians were in place, they started playing "Royal Entrance Fanfare" on their trumpets.

Swag, Tyler, and Midnight frowned and appeared annoyed. Blood, however, took a sip of his water, acting like this performance was normal. The first one to come into the dining room was Madam Lourd. She had locked arms with an Arabian escort. Even though she was an older woman, she looked like Hollywood glamour. She wore a long black satin fabric gown with iridescent sparkles. Swoops and swirls in silvers, blue, and subtle peacock colorings were added in. The dress showed her hourglass figure—she still rocked it. She had on matching black satin heels, and even though her makeup was on heavy, she still looked gorgeous. She was known as the Queen of Diamonds, so bling was everywhere. Her head was covered with a black feather bowler cloche hat, giving screen legend Mae West a run for her money. Her escort directed her to the end of the table, where he kissed her hand and pulled back the chair for her to sit.

After she was settled in, Ivy entered the dining room with a hot Indian escort ready to feast. She wore a long-sleeve leopard print slit dress that showcased her leg tattoo with butterflies of all colors going down her thick frame leg. The dress revealed her big breasts that she loved to show off, and she wore a masquerade mask. Her hair was styled in the famous Halle Berry cut, and a diamond saber tooth-inspired necklace hung from her neck. The escort led her to the seat next to Swag.

He was somewhat uncomfortable with her being next to him, and he hoped she would keep her hands to herself. The second she sat down, she gazed at him with lust filling her eyes. She then smacked the escort on his butt.

"Thank you, baby!"

The young escort smirked and walked away.

Ivy's main focus was back on Swag. "Well, hello, again, sexy. Did you miss me?"

Without warning, Swag felt Ivy's hand rubbing on his thigh. Her touch made him jerk. He looked at her with wide eyes, but she paid his expression no mind.

"Firm meeeow," she purred and moaned. "Mmm, you look delicious."

Blood laughed and took another sip of his water.

Swag looked at him and mouthed, "Fuck you."

Blood smiled.

As the band played on, Josie entered with her male escort. Swag's eyes were glued to her every move. Her long, curly hair was now flat ironed and pulled into a sleek ponytail. Her Revlon makeup was on point with ruby-red lips and cat-eye makeup that brought out the tigress in her. She wore a red Dolce & Gabbana lace trim spaghetti strapped gown that really showed off her dancer/model shape. She also had on a pair of red heels that showcased her long legs. Not only did she have a male escort on one arm, but she also had a beautiful Egyptian Mau cat in her other arm.

Swag smiled as her escort took her over to her seat in between Blood and Tyler. He was excited that they would be sitting near each other. Something inside of him got all warm every time he was around her.

Josie looked around the room and greeted everyone with a smile on her face. "Good evening, ladies and gentlemen."

Her sexy smile brightened up the room and semi-melted the hearts of Tyler, Midnight, Blood, and mainly Swag.

"What's up?" Midnight and Tyler said.

"Hey, baby girl," Blood replied, then leaned in to kiss Josie on her soft cheek.

"Good evening, Uncle Blake," she giggled.

Swag's eyes were locked on the Haitian beauty, but he was also disgusted that Blood's DNA was on her smooth cheek. He just thanked God Blood's venom kiss didn't melt the flesh of her face. Swag wasted no time breaking the ice and putting on his pretty-boy smile.

"What's going on, baby?"

Josie smirked, but deep down, she was blushing. "I'm great, Mr. Solomon."

Swag loved how she called him by his government name. "None of that 'Mr.' stuff. Solomon will do just fine. May I say you look exquisite tonight. Even more breathtaking than I remembered you upstairs."

Josie chuckled and thought about their first, unforgettable encounter. "Thank you, Swa—I mean, Solomon." She almost slipped out his tag name, knowing that it was their little secret.

Swag sucked on his bottom lip and flashed her a sexy smile.

All the flirting was starting to piss off Blood. He was beginning to sweat bullets, so he kicked Swag's leg underneath the table.

"Eww, shit!" Swag reached for his leg to rub it. He glanced at Blood, who had a sly smile on his face.

"Oh, are you okay?" Ivy said, rubbing his shoulder.

Swag knew this was Ivy's act of seduction again. He sat up and shook her hand off of him. "I'm cool, ma'am."

Ivy sighed. She hated being called ma'am. She hated that word with a passion and wished whoever thought of it would burn in hell. In her mind, she still wanted to be remembered as the 16-year-old girl who was the most famous escort in all of San José, Costa Rica. She was even more pissed at Swag because he was the first young man to ignore her advances. She hated that she had to compete with these young chicks, especially her own child. She folded her arms and pursed her lips as she thought about being rejected.

The musicians stopped playing, and Blood stood up. "Stand, everyone."

Madam Lourd, Ivy, and Josie rose as if it were normal. Swag, Midnight, and Tyler looked at them like they were crazy. Blood hissed at them and snapped his fingers.

"Get y'all asses up and show some damn respect!"

Midnight and Tyler hopped up out of their seats like their lives depended on it. Of course, Swag took his precious time getting out of his chair as he was eying Blood. He knew Blood was furious and shitting bricks. Swag put a smirk on his face to irritate him.

Blood winced. In his mind, he wanted to break every last bone in Swag's face. *Keep trying me. Keep trying me,* he thought.

The musicians played a different tune as everyone looked at the doorway. Within seconds, King appeared, looking at her court and her possible future man. Swag's eyes were locked on her. She was sexy as hell in a Rosie Assoulin rainbow-colored, silk-blend lamé halter-neck gown that melted on her perfect silhouette frame. Her makeup was Egyptian-inspired with peacock eye shadow that enhanced her green eyes and gold lipstick on her luscious, kissable lips. She was giving off a Queen Cleopatra-type of vibe. She rocked gold and diamond jewelry from head to toe. A Kundan headpiece was on top of her long, blond hair that flowed down her back. Her gold-painted sharp fingernails had diamond chips on the ends, and she even had on gold Christian Louboutins.

Everyone at the table admired how beautiful she was. Blood licked his lips, wishing it were just King and him in the dining room alone having a romantic dinner. He hated that he had to share her with all her lovers and the world. The first time Blood saw King, he was in love with her right then and there. He was one of many people that saw the softer side of her, and he remembered her always being the person he was so in love with. He'd known her since she was a kid and promised he would protect her no matter what. But he wanted to be more than her protector and confidant. He wanted to be the one and only person in her life. Until he could make that dream a reality, he had to take off a few loose ends . . . and Swag.

Blood got up and walked up to King. He took her hand in his, feeling like one with her. He was determined that King Kia Costello was going to be Mrs. Blake Mario Fernandez by any means necessary. They sauntered over to the table, and he pulled back the throne chair at the head of the table.

King sat on her throne like the true royalty she was. In her mind, it was like *"Fuck the queens. Why be a queen when you can be a king?"* That was a philosophy she'd picked up from one of her idols, King Nzinga of Angola, who believed she was equal to any man.

Once King was seated, Blood took a seat.

"Damn, girl, you look dynamite in that dress. And you are glowing," Blood said, looking at her like a hungry wolf.

"Hmm." King wasn't moved by words she'd heard time and time again.

Swag wanted to laugh because King seemed to dis Blood.

Ivy, though, knew her daughter was the shit. That's what she loved about her. On the other hand, she hated King, because, looking at her child sitting on her throne chair made her think that, that should've been *her* throne. Ivy always felt the Palace, and maybe Costa Rica, could've been hers if King weren't in the picture. Trying to block out her would've, could've, and should've thoughts, Ivy took a deep breath. She wanted to break the ice in the room and semi size up her own child. She got up and straightened her dress.

"My baby and Josephine looking good tonight."

King and Josie looked at Ivy like she was drunk.

What does this crazy ol' whore got up her sleeve? King thought.

"Y'all young boys like these young girls, huh?" Ivy said, laughing.

Everyone sat in silence, looking at her as if she'd lost her mind.

She sat on the table, spread her legs, and let her old puss breathe air. "Why y'all want orange juice when you can have Dom Pérignon." She winked at Swag. "Meow."

Swag wanted to vomit at this pathetic, attention-seeking whore. *Trick, this ain't Basic Instinct, and you damn sure ain't no Sharon Stone,* he thought.

Josie's Egyptian Mau cat crawled on the table and inched toward Swag and Ivy.

"Hey, cutie." Swag rubbed the beautiful cat and tried to block the visual that Ivy was serving him.

King wasn't feeling either one of these scenes. The cat she could deal with, but her mother was another story. Sometimes, King wished her mother would grow the hell up and stop having the mind of the 16-year-old girl she once was. If Ivy weren't her mother, playing these old ho games would've gotten her killed a long time ago. Ivy was still competing with King's girls and giving young boys her money just to sleep with her. One thing she wasn't going to let her do was get to her new catch, Swag. King slammed her hand on the table and screamed at the top of her lungs, "Goddamnit! Get that pussy off the table!"

If there was one thing Ivy knew not to do, that was not to mess with her child. She quickly hopped off the table and got back in her seat.

King laughed at her mother. "I meant the cat." She pointed at the cat.

Swag took the cat off the table and held it in his arms. King looked at Josie. "Didn't I tell you I didn't want that fleabag in my dining room?"

Josie got up. "I know, Mom. I'm sorry, but Chiquita followed me here. I couldn't take her back upstairs because I didn't want to be late for dinner."

She took her from Swag and held the cat like a baby. "Chiquita, hi, baby . . ." Josie kissed her cat on the forehead.

"Chiquita is a cute name," Swag said. "You named your cat after a banana, ma?"

Everyone laughed except Josie.

"No, I didn't name my cat after no damn banana. I named her after the cheetah of my idol, Josephine Baker, that she used in her shows. The cat will have to do since Mom won't let me have a real cheetah."

"You damn right you ain't getting a cheetah in my palace. There's only one boss in this bitch, and that's me."

Swag smiled at Josie and her cat. "She's still a beautiful cat, though."

"Thank you, Solomon. I love her so much, my mini cheetah." Josie kissed her cat again.

King wanted to throw up. All attention was supposed to be on her, and her alone. It was bad enough she had to semi compete with her mother. The last thing she wanted to do was compete with her adopted daughter and protégé. She had to get shit in order before dinner came.

"Cleo!" King yelled.

Within seconds, Cleo walked in and bowed to King. "Yes, my lady?"

"Cleo, my dear, please remove the feline." King pointed to the cat.

Cleo walked over and removed the cat from Josie's arms.

"Thank you, Uncle Cleo," Josie said, handing her over. "Love you, Chiquita." She kissed the cat again.

Chiquita meowed as Cleo exited the dining room with her.

King cleared her throat. "Well, now that the interruptions are over . . ." She glared at her mother. *Bitch, stay in your lane.* She smiled at her crew and guests. "King wishes to eat. Let's have dinner." She snapped her fingers at the musicians to play some music while the chefs started to bring in dinner. The musicians played the famous Japanese ballad from the opera *Madame Butterfly*. Two muscular guys came in carrying a long charcuterie board with a beautiful naked Japanese woman on it. She looked about 18 and resembled a real Barbie with flowers and raw fish surrounding her. They placed the board at the head of the table. Another set of muscular guys came in with another charcuterie board. This time, there was an attractive, naked Japanese man on it with flowers, shrimp, and raw fish surrounding him. They put the board on the table and exited the room. Right then and there, Swag was sick to his stomach. He knew King was crazy, but eating people was insane. At that moment, Swag became a vegan.

Blood smiled as the waiter brought in soy sauce, sake, and gold chopsticks. "Mmm, my favorite." He licked his lips.

Swag and Tyler looked at each other, then at Blood. King rubbed her hands together and was ready to dig in.

Swag decided to speak up. "Uh, King, no disrespect to your sexy hospitality, but this where I put my foot down."

King giggled like a schoolgirl. "Solomon, bae, what are you talking about?"

"I'm not a cannibal, okay? I don't eat people. I'll eat some good punany, but humans, in general, are where I draw the line. Yo' people got any salad?"

King eyed Blood, who eyed Madam Lourd, Josie, and Ivy.

Oh Lord, Swag thought, as his heart started to thump against his chest. Tyler and Midnight shook their heads.

Damn, bruh done fucked up now, Tyler thought, lowering his head.

King and her family started laughing at Swag. Ivy looked at him and giggled.

"Ba . . . by, are you *serious?*"

"Yeah, you really think we some type of zombies about to eye them on the table?" King laughed and held her chest. She was many things to so many people and was a savage beast when it came to her business. But never in a million years would King eat human flesh. Hell, she had to watch her sexy girlish figure.

"Darling, you can tell these Americans have never been anywhere," Madam Lourd said as she took another sip of scotch and pulled out a cigarette. She lit it and took two puffs. Then she started to cough real hard and choked on the smoke.

Midnight jumped from his seat and hit her back. "You okay, ma'am?"

Madam Lourd waved him off. "I'm fine, dear, please, go sit. And none of that 'ma'am' shit. Madam or Madam Lourd will do just fine."

Midnight eased back in his seat.

Madam Lourd, like Ivy, hated the word "ma'am." She hated that she was getting older by the day. She knew it wasn't long ago that she was once the beautiful island girl from Trinidad and Tobago. She was every man's desire. Like the thousands of girls, she was one of many who were sold to the Palace at the age of 8 by her family who couldn't afford to take care of her anymore. They hoped that someone in the Palace would take care of her and make her a real woman. In the beginning, she tried to run away but was beaten by her former madam. In the end, she learned to make the best of a bad situation. She went from house servant to being schooled, to being a sophisticated escort, to sharing her position as a madam with another person whose name she never spoke in King's presence. Now that she was retired from her position, the only thing Madam Lourd looked forward to was traveling, going to high-class social parties, her scotch, her wig collection, and cigarettes.

Madam Lourd looked over at Midnight, realizing she was slightly rude to him. In reality, she was grateful for his swift actions.

"Thank you." She took another puff of her cigarette.

Midnight nodded. "Anytime, ma'—I mean, Madam Lourd."

She laughed and licked her lips. One thing Madam Lourd liked more than old movies was sexy chocolate men with a big stick. Shit, just because she was up in age didn't mean she didn't want to be dicked down good. Madam Lourd tried to seduce him with her eyes and mouthed to him, "Meet me in my room later." She winked at him.

Everyone laughed.

Midnight turned around and tried not to blush. He would screw her in a heartbeat.

King was starving and wanted to change the topic fast. She cleared her throat, and everyone looked at her. The room went completely silent. She addressed Swag.

"Solomon, baby, we aren't cannibals. This dish is called Nyotaimori/Nantaimori. It's a Japanese human sushi bar. Watch." She got out her gold chopsticks, went over to the female body, and removed sushi from her right nipple. She dipped the sushi in soy sauce and placed it in her mouth.

"Mmmm, delicious." She noticed the girl's hard nipple, so she bent over and sucked almost all the sake mixed with sushi juice off her breast.

"Aah," the girl moaned while trying to maintain her pose. After all, she was getting paid for being there.

The guys were turned on by the action—this was one dinner table they didn't mind sitting at. King took one last swipe of the girl's nipple before she sat back down to eat.

"Dig in," she said.

Everyone picked up their chopsticks and dove right in. Swag was trying to get the hang of the chopsticks, but the task was difficult. King laughed, then showed him how to use them.

"Thanks, bae," Swag said, smiling at her.

Blood was hot, but to keep the peace, he didn't say a word. Swag got up to get some oysters from the girl's vagina area.

"Mmm, oysters," Ivy said, purring like the late Eartha Kitt. She rubbed Swag's shoulders. "You know what those can do for a man's sex drive?"

Swag spit the oyster from his mouth. He managed to play it off like he was choking, but he was annoyed by Ivy. She was a pro at getting into people's personal space and didn't think it was offensive. To Swag, it was.

She rubbed his back. "Damn, sexy, you okay?"

He fake coughed some more and shook her off him. "Yeah, I'm cool, mama!"

Ivy took her hands off him after hearing the word "mama" come from his mouth. It sent her over the edge.

"Why, I never!" She stared at him like he had shit on his face. Calling her mama was the last straw. She was done with him.

King had joy in her eyes because she knew her mother was upset. She didn't appreciate her acting thirsty, and without even knowing it, Swag had said the right thing.

Swag saw that the oyster he'd had in his mouth had landed on Blood's head. Blood remained calm about it but reminded himself to deal with Swag later.

"Dang, Blood, sorry about that, bro. I'm sorry, everyone, for choking on this good oyster. I'm so sorry, everyone, especially to my man, Blood."

Blood gritted his teeth. He didn't accept a damn word of his apology. His hand slowly went for the chopstick, but Swag was saved by King when she held Blood's hand and looked at him with those sweet, innocent, green eyes and a sly fox smile.

To some men, that would've been a slight flirt or a let's-have-sex smile. But Blood had been around King for a long time and knew all her motives like the back of his hand. He knew she meant, "Leave him be, and I'll make it worth your while later." Blood loved her "I'll-make-it-worth-your-while" sex sessions. He smiled at her and winked. King pointed to the oyster on his forehead, so he picked up a napkin to remove it.

"Darling, the boy gave you an apology," Madam Lourd said. "It's proper for you to accept it."

Blood looked at Madam Lourd with a slight smile. Then he turned to Swag, who had a smirk on his face.

"Yo, man, it's cool," Blood said. "It was a freak accident." Blood took a sip of sake and continued to look deviously at Swag.

King smiled at both men. She loved how they played with the fake apology. She knew deep down that they wanted to kill each other, and that thought made her moist—her bodyguard and her possible new boy toy being at odds. She took a sip of her sake and looked over at Blood, knowing she had to keep her promise to him. Shit, she was in the mood for fish tonight. Now, she was changing her order to Blood sausage.

Chapter 14

Hey, Brother

In the great room where the legendary, silver-haired filmmaker was, Swag, King, and the others were also there. They were having a dessert called Cajeta De Coco (Costa Rican Coconut Fudge) and Dom Pérignon. Tyler, who hadn't eaten anything because he was allergic to shellfish, was eating the fudge like his mouth was a black hole.

Everyone was irritated by his actions, especially King. Tyler, however, didn't give a damn. He was hungry and was sneaking some of the fudge in his pockets, just in case he got hungry in the middle of the night.

Tyler looked at King as he took another bite of the fudge. She raised her brows.

"Oh, hi, Your Majesty," he said nervously. "Is something wrong?"

King loved that she could put fear in so many people. "What's your name again, honey?"

Tyler had a mouthful of fudge. He held up his finger and chewed, then took a sip of champagne to wash it down. He cleared his throat and smiled at her.

"I'm Tyler, ma'am."

King laughed. "Forget the 'ma'am' stuff. King or what you called me a moment ago will do just fine." She looked down at the six pieces of fudge on his plate and back at him. "Was something wrong with your dinner?"

Tyler shook his head. "Oh, no, King. Dinner looked delicious, but I can't eat it because I'm allergic to seafood."

"Oh, baby doll, why didn't you tell me? I could've had my chef make you something else."

Tyler and Swag were shocked at her response. They expected her to say something different.

Tyler smiled. "Thank you, King, but I don't want to be any trouble."

"Darling, you won't be any trouble at all, because you can't live off fudge. I don't want you to get a sugar high or get fat, because you won't be any good to me if you get fat. What would you like the chefs to make for you? Anything you want will be fine."

Tyler was trying to figure out the statement she'd made about him not being any good to her. He started to ask but decided against it.

"I don't know what I want to eat. I guess I'll take anything, as long as it's not shellfish or pork."

King removed the plate and waved for Cleo to come to her. They talked in Spanish before Cleo nodded and left the great room.

"Don't worry, Tyler. After this, there will be a delicious meal in your room waiting for you."

Tyler grinned. "Thanks, but what is it?"

King laughed. "You'll see." She got up and stood in the center of the room. She clapped her hands again. "May I have your attention, please?"

Everyone stopped what they were doing and looked in her direction.

"I hope you all enjoyed your dinner and dessert. But I have a special treat for you all this evening, mainly for our special Palace guests. I'm proud to present my daughter, who will be doing a piece from *Giselle*. So I would like everyone to clap your hands for my child and protégé, Josephine Batiste."

Everyone clapped their hands as Josie paraded in front of them, looking like a beautiful angel in a white lyrical dress with white ballet slippers. Her curly hair was slicked back into a ponytail. She walked over to King, who kissed her on the cheek.

King sat between Blood and Midnight.

Josie smiled at the audience. She hoped that one day she'd be in front of big audiences, not this, like in Paris where her idol performed in her prime. She even hoped for a life of nothing but dancing, music, acting, and perhaps, a little romance. Until then, she pictured her small audience as a huge, massive one. She looked at the musicians and nodded. They began to play music from French composer, Adolphe Adam's famous ballet, *Giselle*. Josie closed her eyes, and from then on, she was in character. She began to dance to the sound of the music.

Swag smiled at her. To him, Josie had bad-assed skills. It took him back to when his grandmother would take him to his sister's recitals, and he had his headphones on, trying to listen to some music until it was all over. It amazed him how much he had taken precious moments like that for granted. Now, looking at Josie, he could watch her dance all day. She was even more graceful now than when he'd seen her earlier.

Josie was in total eye contact with her audience. She mainly loved how Swag was looking at her moves. She didn't know what about him made her so weak and performed even harder. She was a moth, and he was her flame. But she knew it was a deadly combination, as far as King was concerned. The last thing Josie wanted was to lose the lavish life she was living in the Palace. Shit, it beat the one bedroom that she once lived in back in Haiti. All she wanted to do was keep being in King's good graces, and hopefully, one day, run away to Paris, France, to be like Josephine Baker.

She made a slight leap and gracefully landed on the floor as she let the music take total control and gave it her all.

As Swag continued to gaze at Josie, King looked at him from the corner of her eye. In her mind, she'd be damned if he ended up with her daughter. Hell, Josie, was going to be her masterpiece. King had given her everything that any child could dream of having. She'd brought her up like a little princess. Besides living in a beautiful palace, King made sure Josie had the best tutors and even paid for her to have one of the best dance instructors. She couldn't wait until Josie turned 18 in a few weeks. She wanted to get her out of that fake-ass, Walt Disney princess mode, and teach her to be a hardhearted, street-smart diva like she was, especially if she wanted to rule her empire. She needed to keep Josie focused. The only way she could do that was to keep Swag away from her.

King felt a firm hand on her thigh. She looked over at Blood, whose eyes were directly on Josie, but a smirk was on his face. King hadn't forgotten about her promise to him, and her thoughts made her giggle. She turned her attention to Josie, who was killing a classic routine.

As Josie was about to take another leap, everyone heard a voice sounding both male and feminine coming their way, shouting, "Stop! Stop it now!"

The musicians stopped playing, and Josie stopped dancing. That was one of the seven deadly sins for a dancer. No matter what was going on—a loud noise or if you forget your step—you *never* stop dancing. Everyone looked at where the sound was coming from.

"Come on, Jo-Jo, baby. Come on, you putting everyone to sleep," the feminine voice said as he came into the great room and headed Josie's way.

The guy that walked in looked about the same age as Josie. He was light-skinned with big brown eyes, a nose ring, and a light mustache and beard. He also had a swimmer's build that showed nicely in a tropical shirt, tan khaki shorts, and flip-flops. His hair was cut in a low fade. He walked up to Josie and kissed her cheek.

King jumped up and lashed out at the boy. "Eh, what are you doing?"

He knew his actions would piss off King, and he loved every last minute of it. He laughed.

"Girl, Jo-Jo is boring the hell out of me and everyone else with this prissy white-man shit. Don't y'all want a little more life in here?" He looked at the musicians and spoke in French. Within seconds, the musicians started to play some Reggae music.

The boy screamed and started to dance. Many of the people watching had to admit he had some great dance moves. He grinded against Josie, and to everyone's surprise, she started dancing wildly too. Everyone approved of the dancing . . . except for King.

"Come on, everyone!" the boy yelled with excitement. "Get up and join the party!"

Josie started to twerk and kicked off her ballet slippers. She was getting it in, and as she began to pop her booty, Swag rushed up behind her. At first, she was hesitant because she knew King didn't approve. But it wasn't long before she turned to face Swag and started grinding on him.

Flames of fire shot from King's ears. If she would've had a lighter right now, she'd burn the Palace down with everyone in it. *How dare they disrespect me,* she thought. But as everyone danced and seemed to have a good time, King kept her cool.

"Get up and join the party!" the boy yelled again. He pulled Madam Lourd up from the sofa. "Come on, Granny. I know you still have some moves left in that old body of yours."

Madam Lourd got up from the sofa and looked him up and down. She hated the word "old." It didn't exist in her vocabulary. She asked Tyler to hold her cane and stepped on the floor to give the people a show.

Most people thought Madam Lourd was such a classy, elegant lady who ruled with an iron fist. But she gave everyone second thoughts when she got on the floor because she would put many strippers to shame and out of work. She twerked and did splits in her couture evening gown and heels. Jaws dropped, and nearly everyone clapped and laughed until their stomachs hurt.

"Back that ass up!" Tyler shouted and cheered on Madam Lourd. In his mind, if he were a big spender, he would be throwing dollars at her all night long.

The boy looked over at Tyler and was immediately under his spell. He couldn't believe Tyler was so damn fine. He wanted to do his own special dance with him . . . in his bedroom. He didn't hesitate to mouth, "Hey, sexy."

Tyler brushed off his words and got up. He left Madam Lourd's cane on his seat. He took her by the hand and danced with her.

Not wanting to be outdone by Josie and Madam Lourd, Ivy pranced to the dance floor and started shaking her ass.

"Shit, juvenile couldn't even back this shit up." Ivy rapped an old Trina song.

King folded her arms and rolled her eyes. *No man is going to want that ugly cellulite ass of yours.* King just hated that this was happening in her presence.

As Ivy danced, she looked over at Swag and Josie, who were freaking each other on the floor. She rolled her eyes and decided to show him what he was going to be missing. Ivy stood in front of Midnight, twisting her body. She clapped her ass in his face and watched the muscle in his pants grow. She also looked at King, who was pissed off even more. It didn't bother her one bit, and she continued to seduce Midnight. He looked Ivy up and down and stroked his chin.

"What are you waiting for, handsome?" Ivy said. "You're not just going to sit there and not dance with me, are you?" She reached out for his hand.

"Shit, what the hell," Midnight said, smiling. He joined Ivy on the floor, and they partied their hearts out.

King and Blood were the only ones still sitting and looking like two sourpusses. Blood kept a straight look on his face, but in the back of his mind, he wanted to take King by the hand and have fun like everyone else. He wanted to dance the night away with her. Sometimes, he wished that King would lighten up and have a little fun in life. Everything was always business or sex with her, as far as Blood was concerned.

King was getting frustrated with all the Jamaican music and her guests grinding on each other, especially Swag and Josie. To her, that was the ultimate disrespect and betrayal, all wrapped in one.

Her thoughts were interrupted when the boy got in her face. "Come on, sis! Stop being such a sourpuss and join the party." He looked over at Blood. "You too, Plasma. I mean, Blood." He laughed as he turned around and twerked in their faces.

King turned her focus from Josie and Swag to the light-skinned dude. She wanted to kick him in his face, but before she could, she heard Madam Lourd coughing hard and clutching her chest. Everyone stopped dancing and focused on her. The musicians, however, kept playing their instruments.

King immediately got up from the sofa and helped Tyler get her to the sofa. Madam Lourd continued to cough and choke.

"Damn, ma'am, are you okay?" Tyler asked, holding her hand.

King gave her a napkin, but she couldn't think straight because of the loud music. She didn't know what came over her. She looked at the musicians and screamed. "Stop playing that damn jungle mu . . . sic!"

They immediately stopped playing, and everyone stood there, shocked.

King's focus was back on Madam Lourd, whose coughing and choking started to calm down a little.

"Grandmother, are you okay?" King rubbed her shoulder.

The last thing King wanted was for Madam Lourd to die on her. To her, Madam Lourd was the one person who gave nothing but the unconditional love that her mother hadn't give her. Madam Lourd looked at King and fanned herself with the napkin. Within a few seconds, she started coughing again. King patted her on the back. "Grandmother, please tell me you're okay." She continued to rub her back.

Swag watched the two of them. He loved this side of King, caring for others.

Madam Lourd looked at King as her breathing returned to normal. She nodded as she smiled at her.

"Yes, baby doll. I'm fine." She slightly coughed again. "I'm fine. I keep forgetting I'm not that young sexy island girl I once was." Madam Lourd started to take deep breaths in and out.

"Are you sure? Do you want Blood to go get the doctor for you?" King was still worried. She always had the doctor on speed dial, just in case something was wrong with the family or her workers.

"No, no, no!" Madam Lourd shouted. "I'm . . . I'm tired. I'm very tired. I need my rest. I'm going to retire to my room for my beauty rest."

Madam Lourd tried to get up from the sofa, and King assisted her. She looked over at Blood and motioned for him to come their way.

"Blood, dear, please take Madam to her quarters for the evening."

"Of course, Boss," Blood said, winking at King to let her know he didn't forget her promise.

Madam Lourd held her arms out for Blood. "Take me, Zaddy." She put the biggest Kool-Aid smile on her face.

Everyone laughed.

Blood swept her off her feet and exited the great room. After they left, things started to calm down a little. But something came over King. She appeared possessed by a demon. She walked up to the boy and slapped the dog shit out of him. He fell to the floor and held his cheek.

"What in the hell was that for?" he asked. He kept touching his face and felt wetness on his lips.

King wished she had a switchblade or anything sharp to slice up his face. She started to stomp his face with her heel, but Ivy pulled her back from him.

King looked at Ivy like she had just lost her mind.

"Look, Mother, this doesn't concern you—"

Ivy pointed her finger in her daughter's face. "Look, *chica,* you may rule all of Costa Rica, but at the end of the day, I'm *still* your mother, and you won't ever disrespect me or your brother, Santana!" Ivy pointed at Santana, who was getting off the ground.

Everyone was stunned at the words Ivy spoke to King.

King looked at Santana, who was straightening his clothes. She loved her brother, but she hated him because he was a reminder of something she could never forgive her mother for a long time. And every time she looked at Santana, all she could think of was the past that messed her up for years.

"But, Mother!" King shouted.

"No buts. He is still your brother, and no matter how much you hate him, you don't have to harm him." Ivy gave King a stern look like she were 7 years old.

King looked at Santana. "I wish Ivy would've aborted your ass cause you ain't nothing but a damn mistake, you faggot ass!"

Ivy slapped King, whose jaw dropped wide open.

"Don't you ever, *ever* disrespect Santana!"

King shot her mother an evil glare. Ivy walked over to Santana and embraced him. He kissed her on the cheek, then looked at everyone with a smile on his face.

"I'm still pretty! And by the way, everyone, my name is Santana. Santana Costello at your service." He bowed and winked at Tyler, who ignored him again.

King felt jealous of the affection her mother gave to Santana. She was so pissed off at the events that happened this evening. First, it was Josie doing that ratchet dancing thanks to her brother, and then Madam Lourd had scared her to death. She took a deep breath, threw her head back, and stormed out of the room.

Chapter 15

The Secret

When Blood and Madam Lourd got to her quarters on the other side of the Palace, Blood opened the door to her room, which was incredibly gorgeous. The colors of the room were silver and red velvet—from the walls to the furniture. She had pictures of old Hollywood stars in the golden age of Hollywood. Also, she had a collection of expensive wigs in her closet. She also had a vanity table with bright white lights surrounding it.

Blood put her on the edge of her eighteenth-century bed. Once she was settled, Madam Lourd opened up her nightstand drawer, pulled out a cigarette, and lit it. She took two puffs and blew out the smoke. She crossed her legs and leaned back a little on the bed.

Blood couldn't believe this woman who almost coughed her guts out was now having a cigarette. He just shook his head. *That's Madam Lourd.*

Madam Lourd started to cough.

Blood was worried. "Madam, are you okay? Do you want me to call the doctor?"

She waved him off. "No, no, darling. I'm fine. Like I told King, all I need is my beauty sleep. Now sashay away."

Blood took a deep breath. "Okay, but no more cigarettes for tonight," he removed the cigarette from her hand, "or your nightly dose of scotch." He puffed on the cigarette before putting it out.

Madam Lourd rolled her eyes.

"You want some warm milk and a sleeping pill?" he asked.

"Boy, I'm old, not dead yet. Now, get out!"

Blood smiled and nodded. He leaned in to kiss her. "Good night, Sophia."

She smiled. "Night, boy. King is waiting for you."

He laughed as he walked toward the door. But before he left, Madam Lourd yelled out, "Blake!"

Blood knew whenever she called him by his government name, something was always up. He turned around, thinking she changed her mind about calling her doctor. He went to the bed and sat beside her.

"Yes, madam? Do you need the doctor to come by? Do you want King or Ivy?" Before he could shout for either woman, Madam Lourd touched Blood's arm.

"No, no, darling. Like I said earlier, I'm fine. All I need is my beauty rest." She laughed while licking her lips. "All I wanted to tell you was dick King down good." She rubbed on the dick print lining on his slacks. "Mmm . . . firm."

Blood was shocked. He shook his head and laughed as he got up from the bed. He was ready for King, and after he took his mind off her, his focus was back on Madam Lourd.

"Anything else you need before I head out?"

Madam Lourd uncrossed her legs. She was aroused after feeling on Blood's penis. At that moment, she needed her own bedtime snack—some sweet chocolate.

"Oh, could you tell that fine-ass Midnight to be in my boudoir in two hours. I'm in the mood now for a Hershey's bar with almonds. Mmm . . ."

"But, Sophia, are you sure you need dick right now? I don't want you to hurt yourself. If King finds—"

"Look, dear, forget about King. I'm horny as hell, and I ain't too old to get my freak on. Now, do what I told you to do. I want Midnight in my bed in two hours. Now get!"

Blood nodded. "As you wish, Madam Lourd. Good night."

"Night, darling."

Blood left the room.

Madam Lourd took a deep breath. "Thought the big stud would never leave."

She got up and sat at the vanity mirror while looking at her face that was beat to perfection. She reached for some face wipes to wipe off all her makeup. Once her face was completely bare, she was back to the woman that looked her real age, instead of looking like a film goddess in her 40s. Now she was ready to face her next disappointment, besides losing her beauty. She took off her wig and placed it on the table. She faced herself again, not only looking at her bare foot but also at her partially bald head. Seeing the old woman she really was, Madam Lourd broke out crying. Her dramatic tears were broken when she started coughing hard again. She got a Kleenex and held it over her mouth. When she stopped, she saw blood on the Kleenex. "Damn this stage three breast cancer!"

She wanted to break the vanity mirror but decided not to. She was diagnosed with breast cancer by her doctor six years ago. She did what she was supposed to do. She went to chemotherapy daily and took her medicine. It caused her to lose a lot of weight and made her once thick, curly hair fall out. This made her keep up her appearances so no one would worry. Hell, she was still a boss, even though King had taken her position. In her mind, *she* was in charge of the girls.

When the doctor told her that he would have to remove both her breasts because the chemo wasn't working, Madam Lourd declined. She had already lost a lot of weight and her trademark West Indian hair. But when it came to her Dolly Parton-sized breasts, that was the last straw for Madam Lourd.

Madam remembered the exact words her doctor told her about putting herself at considerable risk for not getting the surgery. Just thinking about the ordeal pissed her off. She got up and went to her bathroom.

She slipped off her gown and was adamant that cancer wasn't going to keep her down. As she looked in the mirror, you could see that her breasts were now deformed and red from the disease spreading. To her, if she were going to die today or tomorrow, she was going with all God gave her to work with. Her mind was made up. It was her time to go, and she was going to be remembered as being a boss and a celebrated escort.

She kept thinking about the doctor she'd paid very well to prescribe her the best pain relief medicine money could buy. It was against the doctor's practice, but with the money Madam Lourd paid, he couldn't refuse. He had prescribed her methadone shots to kill some of the pain. He ordered them every month for her, and Madam Lourd kept him on the payroll. If she needed anything, he'd be there no matter what. Her doctor was putting everything on the line for just one patient. He was putting his license, his practice, family, and reputation in jeopardy for one old lady. Shit, the money Madam Lourd was paying him was enough to feed a small country. Plus, adding a little bonus to sweeten the deal by sending him tail from women or men he could bang anytime for free. Madam Lourd knew the doctor was a happily married man with three adult children. But in her world, all men needed a different variety from time to time. She knew the doctor couldn't pass up free punany. He was a frequent customer at the Palace and never slept with the same woman twice.

Madam Lourd laughed at the thought of her greedy doctor having his cake and eating it too. *Men.* Then a sharp pain went through her chest.

"Oh—"

She held her chest while trying to keep her balance. The last thing she wanted to do was fall and break a bone, knowing her body was so fragile. She didn't want Ivy, King, or anyone else to find her on the floor. She didn't want anyone to find out about her diagnosis. One thing she'd learned in the escort business was never to show fear or weakness. She knew if King ever found out, the first thing she'd do was curse her out. Then fire her doctor and ruin whatever he loved. King would hire the best doctors in the world to keep her alive, and as crazy as King's ass was, she'd hire a voodoo witch doctor to put a spell on her to make her live forever.

She laughed about the idea and tried to ignore her unbearable pain. It was now going down to her stomach, making her want to vomit. She rushed over to the toilet and poured her guts out. She hated being this way some days and nights and wished the pain would all go away, or she'd just die. She stayed on her knees for a moment facedown in the toilet, waiting for more to come out. But nothing did, so she finally flushed the toilet.

Feeling unending sharp pains, she reached for her medicine and injected it into her right butt cheek. The drug hadn't kicked in yet, but she stumbled out of her bathroom, then sat on the bed and opened her drawer to get her other favorite, special "medicine." It was her famous Colombian cocaine. It was the one thing that helped her methadone kick in a little faster and was the very best cocaine in all of South America.

Madam Lourd knew King was against drugs and would flip the hell out if she found drugs on her escorts or her family. But to Madam Lourd, it was being used for medical reasons only. The last thing Madam Lourd knew she wasn't and that was an addict. She snorted some cocaine, then tucked the rest away. After that, she lay down to take a thirty-minute power nap and wanted to prepare herself in case Midnight showed up. She may have been old, bald, and sick, but she was still a woman with needs. She started to get hyped while thinking about all the shit she was going to do to Midnight. The one thing she loved about that Colombian cocaine was, not only was it her healing method, but it also made her feel incredibly freaky. With a creamy buildup between her thighs, she was ready.

Chapter 16

Bed Talk

Tyler stepped off the elevator on the floor to his suite without saying a word to Swag or Midnight. In the situation he was in now, it was every man for himself. He went inside his room and locked the door behind him. Then he looked around at his suite. It was the perfect player's paradise. It was all dark blue and white, from the furniture to the floor. The suite had a more urban vibe to it that Tyler liked. It also had a minibar with an array of drinks behind it. He poured a shot of vodka straight up and tossed it back. After a while, the liquor started to take effect. He stood in the room, thinking about the last few weeks. He thought he was going to get $50,000 to change his life, but this whole ordeal had only become a nightmare from which he couldn't wake. To him, if he hadn't gotten caught and had received the $50K, he would've gotten his own apartment and barbershop. One day, he hoped to be a hairstylist to the stars.

But now, Tyler felt like his dreams were all water under the bridge. He patted his stomach and noticed he was starting to get a tiny gut. It was hardly noticeable, but he was frustrated about everything.

"Damn, King was right. I need to lay off the fudge for a while."

Then again, he was ready to eat whatever King's chef had whipped up for him. He sat on the sofa and propped his feet up on the coffee table. His mind traveled to Travis. Tyler had a gut feeling something terrible was going to happen to his brother. He didn't know for sure, but he always had a spiritual connection to his brother. Tyler loved his brother with all his heart, and he prayed he would see him soon. He wondered if Brad got out of Rio with his female friend, or if they were dead. So many thoughts flooded his mind, and at this point, it didn't seem like there was much he could do.

Still hungry, Tyler's stomach started to ache. He rubbed his belly and wondered what was taking the chef so long with his food. Minutes later, someone knocked on the door. Tyler hopped up and asked who was there.

"It's Chef with your dinner!" a deep, loud male voice said.

Tyler took a deep breath, tossed back more vodka, and then put the glass on the table. He opened the door . . . and it was the last person he wanted to see. Tyler rolled his eyes. *Oh, hell naw. Not this clown.*

"Hey, boo-boo, here's room service," Santana said, smiling and posing with the tray in his hand.

Tyler had a blank expression on his face. *What in the hell? This fruity-ass dude,* he thought. Santana thought Tyler was feeling him. After all, what man wouldn't? Santana just loved turning out the *straight* guys. They were a challenge, and he enjoyed a good challenge. He had a 95 percent success rate turning dudes out, and he was only 18.

"So, are you going to stand there or let me in?" Santana bit his lip and sucked on it seductively.

Looking at this dude, Tyler wanted to punch the shit out of him for trying to make a pass at him. He came from a very religious family, and they always told him and his brother that homosexuals were bad people. Also, they were all going to rot in hell when Judgment Day came.

The smell of food from the tray made Tyler's stomach ache even more. He wasn't about to send Santana away, so he stepped aside and let him come in.

Santana walked in, swishing his butt, and entering the suite like a runway model. Tyler looked at him as Santana placed the tray on the coffee table, then sat on the sofa and crossed his legs.

Tyler rolled his eyes and released a deep sigh.

"Come on. Sit down 'fore your food gets cold," Santana said, patting the empty spot next to him.

Tyler rolled his eyes again and ignored Santana's advances. It was all about the food, so he sat next to him and removed the lid on the tray. He was surprised by what he saw. It was a T-bone steak, baked potato, salad with a side of blue cheese dressing, and strawberry cheesecake for dessert—all Tyler's favorites.

Santana reached for a napkin and tried to put it around Tyler's neck. In reality, he just wanted to feel his skin.

Tyler jerked back so he wouldn't touch him. "Damn, bruh, what's up?"

Santana giggled. "I'm just trying to be helpful. I didn't want you to get steak juice on your chest. Damn, you work out?"

"Yeah, I do, but . . ." Tyler thought about the words Santana said and was heated. "Nigga! If you don't get your faggot ass out of my room . . . Thanks for bringing my plate, but you gotta bounce."

Santana laughed. "Look, man, I'm sorry about that. You straight boys are *so* touchy. Let's start over. I'm Santana Costello." He held out his hand.

"Tyler," he said dryly.

They shook hands.

"Tyler, what?"

"Evans."

"Nice to meet you, Tyler Evans."

Still holding hand, Santana felt a spark.

"Mmm, you got some soft hands. Almost soft like a lady's. What kind of moisture do you use to wash or rub your sexy ass with?"

Tyler snatched his hand away from Santana. He pointed at the door. "Out, dammit, now!"

Santana laughed again. "Okay, I'll leave. But if you need anything, and I do mean—" He paused and looked down at Tyler's pants for a moment. He giggled like a naughty Catholic schoolgirl. Then he looked back at Tyler, "*anything, just let me know.*"

This was a disgusting display to Tyler, and it was starting to piss him off. He got up from the sofa and tightened his fists.

"What I need for you to do is go—go before I drop yo' gay ass!"

Santana pursed his lips. "Oh, so aggressive. That's *so* turning me on."

Santana sashayed over to the door. Before walking out, he looked at Tyler and blew him a kiss. "Good night, boo." He left and slammed the door behind him.

Tyler shook his body. "Eww, fags, eww." He tried to get his mind back on the food, but before he dove in, he looked down and noticed his dick was hard as a rock. He was tired, hungry, and horny . . . but for what?

Blood was in his suite or what he liked to refer to as his man cave. He was taking a shower, washing every inch of his body. He mainly washed his ten-inch penis and made sure his third leg was extra clean, along with his ass. He thought of all the freaky shit he was going to do to King. His nasty thoughts, along with the steamy water pounding on him, made his nipples and his manhood nicely firm. Blood wanted to jack off right in the shower, but he looked down and talked to his dick. "Down, boy. We gotta get ourselves ready for King, my love."

His jock went down slowly. He put the washcloth on his penis and washed it again. *Damn, this feels so good.* His nipples were still hard, and he started rubbing on them. After he was done entertaining himself, he got out of the shower and rubbed his body down with coconut oil. He then sprayed some Ralph Lauren cologne on his chest, wrapped the towel around his waist, and left the bathroom. While standing next to the bed, he put on red velvet silk boxers, which were the ones King loved to see him in. He was almost ready for her, and his excitement was building.

The last thing he did was put on Gucci flip-flops and a black and gold Versace robe that was a Christmas gift from King. He hoped that one day he'd be the rightful king for King, and he smiled at the thought of her making it official.

Suddenly, he heard a knock at the living room door. He exited the bedroom and went into the living area. The knocking continued.

"Hold on! Hold on!" He reached for the door and opened it.

It was Mina and Blacknese looking as sexy as ever. Both women had their long, black hair in buns. Mina wore a short, black satin robe, and Blacknese wore a pink silk one.

"Hey, big daddy," they said, before letting their robes drop to the floor.

Blood wanted to have sex with the ladies, but their timing was off. He was getting ready for King—and King only. He told the ladies they had to leave, and after they put up a fuss, they rolled their eyes, put their robes back on, and left. After they got on the elevator, Blood tightened his robe and knocked on King's door.

"King!" he shouted.

"Come in!"

Blood straightened his robe and opened the door. He walked into the classy living room area that had gold and silver décor.

"Make yourself a drink and relax," King said from her bedroom. "I'll be out in a few minutes."

"Cool. Take your time." Blood walked over to the minibar, where he saw King had his favorite drink ready for him. Two bottles of Imperial beer. He smiled, knowing King was not a big fan of beer at all.

While in her bedroom, King cursed herself. "Dammit! Dammit! Dammit! Dammit!" She wasn't in the mood to fuck Blood tonight. Her plan for the evening was to seduce Swag and make him forget about Josie. That idiot brother of hers totally messed up the evening. Thinking about Santana pissed her off. She loved her brother, but hated him, all at the same time. The past still haunted her. She shook off her thoughts and took a sip of Moët. She was sitting at her vanity mirror, looking at her flawless face. She put on very light makeup and tried to get hyped about sleeping with Blood. She looked back at her hidden cameras. She wished that Mina and Blacknese had tried harder to seduce him so that she could go to Swag. But her girls were slipping, and now she was stuck with pleasing Blood tonight. She took another sip of her drink, trying to wash out the idea. Shit, in her eyes, Blood was the help, bodyguard, and business partner. It wasn't wise to mix business with pleasure, and she'd had a bad experience in the past that she didn't want to repeat. Nonetheless, she felt like she owed Blood something.

Blood picked up both beer bottles and went over to the sofa. He took a seat and finished off one beer. He belched loudly, and as he looked to his right, he saw King's cigar box and pulled one out. After long drags, he felt kind of buzzed and didn't notice that King came out of her bedroom and was standing there looking at him. She smiled while thinking of Swag. With a black lace robe on that left nothing to the imagination, she headed Blood's way. He looked at her, almost choking on the smoke.

"I'm glad I got your attention," she said.

Blood cleared his throat and hurried to get himself together. He wiped the drool off his mouth and sat up straight.

"Damn, King," he whispered.

King knew she was what singer Prince used to sing about, "You sexy motherfucker." But it took everything in her to go along with this.

"So, are you ready to keep your promise?" Blood asked.

King continued to envision Swag on the sofa. "Just as long as you break me off really good."

Blood grinned sinisterly, knowing tonight, *he* was in charge and ready to bring King into sexual ecstasy.

"Take it off," he ordered.

This was the part King was waiting on all night. She started to take off her robe.

"Stop!"

She paused.

"Slowly. We got all night. I'm not going anywhere."

King smiled. She loved the art of seduction that Blood was playing tonight. She slowly took off her headband and let her long hair fall. She then removed her robe and let it slide down to the floor. She stood there in nothing but a cherry thong.

Blood continued to lick his lips and look at her breasts that looked edible. Her nipples were covered with red lipstick, and she started to rub herself.

Blood waved for her to come his way. "Stop playing and come over to papi."

King strutted over to Blood in her heels. She sat on his lap with her titties all in his face. He loved every minute. He sucked on her breasts for dear life, not caring that red lipstick covered them. King dropped her headed back and started rubbing his bald head. She was in total bliss. One good thing King loved about Blood was that he could suck the hell out of some titties. She wondered if Swag possessed the same skill. Just thinking about how he was fucking Desiree on the ship got her wet between the legs.

"Aaah," she moaned.

Blood untied his robe and looked at her. They stared at each other for a moment before indulging in a lustful kiss. During the intense kiss, Blood cuffed her breasts and massaged them.

"Mmmm," King grinded on his manhood, dry fucking him.

Blood liked how she teased him, and he sucked on her neck as if he were Dracula. He stopped kissing her so that he wouldn't come.

"Stand up and turn around for papi."

King licked her tongue on the tip of his nose. "Sure."

She got off his lap and turned around. For that moment, Blood admired her smooth, thick ass. He smacked one cheek.

"Oh, damn, Blood. Don't forget the other one." King turned and looked at him with bedroom eyes.

"Is that what you want, mama?"

"Yes, Zaddy."

Blood smacked her other cheek.

"Ouch," she joked.

Blood saw wetness forming between her thighs. He licked his lips like a hungry lion.

"Spread them legs and bend over."

King loved the dirty talk Blood was speaking. She smiled and obeyed.

"Love them cakes, baby!"

Blood smirked while admiring her ass. He wanted to sex her from behind right then and there, but he contained himself. He smacked both cheeks again, then dropped to his knees in front of her. He wanted to rip her thong off and dig right into her candy dish, but first, he inhaled her scent. He then stuck out his long tongue and licked all over her ass cheeks like they were two big scoops of ice cream. King was trying to keep still, but her legs trembled, and cream started to drip down them.

Blood was hungry for a taste of her. His tongue went up and down her legs, licking every last drop of her juice.

"Aah . . . yes. Drink, baby . . ."

Hearing King's approval excited him. He wanted to be inside of her, but he wasn't done tasting her. He licked her pussy from behind, even though the thong was covering it up. He rubbed up and down her legs with his big hands and teased her with his fingers.

"Yes," King growled. Her legs were getting weak, but she was too turned on to care. She wanted him to take her now. "Yes!" She rubbed her titties.

Blood stopped sucking on her and stood up. They shared another intense kiss, but King was a little disappointed that he hadn't yet removed her thong. She roughly kissed his lips, neck, his tatted chest, and his nipples. He quivered over this feeling, almost screaming like a little bitch. "Aaah!"

King loved how some men got weak when it came to their nipples. She loved power. She continued to kiss and suck on his nipples for a few moments before dropping to her knees. She looked up at him and smiled.

"Take your robe off," she demanded.

Blood obeyed, and King kissed the lining of his dick in his boxers while toying with his butt.

"Don't be playing no games. Serve papi."

King needed some Blood sausage, so she covered his third leg with her entire mouth. Blood loved the warmness of her mouth. She was almost sucking the skin off his penis.

"Damn, girl, where you learn that from?" Blood almost lost his balance.

She stopped sucking him off. Now, she was in the mood for some meatballs. She took his ball sack, kissing and sucking on them one at a time. She even tea-bagged them. One thing she loved about men, especially Blood, was his clean balls.

"Damn . . ." Blood quivered and felt like he was about to pass out and come all at once. "Okay, okay . . . That's good." He patted her head. "Let's go into your room."

King stood and led him to her bedroom that looked like nothing but pure royalty. Blood laid her gently on the high, king-sized bed that was covered with a gold comforter and numerous pillows. The Egyptian sheets soothed their skin, and the angel wings hanging above the bed were looking down on them. King spread her legs and toyed with her clit. She wanted some dick inside of her and needed an orgasm like a drug addict needed a hit. Blood examined her honeypot, which was still dripping through the thong. And to give him a quick taste of her, she placed her fingers in his mouth so he could taste her juices.

"Mmm, good," he said.

"Are you going to lie here with your mouth open, or are you going to get some?"

Blood ripped her thong off and dove in like a hungry dog. King held his head steady and closed her eyes. She was in la-la land, and so was Blood.

"Damn, you taste so good, like raspberries and cream." He knew it was lame, but King's pussy was the best he'd tasted in a while.

He was talking too much, so she pressed his head down to her pussy. "Eat!"

He obeyed and put his fierce tongue in motion. King moaned and groaned loudly with so much excitement.

"Yes!" She was so aroused that she came hard on Blood's face. "Aaaah, baby, yes!"

Blood loved to taste her and loved it when she came on his face. He knew he was doing his job. He knew right then and there her mind was off of Swag. He gazed up at her while tasting her. King closed her eyes as she rubbed her titties while playing with her nipples. Her actions caused his dick to harden. He was getting tired of all this foreplay. Now, he was ready to feel her. He positioned his manhood between her wet folds and drove right in.

"Mmmm," he groaned and stroked in and out of her.

King's eyelids fluttered. She was in sexual heaven but mainly focused her mind on Swag. Blood had no idea as he lifted one of her legs and placed it on his shoulder. He licked and kissed her foot, and his thrusts were faster and deeper.

"Yes! Yes, papi! Faster!" King screamed and had multiple orgasms as she came all over his dick.

"You like that shit, don't you?"

"Yes, papi!"

"What's my name!"

King almost said Swag's name but kept her thoughts together. "Blake!"

Blood loved it when she said his real name. They shared a wet, sloppy kiss as he stroked faster, reaching her G-spot and making her come harder on his jock.

King moaned and screamed even more. Blood loved it. She was tired of him taking control. Now, it was her turn. She scratched his back until she felt and saw blood oozing out.

"Shiiiit," Blood groaned in pleasure and pain.

King got on top like a cowgirl and licked his blood from her fingers. Blood looked at her with some disgust but hid his feelings because of the pleasure she gave him. She bounced up and down on his dick, going wild. Blood's eyes rolled back, and his toes curled. He was in total sex heaven, especially when she sucked his nipples. He could barely hold on to her hips because she was moving too fast. He cuffed her bouncing breasts and started to suck them like a hungry newborn.

Blood felt his juices squirting out. "King! I'm . . . 'bout to come!"

That was King's cue to get off of him. The last thing she wanted was a baby to mess up her body and beauty. Plus, she loved watching Blood come. She rolled off him and lay next to him. Blood jerked his manhood, and they both watched his sperm squirt on his stomach and chest. He quivered and continued to breathe heavily.

King looked at all the sperm on him and smiled. She knew if he'd put that in her, she would've gotten pregnant. The main thing was that Blood was happy. He intended for this to happen again every night. He closed his eyes, believing just that.

Chapter 17

Nightmare

Tyler was asleep in his comfortable queen-sized bed. He had just gotten through eating a good meal, tossed back three more shots of vodka, and jacked off twice to get rid of the hard-on that was driving him nuts. He tried to block out Santana from his thoughts, but Santana clouded his thoughts. Tyler had no clue why, and to him, Santana was like a pesky mosquito that wouldn't go away. Tyler kept telling himself over and over that he wasn't gay. His father would've killed him for thinking or being with another man. But even as a kid, Tyler always had a fascination with the LGBTQ lifestyle. He always played the macho tough guy loving the ladies, but deep inside, he saw men differently.

That evening at the other mansion, Travis was sitting on his bed and looking at his missing finger. He still couldn't get over what King had done to him. All he could think about was payback. He also thought about how stupid he and the fellas were for falling into this trap. They were supposed to be having fun with their new boss. He remembered how Paco hyped him up as well as the fellas, thinking they'd all be rich. His mother used to tell him and his brother, *"If something is too good to be true, it is."*

But being in the mansion wasn't so bad. Travis kept to himself and stayed out of Paco's way, especially since Swag and Tyler had already beaten Paco's racist ass. Travis knew Paco was going to take his revenge out some way. He just had to keep his guard up, since he had no one watching his back or front. He would come downstairs for food and drink and stay clear of Paco and his gang.

Travis yawned, removed his clothes, and got in bed. He closed his eyes and said a short prayer. "Lord, protect me and mostly my twin. Amen."

Downstairs in the mansion's kitchen, Paco, Ike, Rock, Landon, Miguel, and Nash had a meeting. They were trying to come up with a plan to get revenge against Swag, Tyler, Midnight, and King. It shocked the crew, except Landon, who experienced an earlier ass whooping from Paco.

"Why Midnight? Why, homes? That's the homie, man," Miguel said in his thick Hispanic accent.

"For the last time, I don't give a fuck! Midnight is disloyal!" Paco yelled. "He didn't do shit for me. Look at my face!" He pointed at the black marks on his face. "Fuck Midnight. He let that goon and his sidekick kick my ass! So, no! Midnight is no longer my right-hand man. My new right-hand man is Landon!"

Landon sat there, smiling as if he had just won the lottery.

The rest of the crew looked at him with disgust. They knew Landon kissed both Paco's and PJ's asses. If Paco told Landon to lick his ass, he'd lick all the color off until there was nothing but bone.

Nash was a skinny, brown dude with his whole body, including parts of his face, covered in tattoos like a subway in Harlem. He cleared his throat. "Why li'l dude gotta be the fucking sergeant at arms? This li'l bitch ain't nothin' but a punk ass!"

"Yeah, I been with you just as long as Midnight. Not like this gay-ass-looking Diggy," said an angry Ike. "If anyone should be the sergeant at arms, it should be me. Not this li'l bitch!"

"Look, I ain't goin' be too many of y'all's bitches. So, watch it!" Landon pointed a knife at Ike and Nash.

"Oh, I'm scared," Nash said sarcastically while giggling.

Ike brushed Landon off, knowing he was all bark and no bite.

Paco loved the fact that everyone's true colors were coming out. He loved to see friends turning against friends. But to him, in this lifestyle, you had no friends, just associates. As much as he loved the drama, he had to get the show back in order.

"Look, all y'all shut the hell up. A'ight?" Paco stood up. "This may be King's shit, but I'm still the head muthafucka in charge. Hell, maybe if killing my dad and King go right, *I'll* be king of the Hernandez Cartel *and* the Leopard Clit."

"Yeah, right," Rock said softly with a sly look on his face.

Paco and everyone looked Rock's way. Paco was stunned at the words that came out of his mouth, especially since he was almost family. Rock was going with Paco's little sister, who was expecting his child. In his mind, Paco should've killed him when he broke the code of messing with the boss's sister, but he let it slide.

"What was that, crack baby?" Paco's brow shot up. He knew that would anger Rock, whose childhood nickname was that.

Rock winced and shook his head. "Nothin', man."

"Naw. If you got something to say, then say it in my damn face and not no weak-ass shit!" Paco sipped from his glass of alcohol. "Come on, let's put everything out on the table, crack baby." He laughed, knowing he had Rock right where he wanted him.

Rock was livid, and at this moment in his life, he just didn't give a shit anymore. To him, Paco was no boss of his. He felt like it was time to bring Paco back down to earth.

"Man, when I first met you, I loved and admired you. Shit, I wanted to be like you and your father. I'm pretty much family with my retarded seed in ya sister's stomach." Rock cleared his throat, then chuckled. "Now, look at you. You thought you was on some Michael Corleone, Mafia-type shit with King. In the end, you got punked and played by a female. A *female,* punk ass!"

They all wanted to laugh, knowing what Rock said was nothing but the truth. Instead, they remained silent with straight faces. Paco laughed his ass off, trying to soak in what Rock had told him. For years, he saw Rock like a man, friend, a member of the Hernandez Cartel, and soon-to-be brother-in-law that he once loved. Now, all that love was turning to anger and pure hate. Paco took a sip of his beer and cut Rock with the look in his narrowed eyes.

"Yeah, then you got your ass kicked by Swag and Tyler. Oh, and don't forget you got your ass kicked out of King's bed!" Rock laughed to the point of insanity. He really didn't give a shit anymore about anything. In his world, he was his own boss now.

"Calling me weak and slow for years, and yo' ass can't even fight without Midnight to fight your battles. You ain't nothing but a joke. A clown for the Hernandez Cartel. Just like PJ said you were." Rock's laughter continued.

Paco was heated from all the disrespect and venom thrown at him. He saw the real Rock or his government name, Roland Douglass, for the very first time in their almost-a-decade friendship. It was just a pity that his sister was carrying a part of him inside of her.

Landon had gotten an apple and was cutting it into slices while walking around the kitchen. No one paid him any mind except Paco, who was studying Landon but focused on Rock.

"So, do you want out of the cartel then?"

"Yeah. I'm going to turn myself in to the police and confess everything so that I can get a plea bargain. That way, I won't miss much of my child's upbringing."

Paco's pressure rose to the edge, hearing that. To him, the last thing you did in the criminal world was snitch out the crew or the family business. Rock knew that he just signed his death certificate, and he bought himself a one-way ticket to hell. At that point, he didn't care. He was ready to meet his maker.

Paco kept his cool and smiled like he didn't have a care in the world. "All right, Rock. If that's what you want, we'll miss you." He shifted his eyes to Landon.

Rock didn't know what hit him once Landon took the knife and stabbed him in his neck. Blood squirted on Landon, who got a thrill out of watching Rock scream.

"Aaaaah!" Rock held his neck and fell to the floor. Landon stabbed him repeatedly, causing chunks of his pink flesh to fly.

"Stop! Stop! That's enough, Landon!" Paco yelled.

Landon backed away from Rock with blood all over his shirt and shoes. The other men looked on in disbelief. They had been wrong about Landon. It seemed like he did have balls after all. No one was more pleased than Paco. He patted Landon on his back and smiled.

"Good job, man. You passed the test. Now, you have proven your loyalty to me and the new era of the Hernandez Cartel."

Landon smiled like a little kid getting a big bonus on his allowance.

Paco looked down at Rock, who was gasping for air and trying to hold on to the last bit of life he had.

"Heeelp me, pleeease," Rock begged, reaching out for Paco's hand. Paco just stood there, watching Rock die a slow, painful death.

His eyes fluttered, and when he opened them wide, he was face-to-face with Paco, who was kneeling beside him with no remorse on his face. With his last dying breath, Rock told Paco how he really felt.

"See you in hell, pussy-ass bitch!" He spat blood on Paco's chin.

Paco laughed and wiped the blood with his hand. "Yeah, but I hope you can see when you get there!" He snatched the knife from Landon and stabbed Rock's eyeballs.

He screamed in torment as his body flopped on the floor like a fish out of water.

Paco was tired of his screams, so he sliced open his throat. Rock was finished. He was no longer part of the land of the living.

The rest of the crew showed no emotion whatsoever. But deep inside, they were scared shitless of Paco. They knew he had his way of handling business, but what he did to Rock was total insanity at best.

Paco looked back at his remaining crew. "See? That's what happens when you're disloyal or show disrespect toward me." He looked at Rock's lifeless body and kicked his face. "Enjoy hell, and here's a little something to cool you off while you're there." He laughed as he urinated on Rock's corpse.

Once he was done pissing, he got himself in order and looked at everyone. "Now, is there anything anyone needs to put on the table about me as a boss? Speak now or forever hold your peace."

No one uttered a word.

"Snap the fuck out of it! All of you. You act if as you've never seen a dead body before! Let me ask again. Do any of you have any issues with me or my motives?"

"Nah, hell nah," they said in unison.

Paco smiled wickedly, knowing he was back in control. "Good!"

He walked back to his seat with the knife he'd killed Rock with and reached for an apple. He sliced it and ate the apple, even though the knife was still dripping with Rock's blood.

"Delicious. Now, when I'm the new leader of the Hernandez Cartel along with the Leopard Clit, the new motto will be 'Take No Prisoners.' First, I'ma kill that bastard of a father of mine. Then kill Swag, Tyler, Blood, and Midnight. Once I get that bitch, King, alone, I'ma snap that pretty little neck of hers for double-crossing me." He laughed.

Landon laughed along with him.

Paco looked at him. *This ass kisser,* he thought. He appreciated his loyalty, but he didn't like ass kissers. Paco looked down at Rock and back at his crew.

"It's time for you all to show your loyalty to me again."

They all looked at one another, then back at Paco.

"Paco, man, we've always been loyal. Hell, at least I know I've been. We've known each other since we were kids. Man, we family, homes, on real shit," Miguel said.

"Yeah," Ike and Nash agreed.

"Loyalty, my ass!" Paco got mad all over again while thinking of the earlier events that took place. "Where were you assholes when I was getting my ass kicked or when I was getting disgraced by that fake-ass Griselda Blanco?"

Again, the room fell silent. But Ike, Nash, Miguel, and especially Landon knew the consequences if they tried to help. They knew they weren't in Texas anymore.

"Yeah, y'all quiet 'cause y'all know y'all was wrong for keeping me hanging. I should've killed you all in your sleep, but I still have a somewhat forgiving heart. And like Miguel said, we still fam 'til the end."

There was a sigh of relief in the room.

"Don't start exhaling yet! You all still have a debt to pay from earlier."

Eyebrows shot up. They were curious about what he'd said.

"I hope y'all didn't think it was all peaches, milk, and cookies," Paco laughed. "You all, as of tonight, will have to re-prove your loyalty to the new organization and me."

"Re-prove our—" Ike said.

Paco cut him off. "Yes!"

"What we gotta do, Paco, to get back in your good graces?" Miguel asked.

Paco looked up, then back at his crew with a smile.

"What's up with that, Paco?" Nash asked, concerned.

Paco loved the game he was playing with them. "Well, our 'special' guest upstairs is a lost little lamb without its shepherd. It's time to teach the boys from the Lou a lesson. An eye for an eye. It's time to go hunting, gentlemen." Paco held up the bloody knife.

Tyler tossed and turned. He was sweating and breathing heavily.

"Go get a knife, and let's go hunting!" Paco stood up from his seat. "Come on. Let's move." He looked at Rock's dead body. "And after we're done, I need you all to clean up this piece of shit."

The guys nodded and started to get knives for themselves. Landon picked up a sharp meat cleaver.

***

Tyler continued to breathe heavily and talk in his sleep. "No, no."

Paco and the crew went upstairs and headed to Travis's room. Once at the door, Paco quietly opened it. "Idiot wasn't smart enough to lock the door."

"Damn, Paco, this is too easy," Landon laughed, almost giving them away.

Paco told him to hush up. They all went inside Travis's room and formed a circle while looking down at him.

Tyler turned, flipped, and flopped around in the bed. His breathing got worse. He thought he was having a panic attack. "Travis, Trav . . . is! No! No!" His eyes were shut tightly.

Travis slept peacefully without a care in the world. He didn't know a circle of the Hernandez Cartel was watching him. Paco smiled while holding the knife firmly in his hand.

"No one to protect you now," he laughed. "Wake your ass up!" Paco kicked his leg.

Travis woke up, surprised, as he looked around. He was outnumbered. His heart pounded against his chest, and beads of sweat formed on his forehead.

Tyler sweated a river. His heart started to beat faster. He thought he was going to have a heart attack. He closed his eyes tightly with tears coming down his face.

***

Everyone had their weapons up.

"Now, go back to sleep!" Paco shouted.

Travis tried to get out of the bed, but not before Paco yelled, "Now!"

He and his crew began to cut, slice, and stab all over Travis's body.

He hollered in agony, knowing the Hernandez Cartel outdid him. "Heeelp, somebodeeee, pleeease, Tylerr, help meee!"

Tyler jumped up. "Travis!" He was hyperventilating. Tyler needed to see his brother. He didn't know if it were a dream or real. When day hit, Tyler was going to check on his brother. Then his skin got hot, and he started to feel pain in his chest and stomach. "God!" Tyler hadn't prayed or been in church in years. But he needed God's help at that moment. His twin was all he had on this crazy ride they were on. "Please take care of my brother. Don't take him away from me. Protect him."

Travis turned his head, closed his eyes, and took his last breath. Paco smiled proudly at the now sliced, diced, and chopped up Travis. Travis's blood was everywhere—on their clothes and the bedding. The crew looked at Paco.

"Is that it? Have we proven our loyalty to you?" Nash asked with bass in his voice.

"Damn, two bodies in one night," Landon said, high off bloodlust.

Paco walked over to Nash and laughed. Without warning, he cut Nash on the right side of his face.

"Fuck!" Nash held the side of his bleeding face. "Shit, man! What the fuck!"

"Now, we're even." Paco looked over at Ike, who was in disbelief at what Paco had done. Ike was a lot of things, but a killer wasn't one of them.

"Ike, go in the bathroom and get Nash a towel!"

Ike looked down at the floor.

"Earth to Ike!"

Ike looked up at Paco. "Yeah, G?"

"Get a towel for Nash!" Paco snapped his fingers.

Ike cut his eyes at Paco and went to the bathroom. He came out and handed Nash the towel. He pressed the cloth against his face to soak up the blood.

"Thank you all for proving your loyalty to me. Now, go wash up. You gotta get rid of this piece of shit too, and if anyone needs me, I'll be in my room." He walked out while leaving his crew to clean up both messes.

Once in his bedroom, Paco locked the door behind. He lay on the bed, not caring that the blood of two men covered him. He laughed evilly and felt good and proud of his accomplishments.

Chapter 18

Eyes and Ears

Blood and King had finally wrapped up their sex session and kissed each other for a brief moment. He smiled while looking into her beautiful green eyes. The color reminded him of the country plains, where he grew up as a child. Never before had he felt love like this. King meant everything to him. However, in King's mind, she wasn't with that love shit. That side of her died a long time ago. She cleared her throat and tapped Blood on his shoulder.

"Blood, baby, get off me. You're getting heavy and sweaty."

Blood laughed, but before he could turn over, King saw her tablet and started watching the massacres at her mansion. First was Paco's man, Rock, and then Travis.

Blood leaned over and looked at her tablet. They watched and heard everything from the misfits of the Hernandez Cartel killing one of their own, to Tyler's brother and Swag's homeboy. It amused King and Blood. They loved how friends turning against friends resulted in this.

"I don't believe it," King said, laughing. "Paco, this bastard, actually thinks he has a master plan. He has no idea what's coming to him."

Blood laughed and watched as King switched the monitors back to her palace. She checked in on her girls in their rooms. Some were sleeping alone, some finishing up with clients. Then King checked on Ivy. She should've known her mother was with one of her boy toys. She shook her head, but King was just happy she wasn't with Swag. She tuned in on Tyler, who was tossing and turning in his sleep. *Poor guy,* she thought. She didn't know how she was going to explain the gruesome death of his brother. Then King wondered why in the hell she was feeling sorry for someone she barely knew.

She switched the monitor to Josie, who was getting out of the shower and getting ready for her morning workout. King had big plans for Josie later on that day. King was going to check in on Madam Lourd but decided against it. She was eager to check on Swag, and when she did, he was sleeping shirtless wearing only boxers. She zoomed in on his face but was careful not to upset Blood. He looked at the screen with disgust, and trying to distract King from looking at Swag, he started to tease her nipple. It worked because she dropped the tablet on the floor. Afterward, he stopped. King looked at him with confusion in her eyes.

"Why did you stop?"

"Because we need to talk about what we're going to do with our guests at the mansion. Shit, they half-assed did us a favor by killing Rock and Travis."

"Yeah, and they messed up my kitchen and one of my favorite rooms in the house with blood and gore." She stretched her arms out with a big smile on her face. "But don't worry, Blood, I have that all under control."

"How?"

"Don't rush me," she giggled and went over to her nightstand to get her cell phone. She dialed out. After a few rings, someone picked up. "Yes, Cleo, bring them up, please." King ended the call.

Blood looked confused. He and King always discussed plans on how to get money. He didn't know what was up with that.

"King, what in the hell is going on?"

"Shh. It's all in good fun." King rubbed his brawn chest.

Within moments, a knock came at her bedroom door.

"Come in."

Cleo came in dressed in a new black suit with matching black dress shoes. "Good evening, or should I say, good morning, King and Mr. Blood."

Blood nodded. "What's up?"

"Good morning, Cleo," King said.

Cleo stepped to the side and waved his hand. Six beautiful women entered the room in sexy outfits that showcased their bodies.

"Good morning, King," the ladies said in unison.

King smiled while looking them up and down. Blood smiled too.

"Damn." He looked over at King. "I know these ladies are gorgeous, but how do they solve our little problem?"

King got out of bed and flaunted her naked body. Blood's complete attention was on her.

"Ladies," King said and clapped her hands. Without warning, all six ladies were all over Blood like a cheap suit with guns and swords surrounding him. He was outnumbered by six femmes fatales, ready to kill when King gave them the word.

"Any more questions?"

"Nope. They'll do."

King laughed at the fact that Blood was off his game. She snapped her fingers, and the ladies put their weapons in places Blood never imagined.

"What the fuck?" Blood said.

"Go on, ladies. Play nicely."

They left the room with Cleo following behind them.

Blood took a deep breath. *Thank God.* He lay his head on the pillow, thinking about King and her kick-ass assassins. She had never tried that shit on him before.

King laughed, lifted her leg, and kicked Blood on his side.

"Time's up," she said. "Get out!"

Blood cocked his head back and looked at her as if she were crazy. "What?"

"Get out! I need to catch up on my beauty sleep. Thank you for a lovely evening, but we're done." She kicked him again.

Blood's feelings were hurt, but he got up as he was told. "Okay, cool. I'll see you at breakfast."

She winked, but deep inside, Blood was pissed. She'd treated him like he were a common ho in the street without any pay. He left and didn't dare question her actions.

Once Blood was gone, King lay back on her messy bed. Her body was tired yet satisfied at the same time. As she was about to close her eyes, her cell phone rang.

"Hello," she said.

"Is everything ready?" asked a man with a deep voice.

King laughed. "Yes."

Chapter 19

Bed and Breakfast

Later during the morning, everyone was in the dining room enjoying a delicious buffet breakfast of beef tamales, chorreadas (corn pancakes), scrambled eggs, gallo pinto (black beans and rice), bizcochos (pastries), chicharrónes (fried pork belly), and all kinds of fruit, orange juice, and water.

Madam Lourd looked flawless, and she tried to forget all about her slipup last night. She had on one of her wigs and a white silk robe. Josie was still in her jogging suit, with her hair looking pretty. Swag was enjoying his breakfast while wearing a tank top, shorts, and sneakers.

Within moments, King joined everyone. She had just gotten out of the shower and had oiled her body with a jasmine scent. Her hair was wrapped in a towel for it to dry, and a white towel covered her body. She wasn't wearing a drop of makeup and was still tired from last night.

"Good morning, everyone."

They all replied, "Good morning," as she looked over at the buffet. She wasn't hungry, so all she got was a glass of orange juice before sitting at the table with everyone.

Ivy, who looked fresh as a daisy after being dicked down by one of her boy toys, was all dolled up in a blue jean pants suit with her hair slicked back.

"Damn, daughter, what's wrong? You look like someone broke your heart. No makeup?"

King looked at her mother and rolled her eyes. She knew her mother was trying to push her buttons. But it was too early for King to check her. Instead, she sipped her juice. She didn't have time to entertain this petty shit right now. Today, she had bigger fish to fry. She took another sip of her drink when she saw Tyler coming into the dining room.

He nodded to everyone. "Good morning, folks."

"Morning," everyone said.

With cornrows, a T-shirt, denim jean shorts, and white sneakers on, Tyler walked into the room, nervous as shit . . . mainly because he wanted to know if his other half was dead or alive. He kept a confident look on his face as he went over to the buffet to get some food.

King cleared her throat and waved to Tyler. "Oh, Tyler, come here. Come sit next to me."

Tyler looked at her with a blank expression but joined her at the table.

"Good morning, King."

"Good morning, Tyler. How are you?"

"Okay, I guess. I miss my brother. Can I see him today? I just have this feeling . . . Can I see him, King? Please."

King looked at him, knowing the truth. She saw the hurt in his eyes, but she knew he was trying to remain strong and cocky. Deep down, King wanted to hug him and tell him that his brother was murdered at the hands of Paco. But that would spoil the surprise she had planned for later. She just wasn't into that emotional shit . . . hugging and caring. She killed that side of her a long time ago. She needed to remain a hardhearted bitch at all times to keep her respect. She pretended to ignore Tyler's situation, which, to her, was a bore. She wanted to change the subject. She just looked at his cornrows and smiled at him.

"Who did your braids? One of my girls or Santana?"

"Nah," Tyler said. "Hell . . . naw." Tyler realized Santana was King's little brother and changed his tone. "I mean, no. I did it myself."

"Really? You did a great job."

"Thanks. I used to be a barber, plus a stylist back home."

"Really?" King said with amazement in her eyes.

"Yeah," Tyler replied. He tried to get back to the topic of his brother. "What about my—"

"Oh, Tyler, can you braid my hair?" King purposely cut him off, and instead of slapping the shit out of him, which was her way of toughing him up, she was giving him the chance to make her look beautiful and doing something that once made him happy.

Tyler was tired of the subject about his brother being changed, but he had to remember he was now in King's home. He didn't want any harm coming his way, so he just kept up with the program. "Sure." He put on a fake smile. "Sure, I'd love to do your hair."

"Good. You can do mine and my daughter's hair too. Right now. Come on." She waved at him as she got up and looked over at Josie. She waved at her too. "Come on, my child. We have to get ready. It's a special day for you too."

Josie didn't say anything. She just got up and walked over to King's side.

King kissed her on her cheek and looked over at Blood. "Blood, please make sure Swag, Midnight, and you are in your black suits. Be ready in an hour and a half." King looked over at Tyler. "Come, Tyler. We're on a schedule. Plus, there is a score to settle."

Chapter 20

Business Is Business

Upstairs in the eastern quarters of King's Palace was a huge, luxurious, personal beauty salon and spa. It had everything that a real beauty shop had and more. The interior was beautiful, with colors from pearl white, gold, and a touch of diamonds. The only pop of color in the whole space was four statues of leopards to rep King's operation.

Today was a very special day, and King had to go all-out for her beauty makeover. So she had flown in celebrity manicurist to the stars, Oneisha Lamar, to do both Josie's and her nails and toes. It cost King a pretty penny to have her, but it was worth every dime for what Oneisha could do to your hands and feet.

Both ladies got painted nails, except King's were painted her favorite color, gold. Josie stayed girlie and had hers painted pink. As King was getting her feet and makeup on point, she looked over at her child. She was giving her daughter a little insight on what she and her operation did. King knew it was a bit early to show her this since Josie's birthday was coming up in a few weeks, where the *real* orientation was going to begin. King was determined to get Josie out of that fairy-tale, happily-ever-after, pretend world she invented in her mind.

The only reason King was letting Josie practice ballet and design was to have an outlet to relieve stress. King had no plans for Josie to go anywhere with her talents but to serve the Leopard Clit. King wanted Josie to be a future boss and rule over Costa Rica. But until then, she was going to give Josie some training regarding her world slowly.

Once their feet and nails were done, along with their makeup beaten to the gods, King and Josie went to the salon side. They both sat in their chairs to get their hair braided by Tyler.

As Tyler was doing both ladies' hair, his mind wandered over to his twin. He couldn't get Travis off his mind, especially after that horrific dream he had last night. But until he could put all the clues together, he focused on doing hair.

It had been months since he'd cut or styled someone's hair. He was amazed at how everything came back to him, and he didn't know if it were nerves or excitement of being back in his own element.

King had all the styling tools in her salon that Tyler could ever need to perfect both ladies' hair. When he finished, King looked at herself in the mirror. She was amazed at what he had accomplished. He had styled both of their hair into two French braids with curls on the end.

"Oh my God! I love it!" King smiled.

Josie nodded and agreed with her mother.

Next, they got hooked up by an up-and-coming designer who was making waves in the industry. She styled both ladies in her signature sleeveless jumpsuits.

King wore a sexy, lacy, black one that left nothing to the imagination. She even put on some gold heels to complete her look. She immediately fell in love with the look. *Perfect for the occasion,* King thought.

Josie wore a lacy pink one with white heels.

King looked in the mirror and thought of herself as a glam goddess, dressed to kill. Josie, on the other hand, felt so out of place. This wasn't her. She didn't recognize the girl in the mirror, and she felt uncomfortable wearing a jumpsuit that exposed so much skin, including her breasts. She was much more comfortable in her tomboy chic look.

King looked over at Josie, knowing that she wasn't feeling the look. But in King's eyes, this was part of today's lesson: The Art of Seduction and Land Your Prey.

She stood behind Josie and wrapped her arms around her waist.

"What's wrong, my child?" King kissed her cheek.

"Mother, this look. It's . . . It's . . ."

"It's perfect. Sexy and a lesson I'm going to teach you today."

Josie had a blank expression on her face, but she wanted to let King have it. "What lesson?"

"Shh," King massaged Josie's shoulders as they looked in the mirror. "Don't worry, doll face. You'll see soon enough. Now, leave and wait for me at the top of the stairs."

Josie displayed a fake smile. She'd rather be practicing dancing than having to do whatever King had planned.

Tyler washed his hands and dried them with a towel. He looked at King's reflection in the mirror and smiled. "Well, King, if you need anything else, I'll be in my room."

Before he could walk out of the room, King shouted, "Tyler!"

He looked her way. "What's up, ma?"

"You're coming with me today."

Tyler was superhyped. "To see my brother!"

King laughed and looked back at her reflection in the mirror. She posed and admired how good she looked.

"I need you to come with me. I have a surprise for you."

"What kind of surprise?" Tyler asked with a raised brow.

King released a wicked laugh, then snapped at him. "Don't ask so many questions. Just come on."

She walked away.

"Should I get dressed in a suit too?"

She looked back at him. "No." She shook her head. "What you have on is perfect for this occasion. Now, let's hurry."

King and Josie pranced down the stairs, looking like they were ready for the runway. The guys, Swag, Blood, and Midnight, looked clean in their all-black suits and resembled *Men in Black 4,* but in a good way.

King smiled, especially at Swag. The guys were trying to keep their tongues in their mouths, but most men or women could not resist King and her child.

King approved of the men's attire. "You all look good."

"Damn, you ladies look beautiful," Swag complimented.

He looked at Josie, but she turned her head, trying not to smirk. King went over to Swag and checked his wrapped hand.

"When we get back, we'll check on that."

King wasn't going to check on shit. She wanted his undivided attention that was locked on Josie.

"Sure," he said.

King licked his cheek like a sexy kitten. Blood looked at this display with disgust. He was frustrated with King, especially after the way he'd sexed her last night. She could see the fury in his eyes, but King viewed him as a fool.

"Let's not stand here," she said to Swag. "Let's go."

Before anyone left, Tyler rushed down the stairs, feeling out of place. He looked like a common street dude while everyone, including his boy Swag, was dressed to the nines.

"Now that we're all here, let's move out."

A long, black limousine and two silver Rolls-Royces were parked in front of the Palace.

"All right, everyone," King said. "Boys, you all in the limo, and Josephine, you will be in the Rolls-Royce in the middle. Blood, take me to the Rolls-Royce at the end."

Josie was kind of shocked by being in a car all by herself. She wanted to speak up but didn't. She was hoping Swag would be in the car with her. She'd had a weird connection to him ever since they'd met. In her mind, she felt that, next to Madam Lourd, she could talk to him about anything.

Everyone went to their respective cars. Blood escorted King to hers, and he looked at Swag and mouthed, "Punk ass."

Swag mean mugged him and mouthed, "Fuck you" before entering the limousine.

Blood laughed.

King entered the car, and Blood sat next to the driver. The limousine took off with the other cars following behind it.

In the Rolls-Royce, things were heated between King and Blood. He had a straight look on his face. King knew Blood was still mad as hell at her for licking Swag's cheek. She laughed at him.

"You can stop it now."

Blood was caught off guard by her comment. He took off his shades and replied, "Stop what?"

"You heard what I said. Stop being so jealous of Solomon."

Blood rolled his eyes, but he was still in complete shock and amazement by her comment.

"Jealous? Jealous of what? That stupid-ass American? King, please. You know me better than that." Blood put his shades back on.

"Look, I know you and Solomon are trying to see who has the biggest balls, but this is *my* show. And show him a little more respect, because he's going to be with us a little bit longer."

"What! A little bit longer? What's that supposed to mean? No fuckin' way. What can he do? He can't do none of the shit I can do. He will never *ever* be me."

King gave Blood a stern look. She hated when Blood compared himself or any other man to *him*. In King's mind, no one will ever be compatible with *him*, or them, at that. King wanted to kill Blood for letting those words slip out of his mouth, but she was going to let it slide . . . for now. Today, she had a bigger score to settle.

Blood took a deep breath and calmed down. "Look, King, I'm sorry, okay? I just don't trust this man. He's going to bring the whole operation down if we let him. Can't you see that?"

King didn't agree with him. She hated to have negative vibes in her presence.

"I hate him. It should be me and you ruling, side by side," Blood said as he reached back and touched her hand. "Why can't we be together? I love you, woman. If last night didn't show anything, I don't know what else will."

King looked at him in disbelief. She knew Blood had been in love with her since she was a child, but his request was pure nonsense.

"Why, Blake Fernandez," she said and touched his fresh, clean face with her other hand. "Blood, I wish I could say the same thing, but I gave up on that four-letter word a long time ago. I'm never giving my heart to anyone else, ever again. The only people that have 25 percent of my heart are my mother and Madam Lourd. Santana, eh, the mistake. I'm sorry . . . but not sorry. You're just my right-hand man, and that's all, okay? Just be that."

Blood's heart had been stomped too many times by this woman. He had so many women ready to jump on his jock, but he gave his heart and soul to King Kia Costello. He couldn't understand the hold she had on him. At times, he believed a witch put a spell on him that he couldn't break. But even with King's hurtful words, he was even more determined to make her his. In his eyes, King played this hardhearted bitch ready for blood. But he remembered when she was a sweet, innocent little girl thirsty for life. Blood knew deep down in King, that little girl was still in there. But until he could figure out a plan, he would continue to play her right-hand man.

"Yes, King," he said.

King nodded. She looked out the window at her kingdom. People in the market were buying and selling goods. Kids played in the streets. She looked over at the beautiful ocean view and watched people swim. Her cell phone rang, so she pushed the talk button.

"Are you coming?" a mysterious voice said.

"Yes, I'm almost there."

"Hope I'm getting my money's worth."

"Oh, don't worry. It's going to be worth every penny."

They both laughed.

The limousine and two Rolls-Royces arrived at the mansion and parked. The guys got out of the limo and stretched their legs. Then Josie got out and looked around. The Don herself came out with her gunman, and King went over to kiss her child.

"My daughter," she said.

Within minutes, a white limousine pulled up and parked next to the black limousine. Swag looked at Tyler and Josie. They all wondered what was going on.

Midnight, Blood, and King stood there like everything was perfectly normal. The limousine driver, an average-sized Arabian man, exited and opened the back door.

Out came the Original Gangster of the Hernandez Cartel himself, Paco "PJ" Hernandez Sr. He defined sexy with a perfectly trimmed mustache and goatee. Dark shades covered his eyes, and he wore a brown Ermenegildo Zegna, solid wool, two-piece suit with matching loafers. He commanded attention, and the smell of money blew all around him. Getting out on the other side of the limo were two black bodybuilder dudes who would kill King and her gang with just one word from PJ. The last person to come out of the limo was PJ's attorney, Manny Louis.

Swag felt like he was in a scene from a good old gangsta movie. Both PJ and his posse walked close to King and company.

King smiled. "*Hola,* Sr. Hernandez."

PJ laughed. "King, darling, you don't know how you talking in Spanish turns me on."

King laughed and reached out to touch his face. PJ put his arms around her waist.

"Damn, you look beautiful, mami."

Blood frowned. He wanted to slap the dog shit out of this man for touching his lady.

PJ had both her ass cheeks in his big hands. "Damn, that soft phat ass."

King slightly pushed him back. "Damn, baby, you're getting me hot. But passion can wait. First, let's take care of business. Where's the money?"

PJ snapped his fingers. Manny presented a briefcase and held it up. PJ opened it. Inside were stacks and stacks of thousand-dollar bills. It was exactly $60 million in cold hard cash. That put a big Kool-Aid smile on King's face.

"All 60 mill that we agreed on. It's all there. You wanna count it?" PJ asked sarcastically.

King laughed. "No, that's okay."

Manny closed the briefcase, and King snapped her fingers. Blood rushed over and took the briefcase from Manny. PJ held a stern look on his face.

"So, is it done?"

"You tell me." King pulled out her cell phone and dialed. Someone quickly answered. King spoke in another language so that no one could understand. Then she hung up. Seconds later, the six girls from earlier came out of the mansion covered in blood from head to toe. Everyone except King and Blood was worried upon seeing them.

"What the hell is this?" PJ shouted.

King laughed. "You'll see. Come on."

King strutted to the door and looked at her girls. One girl from Nigeria was covered in mostly blood and flesh. King and the chick lip-locked in an erotic way.

The guys didn't know whether to get turned on or grossed out. Josie, on the other hand, couldn't believe what was happening. After the kiss, King winked at the lady and turned to everyone.

"Come now!" She opened the front door wide and stepped inside.

To PJ, what King had done better be worth the money. Once everyone was inside the mansion, they stood in total shock. Everything—from the ceiling, the walls, and the floors—was covered in blood.

This is beyond a massacre, PJ thought while looking at the ghastly display. He thought King and her bloody ladies were insanely mad. Never had he, in his entire life in the crime world, seen anything like this shit. All he could do was shake his head in disbelief while walking around the room.

King looked at him. "Well, was this your money's worth?"

Shit, this was more than my money's worth. Shit. PJ looked down at a body cut in half, looking as if it had been dissected like a guinea pig. "Shit, baby, yeah."

Everyone was horrified, especially Swag.

"This twisted—"

He halted his words when a feminine voice started screaming. Everyone looked back and saw it was Josie. She was scared to death after seeing not only blood and gore but also two heads cut off and three brains lying in blood puddles. It made her sick to her stomach. Josie ran over to the side of the room where there wasn't much blood and started to vomit. In her almost 18 years, she'd never seen anything this gruesome.

Swag rushed over to her and rubbed her back. "Baby girl, you okay?" He looked down and saw the green stuff Josie threw up. She stopped vomiting and started to breathe deeply.

"You okay, ma?"

Josie cleared her throat. "Not really, and I'm so embarrassed."

"Don't be embarrassed. It happens to the best of us." Swag saw beads of sweats on her forehead and gave her his handkerchief. "Here you go, ma."

Josie took it and wiped her forehead and the sides of her mouth. "Thank you."

"Anytime."

King didn't like what she saw and was fuming inside.

"Excuse me for one minute, PJ." She strutted over to where Josie and Swag stood. "What's going on here?"

King was trying to keep herself together. Josie looked at her with so much fear in her eyes.

"Mother, can I please leave and go back to the car? All this . . . is too much. I can't . . ."

Josie was scared shitless. King loved every minute of it and fed off her fears. She understood why she was scared, but for Josie to be the heir of her throne, she needed to have a backbone. King didn't want no gutless chick sitting on her throne. She pulled Josie toward her and slapped the shit out of both cheeks.

"Ouch!" Josie screamed and winced at King with gritted teeth.

She couldn't believe that King hit her the way she did. For the last few years that Josie lived with King, she had never laid a hand on her at all. The only kind of touch King ever gave her was a kiss or a hug.

King grabbed Josie's face and squeezed her cheeks. She spoke through gritted teeth. "Toughen up! *This* is the world we live in!" King motioned her hand to show her the display of the bloody area. "*You* are the heiress to my throne. Boss up! Grow up!" She released her cheeks and pointed her finger in Josie's face. "Shit, you'll be 18 in a few weeks. It's time to get out of that fairy princess, unicorns, and Prince Charming shit. Happily ever after and true love don't exist. Only power and respect rule the world!"

A tear rolled down Josie's face, but King wiped it off. "Toughen up, do you understand me? And don't mess up your makeup."

Josie didn't want to be hit anymore. She couldn't find the words, so all she did was nod. King grabbed her arm.

"Walk with me, my child." She pulled her toward their special guests. She planned to keep Josie as far away from Swag as she could. The last thing she wanted Josie to do was to catch feelings for him.

Swag was seething with anger and was on the verge of doing something that would've gotten him killed. His fist tightened. He couldn't believe how cold that bitch King was. As she walked away with Josie, Swag released a deep sigh. King and Josie walked toward PJ, passing more blood, cut up body parts, water, and glass.

Josie held her stomach as she smelled death in the air. PJ, on the other hand, ignored the disgusting display and was lost in Josie's beauty. He smiled and flashed his pearly whites at her. "King, who is this charming young lady?"

Josie had her head down, but King reached for her chin and lifted it. "Oh, this is my daughter, Josephine. Josephine, this is PJ, the head of the Hernandez Cartel. He's a client we're taking care of."

"Josephine . . . I love it." PJ held out his hand.

Josie looked at his hand for a moment. Since she didn't budge, King pinched her arm.

"Ouch!" Josie whined and looked over at King.

"Girl, don't be rude. Shake his hand."

Josie and PJ shook hands.

"Mmm, you have very soft hands," PJ complimented. "King, she's just as beautiful as you are."

King smiled. Josie saw lust in PJ's eyes, knowing he wanted more than just a handshake. He looked her up and down and laughed a little as he got back to business.

"So, this little tour of a bloody massacre is nice. But where's Paco?"

King put a wicked smile on her face. "I thought you'd never ask." She looked back at the tall, bloody female and spoke in her native tongue.

The bloody woman came over their way. Once there, King asked in her language, "Where's Paco?"

The bloody woman motioned for everyone to follow her. The only thing everyone could wonder was what terror lay up ahead.

***

Upstairs in Paco's room, the door was closed. PJ wanted to open the door, but King slapped his hand.

"Don't kill the suspense, PJ. You stay out here until I call for you."

PJ looked confused, not knowing if he could take any more of the *Nightmare on Elm Street* shit King had pulled.

"Okay, I'll wait."

"Blood, Solomon, and Josephine, come with me."

Blood opened the door as King, Swag, Josephine, and he walked in, closing the door behind them.

In the room, there was only blood—no gore like it was downstairs. Just a few ripped sheets, pillows, and broken glass. King looked up. Paco was tied up bondage-style on the bed with a bucket on his head. He wasn't aware of his surroundings. The only thing Paco was wearing was a pair of boxer briefs. His entire body was cut up, beaten up, and bloody all over.

"Damn," Blood said.

"Yeah, my chicas really know how to slay a guy," King said, standing there proudly.

"You can say that again," Swag said softly.

King looked at him. "What was that, my little lovebug?"

Swag was caught off guard. "Huh? Nothing."

King raised her brow and ignored his little comment. She looked back at Paco's bucket-head body.

"Josephine, take the bucket off."

Josie was scared. "I can't."

King snapped at her. "I said, take the damn bucket off or meet these hands again. First lesson . . . never show any fear. Now, go!"

Josie didn't want to be slapped again, so she walked up to Paco's tied up body. She looked back at everyone.

"What are you waiting for? Go on!" King shouted.

Josie took a deep breath before she removed the bucket from his head.

Paco's face was beaten and bruised badly. His lips and teeth were busted, and his handsome features were gone. He lifted his head and hollered. Josie screamed and ran to the other side of the room. King and Blood just laughed. Swag just shook his head.

One of Paco's eyes was closed shut. He looked at King with the good eye.

"You bitch!" He tried to get loose, but it was no use. He breathed heavily. "How could you double-cross me? We were supposed to be business partners. How could you?" He lowered his head and thought about the crazy shit King's girls did to his remaining crew. But the girls had spared him. He had no idea why. In Paco's twisted mind, maybe King still wanted him for herself.

"Oh, really?" King moved closer to him. She used her long, pointed index nail to cut into his face.

"Aah . . . shit!" Paco jerked his face to the side before looking back at King. He gave her an evil glare. "What did I do to deserve this shit?"

King laughed. "Oh, you don't know?" She went into her purse and pulled out her tablet. She showed Paco the conversation he was having with his late boy, Landon. Paco's jaw dropped, revealing the empty spaces in his mouth where his missing teeth had once been. He looked at the scene, knowing he was cold busted.

King turned the tablet off. She smiled at him, knowing he was frightened. "What's the matter, Paco? Cat got your tongue?"

Paco was speechless, and King laughed sinisterly. "If you like that, you're going to love *this*." She looked at the door. "Come in."

The door opened, and Midnight, Tyler, the two mus-
cled men, Manny, and the real McCoy, PJ, came in the
bedroom.

Paco's good eye widened. "Dad!"

PJ smiled while looking at his bruised son. "Hello, you
little shit!"

Paco looked at King. "What in the hell is *he* doing here?"
He looked at PJ. "Dad! Help me. Please!" Paco knew he
sounded like a punk after wanting to kill his father. But at
this moment, he didn't have any other option. Also, Paco
hoped that PJ would open up his heart to see that his
little boy needed his daddy.

"Oh, *now*, you need my help—but before, you wanted
to assassinate me and tried to take over my organization,
sí?"

Paco was shocked that his father knew everything. He
looked at King. "You snitchin'-ass bitch!"

Everyone laughed.

"No, no, no, she didn't do a damn thing!" PJ shouted.
He walked up to his son and grabbed Paco's bloody neck.
"For one, I've been on you for a while now."

Paco was shocked and could barely speak. "How?"

Midnight stepped forward. "Look, man, you were supposed to be heir to the throne, but my loyalty is with PJ."

Paco was in so much disbelief. His heart was racing.
"Midnight! You . . . You were my friend. Why, man, why?"

"Look at you. You were losing control, and we had to
stop you."

"Yeah, I paid King and Midnight to talk you into part-
nering with King's organization. I knew you would take
credit for it," PJ said with a smirk.

"Damn, you got played badly. You fake-ass Gotti," Swag
said.

Paco looked at Swag out of the corner of his good eye.
"Fuck you, nigger!"

"What!" Swag tried to charge at Paco, but PJ's body-guards kept him back.

King added her two cents. "I know you want to hurt him, Solomon, but you already had your taste of him."

"You got that right!" Tyler yelled at Paco. "Where my brother at? Where's my brother?"

King strutted over to Tyler and opened the tablet so she could show him the video.

Tyler slapped his hand over his mouth. His whole body quivered as he watched. He couldn't believe Travis was dead. The most disrespectable thing he saw was when Paco and his crew set his brother's corpse on fire. His blood boiled. As tears streamed down his face, he started to hyperventilate. He couldn't believe the dream he had the night before was a reality. All Tyler saw now was red.

King smirked and loved every bit of his reaction. After this, she knew he'd be the perfect assassin. She reached into her purse and pulled out her switchblade.

"Here you are. Enjoy." King stepped back. "Come on, everyone, let's leave them alone. Playtime."

Tyler gripped the switchblade tightly while looking at Paco with twitching eyes. PJ looked at his son and shook his head.

"The day of your final destination has arrived. Good luck, son."

They all walked out, including Josie, who raced out of the room first.

"Daaaad!" Paco cried out. "Are you going to let him do this to meeee?"

PJ didn't respond. Swag looked back at Tyler, knowing what he was going to do to Paco. He also knew that Tyler needed his friend. Even though he hadn't seen the video, it pained him that Travis was dead. Swag rested his hand on Tyler's shoulder.

"Tyler, man, it's—"

Tyler shook Swag's hand off his shoulder. "Beat it."

He spoke so softly Swag barely could hear him. "What?"

"Get the fuck out!" Tyler yelled while looking at Paco.

Swag stepped back. He knew his friend's mind was gone. He saw the same thing in Stan back in the Brazil prison. Tyler's eyes were on Paco. He was so focused.

"Oh, the little baby got a knife," Paco taunted him. Shit, he didn't have a choice. If he was gonna go out, he was going out with a bang. "Put that knife away. You ain't gonna do shit. You a bitch like Travis was."

That did it. Rage consumed Tyler. He rushed up to Paco and stabbed him multiple times in his face. He stabbed his good eyeball, and his mouth so he would never speak his brother's name again. He even stabbed Paco in his throat.

Paco screamed in horror. It was music to Tyler's ears.

"Die, you dirty motherfucker!" he yelled and kept stabbing Paco. Within minutes, Paco was no longer a part of the world of the living. Tyler's clothes were covered in blood as he looked at the deformed and deceased Paco. He'd never killed anyone in his life, but Paco's killing of his brother took him to a whole new level.

"For you, Travis. I'm sorry I wasn't here to help you."

Swag couldn't believe what he had witnessed, but he understood why it was necessary. He slowly walked up to Tyler and pulled his arm.

"Let's go, man. It's over."

Tyler yanked his arm away from Swag. His eyes were still on the corpse of Paco Hernandez. He looked down at the bloody switchblade. He then stabbed it in Paco's black heart. Afterward, he walked out.

Swag tried to talk to him, but Tyler moved quickly. Swag looked at his surroundings and saw that everything was falling apart. *What have I done?* was all he could think.

***

Outside, King and PJ shook hands, along with Midnight and Manny.

"It was a pleasure, King," PJ said.

"Pleasure was all mine," King replied.

PJ laughed and looked over at Josie, who was standing by her Rolls-Royce.

"Uh, King, how much you want for that one?" He pointed at Josie.

Josie was stunned at being treated like cattle. King glanced at her, then back at PJ. "She's not for sale."

PJ laughed. "Okay, maybe next time." He looked at Midnight. "Come on, Midnight, let's go back to Houston. I'll take care of everything, and you should be fine."

Midnight nodded. He was so happy that he was going back home to see his family and leaving all this shit behind him. They all went to their respective limousines and took off.

Once gone, Tyler came out of the mansion, looking like a madman. King smiled, admiring her up-and-coming creation.

Chapter 21

Turning Tables

Back at the Palace, things were tense among everyone, but mainly with Tyler and Swag. Tyler was still in shock and rage. He took the place of Josie in the Rolls-Royce, which King thought was best. The last thing she wanted him to do was harm Josie or Swag.

Nobody knew what was going to happen. During the limousine ride, Swag, Josie, and Blood were in the limo together. Swag looked over at Josie, knowing she was still shaken up and scared from the events that happened today. He was just glad she wasn't in the room when Tyler stabbed and sliced Paco. If she had seen that episode, Swag knew she would've lost her mind. He could tell Josie wasn't built for this lifestyle. He wanted to ask if she was okay, but Blood was eye-balling him hard.

Swag felt King was using Blood as a babysitter, or Swag would've consoled and told her that everything would be okay.

Blood flashed his gun at him, wanting to show him that he was still running the show. Swag was sick of him playing that game, so he rubbed his forehead and gave Blood the middle finger.

King, on the other hand, was having a great day. In her mind, her kingdom was safe from fakeness and haters. She smiled at her accomplishments. Her next goals were to bring her father down, train Josie to rule beside her one day, and get to know Swag more. She figured in time, he wasn't going to have anyone to run to but her, since his and Tyler's friendship was coming to an end. She loved the thought of having him all to herself.

Tyler got out of the car, looking like a zombie. He walked toward the Palace doors, displaying so much hate in his eyes.

Cleo knew not to mess with him. He opened the door to let him inside.

Swag quickly got out of the limousine and rushed up the steps to catch up with him.

Once inside the Palace, Tyler walked by the grand room filled with girls and guys with some of their high-profile clientele. Everyone looked at him like he was a madman as he headed to the elevator. Swag followed behind him.

"Tyler! Tyler! Ty, man, wait!"

Tyler ignored him. He wanted to be alone so he could digest his thoughts.

When Swag caught up with him, he looked at Tyler from the side.

They waited for the elevator doors to open. Then Swag took a deep breath.

"Tyler, everything will work out. Trust me on this," he said.

Swag put his hand on Tyler's shoulder, but Tyler yanked it off.

Tyler looked at him with a cold, evil glare in his eyes. "Don't you *ever* touch me again, nigga."

Swag didn't know who Tyler was anymore. To Swag, this wasn't the Tyler he knew. All he saw was emptiness and darkness as they got on the elevator.

Swag figured he was taking a risk by getting on the same elevator with his friend, but he was trying to get through to him. Once the doors closed, things got heated between the two.

"Tyler, man, talk to me. Come on, man." He touched Tyler's shoulder again.

Tyler, however, was thirsty for blood. He pushed Swag back, causing him to fall on the floor. "Get off me, nigga. Didn't you hear what I said?"

Swag sat there with his mouth hanging open. He knew Tyler was pissed, but he didn't like Tyler putting his hands on him.

"Just leave me the fuck alone!" Tyler said, before getting off the elevator.

Swag got up and followed him.

"Ty, man, this ain't you, man. Let's talk about this and try to figure out our next move. Don't you want to get away from here?"

Tyler stopped in his path, trying to hold back his tears. He was filled with so much rage and hate. Swag didn't understand what he was going through, so Tyler swung around and shot him a cold look.

"Are you *serious* right now? I said, leave me alone. Stop asking me questions, and just go!"

Swag refused to leave his friend like this. "Look, man, I know how you feel. Travis was like a brother to me too. Words can't describe how sorry I am right now, but I know Travis is in a better place. *Anywhere* is better than the shit we're in now."

"Stan was right," Tyler mumbled.

Swag didn't hear what he had said. "What was that, bruh?"

"Stan was right!" he yelled. "It's all *your* fault we're in this shit. We lost Stan, we don't know where the fuck Brad is, and my twin got killed by a petty fool you automatically trusted and got us into some even deeper shit. I *hate* you, man!"

Those words, "I hate you," cut Swag's heart in two. He knew this wasn't Tyler at all, but he understood why he felt that way.

"Man, I know you're upset with me, but you don't know what you're sayin'. That's your pain talkin', and I'm hurtin' too. We gotta be strong. We brothers who just lost a brother—"

"*I* just lost a brother—You and me ain't shit." Tyler got into Swag's face and pointed his finger at him.

Usually, Swag would've punched a dude in his face for stepping to him or pointing a finger in his face. But he gave Tyler a pass and remained calm.

"Stay the hell away from me, or I'll kill you like I did Paco," Tyler threatened and walked away.

Swag rushed up again and touched his shoulder. "Ty, man—"

Before Swag could get another word in, Tyler punched him on the side of his face. The hard blow caused him to fall ass first on the ground.

"You are dead to me," Tyler said. "*Dead!*"

He opened the door to his bedroom, went inside, and slammed it.

Swag lay on the floor, thinking about how life was so fucked up. He felt like a big loser and thought about the words Tyler had said, *"It's your fault."*

Swag realized that he had so much blood on his hands. He should've been back in St. Louis kicking it with his fellas, playing with his sons, trying to work things out with Zaria, or moving on to the next best thing. He was determined to fix this, and he prayed for God to give him strength. Tears flowed down his face, even though he viewed tears as a sign of weakness. He was broken. There was no one else to turn to.

While in her suite, King watched the whole showdown with Swag and Tyler. She laughed, especially when Tyler punched the hell out of Swag. She looked at Swag, who looked like he was a sad little puppy that had been abandoned by his owner. She laughed again that her plan to break up Swag and Tyler's friendship had succeeded.

Now that their sorry-ass friendship is dead, Swag will have no one to turn to but me. "Here comes mama," she giggled.

Chapter 22

Would You Mind?

Tyler took a long hot shower to cool himself down. He started to wash off all the blood and essences of Paco Hernandez. He broke down crying, thinking about Travis. So many flashbacks of his brother played in his head. He thought of times when they were little kids, their good and bad times. He even thought of the last few weeks of how his life had turned around. Ending his friendship with Swag felt good. Swag was toxic to him, as far as he was concerned. He was the venom that broke the fellas' bond forever. Tyler regretted not having his brother's back and for not defending him when King cut off his finger. He abandoned him when King kicked him out. He thought that he should've been with his brother. As the water ran down him, he felt if he were with his brother, they could've fought Paco and his crew together. Or they could've died trying to fight for their lives.

An hour later, Tyler got out of the shower and dried himself with a towel. He exited the bathroom, went to the bedroom, put on some clothes, and chilled on the sofa. While in a daze, he stared at the ceiling, feeling dead on the inside. Tyler wanted to cry again, but couldn't. He needed something to stop all the crying and hurt. He leaned back and massaged his aching head. *Damn, Travis! Damn!* A tear rushed down his face, but he swiped it away.

Feeling hungry, he wanted to go to the dining room to get something to eat, but he didn't want to be bothered with anyone. Minutes later, someone knocked on his door.

Tyler hoped that it wasn't Swag, still trying to talk to him. He was done with him, and he meant what he'd said.

"Who is it?"

"Room service! It's Chef!" a man with a deep voice said.

Tyler took a deep breath and opened the door. The last person he wanted to see was Santana Costello, who came in with a food cart that had three different plates on it.

"Hey, friend," Santana said with a broad smile on his face.

Tyler didn't say a word. He just wanted Santana to drop off the food and get out. But then, he took notice of what Santana was wearing. He had on a melon-colored shirt, white pants, and Jordan sneakers. Tyler thought for a gay dude, Santana could dress. He started to feel hot in the room, even though the air was on.

Santana swung around after he set the plates on the coffee table. Tyler looked at him as he took his time bending over with his butt in Tyler's face. Looking at Santana's ass made Tyler's manhood a little stiff. He didn't know why he was having these feelings for another man. In his opinion, all gays had AIDS, which his family believed was God's punishment on them.

Santana looked at him and stood up straight.

"Is there anything else I can get you, sir?" He lowered his eyes to the stiffness in Tyler's boxers.

Tyler bit into his bottom lip. "If you don't mind, could you take the lids off the plates?"

Santana laughed. He knew Tyler wanted to look at his ass again. "Sure." He bent over and took the lid off the first plate, which had slices of a turkey breast, dressing, green beans, and a dinner roll. The second plate was a seven-layer salad. But Santana hesitated to remove the lid off the third plate.

Tyler looked at him with suspicion. "What's on the third plate?"

"That's dessert. A specialty by me."

"Dessert? What kind of dessert? Cake or pie?"

Santana stared at him with seriousness in his eyes. "Nah, it's just a little something to mellow you out. I heard what happened to your twin brother. I'm sorry about that, man."

Tyler lowered his head down for a moment. He sighed before lifting his head. "It's cool. Now take that lid off the plate. I'm the type of dude who eats dessert first away."

Santana removed the lid. The plate was full of pure white cocaine with a razor blade and a rolled-up hundred-dollar bill. Santana knew that King hated drugs in her palace, especially after what they did to their mother. But under the circumstances, he didn't give two shits. Plus, the cocaine he was serving Tyler was the real deal and not the cheap street shit that nickel-and-dime boys passed out. It was pure Colombian cocaine. Santana picked up the first two plates and placed them back on the cart.

Tyler looked at Santana. "Dessert, huh?"

Santana nodded. "Dessert, and it'll make you feel better."

Tyler needed something right now to get his mind off things. He needed to let go. Plus, he hadn't had good cocaine since he'd graduated from high school. He picked up the razor blade and put some of the cocaine in three lines. Then he picked up the rolled bill and used it to snort the cocaine in his right nostril. He then closed his eyes and let the coke take effect.

Santana studied his every move and was surprised when Tyler asked him to sit down.

"Excuse me?" he said, touching his chest.

Tyler laughed. "You heard me. Come sit next to me."

Santana flopped down on the sofa next to Tyler. He didn't know what was going on in Tyler's head, but he loved the mood and didn't want it to stop.

Tyler pushed the plate over to him. "Want some?"

Santana hadn't had his fix all day, and even though he only snorted cocaine two days out of the week, he was stressed out dealing with King. He indulged with his eyes closed. Tyler didn't know if the cocaine was talking or if his true self was coming out, but he thought Santana looked beautiful. At this moment, he didn't give a shit anymore.

He gazed at Santana's half-opened shirt and saw part of a tattoo.

Santana opened his eyes and cocked his head back. "What are you looking at?"

"What's that a tattoo of?"

"Would you like to see it?"

"Yeah."

Santana unbuttoned his shirt and showed off his ripped chest with six-pack abs. Tyler admired the tattoo of a sword in the middle of his chest.

"Damn, that's cool. Who did that for you?" Tyler really didn't care about the tattoo. He was just trying to get to know Santana a little more.

Santana played right along. "I got it done last year in San Francisco, California. Some dude did it during Pride week. I decided to go on a vacation to Cali with this dude I was with at the time. He took me to a tattoo shop there. It took the tattoo artist all day to get it together. For the rest of the trip, it hurt like hell. Shit, for a while, it was almost too painful to touch, but it's better now."

"Nice," Tyler said, then reached over to touch Santana's chest.

His skin felt so smooth, and he touched his nipple, up to his shoulder, and then his washboard abs.

Santana looked at Tyler's hand on his stomach. "What are you doing?"

Tyler looked into Santana's eyes. "Don't you see that I'm trying to seduce you? Besides dealing with the shit I've been through today, I also thought about you. I jacked off in the shower earlier, thinking about you."

Santana was shocked, but then again, he wasn't. "Oh really?" he said, grinning and moving closer to Tyler.

"Yeah."

Tyler touched Santana's face and put his thumb on his top lip. Santana sucked on it while looking at the lining of his penis in his boxers.

Tyler enjoyed the erotic display Santana was giving with his thumb. He didn't even pay attention to Santana opening his boxers and reaching for his penis.

"Mmmm," Tyler moaned and closed his eyes.

The one thing that Santana loved about South American cocaine was it made you freaky as well as high. He rubbed up and down on Tyler's shaft, loving his reaction.

Tyler opened his eyes and tried to process another man touching his dick. At that moment, he didn't care. All he wanted was to be held by someone who could make him feel good. He went along with Santana choking his chicken.

"Please, please, stop. No!" Tyler said.

Santana continued to jerk Tyler's manhood even faster.

"Yes!" Tyler could no longer contain himself. "Oh, Santana, kiss me. Please, kiss me . . ."

Santana stopped rubbing Tyler's penis. He took his hands and pulled Tyler toward him. They shared a kiss with so much passion and fire as Santana laid Tyler on his back.

Tyler was ready to take on a new ride of total bliss and ecstasy.

Chapter 23

Playing the Game

Swag was in his suite, drinking down a whole bottle of Hennessy. He was as drunk as a skunk but could hold his own. He was doing his best to drown his hurt and anguish with the alcohol, especially after his boy, his former friend, ended their long friendship and punched him. Thinking about the punch, if they were back in St. Louis, Swag would've kicked Tyler's ass. But he let it pass since Travis was killed in the worst possible manner. Even though he and Tyler were no longer cool, it was like a bullet in Swag's heart. They all grew up together from partying, smoking blunts, fighting . . . anything you could think of.

Swag sucked in a deep breath, knowing that everything around him was falling apart. He reminisced back to the time when all the fellas were in Brazil and locked in the elevators for days. He remembered the words Stan shared.

"Cool out? Man, don't say shit to us because this is all yo' fault we in this bullshit! I've been trying to keep my mouth shut, but now that we're alone, I could just fuck you up for getting us in this mess!" Stan yelled.

There was no question that Stan's blood was boiling.

Swag stepped forward, moving face-to-face with Stan. "Listen up, motherfucker! I didn't put a gun to your head and make you come to Brazil. So don't put this shit on me. All you saw, bruh, was dollar signs."

Stan cut his eyes before walking a few inches away from him. "Fuck you, man. I hate yo' ass. You ruined my life."

He took another sip of his drink, remembering the words of Tyler from earlier. *"This is all your fault."*

Swag started to repeat those words. "It's . . . all my fault. It's my fault!"

He broke down crying, now knowing the world he knew was really gone. He felt that he'd fucked up all the good in his life, from the loss of his nana to abandoning his siblings and sons. But the biggie was having his boys and his only real family coming out to Brazil to help him. The one thing he remembered was an up-and-coming kingpin back in St. Louis told him to "Never get your family involved with this life ever." Shit, he already sold out his boy, Stan, for falling for Paco's bullshit. Then Brad, the real glue that kept the fellas together. Swag also thought of how he let Paco blindside him. He believed in Paco's hype of freedom and getting money. But Swag's real goal was escaping so that he could be with his sons again.

He realized at this moment that the greatest treasure all this time was his sons. Now understanding that all he cared about was money—getting money and women—he realized that he wasted all the time he should've been spending with his children. Now, he was an international fugitive on the run from the law.

He took another sip, thinking of his sons and what he was now missing out on. His son, Namond, would be 1 in a few weeks, and he wasn't there for him. There was a possibility he was going to miss out on showing them how to be men, how to drive a car, see them graduate, and so much more. The main biggie that got him hurting about his sons was they would be fatherless, just like he was. He couldn't have that for his sons. He needed to get himself out of this bad situation by any means necessary. He was determined to see his sons again.

He lowered his head, getting his sons out of his system for the time being and refocused on the events that happened that day. His mind went straight to Tyler putting his hands on him. Swag knew he put his boys in a messed up situation, but no one put their hands on him. He started to get pissed at Tyler.

Fuck Tyler. Who needs him anyway? I stand alone, Swag thought.

He took the last sip out of the bottle. Tyler was dead to him too. If anyone was going to save Swag, it was Swag. The only way he could do that was the only option he had at this time.

Operation: Get Close To King Kia Costello. She was the key to getting him out of a fucked-up situation.

King, you want me? You got me . . .

Chapter 24

The King's Swag

King couldn't sleep that night. She was on a high from earlier that day. She'd destroyed Paco, who had threatened her throne and his father's also. She had a clear mind and believed that both their operations were safe for now. The biggest kick out of King's day was watching the footage of Tyler killing that clown, Paco, stabbing him with her switchblade over and over again. After Paco was murdered, Tyler stabbed that asshole in his heart to make sure he was dead. To King, that was a total savage move. She loved the new monster she created and couldn't wait to train Tyler to be the next of her assassins. She must have looked at the video five times, laughing every time she watched it.

Since King couldn't sleep from all the excitement, she decided to go into her living room with a glass of red wine and papers she placed on the coffee table. She should've been planning her next attack, which was her father, who denied her for so many years. Instead, she was planning a surprise birthday party for Josie's big eighteenth. She was determined to toughen up Josie. One thing King hated was a prissy and scared-ass female. The way Josie acted with PJ was pathetic in King's eyes. She knew that she had to keep her away from Swag for a while. In King's mind, she already saw Swag and Josie had a connection.

Thinking about them made her wet between the legs. It had been a while since she had this feeling of them taking her places that no one ever had. She shook her head, forgetting all about Josie's birthday and felt more wetness between her legs. As she was about to slip two fingers inside her panties, someone knocked on the door. She was pissed off that she couldn't get her shit off, and she hoped it wasn't Blood thinking he was going to get some of her sweet honey. The banging on the door got harder, so she tightened her robe and headed over there.

"Hold on, dammit!" She opened the door.

The person standing at the door was a huge shock to her, but she was delighted. Seeing Swag put a smile on her face.

"Well, hello, Solomon. To what do I owe this pleasure?"

Swag was still drunk, but very much in control. He stood there in his wife beater, black slacks, and was barefoot.

"King, can I talk to you for a sec?"

"Sure, come on in."

Swag walked in. It was the first time he had ever been in her suite. It wasn't what he imagined. He assumed it would be styled like a butcher shop and torture chamber. He was dead wrong. They walked over to the sofa and sat down.

King crossed her legs and waited for him to say something. There was a long silence before she finally spoke up. "What's going on, sweetheart?"

Swag knew he had to be on his A-game if he were going to win King over.

"King, today was a real eye-opener for what you and the Leopard Clit do. I felt like I was in a Mafia movie or something." Swag took a deep breath. "But Tyler losing his brother the way he did, that was crazy. The real reason I'm here is that Tyler is blaming me for his brother's death, and I feel horrible about it."

King wasn't paying any attention to what Swag was saying. She was just glad that her crush finally got the balls to come in her suite. She finally felt complete with him in her presence. She then noticed his still-wrapped-up hand and his bruised cheek. She was tired of hearing his sad love story. It was time to change the subject.

"Oh Lord, what happened to your face, baby?" King rubbed his face.

Swag brushed it off. "It's nothing. Don't worry about it."

Even though his and Tyler's friendship was over, he still cared about his brother. He didn't want King to harm him before he could get himself, and hopefully, Tyler, out of her world. King continued to play that dumb blonde role. But at the same time, she didn't want anyone to damage her new toy.

"I'm so alone right now," Swag said. "My boy kicked me to the curb. I just don't know who to turn to." Tears ran down Swag's face.

King looked with no emotion on her face. She hated weak men and women in any situation. In her world, if you showed only one sign of weakness, she kicked you to the curb. But King gave Swag another pass. There was something about him that made her warm. She put her hand on his shoulder.

"It's okay. Just forget him. In this life, you have no friends. The more power you have, the better. You don't have any family either."

"True," Swag agreed and thought about his bitch of a mother.

King loved this moment. She was getting to know Swag little by little on a mental basis. "Listen, sweetie. Your King is here, and if you need anyone to talk to, come to me."

Swag nodded as he wiped his tears. "Thanks, King. I truly appreciate that."

"Anytime."

Swag kissed her on her cheek. Her skin was as soft as a baby's bottom.

King smirked at him. She admired him being a gentleman and not being forceful with their first semi-intimate moment together. She also loved her men to be a little forceful and who could take control. She had to remember, though, that she was the ruler.

"Loosen up," she said, pulling Swag closer to her and sticking her tongue in his mouth. They indulged in a heated kiss that gave Swag a woody. King loved this and liked the fact he was a good kisser. She halted the kiss and searched his eyes.

"Oh, baby, stop. You're getting me hot." She knew exactly what she was doing. Any other time, she would've given him something he could feel. But for now, she was just offering him a snack—not the whole kitchen. Swag couldn't believe he was being blown off. Her actions left him with blue balls.

"It's late, so I think you'd better go," she said.

"King, I don't wanna be alone tonight. Can I stay with you?"

King laughed. "You can sleep on the sofa for the night."

She went to her drawer and pulled out some Vaseline and tossed it to him.

"What's this for."

King giggled like a horny schoolgirl. "For your 'friend' down there. Shit, I ain't Beyoncé, and I ain't into that 'Drunk in Love' shit. So jack off and get off. Oh, sheets are in the closet." She pointed to her closet. "Good night." King left him and went into her bedroom.

Once Swag heard the door close, he propped himself on the sofa with a big grin on his face. *So far, so good.*

Chapter 25

Another Right-Hand Man

The next morning, Tyler was in bed, sleeping peacefully. The rays from the sunlight woke him up. He twisted his face while rubbing and covering his eyes. *Why is it so damn bright up in here?* he thought. He stumbled and slowly got out of bed, but he felt a flood of pain in his head, body, and anus.

"Ooh." He put his hand on his butt as he took a deep breath. "What the hell is wrong?"

He stumbled over to the window, and with each step he took, his ass hurt like hell. He needed to close the blinds. It was way too early for all the sunlight. Once over at the window, he took a few more deep breaths. He quickly closed the blinds, but the pain in his head and anus were unbearable. He needed to get back in bed, but before he did, he looked down at himself, realizing that he was in his birthday suit. He also noticed white stains on his chest and stomach. He touched the stains, realizing the white substance was dried up come.

"What? No, God. I didn't! I didn't! Did I?" His head started to pound even harder from just thinking. "Ooh, ouch." He took more deep breaths. "Ouch."

He sat on the bed, then jumped up again. "Shit, what's wrong with my ass?"

He rubbed his temples because he felt light-headed. He began to have flashbacks of him and his wild sexcapade with Santana from the night before. They did it everywhere . . . from the sofa, the bed, the coffee table, and even the shower—in all different positions.

"No, no, I'm not gay. I'm *not* gay!"

Tyler believed the whole situation was a bad dream. He panicked, but could still hear Santana's words in his mind. *"Yeah, it's all mine. Come to daddy."*

Tyler remembered feeling pain but yet pleasure at the same time from Santana. *No, no, this can't be. I'm straight. I didn't do this.*

He hurried to remove the messy sheets, but as he was in the process, Santana opened the bedroom door. Tyler looked at him with wide eyes.

"Oh, you're awake." Santana walked in with two coffee mugs in his hands. "I brought you some coffee." He put the mugs on the nightstand.

"I don't want your damn coffee, Santana!"

Santana picked up one mug and sipped from it.

"What happened to me?" Tyler asked.

Santana laughed and put the mug down. "Nothing more than what you asked for, from the back, flip-flop, sideways, and even upside down. Shit, you a total freak."

Tyler pointed his finger at Santana. "No, you did something to me so you could have your evil way with me."

Santana nodded. "Ty, I didn't make you snort that good-ass cocaine. You did that on your own—like a pro, might I add." He smiled devilishly while grabbing his dick. "Shit, you took more than cocaine like a pro." Santana exposed his penis and put it back in his pajama pants. "If you know what I mean. You sucked the shit outta this."

Tyler got up, still with a sore ass that was hurting and burning like hell. He pushed Santana. "Stay the fuck away from me, you faggot!"

Santana caught his balance and continued to laugh. "Really? I wasn't a faggot last night. I was a baby, boo, and big daddy when you damn near pleaded for me to put this dick inside your virgin ass."

This was pissing Tyler off because, in his mind, he wasn't gay. All Santana was to him was an experiment. Also, a stress reliever from losing his twin yesterday. After last night, he wanted nothing more from Santana. Tyler was still trying to keep his macho, straight man attitude on.

"You took advantage of me at my most vulnerable point. You took my kindness for weakness. You are evil and going to hell. You disgust me! All you gays disgust me! You *all* will burn in hell on Judgment Day."

Santana wanted to say so much shit back to Tyler's homophobic comments, but he held back. He knew that Tyler was still mourning the death of Travis and still holding in a lot of pain. He slowly walked over to him.

"Look, Ty, we can talk about this. I just have this weird feeling that we belong together."

He put his hand on Tyler's shoulder. Without warning, Tyler punched him on the side of his face. He fell on the floor in disbelief.

"Stay the fuck away from me!" Tyler rushed over to the bathroom but turned to look at Santana before going inside. "I'm going to take a long, hot shower to wash off the curse you put on me. When I come out, you'd better be gone."

Tyler went into the bathroom and locked the door just in case Santana got any ideas.

Santana got off the floor and looked at his face in the mirror. It was a little red, but it wasn't anything that he couldn't cover up with makeup. He laughed at the whole ordeal and was happy that his master plan was working. He could tell Tyler was feeling him and would soon be eating out of the palm of his hand. He chilled in the chair and waited on his new man to get clean.

In King's suite, Swag slept like a baby so peacefully after finishing off a full bottle of Henny. King went into her living room with a head wrap on that covered her braids. A white towel covered her naked body after a relaxing morning bath. The smell of jasmine followed where Swag was sleeping on the sofa. She looked down at him, sleeping, and smiled.

"Come on, wake up. No soldier of mine sleeps all day." She shook his shoulder.

Swag twisted his face with his eyes still shut closed. His head was pounding. He had a hangover from the Henny. He finally opened his eyes, which were bloodshot red. Tears started to come down his face.

"Damn." Swag massaged his temples.

"Come on, sit up and drink this," King said, holding a glass in her hand.

Swag wiped his face and didn't want to be bothered. All he wanted to do was sleep all day and maybe get drunk again. He needed some kind of escape from this hellhole and was shocked when King slapped him on the side of his head.

"Come on, Solomon! Rise and shine! I won't repeat it!"

Swag didn't want to upset her. At the moment, he was trying to win her over. He couldn't afford to fuck up the plan now. He slowly removed the covers and sat up.

"Drink this. It'll make you feel better." King pushed the glass of Bloody Mary to him again.

Swag grabbed it, not knowing if the beverage was a real Bloody Mary or real blood mixed with guts.

King smirked. "Down the hatch."

Swag sniffed it. "Eww, it stinks."

King rubbed his shoulder roughly. "Drink."

He stirred the drink with the celery stick, then took a tiny sip.

"Eww." He hated the taste of tomatoes mixed with liquor, but he needed something to break his hangover. He tossed back the drink and gave the glass back to King.

"Good boy. Now, let's go to the balcony."

Swag followed her to the balcony where they overlooked the city of San José, aka King's kingdom. There was a table all set up and ready for them to eat.

"Come sit down and have some breakfast with me," King said, letting go of Swag's hand. Although Swag was tired and sluggish, he had to admit it was a beautiful day. He sat at the table filled with fruit, eggs, bacon, toast, red potatoes, muffins, turkey sausage, freshly brewed coffee, and orange juice.

"Just giving you a little breakfast," King said, smiling. "What do you Americans call it?" King thought for a moment as she reached for a sausage link. She licked and sucked on it before taking a bite. "Oh, yeah. Continental breakfast."

Swag stared at her, admiring her natural beauty. King could tell he was intrigued by her.

"What?" she said.

"Nothing."

"Then stop staring and sitting there with your rumbling tummy."

Swag started to eat and drink orange juice. He glanced at the papers King had on her desk. "So what's that? Your light bill?" He laughed, trying to soften up the mood.

King looked at him with a straight face. "Ha! Ha! Ha!"

Swag knew she was being sarcastic, and he liked it.

"I'm planning a surprise birthday party for Josephine."

Swag lit up when he heard Josie's name. "What! I didn't know Jos . . . Josephine had a birthday coming up soon. How old will she be? What's the theme of the party?"

King's brow went up. "You ask a lot of questions about a girl you barely know. But anyway, she'll be 18. As for the theme, that's the surprise. But the colors will be black, white, and pink."

Swag cleared his throat. "Cool, my oldest son has a birthday coming up soon. He'll be 6 years old."

Just thinking about his son or sons, in general, brought a smile to his face. He hated that he was half a world away from them. Part of it was his fault, and he also had to remember that he was on the run.

King was shocked by his confession and wanted to know more. "A son? You have a child?"

Swag nodded. "Yes, King. I have two sons, actually. I wish I had my phone so I could show you pics of them. I can't log on to my Facebook account without the Feds finding out my location. Dammit!"

King could tell Swag truly cared about his sons. "What are their names?"

"My oldest boy's name is Solomon Jr., aka Li'l Swag. And my baby boy, Namond, is almost 1."

Swag showed King his right upper arm, where there was a tattoo of Li'l Swag when he was first born. He then showed her his left upper arm of Namond at his current age.

"They're adorable, Solomon."

"Thanks, ma."

The last thing King wanted to do was compete with babies or their mother. "So, are you still with their mother?"

That comment caught Swag all the way off guard. "What?"

King pinched his hand. "As I told you before in the limousine, I don't like to repeat myself. I've been letting you slide a few times, but if you want to be on my right-

hand side, I suggest you get with the program. Got it?"
She pinched him again.

"Damn, that hurts, but, yes," Swag said, rubbing his
hand. He hated being pinched. It reminded him of those
days when his nana would pinch him, and that hurt like
hell when he acted up.

"Now, the question is, are you still with your baby
mama?" King folded her arms.

Swag didn't want to discuss Zaria. He felt as if his love
for her was gone. The only piece of love he had for her
was that she was the mother of his sons.

"If you mean living together, yes. But if you mean by
being in love with her, no."

King was surprised. She was expecting a long, written
out love letter on how much he loved her, wanted to
marry her, the white picket fence, and all that love shit
she hated reading about and looking at. If that had been
the case, she would've taken her butter knife and cut off
his balls.

King played the dumb blonde role again. "You live with
her, but you don't love her? Then why stay where you're
not happy?"

Swag didn't know if it was the Costa Rica air, the
excellent breakfast, or King's essence. He was starting
to feel comfortable talking to his soon-to-be new boss . . .
until he remembered that in the very near future, he had
to break away from her slowly. But he played it cool and
answered her.

"Well, at one time, I did love her very much. Shit, she
was beautiful . . . silky chocolate skin, and we had a great
connection."

"Damn, she sounds like a dream."

"Yeah, she has a lot going for her. She's in school to be
a biomedical engineer, which I was paying for since her
family cut her off for being with me. And when she told

them she was pregnant with my seed, she was dead in their eyes. They didn't want their daughter with a street dude. To make things comfortable for her, I bought us a big loft in the loft district. I bought her a Mercedes-Benz and was paying for her tuition at Wash U. She didn't have to work or want for anything. I was taking care of the home, but then, over time, she got greedy."

"Uh, what do you mean by greedy?"

"Well, she always wanted to show up and show out in front of her college friends and cousins. She wanted to go shopping every day and buy up the entire mall. She wanted to go to the club every night to pop bottles. Hell, she forgot all about her schooling, keeping our home clean, and taking care of the kids. When I told her about my concerns, all she said was 'hire a maid or a nanny.' But I wasn't having that, so I cut some of her weekly allowance until she got her shit together."

Just talking about his baby mama pissed him off. So many memories flooded his mind. Mainly, how she flipped out on him and changed toward him. He even got her pregnant a second time, hoping things would get better. Shit got worse after she had Namond.

"Then she started to use my kids against me. She made threats and said if I left or didn't give her what she wanted, she would turn me in to the police."

King shook her head. "Yeah, in this life, one thing you never do is mention the cops. That's a death wish." She cleared her throat. "Go ahead."

"If it weren't for my kids, I would've left. I put up with it for a bit, even while she was cheating on me when I was on my overseas' gigs. I just wanna see my kids, even if it's for one day, to see if they're okay."

King admired how much Swag loved his children. She wished that her father had that same love for her. "Well, Solomon, how would you like if I could do that for you?"

Swag looked at her with confusion. "What do you mean?"

"What if I can arrange for you to see your sons?"

Swag was shocked by those words coming out of King's mouth. "You can? How?"

"Shh, just leave it to me," she said. "Finish your breakfast so that we can take care of business."

As they were enjoying their breakfast, Blood came on the balcony. "King, I—"

He paused and looked at Swag. "What is *he* doing here?"

Blood was furious. He was the only man who was supposed to be in King's suite, having breakfast with her.

"Blood, first off, this is *my* shit! *I* run this, okay? Solomon is my guest and my newest right-hand man in training."

Blood's heart dropped at what King told him. She wasn't supposed to recruit anyone without talking to him first.

"*What?*"

"You heard what I said. Now, you know I don't like to repeat myself, but again, Solomon is my new right-hand man. I want you to train him right, and I want no harm to come to him."

Blood's face was like stone. All he did was turn and walk away.

"Blood!" King shouted.

He swung around with evil in his eyes.

"I'm warning you. I don't want any harm to come to Solomon. Understood?"

"Sure." Blood left . . . ready to kill someone.

King looked at Swag, who was impressed by how she handled business.

"Are you almost done eating?" she asked.

Swag nodded and took a sip of his orange juice.

"I asked because you're going to need all your strength. Today is your first day of training."

Swag choked on his juice. *Damn, already?* he thought.

In the gym in the basement of the Palace, Blood punched the punching bag. He pretended it was Swag's face that he wanted to mess up. He replayed the whole scene in King's suite when she told him Swag was going to be the new right-hand man. He continued to punch the bag like a professional as sweat rained down his face. He started to breathe heavily and couldn't get King's words out of his mind. His frustrations made him punch the bag even harder.

No harm will come to Solomon.

He punched the bag so hard that it busted. Blood wished that it was Swag bleeding and dying a slow, painful death. Soon, his vision would come true. All he had to do was make one simple phone call.

Chapter 26

A New Beginning

Tyler was in the shower, trying to scrub off the events from last night. He scrubbed so hard that his skin was turning red. He even took his braids down to wash his hair real good. His mind also traveled to the murder he'd committed yesterday. All of it was a hard pill to swallow, and he was so confused. He wanted to contact his family to tell them about Travis, but he didn't want to risk getting caught by the FBI. The only thing Tyler could do was wipe his face and forget that he even had a twin brother. The thought of that made him cry harder. He was unable to stop his body from quivering.

Then his mind went back to Santana. For some strange reason, he couldn't get Santana off his mind. He hated to admit that Santana was a sexy-ass dude. And he hated to admit that he enjoyed his encounter with him. Tyler had slept with many females and played with one dude, but nothing serious. But Santana was his first time having sex with a man. No female had ever made him feel this way sexually. Santana helped him realize who he was, but he wasn't fully ready to express that side just yet. Shit, first, he had to figure out a way to get out of the shit Swag had gotten him in.

Right then and there, he had a grand idea. It all started with staying on King's good side. But the biggie was Santana. He figured Santana could one day help Tyler escape from King so he could get back to his family. He had nothing else to lose, and if it took him being gay to get out of Costa Rica, then that was *precisely* what he was going to do.

After almost two hours of washing and reflecting, Tyler finally got out of the shower. He seemed to have a new attitude and appeared ready for whatever was next.

Chapter 27

Back to Basics

Things were going well at the Palace for everyone despite the most recent actions days ago.

Swag had started his training with Blood to be one of King's right-hand men. They did everything from boxing, cardio, to boot camp, day in and out. But the thing Swag was glad to do was gun training. He missed the feeling of having a gun by his side like he'd had back home. His next move was to get King to trust him and give him a gun. Then on his list was to get some money in his pockets to build a whole new stash. After that was done, he would come up with an escape plan to get out of Costa Rica and leave King once and for all.

Blood was doing his best to follow King's orders and get along with Swag. But Blood could see right through him. Until he had some type of evidence, he pretended to be some type of buddy to him.

Tyler and Santana had gotten closer. They were spending more days and sexy nights together. Santana was Tyler's new security blanket, and he needed it with him. King, on the other hand, wasn't going to let Tyler's killer instincts potential go away. He was put into training to unleash the beast within. With King as his trainer, she taught him one thing: When you killed someone, always remember to see Paco's face. That way, Tyler would have no remorse for whoever he killed. After just three days with him, she was even prouder of her new masterpiece.

King had only a few days to plan Josie's eighteenth birthday party. She was also proud of the job she'd done to keep Swag and her child apart. She didn't want Josie with her future man. She didn't want any mistakes with either one of them, but as she was planning Josie's event, she also had something up her sleeve for Swag coming soon.

Chapter 28

Turn Up

Josephine "Josie" Batiste was officially 18 years old and legal to do whatever the hell she wanted. Of course, King decked her child out with expensive gifts. Usually, on Josie's birthday, King would give her ballet slippers, new ballet outfits, artifacts on Paris or her idol, Josephine Baker.

This year, King gave her four birthday gifts. Three were visible, all wrapped up beautifully. King told Josie that her fourth gift was a big surprise.

King smiled. "Go ahead and open your gifts."

The first gift Josie opened up was a pink pantsuit with matching heels. Josie loved them mainly because she loved anything pink. In King's eyes, her child needed a power suit to prove she was a future boss.

The next gift she opened up was a book called *Kama Sutra*. Josie's eyes widened, looking at a few pages in the book with the people performing different sexual acts. It was so nasty to her, and she closed the book. Josie looked at King. "Mother, what kind of story is this?"

King laughed. "Child, you have a lot to learn."

Josie laughed nervously. "Thank you, Mother." Putting the book aside, Josie was trying to get the images of it out of her mind.

Josie went to her last present, and it was a bigger shock than the book. She pulled out a diamond and gold switchblade. She was in disbelief and looked at King.

King smiled. She was so proud of herself for giving her child her first weapon of power. Despite its appearance, it was a beautiful switchblade to Josie. And not to be ungrateful, Josie smiled. "Thank you, Mother. I love all my gifts."

King laughed. "You're welcome, baby."

King leaned over and kissed Josie's cheek.

Josie's skin was so soft, making King want to kiss her on her lips. And now that Josie was 18, King wanted to kiss Josie on her *other* lips, forgetting she was her adopted child. Just thinking about it got King hot all over.

Josie chuckled. "Are you okay, Mother?"

King broke out of her wet dream and cleared her throat. "Of course. Now get dressed so we can go to breakfast."

"Okay," said Josie smiling, wondering what gift number four was.

King took Josie to her favorite restaurant, Villa Haiti, for breakfast. It was well known for some of its Haitian dishes. King knew it was a little something that reminded her of home. Then they went shopping and to the beach to have fun.

When the evening set in, King and Josie went back to the Palace and were ready to be pampered. King knew she and Josie had to show up and show out since it was Josie's birthday. King had ordered the best in couture, heels, and a complete collection of Harry Winston jewelry, from head to toe. Also, she paid the most powerful glam squad to get them on point for the evening. They got Tyler to do their hair since he'd laid them out for the killing of Paco. Tyler styled King's blond hair with thick beautiful curls that hung down her back. Josie wanted to look like her idol, Josephine Baker, and wanted to rock a short cut this year. But she figured King would never let her cut her hair, and she often told her, "Hair as fine as yours should always be shown and not cut." To make King happy, Tyler styled Josie's hair with finger waves and gave her somewhat of Josephine's 1920s vibe. Once Tyler did their hair, a famous celebrity makeup artist did their makeup.

Everything came together perfectly, and when they got dressed, King rocked a Shane Justin crystalized, deep plunging dress and topped it off with silver heels. Josie's look came together in a strapless pink couture gown with high heels. Josie loved everything and thought she was having a quiet dinner with King. Instead, they were headed to her surprise party at one of Costa Rica's hottest new clubs, Club Alcazar.

At Club Alcazar, everyone was waiting for the arrival of the birthday girl. From King's girls and guys, Swag, Blood, Tyler, and Madam Lourd, who was starting to feel a little better about going out, doubling up on her morphine, they all were there. Everyone in the club looked fabulous in their suits and gowns.

The club was decked from top to bottom. The colors were pink, black, and white with the theme, "Paris in the Evening." King figured this was the only way that Josie would ever see Paris. All she wanted Josie to do was focus on being the next ruler of the Leopard Clit. King even flew in a pastry chef to make not one, but *two* birthday cakes for her child. One was a huge cake of the Eiffel Tower and the other of Josephine Baker in her banana costume. Music by Beyoncé, one of Josie's favorite artists, filled the club.

Everything looked very exquisite, and Blood and King knew that Josie would be pleased with the outcome.

Blood got a call from Cleo, letting him know he was outside with King and Josie. Blood had the DJ cut the music off and told everyone to be quiet.

Outside Club Alcazar, Cleo had parked. The club was in downtown San José, not too far from the Palace. King loved the fact that her child was 18, and after the party, she had a special surprise waiting for Josie. It was a significant part of her training, especially if she intended to sit beside King on her throne.

Josie looked a little nervous, not knowing this was the restaurant King was taking her to for her birthday dinner. King told her she had to make a stop at the club to take care of some business so Josie wouldn't get any ideas. She ordered Josie to come with her inside the club.

Josie was hesitant about the whole thing. She didn't want to go into the club. But then her mind went back to the slap King laid on her a few weeks back. She didn't want to be slapped again, especially on her birthday. So, the two ladies got out of the car and walked to the door of the club.

"Open the door, Josephine," King demanded while trying to hold back her smile.

Josie was scared. The last thing she wanted to see on her birthday was another bloody massacre like the one back at the mansion. She took a deep breath, and as soon as she and King walked inside, everyone yelled out, "Surprise!" and "Happy Birthday!"

Josie was shocked, surprised, and relieved . . . all at the same time. She held her mouth in disbelief while they sang "Happy Birthday" to her. Josie started to cry. She couldn't believe that so many people came out and showed her so much birthday love.

King rubbed her shoulder and whispered in her ear, "Stand up straight, Josephine. Remember, you're in couture."

Josie straightened her spine, and King handed her a handkerchief. She wiped her tearstained face, but her makeup stayed on without any damage.

Santana walked up to her, carrying a birthday cake with eighteen candles on it. "Come on, friend. Blow out these candles and make a big wish."

Josie chuckled, took a deep breath, and closed her eyes. *I wish this year that I will get to go to Paris and be famous.*

She blew out the candles, and everyone clapped.

"Okay, everyone. Enough of this emotional shit. Let's get this party started right," Blood shouted into the microphone.

Everyone cheered, and the DJ started to play the latest song by Chris Brown.

As the night went on, everyone was having a great time, especially Josie, who couldn't stay off the dance floor. If she weren't in her birthday gown, she'd really have cut loose. She wanted to show out the strippers King hired.

Swag, on the other hand, was in the restroom taking a piss. Once he was done, he washed his hands and walked out. He looked around the club and noticed the birthday girl having a great time. He smiled and was in awe at how beautiful she looked. Every time he saw Josie, she kept getting sexier.

Then he saw a familiar face he hadn't seen in weeks. It was Tyler, looking sharp in a white silk suit with pink shoes. His face was clean-shaven, and his hair was done in cornrows.

Swag looked at his old friend sitting at the VIP table, sipping on his drink and watching everyone on the dance floor. Swag took a breath, knowing he had to talk to Tyler to make some type of peace. He also wondered if he had recovered a little from Travis's death. Swag walked to the other side of the club and bypassed so many women who wanted to dance or make another trip to the restroom with him. He brushed them off by saying, "Maybe later" or "Not now." That was so hard for Swag to do since he hadn't had sex in weeks and was tired from all the training. At night, Swag thought that his nuts were about to explode, and he didn't like masturbating. When he finally got over to Tyler, he tapped his shoulder.

Tyler turned around and rolled his eyes. If this weren't Josie's birthday party, Tyler would've knocked Swag down again. But Tyler did an excellent job keeping himself calm as he sipped on rum and Coke.

"Hey, bruh," Swag held his hand out, hoping to get some type of love from his friend.

Tyler looked at Swag's hand but refused to shake it. "What up?" His eyes shifted back to the dance floor.

Swag looked at him for a moment. He thought he was looking at some beautiful, exotic beauty on the dance floor. But if only Swag knew who Tyler was looking at. . . .

Tyler wanted Swag to go away so he could watch Santana do his thing on the floor.

Santana was dancing and laughing with Josie. Tyler loved how Santana moved on the floor, and that explained why he was so good in the bedroom. He put a smirk on his face while looking him up and down.

"So, you okay?" Swag asked.

Swag had broken Tyler's focus on Santana.

Tyler finally looked at Swag again. "Yeah, I'm fine. Do you want something?"

Much attitude was on display, and Swag was taken aback. All Swag wanted was for them to settle their differences. He thought if he left him alone for a minute, he'd cool down, but Swag was wrong. He was still willing to give it another try, though.

"Nothing. I just wanted to check on you, that's all. I know that it's been a few weeks since we lost Travis and—"

"Don't you speak his name," Tyler snapped and looked at him with cold eyes.

Swag couldn't hear over the music. "What was that, bro?"

"I said, don't you ever, *ever* speak my brother's name! He's *not* your brother. He's mine! Now, if you're done, your negative energy is bringing me down." Tyler sipped his drink and shifted his eyes back to Santana.

Swag still believed the situation with them wasn't supposed to play out like this. He hoped that he and Tyler would squash this and be boys again. Unfortunately, he was wrong. Tyler signaled for Santana to come his way.

He stopped dancing with Josie but kissed her on the cheek before exiting the dance floor.

Tyler's back was turned to Swag, and the last thing Swag wanted to do was kiss Tyler's ass to be his friend. He knew that this wasn't Tyler talking to him. Swag figured the only reason he was acting this way was that he was still grieving over Travis. Swag wasn't going to give up until he mended their friendship.

"Ty—"

"Hey, Ty, baby," Santana said.

Baby? Swag thought as he looked in the direction of the person speaking. Santana sat on Tyler's lap, threw his arms around him, and smiled.

Swag's eyes widened. "What in the entire hell is this?" He knew that he was in King's crazy-ass domain, but at that very moment, he thought he'd left that world and traveled to the *Twilight Zone*. He always remembered Tyler being the biggest lady's man. Tyler always told him and the rest of the fellas how he'd slept with some of his female clientele. He was considered the biggest player in the group. Swag was speechless, but the next act Santana and Tyler did almost made him vomit up the birthday cake.

Tyler and Santana tongued each other down like they were about to make a porno in the club.

"What the hell!" Swag shouted with a twisted face.

The men stopped kissing and looked over at Swag. Tyler smiled, and Santana laughed.

"Oh, what's the matter? You wanna join?" Santana stuck his tongue out.

Tyler figured that was the key for Swag to leave him alone for good. He assumed Swag didn't want to have anything to do with him after this.

"Nigga!" Swag shouted. "Tyler, you sick, man!"

Tyler laughed sinisterly as he licked the side of Santana's neck. "Damn, you taste so good."

Santana laughed, and they kissed again.

Swag threw his hand back and walked away. He wanted to get rid of his thoughts about those two, and even though he knew Tyler was hurting, he didn't believe that was the route for him to go.

Not looking where he was going, he continued to walk off until he bumped into the birthday girl.

"Oh, I'm sorry," Swag said. Seeing her cleared all the negative images of Tyler and Santana. When Josie flashed her smile at Swag, it melted his heart.

"Hey, Josie. Happy Birthday, ma. I'm sorry about that. Are you okay?"

Josie chuckled. "That's okay. Thank you again for the birthday wishes. And, yes, I'm cool."

Swag couldn't stop staring at her.

"What's wrong?" Josie asked with a smirk.

He shook it off. "Nothin'."

"Where's the fire?"

He knew that she was referring to him walking away quickly from his so-called boy and his new lover. Swag brushed it off.

"Nowhere."

"So where you been hiding at all night?"

"I'm doing my job for your mother and making sure everything is going smooth for your birthday."

"Is everything?"

"What?"

Josie rolled her eyes and giggled. "Secured."

"Oh, yeah," Swag laughed.

"Come on and dance with me." Josie pulled him toward her, but Swag stood in place.

She looked back at him. "Why aren't you moving?"

Of course, Swag wanted to dance with her, but the last thing he wanted to do was piss off King. He was now on her good side while going through all the training and dealing with Blood's ass. He didn't want to screw up everything he was trying to build up. He was going to get out of her world by any means necessary.

He cleared his throat. "Damn, ma. Ain't you tired of dancing? You pretty much outdanced everyone up in here, especially Santa—" Just speaking Santana's name grossed Swag out. But he kept his focus on Josie. "Yeah, don't you want something to drink or some of your birthday cake?"

Josie giggled. She could tell Swag was stalling. "Look, Swag, it's *my* birthday, and I want *you* to dance with me. That's an order. Fuck King. Come on!" She took his hand and led him to the dance floor.

As he followed Josie to the dance floor, Swag was shocked at what she had said about King. The DJ played "I Wanna Dance with Somebody" by the late singer, Whitney Houston. Josie loved this song. She practiced with it so many times. It brought a smile to her face as she started to dance and let Whitney's voice take over. Swag smiled. He truly adored her. Their eyes were locked in a trance, and after Josie pulled him closer to her, they danced like there was no one else in the room.

In the far upper corner of the club, King and Blood were up drinking, eating, planning their next move and watching everyone enjoy Josie's party. King looked down to check on her child. When she looked down, she saw that Josie was dancing with Swag like they were dancing on a Broadway stage. At first, she wanted to get pissed off. But she remained cool, remembering this was Josie's night. She loved how Swag was getting down on the dance floor. She smiled at him, and she believed that if a man moved this good on the dance floor, he would move even better in the bedroom. King signaled for one of her guards and whispered in his ear. After she finished speaking, he walked away.

Blood looked at her with suspicion. "What was that all about?"

"Blood, baby, why don't you take the rest of the night off." She snapped her fingers, and within a few seconds, Desiree strutted over to them, looking sexy with her hair microbraided and a strapless cream-colored dress that showed off her chocolate skin and matching heels.

Just seeing Desiree brought a smile to Blood's face. She'd been gone for weeks with a hip-hop mogul, an oil tycoon, and a member of a royal family. They couldn't resist her addictive chocolate punany. Besides King, Desiree made Blood hard and hot every time he saw her.

"Waah gwaan, love?" she said in a seductive voice.

Blood wasted no time getting up.

"You two have a good time tonight," King said, waving as they walked away. Then she strutted out of the balcony and headed downstairs.

Swag and Josie finished dancing to Whitney. He was almost out of breath and could barely keep up with her. He hoped she would become a famous dancer one day.

He had put it into the universe, hoping that this would be the year that she would become a prima ballerina superstar.

Since Swag was sweating so much, Josie put her hand on his shoulder. "You okay, hun?"

He took deep breaths to get himself together. "I'm good, ma. I just haven't danced like that in a while."

Josie laughed. There was no question she had worn him out. When a Chris Brown song came on, Josie started to shake her hips. She was ready to get down again.

"Come on, Swag, let's dance again."

She took his hand, but he pulled it back.

"Ma, I'ma get me some water. I'll be back, okay?"

Josie nodded, and he headed over to the bar. Josie continued to dance and raise her hands, but her vibe was broken when she felt a cold tap on her shoulder. By touch, she felt something wasn't right. She slowly turned around and saw that it was one of King's bodyguards.

"King wants you to be at the spot," the bodyguard said in a deep, scary voice.

Josie looked at him with concern. "Spot? What in the—"

The bodyguard gripped her shoulder. She felt chills going through her bones.

"Baby girl, I know it's your birthday, but your mother told me to tell you not to ask any questions. Just shut up and come with me as she instructed."

Josie didn't want to make a scene at her own birthday party. She took a deep breath and walked off the dance floor, followed by the bodyguard.

Once the bartender gave Swag his second glass of water, he started to get his breathing under control. He went back to the dance floor to look for Josie. He was ready for another round of dancing, but Josie had vanished without a trace. Swag looked around all over the dance floor, thinking she had found another dance partner, but she was gone. He felt a great disappointment while standing in the middle of the dance floor, looking like Prince Charming, who'd just lost his Cinderella. The only thing he needed was the glass slipper. Then he felt a soft, gentle hand on his back. He closed his eyes with a big smile on his face, thinking Josie was ready for him. King, however, stood with a beauty pageant smile on her face.

He smiled and tried to pretend he was happy to see her. "King."

"Yes, bae. Who did you expect?"

They both laughed.

The DJ decided to slow things down. He played Janet Jackson's "Anytime Anyplace." It was an oldie but goodie to get everyone in the mood.

"Come on and dance with me," King said, placing Swag's arms around her hips and butt. She rested her arms on his shoulders and pulled him closer.

While letting Janet's smooth voice take over, Swag looked into King's eyes and saw a sweet girl, not a gangsta bitch. King put her head on his chest. She felt like one with him. After the song was over, King lifted her head and looked at Swag. "Let's have a quick drink before we leave. I have a surprise for you."

She reached for his hand and led him to the bar.

"What surprise?" he asked with a raised brow.

"If I told you, then it wouldn't be a surprise, would it?"

Beads of sweat formed on Swag's forehead. He knew it didn't come from dancing, but from King's sexy ass, that drove him crazy and made him nervous. Swag needed some water and a nice stiff drink to get through whatever King's surprise was.

Chapter 29

Birthday Present

While driving to the next location, Swag was nervous as hell. He didn't know what King had up her sleeve. King looked at him, loving the fear she'd put in him. She loved keeping him and all her play toys in suspense and on the edge of their seats. She had a couple of surprises for Swag. One was for tonight, and the other she was saving for him in the morning. She placed her hand on his shaky leg and caused him to jump.

"Relax," she said. "I just wanted to see if you were okay."

Swag cleared his throat while looking out the window and viewing downtown San José. "Yeah, I'm cool, ma."

King didn't want to show weakness, but she was ready to mellow out and have a little fun with Swag. She had the perfect remedy to get him in the mood for anything.

She reached into her Gucci bag and pulled out a cigar, along with a lighter. She lit it up and took a hit. After she blew out smoke, she passed the cigar to Swag.

"Oh, nah, ma, I don't—"

"Take it! It'll calm your nerves."

Swag didn't put up a fuss. He took a hit too and blew out a big cloud of smoke. He then sat back to relax. While his eyes were closed, he thought about having sex with King. He was horny and had gotten a hard-on from looking at her sexy, green eyes, titties, and thick-toned thighs. King looked amazing in her dress that fit like a glove. It looked like diamonds were painted all over her curves that Swag couldn't ignore.

He handed her the cigar. "I'm done. Do you want a puff, ma?"

"Nah, baby boy, that's all for you. Just a little party favor I got from Josie's party earlier, so enjoy," King lied, smiling.

"Okay then, more for me," he giggled. Too bad he didn't know the cigar was laced with coke.

Once they got to the Apartotel La Sabana, a luxury, five-star hotel, Swag was so high that he couldn't keep his hands off of King. He touched her in places that she hadn't let a man touch in years. Even though King didn't like drugs or anyone that did them, she was okay with this. The coke made Swag's freak come out. He kissed and sucked her neck like a vampire.

King's panties were wet, but she lightly pushed him off of her. "Oh, baby, you're getting me hot."

Swag was high as shit but was still in control. All his thoughts and concerns vanished after the smoke. All he wanted to do was see what King Kia Costello was working with. From what he remembered in the documentary, he remembered the announcer saying that men found her puss legendary. Just thinking of her pink walls was making his manhood even harder. The driver opened the door, and King stepped out of the limo first, with Swag following her lead. He grabbed her hand, and they went into the hotel together. He eased his arm around her waist like she was his. King smiled as she went up to the front desk, speaking Spanish to the front-desk associate.

Swag couldn't make out what they were saying, and to him, that was sad because he was half Puerto Rican. He regretted not learning Spanish when he was in school.

Either way, King speaking Spanish was a bigger turn-on for him than anything.

Within moments, the associate gave King the room key. She thanked him and gave him a tip. King and Swag walked hand in hand to the elevator. He stood behind her with his arms wrapped around her waist while smelling her hair. King leaned her head back. Her nipples were so hard. She wanted Swag to fuck her, just like he'd done to Desiree on the ship. That fantasy was broken when King pushed the button on the elevator to their next destination, and the doors closed.

King faced Swag, and they shared a kiss. She had waited for this moment for weeks, and the wait was worth it. It was *everything* she had imagined. His lips were as soft as a rose petal. Swag's hands went down her back to her plump booty. He scooped her thick ass with his hands.

King unbuttoned his suit jacket. She wanted to rip off his shirt but refused to do so for now. They stopped kissing. Swag bent down and was face-to-face with her breasts. His hands cupped both of them.

"Aah . . ." she moaned and turned her head. King's body just melted at the touch of Swag's hands on her. She wanted him to rip off her dress and suck on her edibles. Swag's mouth was watering. He was ready to breast-feed on her. He was just about to expose her breasts, but the elevator doors opened. They almost gave a show to a wealthy American couple who were waiting for the elevator. The woman was in total shock. Her husband's mouth was wide open. He *definitely* wanted to see more.

King and Swag got off the elevator. They traveled down the hallway with King leading the way. They were arm-in-arm with each other. Swag looked over at her. "So, what's this surprise you have for me, ma?"

King laughed. "Now, if I told you, it wouldn't be a surprise, would it, silly?"

"Damn, I feel like it's *my* birthday," Swag said.

King laughed.

Once they got to the door, King opened it wide. The room was dark . . . until King clapped her hands. All the lights came on. The suite was painted an eggshell color. It wasn't anything flashy, but it was nice. King led Swag into the master bedroom, where she turned on the light. Josie was sitting on the bed in a red nightie from Victoria's Secret that she was instructed to wear. Her hair and makeup were still fresh from her birthday party. She looked over at King and Swag with confusion and shock.

"Surprise!" King shouted.

Swag was stunned more than anyone. He didn't know whether to get a hard-on or be ashamed of himself.

"Mother, what's this?" Josie questioned with a slight smile on her face.

King strutted over to the bed, admiring Josie's sexy body.

"My child, my daughter. You're 18 now, which means you're a woman. It's time for you to let go of these little girl dreams. Tonight, besides all the birthday gifts you got earlier today, this is the 'special fourth present.' It's your first lesson: The Art Of Seduction. Time for you to lose your virginity."

This wasn't how Josie wanted to lose her virginity. She was scared, but King figured once Josie got into the groove, she would love it. To King, for Josie to rule Costa Rica and one day take over this crime world ruled by men, Josie had to learn the art of sex.

"Josephine, baby, don't be afraid. It's natural, and once you get into it, I promise you'll love it." King kissed Josie's hand, forehead, and lips. Josie moved her head back. She wasn't into women. She was strictly into men.

"Child, don't be afraid of a woman's touch. Your idol, Josephine Baker, was into women too. And you want to be like Josephine Baker, right?" King rubbed on Josie's smooth legs.

Josie breathed deeply. She felt turned-on *and* felt violated. King's touch was soft and comfortable. Josie thought about her idol having a love affair with Mexican painter, Frida Kahlo.

"Yes, I do," Josie said softly.

Swag's heart pounded hard against his chest. He could barely move. He was tongue-tied.

"Good."

As King and Josie shared a passionate kiss, the hump in Swag's pants grew. He didn't necessarily approve of this, but not too many men could stand there and watch two beautiful and sexy women indulge like this without getting hard.

King removed the strap from Josie's shoulder and licked her shoulder. She sucked her neck and started to massage her firm breasts. Josie pulled her head back, but she enjoyed King's touch. Swag, however, was still in shock. He was stuck in the middle, trying to decide if this was the right move or not. At the end of the day, this girl-on-girl moment had his penis about to explode. He felt precome seeping out of the tip of his dick. He was ready to have his fun too.

"Solomon, dear," King said. "Please get Josie and me something to drink." She pointed to the little minibar on the other side of the room.

Swag nodded and went over to the minibar. The only thing over there was a crystal decanter with scotch inside of it. He poured two drinks and gave each of them a glass.

"Thank you, Solomon," King said, holding up her glass. Josie held hers up too. "Happy birthday, my child."

They clinked their glasses together.

King took a little sip, and so did Josie, but King encouraged her to drink more. Josie gulped it down to the last sip and put the glass on the nightstand. King looked at Swag and reached out to give him her glass.

"Solomon, babe, can you finish this up for me, please?"

"Sure, ma." Swag took the glass and gulped the drink down too. "Damn, that's good stuff."

He put the glass beside the other one. King patted the side of the bed. "Come sit and take a load off."

Swag sat next to King and looked at both ladies. He could barely move. To break the ice, King leaned in to kiss him. King didn't know about them, but she was ready to get down with the get down. King stood up and looked at her play toys for the evening.

"So, how should we get this started?"

She kicked off her heels and watched as Swag lay on his back. Feeling relaxed, he tucked one hand behind his head and motioned his finger for her to get on the bed.

"Come here, ma."

It had been a while since King let a man take control. Usually, she was the one taking charge, but she loved his aggressiveness. She crawled on top of him, and they shared a passionate kiss as Swag's hands went down her smooth back and squeezed her juicy booty. King ripped open his shirt and exposed his tatted chest. She played with his nipples before moving down low to lick his belly button. She was on her knees with her legs spread. They both removed his clothes, and with his hard shaft sticking straight in the air, King licked across her lips. It was beautiful in her eyes. She hadn't seen a penis this thick, long, and hard in a long time.

She licked the precome off the tip and then covered his shaft with her whole mouth. An arch formed in Swag's back, and to calm himself just a little, he closed his eyes.

At first, Josie looked on with fear and disgust in her eyes. But then, she felt a tingle in between her legs, and her nipples started to harden as King slobbered on Swag's penis like the pro that she was. Josie crawled over to Swag and turned his head around to face her. She kissed him, the first man she'd ever really kissed, and saw fireworks when she closed her eyes. King was glad Josie had loosened up. She stopped sucking the meat off Swag's dick and watched them kiss. She moved her body to Swag's midsection and told Josie to remove her nightie. Josie did as she was told but left her panties on. King couldn't wait to suck her firm breasts and roll her tongue across her flat, four-pack stomach. Something was in the way, though, so she pointed at Josie's panties.

"Everything off! I want you naked."

Josie's panties were sticky and soaked, but she quickly slid them off and tossed them on the floor. King and Swag's mouths watered as they looked at her cleanly shaved, virgin pussy. King was ready to pop Josie's cherry, but she invited Swag to taste her first.

"Perfect! Put your ass on Swag's face and look at me."

Josie exposed her pink lips close to his mouth and faced King. Swag never thought in his wildest dreams he'd have a threesome with women this gorgeous. It was like a twisted dream come true. He wagged his tongue at Josie's pussy that dripped over his mouth. He was aroused and excited about having one woman on his stomach and the other over his face. It took him a minute to gather himself, so King yelled at him.

"Solomon, don't just lie there. Eat!"

Eat what? Josie thought. "There's no food in here."

King laughed. "That's what you think."

Swag grabbed Josie's thighs and stuck his tongue between her tight folds. She whined and could barely stay still as his tongue traveled farther inside of her.

"Oooh, shiiiiit," she cried out. "What's happening to meee?"

King wanted to calm her, so she stuck her tongue in Josie's mouth, silencing her moans. As they kissed, King massaged her breasts and listened to Josie come many times.

King wondered if Swag would come up for air, but he didn't. He continued to work his tongue magic inside of Josie while King toyed with her pink walls too. Josie was on a sexual high. Her body shook all over. She couldn't believe what was happening to her. King was a little jealous, and as they continued to give Josie so much pleasure, she wanted to feel Swag inside of her. She waited for the right moment, though, and was willing to let Josie have it all first for her birthday.

"Josephine, dear." King looked at how weak her body was from all the action.

Josie's eyes kept rolling to the back of her head.

"Yeaaaah," she moaned.

King held her hand out. "Come with me."

Swag's tongue felt so good inside of Josie that she didn't want to move. She mean-mugged King before getting off the bed.

Swag lay there lost in a trance with Josie's virgin puss juice all on his face and mouth. His dick was still as hard as a rock with even more precome on it. He was ready to feel one of these beautiful ladies.

King and Josie gazed at Swag's penis. "Josephine, this is my present to you. Get on Solomon's dick."

"What, Mother?"

King hated repeating herself, but she did. "Go ride that dick like a cowgirl!"

Josie was nervous, and again, this wasn't the way she wanted to lose her virginity. But after what Swag had done with his tongue and the way his snake looked, she appeared ready. She sat on top of him, and remembering the techniques King had shown her, she passionately kissed him. Swag could tell she was still nervous, so he pulled back his head.

"Are you sure you're ready for this, ma?"

Josie thought it was sweet of him to ask. She nodded, and he positioned himself between her folds. He then slid into her wet walls, and her mouth dropped wide open. She moaned and fell forward.

"Aaaaah," Josie groaned in both pain and pleasure.

"Sit up and look at me," Swag said softly. "I got you, I promise."

Josie sat up, and as Swag guided her hips and moved her up and down on his shaft, she started to feel at ease. Her moans and groans filled the room. It was like music to King's ears. She was getting hot from just watching them. And it wasn't long before she got naked for the world to see and felt ready for anything.

As the threesome continued, Swag wanted to be in control now. He flipped Josie over, and as she ate King's goodies, Swag thrust in and out of Josie. They all were on a sexual high—rubbing, squeezing, massaging everywhere they could—and simply couldn't get enough of one another. Swag pounded Josie's insides harder and harder. King massaged her breasts as they bounced around, and she and Swag kissed.

"Yes!" King pulled away from him and shouted. "I love this!"

King watched Swag suck her breasts while still pounding Josie and damn near ripping out her insides. She screamed and hollered his name and could no longer feast on King's insides.

"Fuuuuck me, Swaaag! Keep fucking meee, please!" Josie shouted.

Yet again, King was a little envious. She didn't want Swag to come inside of Josie, and she wanted to make sure he handed her a chance to feel the inside of her golden pussy.

She moved away from Josie, then pushed her away. Swag's dick slipped out of Josie, who was stuck in a sexual spell Swag had put her under. She rubbed on her nipples while looking down at her vagina. Feeling sexually abandoned, she watched King sit on Swag and push his dick inside of her. She rode him hard, just to let him know that *she* ran this show. Swag had no problem with that, and he welcomed her bomb-ass sex skills. Her pink walls felt like heaven. He massaged her breasts, and they both closed their eyes because the feeling was so good. Josie wanted in again, so she got on the bed behind King. She rubbed her back, massaged her shoulders and licked down her spine. King moaned and came multiple times. She turned her head slightly to the side and shared a romantic kiss with Josie. Yet again, King released her juices.

"Ooooh, I'm . . . about to . . . come!"

The last thing King wanted was to get pregnant. She rubbed on Swag's sweaty chest, and right after Josie and King moved aside, he released several deep breaths and squirted sperm all over his chest, stomach, and chin. Once he was done, he planted a kiss on King, then Josie. King looked at Josie and smiled. "Once again, Happy Birthday, baby."

Chapter 30

The Morning After

The next morning, the smell of hot, sweaty sex infused the air in the master bedroom. Swag and Josie were in bed sleeping after all the energy they'd burned off.

King was sitting in the recliner after taking a long, hot shower. She slicked her hair back into a ponytail and wore booty shorts and a black bra. A Vogue slim cigarette dangled from her mouth as she looked at Swag and Josie in dreamland. She thought of the sexual encounter she had with them. King hadn't had a great sexual experience like that in a while. It was much needed, and it calmed her down more than anyone knew. She was definitely hooked on Swag's dick, and she planned on keeping him around forever.

King blew smoke from her mouth—so many memories flooded her mind. She thought about the past and present. Her mind was on the Palace, her mother, Mr. and Mrs. Santiago, and the life of King Kia Costello.

Chapter 31

The Tale of King Kia Costello

San José, Costa Rica, was Central America's hidden little treasure. It was best known for its beautiful beaches, tourist attractions, fine dining, and its beautiful people of all colors and races.

But the one reason people came to San José was to visit the main attraction, the Palace. The Palace was located in the heart of downtown San José, run by Madam Ingram and Madam Lourd. It was the place where you could fulfill your sexual desires that you couldn't get at home. Whatever you wanted, the girls and guys at the Palace took care of the needs of their clients. The Palace served everyone from the locals, big celebrities, and even the royals of the world. It was also the place that would be the legacy and the curse of the Costello women.

But one day, an Afro-Costa Rican woman from the poor community of Puerto Limón outside of San José showed up. She worked for a coffee plantation and didn't make much money. She had gone to the Palace and told the madams that her husband was dying of cancer. She wasn't able to afford his medical bills and was tired of seeing her child go hungry. The lady took her young daughter to the city of San José and told her child there was a festival. In reality, she took her child to the Palace, hoping to get some money to take care of her husband and to pay some of the bills. She didn't know if she would see her child again, but she knew her little girl would be in a better place, or so she thought. Once she and her child got to the Palace, Madam Ingram examined the scared little girl who was about 8 years old. She had a tan complexion, was very skinny, and long, black hair flowed down her back. Madam Ingram didn't see where the young lady could bring any money into the Palace, and she wanted them both to go away. But Madam Lourd saw that the little girl was scared and hungry. She smiled at the child and asked her name. The little girl looked over at Madam Lourd and then her mother. Her mother nodded.

"Kiara . . . Kiara Costello," Lila said.

Lila felt more comfortable with Madam Lourd than Madam Ingram.

Madam Lourd smiled at Kiara. "Are you hungry?"

Kiara nodded.

"Come with me."

Madam Lourd held out her hand to Kiara, who smiled and took Madam Lourd's hand, and they went into the living room. The mother looked at her child's back and cried, but Ingram slapped the shit out of the woman.

"She's ours now. So take the money and get out of this house." Ingram only gave the woman ten mil Colones (only US twenty dollars). The woman knew this wasn't enough to pay bills or her husband's medical expenses. She begged for more money or her child back. Ingram told her that her child was theirs and had her goons throw the woman out.

After several weeks in the Palace, Kiara still wasn't ready for clients, so she was reduced to the status of a servant. If any of the escorts had children, at a certain age, they all became servants until Madam Ingram or Madam Lourd saw the potential as an escort. Ingram nitpicked at Kiara the most out of all the kids. She made her work harder and gave her shit jobs around the Palace, such as cleaning the outside stairs. Ingram always threatened to kick her out of the Palace if she didn't do what she was supposed to do. Kiara wanted to run home to her family but always decided against it. She didn't want to go back to starving or living in their shack that was on the brink of collapsing.

As if things couldn't get any worse for Kiara, she had gotten the news that her father had died, and her mother killed herself. Alone in the world, she had no one to turn to. The one person she had to console her was Madam Lourd. Madam Lourd gifted Kiara by telling her she was no longer a servant. She was going to put her in school to be an elegant and sexy escort. Ingram didn't want Kiara to be an escort for the Palace because she knew that one day, Kiara would have great beauty, and buyers from all over would want her. They would take her away from the Palace, and Ingram couldn't let that happen. In her mind, if she couldn't leave, neither could Kiara.

After a few years, Kiara had grown into a radiant vision of beauty. By her fifteenth birthday, she filled out nicely and was no longer a stick. Also, she was done with all her training, so on her fifteenth birthday, Ingram thought it was time for Kiara to lose her virginity and make her damaged goods to future buyers. Without the approval of her partner, Ingram sold Kiara's virginity to a Russian grand duke, Ivan Vasiliev. He wasn't a handsome man, but the two things that looked beautiful on him were his green eyes and blond hair. He was also known for his rape fetish—he loved to see young girls in pain. He didn't want to use condoms because he wanted to feel the girls. That was another reason why Ingram wanted Kiara with him, so he could destroy her *innocence* and *maybe her beauty. She even locked the door so Kiara wouldn't try to get out and run to save herself. It was the worst sexual experience for Kiara.*

In the end, Madam Lourd cleaned her up, and even though Ivan raped Kiara, she managed to rip some of his blond hair out of his head. She was glad Kiara's face didn't get messed up, which pissed off Ingram. Once Kiara's wounds were healed, Madam Lourd noticed that Kiara vomited a lot. Kiara learned that she was three months pregnant. Once she found out she was expecting, she didn't want an abortion. She now believed she had something to live for, and she told herself that she was going to save up enough money for her and her baby to leave. The plan was to get out of this bad situation and away from Ingram. Within a few months, and with the help of Madam Lourd, Kiara gave birth to a healthy baby girl she named Ivy Marie Costello. Ivy had changed her whole world. Kiara didn't see her child as a rape baby. In her eyes, Ivy was a blessing, and she was determined to be the best mother she could be.

But in Ingram's shitty mind, she always reminded Kiara that Ivy was a rape baby. Madam Lourd told Kiara to ignore Ingram's remarks.

Madam Lourd was excited for Ivy. She was the first baby in the Palace for years. While Madam Lourd watched Ivy in the evening, Kiara had built her clientele at the Palace. She also had built a rep for being the most desirable woman there. That angered Ingram, knowing Kiara had brought in more money than she or Madam Lourd ever did when they were once celebrated escorts. Deep down, it scared Ingram that Kiara would take her throne one day. Meanwhile, Kiara traveled with her clients. She hated to stay away from Ivy that long, but she knew that her child was in good hands with Madam Lourd.

And when Ivy got a little older, Madam Lourd took her under her wing and trained Ivy as a lady's maid. She tried to keep her out of the hands of Ingram, who she knew would brainwash the girl.

One client craved Kiara's service all the time. He was Raza Hussain, better known as the crown prince of Dubai United Arab Emirates. He was infatuated with the island beauty and hated sharing her with so many men.

When she left him to go back to Costa Rica, he got upset and wanted her by his side all the time. At first, his father was against his son making some whore his new wife and bringing her into the royal family. But when Raza used the Cinderella story on him, his father gave in. Raza went to the Palace with a fat wallet ready to buy. This excited Ingram because she figured it would be big money for the Palace—and mainly for her.

But when Raza told Ingram that he wanted Kiara, that made Ingram furious. She tried to tell him lies about Kiara, which Raza didn't believe. Then Ingram offered him other girls who were virgins, who were worth a pretty penny. But despite Ingram's efforts, Raza still wanted Kiara. To shut Ingram up for good, Raza gave her 25 million, plus 10 million in goods and a $25-million bonus. Ingram took the deal and asked if Prince Raza wanted Kiara gift wrapped.

When it got out that Kiara was sold, she was crushed that she had to leave Madam Lourd, her second mother. More so, her now 10-year-old daughter. Kiara tried to get Raza to take Ivy, passing her off as her sister, but Raza refused. He promised Kiara a life of luxury, a marriage proposal, life in a real palace, and that she would be an actual princess. The day that Kiara left, she told Ivy that she would have to leave her for a while. She also promised she'd talk to Prince Raza into getting her soon. Lastly, she told Ivy to be happy and behave.

Ivy was saddened for weeks, feeling that her mother left her forever. She hoped one day her mother would come back and make her a princess too. She even read stories in magazines that said her mother was Prince Raza's sixth wife.

Another article said that Kiara was pregnant with Raza's firstborn son and heir to the throne.

It had been two years, and Ivy didn't hear a thing from her mother. She believed that Kiara had forgotten all about her and was content with her new, fabulous lifestyle, along with her half brother, who was a baby prince. Ivy promised herself to get out of the Palace.

Ingram was still pissed about Kiara having a lavish life and getting everything she wanted. And that didn't mean that Ingram couldn't take it out on her child. She was going to get her revenge on the Costello women. In Ingram's deceitful little brain, she was going to pretend to be Ivy's friend. She told her she could be just like her mother and that she would train and guide her. Therefore, Ivy quit being Madam Lourd's lady's maid and started training to be a sexy escort.

Years passed. Ivy was 14 and sexy as hell. That was the year Ingram had a ball at the Palace for some of the wealthiest men in the world to take their pick of some of the most desirable women in Costa Rico. But to Ingram's surprise, none of the men wanted her, and they felt Ivy just looked like the average classic island girl. Ivy was a cute girl who stood five feet four with long, light brown, curly hair and a shape any supermodel would kill to have. Ingram couldn't believe the men always wanted something extra.

Hurt by the men's rejection, Ivy decided to give them what they wanted. She cut her hair into a buzz cut, dying it platinum blond. She wore bright red lipstick and wore sexier outfits. Ingram had another ball, and this time, Ivy caught the eye of a young, hot, Italian eye-candy who was 16 years old. Bruno Bello was an up-and-coming mob boss who was following in his father's footsteps. But like many teenagers, he rebelled and lived life recklessly. He was attracted to Ivy because she was a rebel herself. He was also the man who had taken her virginity. After having her good pussy, Bruno didn't want any other man to touch her. He made sure Ivy had the best of everything. The best clothing, a private car, and the best room to see her in whenever he came to town.

He would also fly her out to St. Louis, Chicago, or Italy to his family's homes. For over two years, Ivy felt like a princess when with Bruno. She thought Bruno would be her Prince Charming, buy her out of the Palace, they would get married and be a family. But all that changed when Bruno came for one of his visits, and Ivy kept getting headaches and vomiting. Bruno took Ivy to the best hospital in San José, and it turned out that she was four months pregnant. From that point on, everything he did for her stopped. He halted the visits, weekly allowances, and even stopped sending payments to Ingram, which really pissed her off. Ivy was kicked out of her luxury suite by Ingram, but Madam Lourd moved Ivy into her room until her child was born.

By Bruno leaving her with no letter or explanation, Ivy fell into a deep depression. She hated the fact that she would never see him again. She tried calling him, but all of his phones were disconnected. The last time she'd heard about him was in Entertainment Weekly. *He was engaged to a Swedish model. At that point, Ivy wanted a drug to relieve her pain. All she had in life from him was her unborn child. She tried to remain strong for her child, and five months later, Ivy gave birth to a beautiful baby girl. The name came simply to Ivy because she believed that her family was of royal blood. Kiara was now a princess, Ivy lived like a princess for a while and had a very powerful mobster prince in Bruno. She didn't believe in queens, thinking they were weak. She named her daughter something higher than a princess and a queen. She called her child King Kia Costello.*

By the baby being so beautiful, and Ivy owing a big debt to Ingram, who'd lost a lot of money because of Ivy, Ingram wanted her to sell her baby. Ivy refused. Her refusal to not give up King and pay Ingram her money caused a huge fistfight between the women, which caused Ivy and King to be banished from the Palace forever. But Madam Lourd gave Ivy money to last for a while.

Not knowing anything except for living a glamourous life at the Palace, the streets of San José were a scary sight, particularly landing in the streets of La Carpio, one of the worst ghettos of Costa Rica that was known for drugs and crime. Ivy didn't have any skills, and she wasn't going to work as anyone's maid. So she went back to the only thing she knew to support her and King, which was whoring. Sometimes, she would leave King with strangers.

When King was 3 years old, Ivy met a Jamaican pimp named T-Weed, who provided a home for Ivy and King and protection with Ivy working for him. Ivy agreed, and to sign the deal, she became pregnant with T-Weed's child. Nine months later, Ivy had King's half brother, Santana. After Santana's birth, T-Weed pimped Ivy and his other girls all over Costa Rica and took all their money. By the time King was 8, T-Weed had introduced Ivy to coke and later on, heroin, making Ivy his zombie. He'd made her shut up about Bruno and the life she should've been living. His only words to her were, "You're not a princess anymore, bitch!"

With Ivy doped up all the time, T-Weed had bigger plans in turning King out, who, day by day, was turning into a beauty. Especially with her smooth fair skin, exotic features, and her beautiful green eyes and natural blond hair that she inherited from her rapist grandfather. T-Weed knew one day King would be worth big money and was thankful Ingram threw her and Ivy out. When King would be of age, he would be the first to pop her cherry. He was getting tired of fucking Ivy and his other girls whose looks and pussies were fading. He was determined to get some of that young meat.

King was aware of her surroundings, and she knew that T-Weed was up to no good. She wanted to help her mother and protect her little brother. Ivy was in the streets turning tricks to get T-Weed his money and polluting her mind due to her drug habit, not knowing she was on this earth much of the time. When Ivy was semicoherent, she would tell King that she was of royal blood. She told her about her grandfather, grandmother, and how, back at the Palace, she used to live the life of a princess thanks to King's father, who was now a big mob boss. Ivy also wanted King to reclaim the Costello family honor. First, the Palace, then Bruno and Ivy's mother. King took her family roots to heart. She kept her mind strong and made it her mission to fight for her rightful place on her throne. Lastly . . . not to take shit from anyone.

When King was 12 and had her first period, T-Weed wanted her to feel like a woman. In King's mind, she wasn't going to let that lowlife take what was hers. When T-Weed tried to rape her, she fought back and kicked him in his balls. Then she ran out of her room, but before leaving the house, she grabbed a knife.

It wasn't long before T-Weed caught up with her. He tried to pull King back into the house, but she wasn't going in without a fight. King pulled out the knife and stabbed T-Weed in his side. In anguish and pain, he screamed, "You little bitch!" King had heard that word all her life from T-Weed, who called his three other girls and her mother the same thing. But not King—the next heiress to the throne. She was even more determined to rid the world of this piece of shit, so while T-Weed was down, King continued to stab him. She tasted his blood while stabbing him in his face and neck. She watched the blood flow from his body as he screamed in pain, slowly dying. She smiled at his lifeless body with no emotion.

As King looked over at T-Weed's corpse, she didn't know that a black limousine was parked nearby, and its occupants were watching her every move. It was husband and wife, Zeus and Lewa Santiago. They were the king and queen of Cuba and the gods of the crime world. Whatever they said was bond in the bloody underworld of crime. They controlled everything from drugs, sex, and whenever the Santiagos told a politician to jump, he'd ask how high.

Instead of being grossed out at what King did to old dude, they were actually impressed with her killing technique. They didn't know what it was about the young girl, but they got totally turned on by her skills. In their eyes, King was a homeless child with no family, and she had escaped the world of the sex trade from the hands of a pimp. Lewa, who didn't have any children of her own, sympathized with the girl. She hated to see any child unwanted and alone in the world. So many memories flooded Lewa's mind as she held back her tears. She tapped her husband's shoulder and made a request. Blake Fernandez, their right-hand man, looked at the couple with a smile. Blake envied their love, and he wished he could clone Lewa. The Santiagos' love for each other was pure and genuine. Lewa smiled at her husband.

"*Zeus, I want her. Bring her to me.*"

They shared a romantic kiss. "*Sure, anything for you, Mrs. Santiago.*" *Zeus gave Blake an order.* "*Blake, you heard Mrs. Santiago. Bring the blond doll to us.*"

Blake nodded. "*As you wish.*"

Blake got out of the car and rushed toward King. Her back was turned as she looked at her mother's bloody former pimp and her half brother's father. Blake grabbed her. King fought back with everything she had. He carried her to the limo, and after opening the door, he threw her inside. King screamed and tried to get out.

"*Calm down!*" *Blake said forcefully.*

King continued to fight. She didn't calm down until Zeus pulled out a switchblade and pressed it against her neck.

"*The man said, calm down!*"

King looked at the switchblade and quickly obeyed.

"*What do you want from me? If it's money, I don't have any. Help!*"

The Santiagos and Blake laughed.

"*No, child, we don't want money. We want to help you,*" *Lewa said, looking at King with gentle eyes.* "*No one is going to hurt you, my dear.*"

King didn't know why, but she felt that she could trust the beautiful stranger. In her young eyes, the woman was simply gorgeous. She had a classy type of beauty with a china doll face. Her skin was dark chocolate, and her hair was cut short. Lewa's smile melted King's heart. It was the first time in years that anyone treated her nicely.

Zeus removed his switchblade from her neck and placed it in his coat pocket. King looked at the strange man next to the woman. She had to admit he was the most handsome man she had ever seen. His white skin was flawless with a five o'clock shadow that made him even sexier. He looked of Cuban and Italian descent. His hair was cut short like film legend James Dean. His body showed well in a gray Tom Ford suit. Lewa looked at King's dirty clothes. It was difficult to ignore the stench coming from her body.

"You look like you could use a meal, a hot bath, and some new clothes. Would you like to come with us? I promise we won't hurt you, child."

Lewa's words were like music to King's ears. She nodded, and the car sped off.

As they rode to the hotel, the Santiagos and King talked and introduced themselves to one another. And when they arrived at the Apartotel La Sabana where the Santiagos had a whole suite, they put King in the tub so she could wash herself up real good. While she was bathing, they didn't know King had ordered nearly everything from the menu. Room service delivered the food, and when King got out of the tub smelling like jasmine, she devoured food like she hadn't eaten in days.

While hanging out with the Santiagos, King learned that Lewa was originally from Sierra Leone and that Zeus was from Havana, Cuba. They still lived in Havana and had many businesses. When they asked what King's name was, they thought King was an unusual name for a girl. Then King told them about her family history and that one day she was going to be on top and reclaim her family honor. She also told them about wanting to get revenge on those who shamed her family. King had heard from a source that her father was living a lavish life back in America and running many businesses. Lastly, she wanted to get her hands on that fat, pig-faced bitch Ingram that Ivy told her about, and more than anything, she was going to take control of the Palace and Costa Rica.

After listening to King's story, the Santiagos loved her determination for power. Zeus saw that King had the potential to be a good femme fatale and a future boss with the right mentoring, training, and guidance. He hoped within a few short years, she would be ready for anything. He offered to help her if she agreed to follow everything he and his wife were going to teach her. King agreed. She was ready to take back what was hers.

When Blake came back from the mall with a few outfits for King, Lewa taught King her very first lesson, and that was looking the part of a boss. She put on clothes with all designer labels and felt like a princess. But to her, King was equal to any man. Zeus taught her how to start her own empire. He told her since she killed T-Weed, she was going to take his place and pimp the three girls, but not her mother, to get whatever she wanted. She was advised to get some poor boys from the neighborhood that would kill for her and protect her. King was soaking in everything the Santiagos told her.

When they dropped her off at her home, a new King had emerged. Without T-Weed's leadership, the three girls and Ivy were lost sheep without a shepherd. With new leadership skills, King took charge of the girls, and with Zeus' switchblade and T-Weed's guns, the girls knew King meant business and went to work.

Within a year, King had T-Weed's ghetto, piss-smelling home looking like a royal palace. She formed her own little organization called The Leopard Clit. No one dared to fuck with her, thanks to the new protection and hidden protection the Santiagos hired. For many years, the Santiagos would travel back to Costa Rica, continuing King's training and were impressed at all she had done. They even taught her how to read, write, and informed her of the keys to survival in the crime world. That consisted of book knowledge, along with a street education, as well. Her favorite book to read was Dracula. She loved his thirst for blood.

When the Santiagos came into town, they took King with them on trips and taught her how to buy and sell workers, even how to set up shops in other countries. They also taught her how to steal, not cheap shit, but diamonds, gold, and artwork so she could sell them for millions to buyers who wanted them on the black market.

With the money King made, she moved herself and her mother, who was trying to kick her drug addiction, to a fancy hotel on the other side of town. King wanted to pimp out Santana. She both loved and hated her half brother, all at the same time. He looked like a light-skinned version of T-Weed. She wanted to kill Santana too, but she decided against it because it wasn't his fault.

King continued to do her business in La Carpio. She made even more money and was feared by all other gangs in the area. It was all thanks to the guidance of the Santiagos, who she regarded as her mother and father figures. Since she didn't know her own grandparents, Madam Lourd always came around visiting them in the hotel and helping Ivy with her withdrawals. She got Ivy morphine to kick the habit.

The next lesson the Santiagos wanted to teach King was the drug game, but she wasn't interested, especially knowing what it had done to her mother. The main lesson King wanted to learn was about murder. The Santiagos gave the 14-year-old her first assignment to kill an American judge who was wrongfully putting young black men in prison on trumped-up charges. One man the judge imprisoned was the leader of the powerful St. Louis organization, The Empire, that wanted the judge dead. King killed the judge, and the Empire's leader was released, and the evidence disappeared. The

Santiagos loved the masterpiece they'd created and thought it would be a good time to leave King, but not until after teaching her one more lesson.

By the time it was King's sweet 16 birthday, the Santiagos had thought it was time to teach King her final lesson: The Art of Seduction. That was also the night they took King's virginity and told her to use her pussy to get all she wanted from the enemy. And that was the night King fell in love with them and wanted to run away with them to Cuba.

The next year, the Santiagos didn't come back. Only Blake did with a note:

> Sorry we have to leave you, my child.
> Your training is complete
> But now it's time for you
> to take your throne.
> Rule like a king and fuck the queens.
> P.S.
> Blake is our going-away present to you.
> Use him well.

King cried like a baby after reading that note. She hated and loved them for leaving her like that. They were her drug and heart. She needed them. In a rage, she ripped the letter into small pieces and let it blow in the wind. She breathed heavily while looking over at Blake.

He looked at her with a stern gaze. "What do you command of me, Boss?"

King still had the animal hunger in her. Her eyes stayed on Blake like he were her prey. And out of nowhere, she punched him in the nose. He never budged, not even when blood poured out of his nose. To King, the ruby-red blood looked beautiful on his skin.

"Blood." King used her fingertip to wipe the blood from off his lip and taste it. "From now on, your name will be Blood. You are my right-hand man of rage."

"As you wish, King."

King was still enraged about how the Santiagos just left her behind. With all that rage and hatred, she now thought it was time to reclaim what was hers. She was tired of living in a hotel. It was time to get her palace and her kingdom and live like the king she was born to be. She looked back at Blake, now Blood. "Get my goons together. I have a score to settle at the Palace."

King called Madam Lourd to the hotel and told her that Ivy needed her now. Once Madam Lourd was gone, only Ingram remained there. King, Blood, and her goons attacked Ingram and tied her up like the pig she was. If anyone got in their way, the Leopard Clit killed him. Once all tied up on a stick, looking like a pig ready to be roasted, King looked at Ingram's fat, nasty-looking body that made her want to vomit.

Ingram was frightened and scared, knowing that her reign of being the queen of the Palace was ending. Ingram knew her Karma was going to catch up to her one day, but she didn't expect it so soon. She looked at King. "Who are you?"

King looked at her and shook her head. "Fuck the queens! I'm King Kia Costello. I'm taking my place on the throne."

King punched Ingram hard in her mouth, knocking out some of her teeth. "That was for my mother." King then took out the switchblade that Zeus gave her and cut out both of Ingram's eyeballs. Ingram screamed in agony and shook like crazy.

"That's for me, bitch!"

Ingram continued to scream, and that made King regret cutting out her eyes. She wished Ingram could *see the sinister smile King displayed. King realized that she wasn't deaf, so she laughed evilly. Ingram was in pain and angry, but she fought through the pain.*

"Fuck you! Fuck you! You high yella bitch and your family. Fuck you all!" She wished that she wasn't tied up so she could hit King's pretty face.

King smiled. "Shut up!"

Ingram continued cussing her out and calling her names other than her royal title.

"Boys!" King yelled.

Her goons came in and bowed down to her. "Yes, King!"

King came up with a brilliant idea. "Cut out her tongue, and skin her alive. I don't want any piece of skin left on that bitch!"

The goons obeyed. "As you wish, King!"

"What!" screamed a bloody, blind Ingram. "Noooo!"

The goons started to cut Ingram, who screamed hysterically. King laughed as Ingram's blood, tongue, and flesh hit the floor. Ingram's screams faded by the second as she was dying.

King inspected Ingram's bloody, skinless body. It seemed like she was trying to hold on for dear life. "Oh, how the mighty has fallen." King looked back at her goons. "Burn her! I want to make sure this bitch is dead."

The goons burned Ingram, and her death was confirmed. King smiled and left, very pleased that day. She knew, at that moment, it was the rise of a hardhearted King, and love didn't live in her heart anymore.

Chapter 32

Back to the Future

King was done with all the reminiscing about her rise to power and her long lost loves, Mr. and Mrs. Santiago. Her eyes were still glued on Swag and Josie sleeping peacefully. Then King's cell phone went off. She picked it up and read the text message from Blood.

They're here.

King smiled, knowing that text made her day. She texted back.

Good. Meet me at the beach.

Blood responded: Will do boss.

King put down her phone and looked back at Swag and Josie. She'd had enough of this now, and she didn't want her future man and her child to get any closer than this.

Time to break the mood, she thought.

She put the cigarette out, stood, and clapped her hands. "All right! All right! Time to wake up, you sleepyheads! Wake up!"

Both Swag and Josie's faces were twisted. They were still tired as hell from last night's events.

"Come on, let's move!"

Swag and Josie got out of the bed, covering themselves up.

King laughed. "It's too late to cover that up. I already seen it and felt it all."

Swag and Josie felt embarrassed.

King looked over at Josie. "Josephine, get your clothes together. The car is waiting downstairs for you to take you back home."

Josie removed the sheets and quickly put her clothes back on. After she got herself halfway together, she left the room. King and Swag were now alone in the suite. She loved the idea of being alone with him, and she wanted some more sex. But right now, sex had to wait until later. King walked over to him and touched his tatted chest.

"Damn, last night was good." She kissed him.

Swag was pleased too. He thanked God for letting him have the strength to handle King, but his head started to hurt a little bit.

"You okay, baby?" King asked in a soft voice.

"Yeah, my head is just a little out of it."

"Aww, poor baby." She kissed his cheek. "Why don't you take a shower? When you get out, I'll have something waiting for you for that hangover." She kissed him again.

He smiled. "Okay."

As Swag headed to the bathroom, King smacked his ass. After he closed the bathroom door, she sat on the bed, picked up the phone, and called for room service.

Swag had wrapped up his shower. He rubbed himself with lotion and brushed his teeth. He felt like a million bucks as he wrapped a towel around his waist and walked out. The suite was clean to perfection and smelled like vanilla. He looked over at King, who was smiling and sitting on the bed. She had a shopping bag sitting next to her. Swag looked at the bag with suspicion.

"Hey, King."

King carried the bag over to him. "Here. I had the hotel pick up some things for you. Put these on and be down in the lobby in thirty-five minutes." She kissed him again and exited the room.

Swag sighed from relief and shook his head. He was tired of being fake to impress a woman that could kill him in the blink of an eye. And after last night, not him, but Josie too. He had to admit that King's puss was the bomb. The shit was addictive. He thought about banging her a few more times before escaping. He even thought of Josie and having taken her virginity. He hadn't had a virgin since Brazil. At other times, he would've loved to have a virgin, but this time it was different. Josie was still a child, and he felt like it was rape, knowing she was only 18. But even though he was forced to sleep with her, Swag still felt a connection with her. It was the feeling he had with Zaria, once upon a time long ago . . . until he messed up with his cheating. Swag's mind was all over the place. He looked over at the clock to see he only had twenty minutes left. By then, Swag got his shit together and opened the bag. Inside were floral swim trunks with a matching shirt and flip-flops. He looked at the items and rushed to put them on. The last thing he wanted to do was piss off King. He'd come too far now to mess up.

Swag went down to the hotel lobby, where King waited for him. He smiled at her as he walked up to her and kissed her. King giggled. She loved this side of him.

She checked him out. His attire was perfect. "Looking good," she said.

Swag nodded. "Thanks, ma."

"Now, come on. Let's head on out. I still have the other half of your surprise."

Swag had utterly forgotten about the secret surprise King had planned for him after a wild night of sex. He didn't know how much more he could take from this woman. King took his hand and led him out of the hotel.

While driving down the streets of Costa Rica, which felt like forever, the driver finally reached Puerto Viejo de Talamanca. It was the most popular beach destination on Costa Rica's Caribbean coast. It was a beautiful day to go to the beach. The sun shone brightly, the breeze was perfect, and it was peaceful. The beach looked vacant, but there was a picnic table waiting for someone and a carnival on the other side of the beach. Swag wondered what in the world was going on and if he were being set up.

"Come," King said as she got out of the car.

Swag got out, and they walked on the beach to the picnic table where some food and goodies were set up. Swag loved looking at the carnival down the way, and he thought of how much his boys would've loved it. His mind then shifted to what had happened last night. He figured King wanted to have a romantic date on the beach. He smiled and didn't think it was a bad idea.

"Solomon, have a seat and enjoy this brunch." King was excited about the surprise she had bottled inside of her.

Swag thanked her and got a plate with French toast, some fruit, and a glass of juice. As he was eating, he could tell King had something else up her sleeve. She took her hair down and let it blow in the wind. As Swag watched her, King poured herself a glass of champagne and dropped two strawberries in it. She looked at the beautiful blue water. She had seen it so many times before, and it never got old. Then her cell phone rang. It was Blood.

"Yes."

"We're here, and I see you."

"Good. Come down."

She turned off her phone, put it in her pocket, and looked at Swag, who was chewing and cutting up his food.

"Good food?" she asked.

"Oh, yes. It's great."

King turned around, so Swag looked to see what she was gazing at. Almost immediately, his eyes grew wide, and tears filled them. It was like God had answered his prayers. Blood had Swag's oldest son's hand, and Desiree was holding his baby boy. As they got closer to him, Swag couldn't believe this was real.

"My boys!" Swag looked over at King.

King smiled. "Surprise!"

Swag was in shock. He couldn't believe King had pulled this shit off. He thought she was joking earlier about seeing his children again. He was still a fugitive and didn't believe it would ever happen. Swag knew that King hated to be questioned, but he couldn't hold his questions any longer.

"King, what? How did you—"

She clamped her hand over his mouth. "Shh . . ." She laughed. "Go over and enjoy your sons and celebrate your oldest boy's birthday."

"King, you know I'm a fugitive, right? How'd you get my boys over here?"

"Solomon, dear, I just had some of my goons go to St. Louis and do a little overnight delivery for me. But don't worry about the law. As far as I'm concerned, I *am* the law. Get up and enjoy your family. Let's just say this is an early X-mas gift from me. Enjoy."

Swag took a deep breath. For the moment, he was going to make the good out of a fucked-up situation. He wiped his tears and rushed up to his sons.

"Daddy," Li'l Swag said.

Swag fell to his knees and kissed his son's smooth face. This was surreal to him. He was overcome by his emotions. He stood and removed Namond from Desiree's arms. In Swag's eyes, his baby boy had gotten so much taller since the last time he'd seen him. Swag smiled at his baby.

"Hi, Namond. I'm your daddy."

Namond looked at Swag and smirked at him.

His smile melted Swag's heart, and at that moment, nothing else mattered to him.

"Solomon, why don't you take your sons and enjoy the beach? And don't forget the carnival around the way. This is your day to do whatever the hell you want."

Swag smiled at King, who was smiling too. "Thank you." He looked at Namond and down at Li'l Swag. "Come on. Let's go."

They rushed over to the water and left King, Blood, and Desiree to themselves.

King thanked Blood and Desiree, and she gave Desiree a passionate kiss. The ladies stopped kissing and looked at each other. King told her to take her car back to the Palace and be in her suite when she returned. Knowing what was in store for her, Desiree hurried to the car and left.

Alone with Blood, King went into boss mode again. But before she could say anything, Blood asked, "Are you out of your fuckin' mind, King? Bringing that bitch's little bastards across the world, for what? His ass! Woman, what kind of spell does this American have on you? This isn't the King *I* know."

King sat down, took a sip of her drink, and didn't trip. Blood's words went in one ear and out the other. She looked at the ocean and checked out Swag and his sons, who were splashing water on each other.

"King, are you listening to me? You know by doing this, it could put the organization at risk. What if—"

King couldn't take any more of Blood's mouth. She jumped up and slapped the dog shit out of him. "Shut up!"

Blood grunted and mean mugged her. His first thought was to choke the shit out of her ass for disrespecting him. He didn't go there because he figured King's spies were on the beach, and they would surely kill him. She pointed her finger in his face.

"First off, you'd better put a smile on that face."

Blood straightened his face, but on the inside, he was boiling mad.

"Second, *I* run this damn show and *not* the other way around. So, I suggest you wait in your car and cool down until I'm done."

Blood just stared at her without responding.

"*Now,* dammit!"

He tried to hold back tears of rejection and disrespect. He couldn't believe how much he hated this woman but was still in love with her all at the same time. He shook his head while walking back to the car.

It was starting to get a little warm, and King needed a cool drink. She got one and continued to look at Swag and his boys. She loved the view, and while thinking about them, she pulled out her cell phone to check the latest news. One of the headlines read: Two siblings abducted in a St. Louis Park.

King pressed the link, and the video of the whole story appeared.

"I'm Greta Armstrong of CNN, and I'm here with the latest news. This story has made national headlines. Recently, two brothers, Solomon and Namond Carter, were abducted from Heman Park in University City, Missouri. What was supposed to be a nice family outing turned into a mother's worst nightmare."

The news showed pictures of both brothers. Then Greta showed the boy's mother, Zaria Mitchell, who had recently graduated from college a few weeks back. There was more footage of Zaria crying hard with her mother and boyfriend consoling her.

Zaria broke down and said, *"All I want are my babies. Bring them back!"* she screamed at the camera.

King laughed at the whole situation. *Who is her acting coach?*

Then the camera went back to Greta.

"The children were taken by masked men who didn't leave many clues. The FBI isn't sure what the motive was for taking the boys. The boys are the sons and cousins of Solomon Carter, known as Swag on the streets, and Brad Carter. Both men are international fugitives wanted in Brazil."

Both Brad's and Swag's mugshots flashed across the screen.

Then the focus was back on Greta.

"If anyone knows the whereabouts of the boys or the fugitives, Solomon and Brad Carter, please call your local police."

King turned off her cell phone and continued to enjoy the view.

In the car, a raging Blood wanted to tear it apart. He wanted to beat the shit out of King. He was a man—a *real* man. His mind was in limbo over what he should do about this situation. He knew he loved the old King, but this monster she was daily becoming he didn't like. And to put the frosting on the cake, Swag made it worse. Blood had to keep her tame. He still wanted her to be his. He scrolled through the names in his cell phone, looking for a bag of his own little tricks. He was determined to get some type of control. Finally, he found the name he was looking for and dialed it.

Within moments, someone answered. "Yes."

Blood took a deep breath. "I need help, G."

The person laughed. "Lucky for you that I'm in town visiting one of my ladies."

"Good, let me call the other guest, and let's meet up at the Apartotel La Sabana Hotel in an hour. I'll tell King I'm meeting some fellas for drinks."

"Cool, see you then."

Blood hung up, ready to get some shit moving now.

Chapter 33

The Rat Pack

Blood soon went to the Apartotel La Sabana Hotel and actually went to the same suite where King, Swag, and Josie had enjoyed their threesome. He looked around the room, and even though it was clean, he sickened at the thought of King with Swag. Blood shook his head, trying to eliminate the nasty thought from his mind.

He sat at the table, putting his briefcase on it. Blood pulled out a Cuban cigar, lit it, and took a few pulls. Then he blew out thick smoke, filling the room.

So many things ran through his mind. *What happened to King? She is so blinded by that pretty American boy, wanting the same thing she saw in Zeus. She's starting to lose focus on the business and me.*

His mind was filled with images of King, aka his love. He didn't know why he was so obsessed with her. He couldn't deny that she was sexy, a killer, and she had a fire for life that wouldn't blow out.

When he first met King as a young child, he thought she was a dirty street girl destined to be a common whore. But after Zeus and Lewa groomed and trained her for the game, she was now a sexy boss.

He used to be mad at the Santiagos for leaving him with King, but after years of being with her, he fell in love with her.

So many times, he tried to express his love to her, but King always shut him down. King teased him with her good punany, and that's the only reason he stayed with her.

But now, Blood was tired of playing games with her. He wanted King all for himself. He had decided in their future life together, if King were a good girl, Blood would occasionally allow another woman in their bed for a little fun. Just the thought of him, King, and another woman gave him a woody. That put a big smile on his face.

But his horny thoughts were interrupted by a noise on his cell phone. Blood looked at the text.

We're here.
He smiled. *Right on time,* he thought as he sent a text.
Come in. It's open.

Blood was ready for business.

The door opened, and three men came in the suite.

Blood stood. "Gentlemen, welcome." He then looked at the tall Sicilian man in a tight-fitting dark blue suit. "And, you, welcome to San José."

The men shook hands, greeting one another. Blood told them all to have a seat and offered them drinks and cigars. The men passed on the drinks.

"Nope, let's get to this business," said the Sicilian in a serious tone.

Everyone looked at the Sicilian crazy.

"Okay, G, damn," said Blood looking him up and down. "Just one question before we start."

"And what's that?" asked the Sicilian as he took a cigar.

"Where is B at? I thought he would be here to discuss our problem."

"Oh, B, couldn't come. He had bigger fish to fry in the Midwest back in the States. But don't worry. He isn't backing down. He's waited a long time to bring King down."

Then one of the other men who was at the table, the police chief of Costa Rica, cleared his throat. "So, Blood, what do you have for us to bring this bitch down for good?"

"Yeah," said the other man, who was the police chief's assistant.

"Okay, gentlemen, I got you all," said Blood.

"You better, Fernandez. The president has been all over my ass about bringing this bitch down for years."

"Yeah, and my boss just wants that little moolie whore the hell away from him with all her lies," said the Sicilian.

Blood laughed as he went into his briefcase, pulling out many documents, photographs, and video leakage of King's guilt with the blurring of other people's faces that she's worked with to protect their business relationships.

The men looked over all the evidence.

"Perfect," said the police chief.

"Yeah," said his assistant.

The Sicilian nodded.

"I say we bust the bitch right now!" yelled the police chief.

"No! She deserves much better than that," said Blood.

The men looked at him with a "Why not?" look on their faces.

"I'm in charge of this operation. And what I say goes, got it?" Blood smiled. "And if you burn me before this shit hits the fan, I have photos of you, Police Chief, with the best girls in the Palace I hooked you up with."

The cop had a lump in his throat that was hard to swallow. He was nervous as shit knowing the photos or whatever Blood had on him could damage his career.

Blood smiled at him, knowing he had him. He looked over at the Sicilian. "Now, G, I know you and your boss are already going to work up a plan. If you do—" Blood went into his briefcase again, pulling out a picture and handed it to the Sicilian.

The Sicilian looked at the picture and back at Blood. "Who is this?"

Blood smiled at him. "That is Solomon Carter, aka Swag. He's a fugitive and one of King's upcoming soldiers."

Both the police chief and his assistant looked confused.

"Oh, he's one of those moolies that escaped the Brazilian prison," said the Sicilian as he looked back at the picture. "But what does he have to do with bringing King down?"

Blood laughed. "Glad you asked. He'll be our star witness for taking King down. And it'll keep King from suspecting all of us. Just keeping our hands clean."

"Well, Sherlock Holmes, how are me and B going to get this eggplant to testify against all King's crimes?"

"Now, G, you know these Americans will do anything, if persuaded right. So, you and B can figure all that out. Shit, you have all the information, so come up with a plan."

The Sicilian nodded. "We'll keep that in mind."

Blood smiled. "Good. Let's bring King and Swag down." He looked at his watch. "Now, excuse me, gentlemen. I have another engagement to get to." He stood up. "Have a great day, gentlemen, and wait for my signal in due time."

"Uh, Blood, one question comes to mind," said the Sicilian.

Blood looked at him. "What's up, G?"

"Why do you want to bring down King so badly? I thought you were her boy? Why destroy what she's built? She's so beautiful and young. What a waste."

Blood chuckled, having his own secret plan worked out in his head. "It's personal. Just be ready when I call." He walked out of the suite, ready to put his plan to action . . . getting rid of Swag and making King his at last.

Chapter 34

All Good Things Come to an End

The last few days had been like heaven for Swag. He loved waking up in the morning, seeing his sons.

He asked Li'l Swag how he and Namond got from St. Louis to Costa Rica, knowing little children his age can't lie. Li'l Swag told him that the family was in Heman Park celebrating his mother's graduation party and that she had a new boyfriend by the name of Garrett.

Swag only knew one Garrett, and he was the disease of the fellas from getting Tyler locked up to going down on Brad's former girl, Nichelle. Now he was dating the mother of his two boys.

He wanted to throw something—anything—across the room but remained calm because of his son. All he told himself was that if he ever got out of this mess, he was going to handle that Garrett situation. But until then, he listened to Li'l Swag.

His son told him some masked men in clown suits came by. And that everyone thought the clowns were for Li'l Swag and Zaria. Li'l Swag said that the clowns put on a show for them, and all of a sudden, smoke was everywhere. And before Li'l Swag knew it, he and Namond were with Blood or as Li'l Swag called him, Mr. Blood.

Li'l Swag even told Swag that Blood fed them and entertained them, telling them he had a big surprise for them and Li'l Swag's birthday.

Swag asked Li'l Swag if he had been afraid when taken away from home and if Blood treated Namond and him right.

Li'l Swag stood up and told Swag, "I'm a soldier. I ain't neva scared. You taught me dat. And I missed my real daddy."

Li'l Swag went on to say Blood was cool.

Swag laughed at the thought of his son, a soldier. Then Swag almost choked when Li'l Swag said he missed him. But he was glad his boys were there, no matter how they got there.

While Li'l Swag and Namond were in San José, Swag spent as much quality time with his sons as he could, not knowing how long they would be there with him. Swag wished he had a camera to cherish these precious moments. He loved bathing them and taking them to the beach. He even enjoyed changing Namond's diapers, despite the shitty smell. But even with the bit of happiness, Swag sensed hate always filled the air.

Tyler couldn't believe that King did that shit for Swag. Don't get him wrong. Even though he hated Swag to the core, he still loved his godsons with all his heart. But even though he loved them, Tyler wanted to do something to Swag to pay him back for the murder of Travis. When he was alone playing with Li'l Swag, he wanted to rape him and take his childhood from him, but he couldn't go through with it. He just couldn't take the innocence of a child. So after the first time seeing the kid, he kept to himself and stayed in his room with Santana.

One day while Swag was training, Madam Lourd was watching both of his children. Even with her illness, Madam Lourd still loved to see the joy of children. But that day, Li'l Swag broke away from Madam Lourd to explore the Palace. He finally made it down to Josie's room, where she was practicing. She was happy to get a break from her training of being the future leader of the Leopard Clit. When she finished her dancing, she looked over and saw the boy. She loved children, and she hoped after her dance career died down, she'd have a child of her own. She played with him, and Li'l Swag warmed up to her. He asked her about her dancing and what she was doing. She showed him a few moves, and he tried them too. To Josie's surprise, the little boy was very flexible. She went on to teach him some more dance moves. Not only did Josie want a successful dancing career and a family, but she also wanted to teach dance one day too.

At the same time, Swag looked all around the Palace, losing his mind while trying to find Li'l Swag. He finally decided to check another place he knew that was forbidden, as far as King was concerned. But at that moment, he didn't care what King thought because his baby boy was more important. When he opened up the door, he was amazed at what he saw.

Li'l Swag and Josie were dancing. But it wasn't any of that boring stuff that Josie danced to. She and Li'l Swag were dancing to "Every Little Step," an old Bobby Brown song. Swag calmed down, and he smiled. Looking at his son and Josie caused a warm feeling to come over him that he hadn't felt in years. He was glad that his son was so comfortable with Josie. The song was in the middle, and Swag went into the room, showing off some of his own dance moves. He had Bobby Brown moves too. Both Josie and Li'l Swag laughed when the song ended.

Swag walked over to Li'l Swag and picked him up. He was grateful that he was in good hands.

"Thank you for finding my son."

Josie laughed. "Actually, he found me. He's a great dancer."

Swag laughed and put down his son. "Come on, man. Let's leave Ms. Josie to her dancing."

"Oh, Daddy, I wanna dance some more. This lady is so much fun. Can I stay? Please." Li'l Swag was cheesing.

Josie giggled.

Swag looked down at his son and was unable to resist his smile. "Okay, you can dance a little more while me and Ms. Josie have a little talk."

"Okay," Li'l Swag said.

Josie put on some more music for the child to enjoy. As he was dancing his little heart out, Swag and Josie sat in chairs. Josie's hair was in a ponytail, and she wore a lyrical dress. He wanted to know if she was all right after not seeing her since her birthday.

"So, are you okay?" he asked.

"Yeah, I'm fine. Why do you ask?"

Swag cleared his throat. "Well, I didn't know you were a virgin at the time. I know that wasn't the way you wanted to lose it. And—"

"Look, Swag, what's done is done, okay? Besides, if we didn't do it, King would've had our necks. I'm trying to get away from here as soon as possible. King is an evil bitch. I didn't see it until now. I just want to get enough money so I can go to Paris and forget this part of my life ever happened. Dance is my life, not being a femme fatale."

Swag was stunned that Josie wanted to get as far away from King as he did. But he also knew that she couldn't pull this off by herself and would need some help.

"Josie."

"Yeah, Swag."

"If you want, I was going to take Li'l Swag up to the beach tomorrow for some more fun. Would you like to join us?"

Josie was stunned at his invitation. She knew Swag was playing with fire, and King would be pissed. King already thought Josie and Swag was a couple. And if she found out about the two of them being together, she'd have them killed.

"Swag, I don't think that's a good idea. May—"

"Look, come on, ma. Live a little bit and let's hang out. You can dance on the beach."

"What about King?"

"Fuck King! Just tell her you're going to the mall or something."

Josie smiled.

"Well, well, well. What's going on here?"

Swag and Josie turned their heads. Their hearts dropped as they saw King in the doorway. Even the music stopped.

"I thought you were looking for the little boy," King said to Swag.

Swag laughed. "Oh, he was in here with Josi—I mean, Josephine. She was showing my son some dance moves."

King chuckled, not giving a shit about Li'l Swag. All she wanted was for Swag to get the hell out of this room and away from Josie. For some strange reason, King was so afraid they would try something behind her back. The way Swag looked at her daughter said everything. King never felt this way about a man since Zeus Santiago. In her mind, she'd lost one man. She wasn't going to lose another one.

"Solomon, let's go. It's almost time for dinner. I want everyone to be clean and dressed."

King pivoted and left the room.

Swag and Josie looked at each other. Josie whispered, "Tomorrow."

Swag nodded.

"Solomon!" King yelled from the hallway. She was ready to claw her nails at him if he didn't come out of Josie's room.

"Coming," he said.

He took Josie's hand and kissed it. After picking up Li'l Swag, he walked toward the door.

"Bye, Ms. Josie." Li'l Swag waved at her.

She waved back, and after they were gone, she thought about her master plan to get away from King. Her plans changed as Swag entered her mind.

That evening after a wonderful meal, King was in her room watching her monitors and checking all the surroundings of her place. She saw that her girls and guys were taking care of their clients. She also checked in on her mother, who was with her latest young man. King shook her head, wishing that Ivy would just find a man her own age and act her age. Then King checked in on Tyler, who was bare-backing Santana and making him scream for God. They were even snorting cocaine in her place, which she hated. She was giving Tyler time to grieve over his brother, but starting tomorrow, she was going to start beating Tyler and Santana's asses for bringing drugs into her palace.

Then she checked in on Josie, who was getting ready for her evening jog. She smiled at her child, but she was pissed off at the interaction Josie and Swag had earlier that day. She played back the footage over and over again and tried to make out their conversation. The music that played was too loud to make out anything. King hated it when she didn't know every little detail going on in her place. She observed how Swag and Josie looked at each other with so much passion. King couldn't get over that Swag never looked at her like that. But then again, King didn't want her hard heart to melt. She didn't want a repeat of what happened between her and the Santiagos again. She couldn't live with more heartbreak.

King cleared her throat and tried to forget about Josie and Swag's encounter from earlier. In her mind, Josie wouldn't dare touch one of her mother's side dishes. King then switched her screen over to Swag's room. Swag was putting the baby in his crib and tucking Li'l Swag in the bed. *So many setbacks,* King thought.

She hated competition, especially when it came to children and Josie. She thought that Swag was losing focus and fear, which all equaled King. She laughed because it was time to switch things up a bit. And as more thoughts came to mind, she reached for her cell phone to text someone. Once she finished, she laughed.

Swag was in his suite, tucking Li'l Swag in bed after putting Namond in his crib. "Good night, Daddy," Li'l Swag said.

"Night, son."

Swag kissed his son's forehead, then walked out of the room, only to be startled by Blood, who was only wearing boxer briefs, and Madam Lourd in her nightgown.

"Blood and Madam Lourd, what's up?"

"King wants to see you right now in her room," Blood said in a dry tone.

"But, but who's goin' to watch the kids? I can't leave—"

"Forget all that! King wants to see you now!"

Mama Lourd stepped up to Swag. "Don't worry, my boy. I'll look after the little darlings." She patted him on his back. "Run along."

Swag didn't want to keep King waiting. He headed out of the room, but not before he and Blood glared at each other.

Swag knocked on King's door.

"Come in!"

He walked into her suite and closed the door behind him.

"Please, sit in the living room and help yourself to a drink. I'll be there in a minute."

"Cool." Swag poured himself a glass of whiskey and relaxed on the sofa. Just after a few sips of the whiskey, King walked out wearing a black lace nightie with her hair hanging down. She looked at the back of Swag's head while holding a switchblade in her hand. She debated on slicing his neck open, but decided against it, knowing that her big master plan was already in play. She put the switchblade on the counter and walked over to him.

"Good evening." King sat down with a flirty smile on her face.

Swag was excited to see her. Her sexiness always made him hard.

"Hey, King. What's up?"

King crossed her legs. "Nothing much. Are you having a great time with your children?"

Her words brought a big smile to Swag's face. "Man, I've been having a blast with my boys. I never thought I would see them again. Seeing them was like Christmas, my birthday, and Thanksgiving, all in one. I thank you for all these precious moments."

And all good moments come to an end, King laughed wickedly.

"What's so funny?"

King cleared her throat. "Nothing." She uncrossed her legs and showed her puss to Swag. "Get on your knees, Solomon."

Because he was ready for more of her, he obeyed.

"Don't just look at it, boy. Thank me. It's time for payment."

While having sex, King's cell phone went off. She could barely reach over to get it, but when she did, she read a message from Blood.

It's done.

King sighed from relief and released the biggest orgasm ever. *No one outshines the King,* she thought.

Chapter 35

Back to Normal

The next morning after a sexy night with King, the sunlight hit Swag. He was in an unfamiliar bed, lying on his stomach, buck naked. His head started to hurt from the scotch he had drunk last night. He used the sheets to cover himself up and lay back on the pillow while thinking about the wild night he and King had.

Within moments, King came into her bedroom with a breakfast tray. She was only wearing a bra and thong with a big Kool-Aid smile on her face.

"You hungry, Solomon? I made you some breakfast."

He stared at her and got excited again. She noticed his hump growing underneath the sheet, but there was no time for what he wanted to do. She placed the tray beside him. He looked at the bacon, eggs, and a Belgian waffle. Li'l Swag loved waffles, and at that very moment, his thoughts shifted to his kids.

"Oh my God! The kids!"

He hopped out of bed and searched for his clothing. He rushed to put them on and ran out of King's suite. When he arrived at his room, he found the bed made up, and the baby crib was gone. Swag was in pure panic mode. He looked all around the suite for his boys, but there was no sign of them.

"Li'l Swag! Namond!"

He rushed down the hallways of the Palace to find his sons. And in King's room, she could see him on the monitors going crazy. She loved to see the fear on his face. It gave her so much power. She figured since Swag's kids were back with their ratchet-ass mother by now, she was glad she was going to be his main focus. She lit another cigarette, proud, again, of what she had accomplished.

Swag continued to look for his boys like a madman. He checked nearly every room. He'd caught many escorts and their clients in uncomfortable situations, and all he could do was apologize. He couldn't rest until he found his sons. He was now on Tyler's and Ivy's floor, still looking for his boys. Ivy, along with her new boy toy, came out of their room, and even Tyler and Santana came out looking at Swag like he'd lost his mind. Swag was sweating all over. That was a huge turn-on for Ivy, who still lusted for him.

"Solomon, darling, what's wrong?" Ivy questioned with concern in her voice.

Swag looked at Ivy, who was wearing a pink silk robe. Her lover was naked. Swag didn't care about any of that. All he wanted to know is if anyone had seen his boys.

"Ivy, have you seen my sons? One—"

"Oh, honey, King sent them back home last night," Ivy said. "Didn't she tell you?"

The words that came out of Ivy's mouth floored him. "What was that?"

Ivy took a deep breath. She hated to repeat herself too. "That li'l jealous bitch of a daughter of mine had Blood take your children back to where they came."

Those words were like bullets that shot through his chest. He couldn't believe King would do something like that to him. Then again, he believed it. He didn't even get a chance to say goodbye or touch them one last time. Swag's whole world crumbled. His sons were the one thing that kept him sane in this place. His heart felt empty. He lowered his head and tried to hold back tears. Flashbacks of memories of his boys flooded his mind.

He walked down the hallway and saw Tyler standing near the doorway to his bedroom.

"Now you see what it feels like to lose someone you love."

Those words caused Swag to stop dead in his tracks. He slowly turned, looking at his former friend and give Tyler an evil glare. "What was that, faggot?"

Tyler laughed and let that word brush off him.

After being and doing Santana for the last few weeks, he was now even more comfortable with his newfound sexuality.

"You heard what I said. You took my brother away from me, and King took your boys back to the States. Now you see what it's like to lose someone you love. Just be lucky they're not dead, cut, or burnt up. You better be glad no one in this hellhole tried to rape your sons or kill their sanity like you did mine."

Swag couldn't believe the words that were coming out of Tyler's mouth. *Did this nigga just say rape? Did he mean that he wanted to rape my kids while they were here?* The entire bull in Swag came out. All he could see was red. Swag understood the pain Tyler felt, but talking about rape and his sons had crossed the line.

Without out any warning, Swag punched the shit out of him. Tyler fell into the door and bumped his head on the floor. Swag punched him repeatedly, breaking his nose and kicking him in his back and stomach.

Santana yelled. "Hey! Get off him!"

Santana wanted to help Tyler, but he was too pretty to have Swag mess up his flawless face. So Santana did what he did best. He ran into the room, got his cell phone, and called security. Within moments, King's security team came up to get Swag off of Tyler.

Swag pushed the security away from him. "Get off me, man! Get off me."

He looked down at Tyler, who was coughing up blood and trying to catch his breath. He pointed his finger at his ex-friend. "You're dead to me!"

Swag stormed away. He was pissed at everything and everyone, especially Tyler and King. He got on the elevator, and once he was on the first floor, he hurried outside and started running. Josie saw him and followed him.

King was in her suite, watching the whole scene. She saw Swag leave the Palace and was almost ready to send her security after him. Eventually, she decided against it and gave him time to calm down. Her cell phone rang. It was Blood calling again.

"Yes."

"It's done. The brats are back in St. Louis."

"Excellent."

Blood cleared his throat.

"Anything else, Blood?" she asked.

"Nope."

"Good. Now hurry back home."

Chapter 36

Getting to Know Ya!

It seemed like hours that Swag was running down the streets of San José, not knowing much about the city or the language. Now, more than ever, he wished he'd learned Spanish a long time ago. After all the running, he stopped, out of breath and sweating. He started to walk and passed by some of the locations King had taken him to. To him, if he weren't on the run, he'd have a real ball in San José.

Within moments, he heard a car horn honk and snapped his head to the side. He assumed King had already sent her goons after him to drag him back to the Palace. But when he looked, he saw a candy-apple-red Lamborghini parked on the other side of the street. The last person he expected to see popped her head out of the window. It was Josie.

"Swag, are you coming over here or what?"

Swag crossed the street and got in the car.

"Ma, is this your car? Did you follow me?"

"Yes and no. The car belongs to Uncle Blood. He'd kill me if he found out I was driving it."

"And you goin' risk your own life?"

"Frankly, I could give a shit right now." She drove off. Swag couldn't believe how well Josie was driving the car.

"So, why did you run off? What's going on?"

Swag scratched his head. He was frustrated. "They're gone."

"Who?"

"My sons. King sent them back to St. Louis. I didn't even get a chance to tell them I love them or goodbye."

"Now that's some coldhearted shit she did."

"No shit."

Josie felt so sorry for Swag. She liked his son, Li'l Swag, who, she believed, had a career in dance. She wanted to make Swag feel better. Then a lightbulb came on in her head, giving her a great idea. She did an illegal U-turn on the street and freaked Swag out.

"Holy shit! What the hell are you doing!" he yelled and held on to his seat belt.

Josie laughed. "It's a surprise."

Swag shook his head and thought about King with her bullshit surprises. Now he wondered what in the hell Josie had in store for him.

They reached an area of San José that looked like the slums of Costa Rica. It kind of reminded Swag of the slums of Rio, where Armand had him and all the fellas hidden for a while until shit cooled off.

They arrived at an abandoned building that looked like it was about to collapse. Josie parked the car and got out. Swag looked at his surroundings. This part of the town looked dirty and forgotten. He was scared to get out of the car, not knowing what was going to happen. Josie tapped on the window.

"Come on! Hurry up!"

He got out and looked around. "What is this place?"

"You'll see."

Josie opened the door to the abandoned building, but Swag was hesitant to enter.

"Swag, are you coming?"

Swag was still near the car. "Are you sure it's safe to go in that building, or is it safe to leave Blood's car out here in this area? If it gets fucked up or stolen, Blood will have your neck—if King doesn't get to it first."

"Don't even worry about that. The car will be fine. Now, come on!"

The only thing Swag could do was take Josie's word for it. He just prayed nothing bad happened to the car—or them—while they were in the building. They went inside. Swag was amazed by what he saw. He thought the old building was run-down with rats everywhere. But it was a semi-decent dance studio with everything any dancer would need. He also noticed kids were stretching and getting ready to dance. Josie smiled and walked over to the children.

"Hola, *chicos* and *chicas*." Josie spoke to the kids in Spanish.

"Hola, Madam Josie!" shouted the students.

Josie took her jacket off and showcased a ballerina outfit. She put her curly hair in a bushy ponytail. She said something else to the kids, and they all looked at Swag and spoke.

"Hola, Señor Swag."

He smiled and waved at the children. Josie had all the children gather around on the dance floor. Swag stood against the brick wall and watched. Before long, they were practicing a dance Josie created. To Swag, the dance looked like something she practiced earlier in the Palace, the first day he arrived. The dance had a mixed African and Haitian flavor to it. Swag loved to see the children dancing and having fun. He especially loved how Josie took the time to help needy children and teach them to dance.

After a while, Swag joined them and had a good time. It was as if his troubles had almost melted away. When class was over, Josie told the children to meet her back there next week, and they left. Now, Swag and Josie were alone.

Swag told her that he admired her for what she was doing for the inner-city youth of San José.

"Thanks. I take some of the money King gives me and use it to do some work on this old dance studio without King's knowledge. I just want these kids to have some type of hope so that they won't be on the streets selling drugs or one day be working for King at the Palace."

Swag nodded his head in agreement with her. At this very moment, he wanted to know everything about Josie. He knew there was more behind her than dance and being the heiress of the Palace. He cleared his throat and held her hand. She searched his eyes.

"So, J, how did you end up with King?"

Josie was in complete shutdown with that question. No one had ever asked her that. "Excuse me?"

"How did you end up with this King chick?"

Josie sighed and let go of his hand. She didn't know what to do. Her heart told her she could trust him with this secret. "Let's sit on the floor. Relax. Because this is a long story."

Chapter 37

Haitian Beauty Secrets

Josie went into one of the closets and pulled out a radio and pushed *play*. The tune that came on was sentimental. She walked over to the middle of the room and stood there. Next, she began to tell her story through dance.

Swag loved her dancing and started to understand her method of storytelling.

Josie remembered her grandmere Dunham and grandmother Marie back in Port-au-Prince, Haiti.

Dunham Depaul, a beautiful, brown-skinned Creole Haitian, was born to an upper-middle-class family. But the one thing that no one could touch her on was her singing voice. Everyone told her that she could've been the Haitian version of singer Lena Horne. Most people put into her head that she was the most people-woman that they ever saw, but it was also her curse, which led her to get raped by her first cousin, Pierre Batiste, at the age of 15.

Swag cried at the thought of any man raping a woman.

Josie continued to dance, telling her family's story and thinking about how Dunham was treated and how she treated her child.

When she told the family about the rape, no one believed her. And to make matters worse, she was pregnant with Pierre's child. Immediately, Dunham wanted to abort the baby because it was a rape child. The family told her she was going to keep the child. And the one thing that made Dunham almost kill herself was they made her marry Pierre. After marriage, her life was pure hell. Her rapist husband would always beat and rape her every day of her life while she was pregnant until she gave birth to a beautiful baby girl, Marie Louise Batiste.

All while Marie was growing up, Dunham called her a rape child and an abomination against nature.

Tears came down Josie's eyes, and the music started to end. She stopped dancing for a minute.

Swag started to get up to console her, but Josie held her hand out, telling him to stay.

He sat.

Then the radio played a jazz tune called "Go Down to New Orleans." Josie wiped her tears and had a big smile on her face. She started to do a jazz routine thinking of Marie and happy times in New Orleans.

So when Marie was 16 and graduated from high school, she went to join her father in New Orleans. Marie went to Central LA Tech Community College and majored in fashion design. If there was one thing she loved, it was clothes. Even when her mother made her wear rags, she, along with her maid, would sew and make Marie her own style of dresses, and that pissed Dunham off even more. When she graduated, Marie tried to sell her designs to local boutiques or to whomever she thought would give her a chance. But in those times, it was hard for a woman to be a designer, especially a woman of color, to make it in America. Marie worked as a seamstress at a local cleaner and was a part-time hostess at a restaurant. Even though she was tired from working all day, she would use her free time to design her own creations. At times, she almost gave up hope . . . until one evening, she was taking a smoke break at her second job, and she got the attention of one man. He told her that he admired her work.

Marie pretended like he didn't exist, but he came around for a few days and introduced himself as Jean Pierre Mereaux, a rich, white Frenchman that promised to back her dreams.

Swag smiled at how happy the performance was.

Josie turned, leaped, turned again, and held herself, thinking of the grandmother's sadness and Jean's betrayal.

Marie believed that their love would be forever . . . until Marie found out she was a few weeks pregnant. Excited, she had a vision that she and Jean would be one big happy family and live happily ever after. But her dream was crushed when Jean told her that he couldn't marry her, mainly, because he was already married with three children back in the south of France.

Marie begged Jean to be with her and their unborn child. He told her that he couldn't, but he asked Marie to be more patient with him and wait until the right time.

Marie agreed to wait for him, but deep down, she knew she was lying to herself. She felt like a fool. She had been lied to and deceived by Jean, a man she loved and put before everything else, even before her designing. Depressed and saddened about raising her child as a single mother, she packed up and took her life's savings and moved back home to Haiti.

The song ended, and Josie dropped to the ground.

Swag looked at her for a moment until Whitney Houston and Mariah Carey's "When You Believe" played.

Josie stood up, thinking about Marie going back to Haiti and her own mother.

When Marie arrived in Haiti, she found that her mother lived in a new home in Pétion-Ville and was now married to a wealthy businessman. At first, Dunham didn't want her rape child and soon-to-be bastard grandchild to mess up her newfound lifestyle or money. Marie had made up lies about being married, and her child's father died in a tragic car accident. Her purpose for coming home was she needed to be with family right now. In Marie's mind, Jean was dead to her, but in the back of her mind, she hoped he'd find her and somehow make things right.

William Joseph, Dunham's new husband, allowed Marie to stay with them for a while. Within months, Marie gave birth to a beautiful baby girl, Mereaux Jean Batiste. Dunham loved her new granddaughter. Mereaux had beautiful, thick, curly hair, soft brown eyes, and she could pass for a white child.

Once Marie was better, she started work as a maid and a seamstress. When Mereaux got a little older, Dunham put her in dance school, and she even became Mereaux's personal vocal coach. Dunham thought since she couldn't live her dream, she might as well live her life through Mereaux.

As time went on, Mereaux became an exquisite dancer, and her singing voice was to perfection. She went on to dance and sing in shows through the Caribbean. Not only was Mereaux a great performer, but she also grew into a beautiful young lady, thanks to Marie, who did her makeup and costumes.

Everyone was so into Mereaux's style. She had the finest fabrics, and all dancers and studios asked Marie if she could design costumes for them. In time, Dunham was impressed by how Marie designed clothes, and she asked her child to design an evening gown for her. In Marie's mind, it was a way to build a mother-daughter relationship—something she always wanted.

By the time Mereaux turned 16, she had excelled as a dancer/singer. She won awards in both the Caribbean and even America. But her mind wasn't always focused on her craft. She had fallen in love with a young man in school named Joseph Mathis.

During her last year of school, Mereaux performed in Miami, Florida, where she, Marie, and Dunham met a white businessman who said he wanted to be Mereaux's manager. He wanted to take Mereaux under his wings and have her travel and dance in places like Paris, Italy, and even Asia.

Mereaux was hyped up and ready to get her career as a performer off the ground. Both her mother and grandmother looked at the sparkle in Mereaux's eyes, but they could tell the man was a con artist right away. They didn't want Mereaux to get her hopes up, only to be let down. They remembered how both their hearts were broken so many times. They didn't want Mereaux to end up the same way. Both women told the man thank you, but no thank you. The man begged them to let him take Mereaux to one of his clients. He'd never seen talent like hers in his years in show business, and he wanted to make her a star. Mereaux believed the man could make her a star, but Marie and Dunham continued to say no.

Mereaux and the man were disappointed. She felt like her mother and grandmother had destroyed her dreams of being a star. Then back in Haiti, Mereaux started to skip dance and voice classes. She began hanging out with Joseph, falling deeper in love with him. He'd gotten a full soccer scholarship to go to St. Louis University in the States, and he wanted Mereaux to go with him. He even asked her to marry him.

Of course, she said yes. And when they graduated from school, the couple eloped to St. Louis, Missouri, which was a huge disappointment to Dunham and Marie.

The music ended, and Josie stopped dancing.

Swag was amazed that Josie's mother went to St. Louis.

Then an instrumental version of rapper Nelly's "Just a Dream" played . . . And Josie started to remember her mother and her asshole father.

Once in America, Mereaux thought her life would be like in the movies, with a good ending, but her journey was far from that. She and Joseph got a small apartment in the city of St. Louis that Mereaux fixed up right away. Joseph spent more time in school or on the soccer field. Mereaux wasn't in school, and not with many skills, other than dancing and singing, she took a job as an exotic dancer. It helped pay the bills since Joseph didn't work. When she had free time, she tried to spend it with Joseph, who was now hardly ever home. And when he was, he was either drunk, bullied her about dancing naked for other men, harassed her for sex or money, and was very abusive.

Josie started to cry again about what her father did to her mother as she let the music take over, thinking of Mereaux's strength as a woman.

Mereaux hoped that things between Joseph and her would get better. She started going to college too. In the daytime, she attended Sanford College for typing and bookkeeping. She didn't want to dance half-naked for old men forever. It was hard trying to go to school and work, but it was all worth it.

Two years later, they both graduated college, and to celebrate, they made love like they never had before. Joseph even told her that he had gotten an offer to play pro-soccer for the New York Red Bulls. She was excited for him, and she told him her good news . . . that she was pregnant. He pretended to be excited, but he wasn't ready to be a daddy. Mereaux asked when they were moving to New York, but Joseph lied and told her he was staying with a friend, and there wasn't enough room for her. He told her to wait for him, and when he had enough money, he'd send for her. Being in love, she believed him.

While Joseph was away, Mereaux saw him on TV. However, he sent her very little money. She still had to work as a dancer just to get by. Months went by, and Joseph no longer called, and he stopped sending money altogether. She had her baby all by herself and named her Josephine Dunham-Marie Batiste. She didn't name her after the child's father, but after St. Louis's own, the first black superstar, Josephine Baker.

Swag's eyes widened in disbelief that Josie was born in his hometown, clearly making her an American citizen.

Josie continued to leap and dance, thinking about her mother leaving America forever.

After the birth of Josephine, Mereaux tried calling and writing Joseph, with no luck. With no other choice, she took all her life's savings and flew to New York. When she located him, she went to his home in Hampton, New York, and found him in bed with another woman. Mereaux hated him and did the only thing the Batiste women knew how to do. She took her last bit of savings and her child and went back home to Haiti. She even changed her last name back to Batiste.

While back in Haiti, she renewed her relationship with her mother and grandmother. Within three years, she reclaimed her love of dancing and started to teach her child. When she heard that her elderly dance teacher was selling her old building, with the little money she had, Mereaux bought the building from her. With money loaned to her by her grandmother and mother, she rebuilt the old studio and started her new career as a dance teacher. She taught and did a little traveling. She taught her child how to dance and told her that she was going to be the next Josephine Baker. Mereaux wanted Josephine to go to Paris one day. The Batiste women looked as if they were going to have a good future . . . but the universe thought otherwise.

The song stopped, and the last song that played for Josie was Maggie Eckford's "Everything Is Lost." Josie had to keep herself in order going back to the day she lost her family forever . . . and how she hooked up with Satan in heels. She let the last memory flood in.

When Josephine was 12 years old, Haiti faced its worst earthquake in years. It destroyed homes, the city, and killed many, including Josephine's family. Her family's home and her mother's studio was gone. She was alone and tried to find ways to survive, like other children that lost their families. Many were even trying to get off the island to start a new life, not realizing some organizations were trying to get the children into sex slavery. Josephine stayed to herself. She didn't trust anyone until she'd met a beautiful woman who had the same complexion as her mother. She was dressed to kill and lovely, like an angel with green eyes. She offered to help Josephine. The woman saw a lot of herself in the brown girl. She could see that Josephine had the potential to be great. Josephine felt a warmness about the woman and took her helping hand. She then asked the woman her name.

"King Kia Costello."

At that time, Josephine saw a woman that would love and take care of her, not knowing that one day, she would have to pay back that kindness.

The song ended, and Josie fell to the ground staying there. No more music played.

Swag stood up and went over to her to see if she was all right.

She sat up and looked at him.

"Are you okay, Josie?" he asked with concern.

Josie nodded. "Yes, I'm fine."

"Wow. And you've been with King ever since?" Swag was amazed at her story.

"Yeah. At first, it was great being with her and Madam Lourd because it filled a hole in my heart where a mother's love should be. They gave me a place to stay, schooling, dance lessons, and whatever else I wanted . . . until now. After the killings, and having sex with her and you, I don't know about this. Plus, taking over the Leopard Clit isn't what I want to do. I want to be able to live out my dream as a dancer or go to Paris to be the next Josephine Baker. King's not my mother, and she's a lying, evil bitch. Now, I want to get away from her. I'm torn between leaving Madam Lourd and the kids, but I have to be happy at the same time."

Swag nodded. "That's true, ma. You have too much talent to let it not be seen by the world."

Josie smiled.

"But you shouldn't leave alone," he said. "How about I go with you just for the company?"

Josie looked at him like he had lost his mind. "Are you serious? King is totally digging you. If she found out that we were in this building together, she'd have Blood kill us both. I don't want her or him to hurt you, and—"

"Look, I don't care about King or that asshole Blood. Where I come from, I'm a soldier, so I ain't never scared." Swag took her hand and held it tightly. "Let's work together and get the fuck out of Costa Rica and go to Paris. I may be on the run, but I want some type of happiness until I get caught. But, Josie, you're a young, beautiful woman, and you deserve to see your dreams come true. I want to see your name in lights. So what do you wanna do? Stay here, or are we goin' work together?"

Josie liked his idea, and since she was going to Paris, she sure could use the company. Hell, they both were going to be like Jay-Z and Beyoncé, "On The Run," but for real. Josie sealed the deal by kissing Swag on his cheek.

"Before we leave," Swag said. "I ask you for one request."

"And what's that?"

He got off the floor and dusted himself off. Then he went over to the boom box and turned on an old Janet Jackson song. He held out his hand to hers.

"Come and dance with me. To confirm that we're equal partners."

Josie laughed as Swag pulled her up. They slow danced to Janet's sultry voice.

The heat between them was powerful. It was a feeling that he was in love that Swag hadn't felt in years. Josie loved Swag's gentle touch, and she knew he was a beast between the sheets. She didn't want to have sex with him. Instead, she wanted them to make love.

They looked into each other's eyes as Janet sang the last verse. Then they kissed passionately. After what was supposed to be one of the worst days of Swag's life, he found happiness in the old building with Josie.

Once they were outside, Swag saw that Blood's car was still out there in one piece. He was relieved.

As they drove back to the Palace, they laughed and talked, not realizing a relationship was growing. When arriving at the Palace, Josie parked the car in the back. She thought she and Swag should enter the Palace separately, not giving King any reason to suspect anything. Swag got out of the car first and walked around to the front door, where Cleo opened it for him. Cleo shook his head, knowing what was up. Minutes later, Josie walked to the door.

"Hey, Mr. Cleo." She kissed him on the cheek.

Cleo smiled and put his hand on her shoulder. "Be careful, baby girl." He winked, and she nodded before walking inside.

"Young fools," he whispered.

Chapter 38

Stir-Crazy

That evening, things started to wind down in the Palace, and soon, everyone was either asleep or clients were getting turned out. During that day, when Swag and Josie had disappeared, King was going stir-crazy, wondering about the whereabouts of her child and future man. Her spies couldn't give her enough information, and they couldn't find taps on either one of them. That pissed King off, and to top off her frustrations, Blood's plane was delayed. He wasn't able to come back for a few days. In her mind, if she wanted shit done right, she had to do it herself. She put on a little makeup and brushed her hair in a sleek ponytail. Then she put on a black lace bra, ripped up booty shorts, and black heels.

She left her room and went over to Swag's room first.

Swag had just gotten out of the shower. He went into the bedroom and didn't pay attention to his surroundings. If he would've, he would've seen King sitting in the recliner, smoking a cigarette.

"Oh, King! It's you. You scared me."

"Good," King said dryly, blowing out the smoke.

She glared at him with her legs wide open. Swag looked at him like the creep keeper's sexy sister. So many things went through his mind. He wondered about her reasons for sending his sons away and if she knew he was with Josie today. He was also concerned that she was planning to kill him.

"Why are you here?" he asked.

She pointed at the edge of the bed. "Sit down."

Instead of sitting on the bed, Swag lay on it.

"Uh, no, playa. It ain't *that* type of party. Sit your ass up! Now!"

Swag didn't want to argue with her, but he did want to know about his sons.

King put the cigarette out and stood up. She stood over him and looked down.

"Solomon, I've been good to you since I saved you from that shithole in Brazil." She paced the floor and kept her eyes on him.

"What is this all about? And where are—"

Before he could say another word, King reached out and slapped the shit out of him. His head snapped to the side, but remaining strong, Swag tried to show no reaction. All he said was, "Damn. Really?"

King attacked him with more words. "Now, when you first met me, I was a straight-to-the-point kind of chick. And I don't like to repeat myself. If you don't want to meet these hands again, please answer the question. Haven't I been good to you?"

Swag rubbed his face and cleared his throat. "You've been really good to me, King. Shit, you gave me my own room, sex anytime I want it, money, making me your new right-hand man in training, and you spared my home-boy's life until Paco killed him. So, yeah, you've been good to me. Thanks, but what happened to my sons?"

King paced back and forth. "Good answer, and we'll talk about your sons when I'm ready. Since I've been so good to you, that makes you loyal to me. And you will be completely honest with me about anything, right?"

Swag shrugged his shoulders. "Yeah, sure, ma. Anything you need to know, I got you."

"Good." King stopped pacing and faced him. "Where have you been all day? I want the truth."

Swag started to sweat. If she had found out that he and Josie were together or in the same room without supervision, King would rip his dick off and grind his balls into salsa. So he did what he did best and put on his best acting performance. He cleared his throat one more time.

"Well, after my boys were sent back without me saying goodbye to them, I was so mad to the point I sucker-punched my ex-friend for saying some slick shit about what he would've done to one of my kids. I was so disgusted that I just ran out because I needed some air. I needed to clear my crazy thoughts, so I went for a long walk. Nothing against you, King, but I was about to lose it."

"Hmm," King looked him up and down. "You were gone all day. What did you do and where did you go?"

Swag chuckled. "To be honest, I don't even know. My mind was so messed up that I wasn't even thinking about where I was. After a few hours alone, I realized I was lost. If it weren't for Josephine finding me and driving me back here, I would still be out there somewhere. I was glad to be back."

"You sure you didn't go anywhere with my child?"

Swag nodded. "After she found me, we had lunch. It was nothing special."

Without her spies on their job, she had to take his word for it. "Okay." She bent over and kissed him. "I believe you, and I'll get you some ice for your face." She went to the door, but before she walked out, she called his name.

"Yes, King."

"Stay away from my child and don't burn me." She closed the door behind her.

Swag took a deep breath and shook his head. All he wanted to know was more information about his sons. But his gut told him not to push King. The timing wasn't right, and he sensed that she was on the verge of losing it.

Even after her interrogation of Swag, she wasn't done. Her next stop was Josie's room.

Josie was sitting at her vanity mirror, wiping off the little bit of makeup she had on. She only had on her nightgown as she brushed her hair. At times, she hated having such long hair. She wished that King would let her cut off just a little bit of it. Her dream was to either rock the famous Halle Berry short cut or a buzz cut like Amber Rose. She knew once she got away from King for good in a few weeks that she would be able to do whatever she wanted. She was tired of being her real-life Barbie doll. As she brushed her hair, she felt warm hands on top of hers. Startled, Josie looked back to see who it was. It was King.

Josie looked at her and displayed a fake smile. "Hey, Mother."

King removed the brush from Josie's hand and started brushing her hair. "Just look at your reflection in the mirror. I got you."

Josie looked at the mirror while King brushed her hair.

"So, how was your day, my child?" King hoped this interrogation would turn out even better than the one she'd had with Swag. In her mind, she thought it was easier to get information out of a woman than it was a man.

Josie knew King's games all too well. "It was okay."

"You were gone most of the day. You even missed training today. How do you expect to be the heiress to my throne if you can't commit? Where were you today?"

Still having her game face on to perfection, Josie was in deep thought until King purposely yanked her hair.

"Ouch!"

"Sorry, sweetie. You had a nasty knot in there."

Josie knew damn well what King was doing. She didn't like waiting for answers.

"So, again, where were you most of the day . . . before I find another knot?" King smiled at Josie's reflection. She could see the fear in her eyes.

Josie coughed and spoke up. "After my morning jog, I wanted to go to the mall. I didn't see anything I liked, so I went for a drive in downtown San José and did some volunteer work. Mainly, I taught some dance skills to some of the poor kids in the area. Just trying to make a difference in their lives."

King continued to read between the lines. She knew there was some truth to what Josie had said, but she was sure there were more pieces to the puzzle than met the eye.

"That's it? The mall and those little bastards in the slums."

Josie hated that King called the children bastards. They lived in the same place she once did.

"Yes."

"So, you didn't see Solomon on your way to do your thing."

Oh my God! Does she know? The kiss? The plans? Josie took a deep breath and thought quickly before King found another so-called knot in her hair.

"Well," Josie cleared her throat. "Excuse me. After I left the mall and the kids, I drove through the city and saw Swa—I mean, Solomon in the downtown area looking sad and crying. I picked him up, and we stopped at a nearby café and talked. He told me his boys were back in the States. We talked a little, and I was able to calm him down. I told him that everything would be okay and warned him not to piss you off." Josie figured that the last comment was the icing on the cake.

"Hmm," King stopped brushing Josie's hair. She put the brush down and rubbed her shoulders and neck. At first, the rubs were soft, but then they turned rough.

"Was that *all* you and Solomon did? Talk and drink coffee? Nothing else happened, right? No hanky-panky or lip-locking, besides that one night?" King began choking Josie. "The last thing I want the heiress to the throne to be is attracted to some man. I want you to be feared, strong, and not afraid of anything."

Josie gagged. She didn't know if King was going to snap her neck or choke her to death. King let her go and swung her around so they could be face-to-face.

"Josephine, I want you to tell me the truth. Did you do anything, no matter how small it is? Did you fuck Solomon today?"

Josie rubbed her throat and coughed a little. "No, Mom, we just talked. That's all, nothing more."

King stared into Josie's eyes. She had to take her word for it. "Okay. Just stay away from Solomon. He's mine." She softly touched her face. "I love you so much. Don't disappoint me." King kissed Josie on her forehead. "Good night, my child."

Josie smiled. "Good night, Mother."

King patted her head and left the room. Once she was gone, the iciness disappeared. Josie took deep breaths. She wiped her face all over again and thought about how fast she needed to get out of there.

King walked down the hallway more pissed off than she was before and ready to kill someone. She was heated about the situation between Swag and Josie. She needed some sweet chocolate to cool her down, so she decided to head on down to Desiree's room.

Chapter 39

Payback Is a Mutha

Tyler and Santana went out on a date that night after all the shit Tyler went through with Swag. In Tyler's mind, it was official that Swag's and his brotherhood and friendship were dead forever. Tyler saw red and wanted complete revenge on Swag for fucking up his life. He wanted to see Swag's blood spill, but he knew that was impossible with Swag being under the protection of King. Tyler knew the only person that could save him was none other than Santana.

After the altercation, Tyler and Santana spent most of the day together. The first thing Santana did to make Tyler better was they had sex. Soon after, both men worked up an appetite, so Santana took Tyler to one of his favorite restaurants where they ate like kings. Also, they went to the beach for some fun in the sun and more sex. They knew people were around, but they didn't care. Then they went to the mall for some new outfits.

When night settled in, Santana took Tyler to The Dungeon, one of the hottest gay clubs in San José where anything and everything went down . . . from dancing, drugs, to everyone having sex in the bathroom or club basement. People got their freak on. The music was lit. It was Tyler's first time in a gay club, but he was going to hang with the best of them. He was still trying to get used to what he and Santana were doing with each other.

He wasn't fully ready to accept the fact that he was a gay man. He still believed that he was bisexual and found women as desirable as a man. Santana, on the other hand, just took it one day at a time with Tyler. They spent half of the night dancing, tonguing each other down, snorting cocaine, and drinking.

Tyler stopped dancing for a moment and went into the bathroom. Once there, he saw a man suck another man off. In the past, he would've gotten turned on, but he had to take a leak. Once he was done relieving himself, he went to the sink and checked out his reflection in the mirror. He looked at his bruised cheek. All his thoughts went back to the events that happened earlier between Swag and him. He hated thinking about him. In his mind, Swag had died and gone straight to hell. Only two things would give him complete sanity for all the shit he'd been through: One, get the hell out of Costa Rica, and two, see Swag's head on a silver platter.

After he washed his hands, he went to the booth Santana had reserved for them. Santana snapped his fingers to the music while snorting cocaine on the table. He and Tyler were full-blown cokeheads, but it was all about celebrating that night. Santana knew Tyler was hurting from his losses, but in Santana's mind, it was like, damn. He figured if he were going to keep supplying this sweet cocaine to Tyler, he needed to start kicking in. The shit was expensive, but for the time being, Santana just loved having the guy of his dreams by his side.

Now that Santana had his prince beside him, the other thing he wanted was his own empire. Santana was tired of living in the shadow of his big half-sister.

Tyler stopped snorting and had a sad look on his face, which caught Santana's eye. He tapped Tyler's shoulder, which startled him. Being around King, her goons, and Blood for so long made Tyler jumpy.

"San, you scared me."

"Sorry about that, bae. What's up with you? You okay?"

"Yeah, I'm good," Tyler said, lowering his head.

Santana lifted his chin. "What's up?"

"Nothin', man. Just thinking about my brother. I miss his ass so much."

Santana sometimes envied the relationship Tyler once had with his twin. Tyler told Santana stories at night about him and Travis growing up. Santana had always wanted that sibling bond with King, but she hated him, mainly because of his father. If it weren't for the love of his mother and Madam Lourd, he would've killed his sister a long time ago. He had a feeling she had her hand in his dad's death. In Santana's mind, King was beginning to lose her way as a ruler. It was time for a new emperor of Costa Rica, and that was him. Santana was working on new ways to build his upcoming kingdom. He worked with an up-and-coming drug dealer that sold good-ass dope. He hated that King let all that good drug money slip on by. If she hadn't, she'd have more money than God. In Santana's eyes, it was the dawn of a new era, and all the competitors saw it. King was so wrapped up in Swag and Josie that she didn't realize that she was breaking her own rule: Love was weak. Santana believed it was finally the right time to make his move.

He continued to chill and wait for the big puzzle for tonight's outing. He took a sip of his drink and looked over at Tyler, who went back to snorting.

"You need to slow down on that shit," Santana said.

Tyler wiped the tip of his nose. "Man, I can handle this. I've been doing shit like this since I was in middle school. I got this."

Santana took his hand. "Just chill on that shit, man. I brought you here to take care of this business. You want revenge on that bastard Swag, right?"

Coldness was trapped in Tyler's eyes. Just thinking or hearing about that dude pissed him off all over again. He was even pissed at himself that he'd let his guard down and had gotten his ass kicked. Tyler had erased every good memory of Swag and him.

"Fuck, yeah, I want revenge on that son of a bitch. When the time is right, his ass is mine." Tyler punched the table.

Now, that's *the man I fell in love with,* Santana thought.

"So, San, how are we goin' to do that?"

"You'll see."

As the night went on, the music in the club got louder. The dance floor was packed. Suddenly, out of nowhere, a very special guest came to their booth.

Santana shook his hand. "What's good, Blake?"

"What's up, li'l brother?" he said.

Tyler's eyes widened. He couldn't believe Blood was in their booth.

He looked at Tyler with disgust, mainly because he couldn't stand Swag. Also, he didn't like fruity-ass men, and he couldn't believe how Tyler turned gay overnight. Blood didn't know what kind of spell Santana put on these straight guys, but Blood was just glad his black magic didn't work on him. He hated being in a gay club, especially when King wanted to go to get action or turn one of the boys out. For him, though, it was a good meeting place because King thought he was still stuck in the States. Blood looked at Santana.

"San, what's *he* doing here? This is supposed to be a business meeting."

"Don't worry. He's cool."

"I don't know, San. I don't trust your newest boy toy like I don't trust Swag's bitch ass."

"Seems like we got more in common than you think," Tyler said.

Both Blood and Santana looked at him.

"I want that fucker to pay for what he's done to my family and me. I want his head on a silver platter so badly I can taste it."

Blood's frown turned into a big smile. This even brought a smile to Santana's face as well.

"Please, Blake, sit down."

Blood was glad to sit. He got tired of all the dudes looking at his ass and calling him daddy or DILF.

"So, what's the deal, Blood? Is it still on?" Santana asked.

"Yeah, it will go down in a few days."

"What's going down in a few days?" Tyler asked, curious.

Not wanting to leave his man in the dark, Santana replied, "The Destruction of King Kia Costello."

Tyler almost choked on his drink. "What? King? Are you insane? She'll kill you. Why?"

"Because she's a bitch and slowly losing her mind. I think the Leopard Clit needs some newer and younger blood to be in charge of it. And that someone is me." Santana pointed at himself.

Tyler didn't know that Santana had so much hatred for King—his own sister. He looked at Blood.

"And *you?* I thought you were King's number one guy. What's your part in all this?"

Blood cleared his throat. "Don't worry 'bout that. I have my reasons, boy. Just keep suckin' off Santana, and you'll see what'll go down."

Blood hoped with this plan that King would have no one to run to but him. And that Swag would be completely out of the picture.

Tyler felt like he was in the crime version of *The Twilight Zone*. He just sat back and let Santana handle shit like a true future boss.

Chapter 40

Change Goin' Come

Things around the Palace seemed to be normal for the past few days. The girls and guys were continuing to make that money for King.

Blood had finally gotten back in town, even though he had been there all this time without King knowing it. He continued to train Swag. King was still training Josie—sometimes, keeping her longer so she wouldn't see Swag.

The only time Josie and Swag saw each other was either at breakfast or dinner. They still weren't able to talk about their plan to get away from King.

King was content with her plan. She hoped with the loss of Tyler's friendship, Swag's sons gone, and him not being able to talk to Josie, he'd come to her more often. But there was a major event coming that would change King's life forever.

Chapter 41

Queen Mother

One night at dinner in the dining room, everyone was dressed to kill. The color theme for dinner was white and gold, making everyone feel like royalty. The feast on the table was like a Thanksgiving feast in Swag's eyes. But his eyes were on Josie, and he tried to avoid eye contact with King. King enjoyed the feast. She didn't seem to have a worry in the world because she ruled the world and was on the verge of having the man she wanted.

Ivy was busy flirting with her new young boo thing. King shook her head at her mother's nasty display, and then shifted her eyes to Madam Lourd, who had barely touched her meal. King also noticed that Madam Lourd appeared very sleepy, and she kept rubbing her chest. Madam Lourd was even coughing more than usual. King kept asking if she were okay, and Madam Lourd said she was fine.

Madam Lourd didn't want her baby to know about her illness, even though she felt herself getting weaker by the minute. She could tell she was losing her fight with cancer. Even though today was the worst day ever, she still looked beautiful at dinner. Her MAC makeup was on point, and she wore an all-white suit with a sleeveless leopard shirt. She accessorized it with gold and diamond jewelry, and to top off her look, she wore a black Afro wig. Not feeling hungry, Madam Lourd excused herself from the table.

"I'm going to retire to my quarters for the evening."
King nodded.

As Madam Lourd got up from the table with her cane, she started to stumble.

Everyone was stunned and stood to help her.

"Madam Lourd, sit down. Are you dizzy?" King asked fearfully. She sensed something was very wrong, but Madam Lourd blew her off.

"I . . . I'm fine. Enjoy your din—" She paused and rubbed her head. Of course, she felt dizzy, and it wasn't long before she hit the floor and passed out.

"Oh shit!" someone shouted.

"Hurry! Get her some help!" another person yelled.

King rushed to Madam Lourd's side. "Madam Lourd! Madam Lourd! Wake up! Wake up!" King yelled for someone to call an ambulance right away.

Blood reached for his phone and called the doctor. King looked at Madam Lourd with Ivy by her side. "Come on, Madam Lourd, stay with us. Help is on the way."

Madam Lourd continued to cough up blood. She tried her best to hold on.

At Clinica Biblica Hospital, King made sure Madam Lourd had a private room and fixed it according to Madam Lourd's style. King, Ivy, and Blood looked at Madam Lourd lying down in the bed. She was knocked out with tubes and IVs in her mouth, arms, and nose. It was the first time King looked at Madam Lourd and realized how old her adopted grandmother had become. By King being around her for so long, she never paid attention to her looks. The person she was looking at now . . . She didn't know who this woman was without the makeup and wigs. She noticed the wrinkles on her face and saw she was utterly bald. King wanted to know

who this old woman was and what had happened to
Madam Lourd.

After hours of waiting, the doctor finally came into the
room. Everyone stood up and rushed to him. The doctor
felt uncomfortable, so he slowly backed up.

The doctor was a brown-skinned, middle-aged man.
He smiled at everyone. "Good evening, everyone. I'm
Dr. Garcia." He shook their hands. "Who are you to Ms.
Lourd?"

"I'm her child, Ivy," Ivy said softly. She was still shocked
by what happened to Madam Lourd earlier.

King looked at Ivy with a twisted face. "I'm her grandchild, King Kia Costello."

"I'm just a good friend of the family," Blood added.

"Enough of the intros, Dr. Garcia. What is going on
with Madam Lourd? Is she going to be okay?" King
wanted answers.

Dr. Garcia took a deep breath. "Family, you may want
to sit down."

King knew when the doctor said that, it meant matters
were getting worse. So while Ivy and Blood sat down, she
remained standing tall.

The doctor looked over at King, "Ms. Costello—"

"King will be fine. And I prefer to stand. Now, tell
us what's going on with my grandmother." King's real
emotions were boiling inside of her.

Dr. Garcia knew damn well who King was, so he
quickly spoke up. "Well, after testing, we find that Ms.
Lourd isn't doing so well. It seems that her stage three
breast cancer has worsened to stage four. I—"

"What? Wait. Breast cancer? Are you serious? Breast
cancer? No, no, no. Madam Lourd can't have that." King
was lost and confused.

Dr. Garcia nodded. "Yes, she's had it for quite some
time. She didn't tell any of you at all?"

King, Ivy, and Blood looked like total idiots in the room. None of them knew what was going on with Madam Lourd. There weren't any signs in the beginning that she was an unhealthy woman. She always exercised and ate right to keep her tight body fit for a woman her age. Then King started to remember the coughs, Madam Lourd touching her chest, her feeling so tired that sometimes she would stay in her room for three days or more.

"How could I have missed this?" King mumbled and felt like she was slipping.

Ivy started to cry. "No, she didn't say anything to me or any of us at all." She cried even harder and covered her face.

Blood consoled her. She started to shake. King rolled her eyes at her mother, whom she thought was so weak. She hated to see tears unless they were from someone she was killing or fucking. She looked back at Dr. Garcia with her signature straight face and was ready to take care of business. Inside, though, she wanted to break down and cry like her mother.

"Doctor, how has Madam Lourd been hiding her cancer for so long without showing any signs until tonight?"

"Well, Ms. Lourd decided not to go through chemo or have a mastectomy. Her physician gave her morphine, and while conducting tests on her, we detected cocaine in her system. She must have been using these treatments to ease the pain. It worked for a while, but after we did more tests, we found that cancer had spread to her liver, stomach, and lungs."

King couldn't believe that Madam Lourd's cancer was so serious. She looked down at Madam Lourd. *Why didn't you tell us anything?*

King finally realized why. She knew Madam Lourd was a woman full of too much pride and too much into her looks. Madam Lourd never wanted anyone to worry about her.

King looked back at Dr. Garcia. "Okay, Doctor, how much?"

"What do you mean, King?"

"I only want the best doctors for Madam Lourd, to keep her alive. Whatever it'll cost, I got it. So, where do we go from here?"

"King . . ." Dr. Garcia paused. He could tell everyone in the room loved Madam Lourd. He knew what he was going to say to them next would change their lives forever. He took another deep breath and put his hand on King's shoulder. "King."

"Please take your hand off me and answer my question."

"Sorry." He straightened his tie. "Ms. Lourd only has a few days left to live. The only thing we can do is make her as comfortable as possible."

Everyone just stopped upon hearing the doctor's words, and a chill came over the room. They looked at Dr. Garcia like he had stabbed their hearts with a sword.

"No, no, Doctor. Not Madam Lourd. Not Madam Lourd!" Ivy shouted and moved away from Blood. She ran up to Dr. Garcia. "There has to be *something* you and your team can do. Like my daughter said, we can pay for the best doctors in the world. You have to keep her alive. Please!" The last thing Ivy wanted to do was lose the one woman who was a real mother to her. In her eyes, Madam Lourd was the glue that kept the Palace together. "Please!"

"Ms. Ivy, I'm sorry for the pain you and your family are going through. But it's out of our hands. The only thing we can do is make Ms. Lourd as comfortable as we can."

Ivy broke down, and Blood rushed to her side again. He looked at King, who still had no emotion on her face. He wished it were King that he was holding, not

Ivy's cougar ass. But he didn't have much to worry about, knowing that once his plan was carried out, King would be eating out of the palm of his hand. His focus went back to Ivy.

"Shh, Ivy, it'll be fine. Come out of the room for a while." He looked at King. "I got her."

King nodded and watched as Blood and Ivy left the room. That left her, Madam Lourd, and Dr. Garcia alone.

"So there's nothing that can be done, Doctor? Are you sure?"

"Positive."

"Okay." King reached into her Gucci purse and pulled out $20,000. "Make sure she is very comfortable and redo this room within the next twenty-four hours. I want the room styled in old Hollywood, glam mixed with chic." She gave the doctor the money.

Dr. Garcia nodded.

"And one more thing, Doctor. I want her talking in a few days. Is that clear?"

"Ms.—"

Without warning, King took her long nails and scratched him on his right cheek.

Dr. Garcia held his face and looked at her as if she were crazy.

"Is . . . that . . . clear?"

"Yes."

"Good." King looked at Madam Lourd, then back at the doctor. "Talk to you soon, Doctor." After that, she left the room.

She walked over to the waiting room and saw that Ivy had calmed down. So had Blood. They both stood up.

"You okay, King?" Blood asked.

"Yeah, I'm good. I'm ready to go home."

"Me too," Ivy said, still shocked and tired.

King flicked her hair back. "Okay, but first I have to go to the restroom."

She walked off and went into one of the private restrooms, making sure the door was locked. She looked at herself in the mirror. Visions of Madam Lourd flooded her mind . . . All good memories of Madam Lourd teaching her everything and loving her unconditionally. Now, part of the love she had next to the Santiagos was dying, and it was one thing she couldn't fix. After thinking of today's events, tears rushed to King's eyes, and she broke down crying. She fell to one knee and felt as if her world were crumbling in front of her. She hated feeling weak, but at this point, she didn't give a damn. *Madam Lourd. Queen Mother . . .*

Chapter 42

Timing

For the next few days, things around the Palace were crazy. King, Ivy, and Blood spent a lot of time at the hospital every day, making it their second home. They wanted Madam Lourd's last few days on this earth to be as pleasant as possible. No one in the Palace could believe what was happening to Madam Lourd. She was like a surrogate grandmother and aunt to all the escorts in the Palace. They all prayed that she'd get better quickly. And even without King's presence, the escorts continued to work on their clients in honor of Madam Lourd.

With King being more at the hospital and not taking care of her affairs, she had Blood handle her business, which he did with pleasure. It gave Blood, Blood's business partners, and Santana time to organize their plans to bring down King, once and for all. He even loved the state she was in over Madam Lourd. Though King didn't show it, he knew she was going to flip out over Madam Lourd's death. And she would run into his arms, and he would be her Superman.

Not only were Blood and Santana plotting against King, but also it gave Swag and Josie time to formulate their plan to escape. They spent days planning every little detail down to the day they intended to run, how they would arrange it, and discussed what they would do for money. Josie had that all handled.

With King gone, she had stolen some of Madam Lourd's jewelry, King's jewelry, and Josie took some of hers that had been gifted to her. She even had some of King's bank account numbers. In one of the accounts, she found $50 million. She created a new bank account under a fake name in Paris, France, and had the money transferred over there. Swag couldn't believe that Josie was so sheisty, but then again, he could believe it by her being around King for so many years. So, of course, Josie was going to pick up a few tricks from the crime trade.

Without King guarding them, Swag and Josie got to know each other even better. They'd spent many breakfasts and dinners alone, enjoying each other's company and getting closer by the day. Everyone seemed to go their separate ways. Even Santana and Tyler hadn't been seen in days. It worried Swag that everything seemed to be going so smoothly, but he still kept a positive mind, believing that he and Josie would have their happily ever after.

Chapter 43

More Changes Are Coming

Swag and Josie were in his room, a place they'd been all day since King was at the hospital with Madam Lourd. They could also relax and sneak a kiss without King knowing.

They talked as they listened to music and played gin rummy. They discussed their plan to leave within twenty-four hours. Josie had everything set up from the airplane tickets to their fake passports, and the stolen goods she had hidden in her dance studio, along with her cat. She was scared shitless and didn't know what the outcome would be. Nevertheless, she was excited that she was going to the place her grandmother and mother had wanted to go for many years. She was glad to say she was the next generation that was going to Europe to be a star. Swag looked over at Josie and could tell her mind was in another place. He couldn't blame her because they both were about to escape this nightmare.

"Ma, you good?" Swag asked.

Josie snapped out of her trance and looked at him. "Yes, Swag. I'm just excited and nervous that I'm finally leaving this beautiful nightmare and that I'm finally going to be living my own life. No more blood, pain, drama, or King."

Swag felt her on that one. "True."

He put his hand on her thigh. Josie loved Swag's soft, tender touch. She loved her idol, Josephine Baker, but she knew she wasn't bisexual. Even after the night with Swag and King, she wasn't into chicks. Josie was strictly dickly and loved the touch of a man. She started to get turned on by Swag's touch and shot him a seductive smile.

Swag chuckled. "What's that smile about, baby girl?"

She leaned in to kiss him and put her hand on his jock. Swag was all for it. Josie turned him on, and he was ready for a do-over.

"Swag, this is our last night in this house. I want to make the most of it."

"How's that?"

"I want you to make love to me. Right here and right now."

Swag swallowed the lump in his throat. "Now?"

"Yes. I want you to make love to me now. I ain't on no lesbian shit like on my birthday. I'm strictly for the beef. I want you not to fuck me, but make love to me. Make me feel good."

Swag was in a loop because he hadn't made love to a woman since Zaria—when they were on good terms. All he'd done to females was screw them and got out. The other worry was his suite was next to King's and across from Blood's room. Either one or both could catch them in action and kill them. He brushed off his worries and said, "Fuck it."

It was their last night in San José, Costa Rica, and what better parting gift to give King and Blood than the smell of their lovemaking. They kissed, fell back on the bed, and were ready to get it in.

If Josie and Swag only knew that Blood was outside in an unmarked car, watching all the footage, giggling, waiting for the shit to hit the fan—and was ready for his game plan to begin.

At the hospital, Madam Lourd was in the final moments of her life. The tubes were out of her mouth. She opened her eyes, looked over at Ivy and King, and tried to stay awake. But at this point, she was tired of suffering and wanted it all to end. Her eyes shifted around the room that was almost identical to her apartment back in the Palace. King could tell Madam Lourd was happy. She looked at King, held out her hand, and painfully cleared her throat.

King rushed over and took her hand. "Do you need your doctor?"

"No, no, child. I just want to look at you for one last time." Madam Lourd touched the side of her smooth face.

To King, her hands felt like icicles. But she was going to make the best of every moment she spent with her grandmother. "Madam?"

"Yes."

A tear rolled down her face—something she always tried to hold back since she was a kid. King turned her head, but Madam Lourd turned her face and made her look at her.

"It's okay. Let them flow. This is the most beautiful I've seen you in a long time." Madam Lourd didn't see her as King, but as the child she once was.

"I love you, Grandma, or should I say, Mother? Because that's what you were."

Madam Lourd chuckled. "I love you too, child. Be careful and stay hardhearted."

King closed her eyes and let the tears come down. She felt Madam Lourd's hand fall. The machine's lifeline was flat. Madam Lourd was no longer part of this world. And out of nowhere, King's screams filled the room. It woke up Ivy and the entire floor.

Ivy rushed over to Madam Lourd's bed and couldn't believe her mother and mentor was dead and gone. Ivy, along with her child, screamed and cried hysterically until the doctor rushed in.

After almost two hours of screaming, crying, and hugging, King and Ivy got themselves together and left the hospital. They took the car back to the Palace, but not with their greatest treasure. King needed to take a nap and a Xanax. She tried to call Blood, but he wasn't picking up. She even tried calling Santana, but he didn't pick up either. She figured he was somewhere sucking off Tyler. Still, she couldn't believe this shit. The main person she needed the most had gone ghost on her. She didn't want to look like a punk when she went back to the Palace, so she wiped away all the tears and tried to fix her makeup.

While on the ride to the Palace, Ivy's cell phone rang. King looked at her, hoping it was Blood or Santana.

"Hello," Ivy said with a concerned look on her face. "Yeah, uh, okay. See you soon." She hung up and put her phone back in her bag.

King looked at her mother with suspicion. "Who was that? Blood or Santana?"

Ivy was a nervous wreck. Not only did she have to deal with the loss of Madam Lourd, but also her crazy-ass daughter and the call. She was rattled, but she remained calm.

"That was one of my little toys who's in town and wants to meet up. To be honest, after all of this, my kitty kat needs some relief today."

King winced and looked at her with disgust. She thought that after Madam Lourd's death, Ivy would start acting like the real mother she needed. To King, her mother was always going to be 16 in her mind and chasing after the youth she was never going to reclaim again.

When they finally reached the Palace, the driver opened the door for them. King got out and looked back at her mother. "Are you coming, Ivy?"

Ivy cleared her throat and was nervous as shit. "No, I'm going to go to the mall and get me a nice outfit. Maybe even get my face beat. I'll be back soon."

King just shook her head and sighed. "Okay, have a good time."

Ivy chuckled. "I always do. I love you, King."

King's facial expression changed. It was the first time in years that she'd heard her mother say those words. But being the emotionally unavailable chick that King was, she turned and headed to the door.

Ivy looked at the driver who closed the door. She whispered, "Goodbye, my child."

As the car sped away, Cleo opened the door for King.

"Thank you, Cleo," King said.

He could tell by the look on her face that Madam Lourd was gone. A tear slid down his face. King patted him on his back before going inside. Things inside looked as if it were business as usual in the Palace. Her girls and guys were fulfilling their clients' wildest fantasies. Watching all this eroticism was getting King turned on and almost making her forget about the passing of Madam Lourd. King was moist between the legs, especially after she saw one of her celebrity clients, a basketball icon with a few businesses under his belt, getting dicked down by a transgender escort. King smiled for two reasons. One, thinking if only the media knew about this American sports hero, and two, this scene was totally turning her on. King looked at the transwoman's penis and needed some dick. She needed some type of relief, after what she'd been through the last few days. She wanted Swag inside of her. He was the closest she was going to get to Zeus Santiago, so she got on the elevator to get her future man.

"Aaah, yes, yessss, Swag," Josie crooned as Swag was inside of her. He took his time with Josie and didn't want to go porn star on her like he'd done on her birthday. He wanted to feel her on a physical *and* mental level. As they made love, they felt like one. They were wrapped in each other's arms with sweat raining down their bodies.

As soon as she got off the elevator, King smelled a funky scent. She looked at Blood's and Swag's doors, wondering which one of them was having sex. She figured it was Blood. After all, it couldn't have been Swag. Just to be sure, though, she went into her room and looked at the monitor. There was no sign of Blood in his room, so she turned on the one in Swag's room. What she saw put a sour taste in her mouth. At first, she thought her eyes were playing tricks on her, but the realization came when she saw Swag and Josie in the room next to her making love. King's heart stopped beating for a moment. She was enraged and couldn't stop gritting her teeth. She pounded her fist on the table as her thoughts flew all over the place.

Those bitches. All the lies and the deceit. I knew it! I knew it! They waited for me to leave to make their move. King's face appeared distorted, she was so mad. *Why does he even want her? He could've had me! Someone sexy and powerful. That little bitch, Josie. I took her out of Haiti and gave her the life of a princess. And this is how she repays me? To think I was going to give this little backstabbing bitch my empire. I should've brought her up and made her a slut like she is.*

King's thoughts were everywhere. She had been through too much today, and this betrayal was the last straw. Now, all her plans with Swag had gone to shit. At first, King wanted a good dick down, but now, all she wanted was the taste of her favorite treat: blood. King wanted to cut, slice, and stab them both. She wanted to eat their organs and swim in their blood to absorb their energy. She snatched her drawer open and pulled out her gold gun and old switchblade.

"Somebody's about to die," she said, storming out of the room. She was ready to create a massacre that the Palace would never forget. "No one fucks with the king—ever!"

After their lovemaking session and not aware of what was coming their way, Swag and Josie held each other's sweaty bodies. They were relieved, and their emotions were everywhere. Swag felt like a teenager again who had just lost his virginity to his sweetheart. Even Josie felt like she'd lost her virginity again, but this time, the right way. She felt so connected to Swag, more than ever. And she was even happier than ever that she was running away with him to Paris. They looked into each other's eyes and smiled.

"I love you, Josie," Swag said, kissing the tip of her nose.

Josie got bright-eyed and giggled. "I—"

Her words were cut off when a gun went off. Both of them jumped up with huge eyes. They saw King standing in front of them with the golden gun pointed at the ceiling.

King's eyes stayed glued on them. They couldn't believe they didn't hear her coming. She'd sneaked in on them like the leopard she was. She put on her Miss America smile and questioned Josie.

"Didn't I always tell you it's better to be feared than loved, my child?"

Josie's heart was beating fast. She was speechless, so Swag cleared his throat and answered for her.

"King, baby, this ain't what it looks like." He tried to work his charm on her as he got out of the bed. But before he could make another move, King pointed her gun at him.

"Get your ass back in the bed." She pointed the gun at the wall next to him and shot a hole in it. Swag hurried back in the bed and kept his mouth shut.

King paced the room without taking her eyes off them. She wanted to vomit at the sight of these lovebirds.

"You lying, sick muthafuckas. After all I've done for both of you, *this* is how I'm repaid? Fucking behind my back, even after I told you two to stay away from each other."

"Ma, I mean, King, we're not toys you can play with and put back on the shelf. We're people, and we do what we want!" Josie shouted and stood up to King for the first time.

King mean mugged her while waving the gun around. "So, it's King now, is it? Not the mother that loved and raised you like you were my own?" King pointed the gun at Josie, but she ducked. "Another thing, you little bitch. You're whatever the fuck I want you to be. And what I want you to be now is dead."

King cocked her gun, but with quick thinking, Swag took one of the pillows and threw it at her. She dropped the gun. It went off and put a hole in the closet.

"Run, Josie! Run!" Swag yelled.

Josie snatched the covers off and ran toward the door. King stopped her with a switchblade in her hand. King wanted to slice up Josie's pretty little face. She waved the switchblade around, toying with her.

"Come on, you little bitch."

"Fuck you!" Josie stood her ground, but she was still scared.

King tried to tackle her but failed on her first attempt.

"Run, Josie! Run! I'll join you later! Run now!" Swag yelled.

Josie snatched up Swag's long T-shirt and ran out of the room. Once she was outside in the hall, she rushed to the elevator, hoping it would quickly open. Tears streamed down her face. She was scared and happy all at the same time. She was finally going to get her rightful freedom. And when she reached the first floor, she ran like a madwoman with her hair flying all over her head. The escorts and clients didn't know who the hell she was. They figured she was a maid and paid her no mind. Once she was outside, she ran to Cleo for help.

"If you wanna live, child, I suggest you run now! If she asks, I'll lie. Now, go!" shouted Cleo.

Josie kissed him on his cheek. "Goodbye, Mr. Cleo."

Cleo smiled. "If you're going, then go, child."

Josie ran into the streets of San José. She felt like a heavy weight had been lifted off her shoulders as she ran and tried to make it to her building. In her mind, if Swag didn't make it to the location within twenty-four hours, she had to start her new life without him.

She never noticed the black limo in which Blood sat watching the whole ordeal and looking at Josie run toward the direction of her building to collect her things. He smiled, knowing that his "niece" was able to escape.

Good luck, girl, he thought. He then took out his phone and dialed.

"Yeah," said a deep voice.

"It's time!" shouted Blood as he hung up. He smiled, knowing that his plan was coming to full circle.

Meanwhile, back at the Palace, Swag and King were on the floor fighting their battle to the death. Swag was on top of her, trying to keep her hands down. But King wasn't no punk. She wasn't giving up without a fight. The leopard inside of her took over. She saw the switchblade to her left and scrambled to get it. After she got it, she sliced it across the right side of Swag's face, barely missing his eye.

"Ah, shit!" Swag shouted and released her.

King used his moment of weakness to knee him in his nut sack.

"Fuuuuck!" Swag grabbed his balls and fell over her. She pushed him off her and felt undefeated as Swag yelled and cried in pain.

King got up and watched him squirm on the floor. *What a little bitch,* she thought. *What in the hell was I thinking of letting this American rule beside me?*

She hated to say it, but Blood was right about Swag. He sure wasn't Zeus Santiago. All she saw on the floor was a weak-ass, lame, nickel-and-dime boy, which in King's mind, wasn't a cute look. He was just another piece of shit.

King wanted to take her switchblade and cut up Swag's entire body. But she was enjoying seeing him writhe in pain. She laughed and searched the floor for her gun. She hurried over to get it and aimed it at him.

"Turn your ass over!"

Swag was in too much pain to obey. King fired twice into the ceiling and repeated herself. "I said, turn your ass over."

Swag slowly turned on his back. His face was very bloody, and his balls hurt like hell. He looked at King. He didn't see the sexy woman he'd first met on the ship that had spared Travis's life. He was now looking at a beast. Her hair was all over the place, her shirt was damn near ripped off, exposing her bra, and her thick thighs and legs were red. She looked like an urban Amazon woman.

King's emotions were mixed with hurt and hate. After the loss of Madam Lourd, she thought Swag would be the cure to take some of the pain away. She also couldn't believe that she would go this deep for a man. She'd broken her own rule: never fall in love.

She pointed the gun at him. "Any last words, muthafucka, before I blow you to hell?"

Swag looked at her like the natural-born savage he was. Shit, he didn't care if he lived or died anymore. He'd lost enough already, and all he cared about was that his sons made better decisions than he had and that Josie was free and happy to follow her dreams as a prima ballerina. Swag smiled at her. He was a soldier and was never scared.

"Fuck you, King! Fuck you, bitch! Go ahead and kill me. I've seen everything except Christ."

That angered King. She finally saw Swag's true colors. He was a no-good-ass American nigga.

"You stupid piece of shit." She twisted her lips as she cocked the gun. "You could've had a future."

As she was about to pull the trigger, the police and FBI swarmed into the room and pointed their guns at both of them.

"Put the gun down, Ms. Costello! Now!" shouted one of the FBI agents.

King was shocked but kept her composure. She wasn't one of those insane criminals who was going out in a blaze of glory. In her mind, these agents weren't going to shoot up her beautiful body with bullets. She smiled at them seductively.

"All right." She slowly lowered the gun to the floor and stood up straight.

"Now, back away from the weapon and put your hands in the air!" yelled the police officer.

King did as she was told. One of the officers cuffed her. She blew him a kiss.

"Hello, Alfred," she chuckled. "Are you here for business or pleasure?"

The officer was one of her many clients. Almost every year, he spent his Christmas bonus for one night of pleasure with her girls.

He mean-mugged her. "Shut up, bitch! You're under arrest. Now, let's go!"

He escorted her out of the room. She looked at Swag and mouthed, "It ain't over, bitch."

Once King and the officer exited the room, Swag sighed from relief. He had never been happier in his life to see the police. He was still a wanted fugitive, but that was better than being dead.

Two big FBI agents picked him up and questioned him. "Solomon Carter, better known on the streets as Swag, right?"

At first, he was going to lie, but he wanted to come clean so that he could face the next journey in his life. Swag nodded. "Yes."

"Do you know how much trouble you're in?"

Swag shamefully lowered his head.

"Solomon Carter, you're under arrest for drug trafficking, murder, and kidnapping. Take him away, boys."

The agents handcuffed Swag and walked him through the Palace. They raided the place, and with so much chaos going on, people were crying and confused. Once Swag was downstairs, the agents escorted him out to the

SWAT car. But before he got into the car, he saw a cop car driving off with King in it. Swag smiled and shouted, "Free at last! Free at last! Thank God almighty, I'm free at last!"

"Shut up, punk, and get your naked ass in the car. We got a long flight!"

Swag didn't care where he was going as long as he was free from King's crazy ass forever.

Chapter 44

Unexpected Visitors

The "King Kia Costello Story" and the "Solomon Carter, aka Swag, Story" had been blowing up in the media for the last few weeks. With lines such as *"The Fall of a King,"* or *"The Fugitive Finally Caught,"* everyone from BET, CBS, and even The Shade Room wanted a piece of the story. It was definitely newsworthy, and the famous people of the world who were in the Palace at the time of the raid were catching hell. They'd been exposed, and the media had a heyday showing the sexual escapades and the use of illegal drugs that took place at the Palace.

King denied everything to the Feds. All she wanted was to get the rats that set her up. She wanted blood and revenge, but she couldn't get out of jail because no bail had been set for her. So, with all the hookups she had in jail, she tried to make it a mini-vacation. She didn't have to eat the shit they called food, she took private showers, and she got to make as many phone calls as she wanted. She tried to call Blood, but his number was disconnected. Even her mother's and Santana's numbers were disconnected. She felt so alone but was glad she'd made arrangements to have Madam Lourd's body cremated and ashes sent to her. She called her lawyers that had gotten her off so many times. All her lawyers told her was that without bail, all she could do was sit back and wait for her trial.

***

Swag was back in Rio de Janeiro, where all the bullshit had started. This time, he was all alone. The only thing he wondered about at night in his private cell was how the Feds caught him . . . but not Tyler. He knew something wasn't right with that picture. Day after day, the Feds asked him where the rest of the fellas were, but Swag always said he didn't know. In the Feds' minds, they knew he was playing the dummy role. That didn't stop them from threatening Swag, though, if he didn't speak up. They told him he would go down with the massacre that happened back at the prison and face a possible life sentence without parole or even the death penalty.

But one day, several men came to Brazil to give Swag an offer he couldn't refuse. Costa Rica wanted King buried under the federal prison forever, and they figured their only ammunition was Swag, but they all needed to keep their hands clean just in case things went left. They were in the interrogation room waiting on him. Within moments, Swag entered the room wearing an orange prison jumpsuit with his hands and legs chained. Even though he was like an inmate, he still rocked the jumpsuit like he was rocking a white tank top, baggy jeans, a fresh pair of Jordans, and the handcuffs like platinum watches.

Swag looked at the men. The first one he knew right away was none other than mobster Bruno Bello. Bruno looked fresh in a gray Tom Ford suit with matching shoes. His salt-and-pepper hair was slicked back, and his beard was nicely trimmed.

Swag stood there looking at the men with a rough look on his face. "So, what's up?"

"Mr. Carter, please sit down," Bruno said in a smooth, deep voice.

Swag did as he was told and kept his eyes locked with Bruno's.

"If you don't know who I am, I'm Bruno Bello of the Bello Crime Family."

The two shook hands, and Swag nodded.

"Let me introduce you to our other guests." Bruno looked at the first man, a Sicilian in a tan khaki suit, looking like a crooked bookie. "This is my attorney, Georgie Falone."

Both men nodded. Bruno looked at the two other men who seemed to be of Latin ancestry. They were dressed in tailored suits. "These are some good associates of mine and very important men. This is the president of Costa Rica, and he is the vice president of Costa Rica."

"Hola, Señor Carter," both men said.

Swag nodded, then looked back at Bruno. "So, what do you all want with me?"

They all laughed.

"Don't you get it? We want to help you," Bruno said with a slick smile.

Swag twisted his lips and cocked his head back. "How the hell you goin' help my black ass? Shit, between the law and the media, my fate has been signed, sealed, and delivered. There ain't no—"

"Mr. Carter, will you just shut that hole in your face and hear us out?" Georgie said.

Swag crossed his arms and listened. "Okay, shoot."

"Señor Carter, I know you're an international fugitive, murderer, and kidnapper. But none of that matters to us. All I want is that bitch, Costello, behind bars forever! Her reign of terror has to come to an end in my country," said the president in his native tongue.

"What he's saying is, he wants King's ass underneath the jail forever. And with your help, we can get her there."

Swag was confused, especially since Bruno was King's father. "Oh, Bruno, a few questions come to mind."

"Shoot."

"Why do you need my help? I looked at the gangland documentary about King. It's rumored that King is your child. So. why in the world do you want your child locked up?"

Bruno laughed, but Swag sat there with a straight face.

"Son, look, I have a lot of children by a lot of different women of all colors, but this one is the Antichrist. I want her to disappear forever out of the Bello bloodline. I need her to be locked up before she becomes a danger to herself and others. So, are you going to help us or not?"

A lightbulb went off in Swag's head. He realized this was his golden chance to get whatever he wanted out these gentlemen. "So . . ."

"So, what?" asked Bruno, knowing precisely what Swag—or a high yellow moolie he saw him as—wanted. In his Italian mind, he knew moolies like Swag always wanted something for their services to the Bello Family.

"What's in it for me if I help you out? Because you want something, and I want something. Seems like it's a win-win deal, so what do I get in return if I agree to help you all bring King down for good?" Swag had a slick smile on his face.

Bruno sat back in his chair, nodding his head. He chuckled and sat up. "Okay, Swag, if you agree to help us, I can make sure Costa Rica drops all charges against you. And, to cut your sentencing real short back in Brazil and make sure you arrive safely back in the United States."

So far, Swag loved what he was hearing. He nodded his head with a smile.

"Also, my friend, I've done my research on you back in the States, and I see that you have a few warrants for your arrest for distribution of an illegal substance, possession of a weapon, and even armed robbery. To top it off, you're a convicted felon. Am I right?"

Swag was shocked at what Bruno knew, but he had to remember who he was dealing with.

Bruno smiled. *Got his ass,* he thought. "To sweeten the deal, if you agree to help my friends and me, I'll make sure all your US charges are dropped, and I can get that title 'felon' off your record forever."

Swag's eyes widened. He couldn't believe the words coming out Bruno's mouth, especially getting the convicted felon label off his record permanently. Swag could start his life over again as a new man.

"Are you serious, Bruno? You can *really* do that?"

"What do you think, Swag? I'm giving you the chance of a lifetime that many black men in America wish they were getting. It's a chance for a new beginning."

Swag thought of so much he could do with his new life if he agreed to help Bruno and company. He could get his GED, get a real job, and maybe go to school. He even thought about being back in his sons' lives forever. So much was going through his mind.

"So how about it, Swag? Are you in or out?"

Swag was still caught up in his thoughts, thinking more about his new beginning.

"Earth to Mr. Carter. Come in, Mr. Carter!" shouted the vice president.

Swag was still in a trance. "What?"

"So, what's it gonna be? Freedom, or would you rather live in a rat's nest forever?" Bruno asked.

Swag took a deep breath. "If I agree to help you, I want terms."

"It depends."

"Okay, while I'm in prison, I want protection since I am going to be a world-class snitch. Two, once I get back to the States, I want to have a place and a job waiting for me. And a bank account with $500K to get me started. Is that too much to ask?"

Georgie nodded. Bruno looked over at Swag. "If those are your terms, then we have a deal."

Swag nodded. "Deal."

Swag hated to be a snitch, but if it gave him the chance to start a new life and be back home with his boys, then he was all for it. *I'm almost there,* he thought.

Georgie then gave Swag an envelope.

Swag had concern etched on his face as he looked at the envelope. "What the hell is this?"

"Just have these notes memorized by the trial, and we'll do the rest," said Georgie.

Swag picked up the envelope, looking at and back at the men. "Cool, just remember my terms."

Bruno twisted his lips. "Guard!"

A big guard came in.

"You can take him away until we need him again. Swag, just remember to memorize your notes and testimony."

The guard took Swag away, leaving the men alone in the room.

"Do you think the American will go for this?" asked Bruno.

"Of course, sir. Like Blood told me, these eggplants will do anything for money," said Georgie smiling.

Bruno, the president, and the vice president smiled. They finally had enough info to bring King down. Swag was their paid alibi to keep eyes away from them.

Chapter 45

Lady in Gold

After a month, the trial of King Kia Costello was finally taking place in front of the Supreme Court of Costa Rica. The media had a field day with her trial. Everyone expected her to look stressed out and rough-looking when she exited the limousine. But she had them all completely fooled. She looked so good that she wanted to tell them what Beyoncé used to say, *Bow down, bitches.* She came out wearing a custom-made Neiman Marcus couture gold gown, looking like the royalty she was. Her makeup was on point, thanks to her glam squad. Her long hair was braided into a ponytail with flowers in it. And she wore gold Manolos on her perfectly pedicured feet.

People didn't know if it were a trial or fashion week in Paris. Jaws dropped everywhere. They couldn't believe a woman as beautiful as King was a cold-blooded killer. Many photographers rushed to take pictures of her. She posed for the cameras, knowing she had an open-and-shut case. Reporters asked her who designed her gown and had who done her makeup, totally forgetting the questions related to her trial. King loved every bit of it.

Finally, federal marshals stepped in and forced the media to back up. King continued to smile, knowing the marshals were feeling her as well. She blew them kisses and winked at them.

"Come on, lady, move it!" one of them said, who gripped her arm.

"Oh, baby, I like it rough," King said seductively.

He rolled his eyes but instantly got a woody.

During the trial, the prosecuting attorney asked questions about the drugs found in her place, her whorehouse, and the well-known people that they couldn't name who came to the Palace. King knew her rich and famous clients paid their lawyers overtime to keep their so-called good names out of this scandal. She answered the prosecutor's questions smoothly and told him that she didn't allow drugs in her place. She also reminded him that prostitution was allowed in Costa Rica.

The prosecutor went on about the many murders that she was suspected of being involved in throughout the years.

King smiled at him, telling him that she didn't know what he was talking about. She felt extremely confident. Her legal team was good at cleaning shit up.

All King wanted the judge to say for the eighth time was, "Not guilty for lack of evidence."

"Oh, really?" said the prosecutor as he went into his briefcase and pulled out a DVD. He presented it to the court.

"You all are so busy looking at Ms. Costello's beauty, not noticing under all that CoverGirl makeup, she's a monster. I have evidence to prove it."

He put the DVD in and let it play for the entire court to see and hear. On the screen, Swag popped up. King frowned, but at the same time, she was kind of turned on seeing him in prison garb.

Swag talked about the time he'd spent with King. He told them how Paco helped him and his friends break out of the Brazil prison. How King brought them to San José, He continued to sing like a bird talking about all her past crimes and murders. Swag's last sentence was that King was an evil bitch. The prosecutor turned off the TV.

King was pissed, but at the same time, not worried. The prosecutor looked at King, who had a straight face.

"So, Ms. Costello, what do you have to say to that?"

King smiled. "It's my word against his."

The prosecutor went to his briefcase and pulled out photos and played more video recordings of her murdering ways throughout the years until recently. He presented all information to the court.

King was speechless, not believing this was happening to her.

"Now, this is you, am I right, Ms. Costello?"

"Yes," King said softly.

"What was that?"

"Yes!"

"I have no further questions."

The prosecutor looked at King's attorney. "Your witness."

King knew she was fucked.

It took the jury almost half the day to deliberate, but the next day, they rendered their decision. King kept telling herself that it was an open-and-shut case. And even if she had to go to jail, she'd only be in there for ninety days. The jury, however, found her guilty of multiple murders, drugs, kidnapping, and harboring fugitives. She was sentenced to thirty years to life in a maximum-security prison in Costa Rica. King stood tall, but on the inside, she was broken. The only thing she valued the most was her freedom, and now it was taken from her.

She got herself together as she was being escorted out of the courtroom. Reporters continued to ask her questions, but she ignored them all. The only thing on her mind was getting revenge on the people who had fucked her over. She wanted Swag's head on a silver and diamond platter. If it weren't for him being a snitch bitch, King would've walked. Then she thought about Josie, and that pissed her off even more. A smile came on her face as she got into the limousine. She used her attorney's phone and dialed one person she knew would have her back.

Within moments, a female voice picked up. "Hello, girl."

"So, do you still wanna be even more famous than Superhead?"

"Of course."

"Good. Release the cheese and blow up Hollywood, Desiree."

"Anything for you, lover."

If King had to go behind bars, she might as well fuck up shit until she got back her freedom.

Chapter 46

Scandal

Weeks after the trial of King, her girl, Desiree, did what she was asked. Desiree released every last video she'd kept hidden for King. She sold them for high prices on celebrity blogs like Hollywood Unlocked, Perez Hilton, Bossip, and even Pornhub. The videos showed every famous person that came to the Palace—from actors to the religious leaders. Hollywood was going crazy and paid their staff double overtime to make the shit go away. Many denied everything from going to the Palace to their true sexuality.

Desiree had pictures that magazines wanted, but she turned them all down. A big publishing house in New York gave her an offer she couldn't refuse. They offered her a $100-million, two-book deal with a $60-million advance, to write a tell-all book about her life at the Palace and the high-profile men with whom she'd slept. When the media confronted King about the matters, all she said was "no comment." To her, if she were going down, she was going to take a bunch of motherfuckers with her.

Chapter 47

Smile

Weeks later, with all the media about King's trial, the Hollywood world went into a frenzy. Desiree's tell-all book was in the works, and Swag's trial finally came. As promised by Bruno and the city of Costa Rica for ratting out King, Brazil sentenced Swag to five years. He would be up for parole in two. The negative press called him a snitch, and rappers came up with rhymes saying it was messed up to rat out a powerful woman like King.

Even with all of the shit that was going on with him, he tried to make the best out of a bad situation. As Bruno promised, Swag had round-the-clock protection and his own private cell with a TV so that he could keep up with the outside world. At night, he thought about the wild ride he'd been on. He thought about what could've been with Josie. He wondered if she ever made it to Paris, or if she were still dancing. He just hoped wherever she was, she was happy. Also, there were days he felt so lonely. He missed his sons and his only real family . . . Brad, Tyler, Travis, and Stan.

One day, while Swag was watching TV in his cell, he'd been flipping channels until he flipped over to CNN, where a story caught his attention.

"Hello, I'm Della Ryan, and I'm in Puntarenas Province in Chacarita, Costa Rica, where a terrorist attack took place in La Reforma Prison. Many died, including the notorious crime lady, King Kia Costello. The cold-blooded femme fatale was burned to death in her cell with all her teeth, toes, and fingers missing. The Costa Rican authorities don't know if this was something aimed at another terrorist or Costello. We'll have an update in a moment."

Swag turned off the television and couldn't believe what he'd just heard. "King?" *King is dead? Damn, King is dead.* Swag leaped out of his bed and jumped for joy. "Aah! The bitch is dead!"

He started to dance, even did some old dances like the Harlem Shake. He was so loud the guard came by and banged his baton stick on the cell door. Startled, Swag turned around to face him.

"Hey! Where the hell you think you at?" said the guard. "No club for you for a few more years. Go to bed. It's almost time for lights out!"

The guard walked away from his cell. Swag smiled and sat on his bed. *Fuck a club,* he thought. He had better things to do with his life.

Swag was happy that his real living nightmare had died and gone to hell. In his mind, he was going to turn up all night long. As the lights went off, he closed his eyes and smiled, knowing pleasant dreams were coming.

Chapter 48

Swagger Meets Swagger

It had been two months since King's death and the attack on the prison. It was still being investigated, and the motives were still unclear. It got to the point where Swag was even questioned about the whole ordeal. Also, the terrorist attack was a good thing for Desiree, who was now going by Desiree St. Clair. Sales were rising on her upcoming book, *Foreign Fruit of an Island Girl*. The book was due out in a few months, and everyone was anticipating a juicy read. It was going to sell more than the Vixen series, and Desiree was milking the wealth.

Meanwhile, back in his prison, Swag was hitting his punching bag while trying to stay healthy. There was nothing else for him to do in his private cell. His days were spent eating, watching TV, and working out to keep his body and mind right. He used the punching bag, did push-ups, and sit-ups. He even put in his mind that when he got out of prison and back on US soil, he was going back to school. Not to only get his GED but also to learn to be a fitness trainer. Being in the cell all day, he loved working out and staying fit. He hoped that he could share some of his knowledge with other people. He even had his mind on opening a gym.

As he was punching the bag, he thought of his beloved Josie. He wanted to know how she was or if she heard that King was dead. He hoped she was living her Josephine Baker dream in Paris. His mind switched to Blood and Tyler. Now, he punched the bag harder. He was so focused that he didn't hear his cell door opening.

"Okay, Carter, let's go!"

Sweat dripped down his body, and he was only wearing shorts. He didn't know what the guard meant, and he didn't move.

"I said, let's go!"

Swag's brows rose. "What's going on?"

"You a free man. Someone paid to get you out of here. I think that's crazy as cat shit, but I don't run nothing around here."

Swag froze and thought about the words, "*You a free man.*" To him, it felt like a huge weight had been lifted off his shoulders. He assumed Bruno was behind the payment, but at that moment, he didn't care. His mind was all over the place as he thought about his newfound freedom and life.

"Are you coming, or do you wanna stay here?"

Swag rushed out of the cell, took a quick, hot shower, and waited for the guard to tell him his next move. Within the hour, the guard was back. He gave Swag a bag.

"Get dressed!" shouted the guard. Then he walked out.

Swag looked inside the bag and saw there was a white Gucci shirt, jeans from True Religion, fresh socks, fresh underwear, an STL baseball cap, and a pair of the latest Jordans. Also in the package was a platinum watch and chain with diamonds. Swag was shocked. He couldn't believe Bruno had gone all out for him like this.

After Swag put on the clothes and jewelry, he looked at himself in the mirror. He was starting to feel like the pretty boy from the Lou again. But this time, a do-better pretty boy. He even thought about going under his government name, but he looked at his reflection again and decided to go under Swag and continue to sport his swagger. Once he finished admiring himself, two guards escorted him outside. It was a beautiful, sunny day in Rio, and he stood for a moment to let the sun hit his face and breathe in the fresh air. It smelled like sweet honey mixed with gasoline.

He looked around at his surroundings and spotted a taxi. The thing that almost took his breath away was a sexy, brown-skinned chick leaning against the cab. She wore big Fendi shades to cover her eyes, and her hair was cut into a short pixie cut with purple highlights. The tight khaki jumpsuit hugged her curves, and black Prada suede sandals were on her feet. She looked at Swag with a big smile that could brighten up any room. Swag smiled, knowing it was Josie. His heart almost stopped. He couldn't believe that she was the one who'd paid to get him out. In his mind, Swag thought Josie had forgotten all about him. He thought she was living her best life with the money they stole from King. Swag walked up to her with the biggest smile on his face and held his arms out.

"Come here," he said.

"No. You come here," Josie replied.

Swag rushed over to her, hugged her, picked her up, and kissed her. He spun her around and felt like he was in one of those romance novels his nana used to read all the time. He smelled Josie's scent, White Diamonds perfume.

"Thank you for helping me get out. How did you do it?" He put her down.

Josie laughed. "I have connections too, and I worked my magic on some very high-profile people. I didn't want you to be in there a minute longer. They didn't either, and I couldn't leave you in that roach motel to rot in for years."

"True."

They both laughed.

"So, where do you wanna go?" Josie asked.

Swag thought for a moment. "I wanna go to St. Louis to be with my sons. I really miss them."

"We can go anywhere you like."

They kissed again and celebrated their reunion.

"Let's go," Josie said, opening the door for him.

As the cab was driving down the streets of downtown Rio, so many memories flooded Swag's mind. He thought of the good times when all the fellas arrived in Brazil, to the nightmare which led to Stan being killed. Not wanting to show his emotions, Swag cleared his thoughts. He and Josie talked about what she'd been up to. She told him that when she arrived in Paris, she toured the city and visited the famous sites and home that belonged to Josephine Baker. She even got a small apartment in downtown Paris. She took up dancing again, and in a few weeks, she had an audition for one of Paris's finest dance academies. She hoped she'd be performing on a stage soon.

The couple cuddled in each other's arms. They saw nothing but a great future ahead. They were caught in a big traffic jam, but they didn't care. They enjoyed their time together and couldn't stop talking about what they'd been up to.

People, however, were going crazy in the street. The cab driver swerved so he wouldn't hit a car that had pulled in front of him. Out of nowhere, a bullet came through the window and went straight through the driver's head. His brains splattered on the windshield, and some of it landed on Josie and Swag. Josie screamed hysterically.

Swag took her hand and tried to get out of the cab. It was too late, though. Four masked men stood outside the cab with machine guns pointed at them.

One of the men yelled, "Don't you fucking move, or you'll join the cab driver in hell!"

Swag was in disbelief. His heart raced fast. In his mind, he thought this shit was over, but he was *way* off. One of the men pulled the dead driver out of the cab and took his place. Two other men got in the back with Swag and Josie, crushing them.

Swag looked at the man who pointed his gun at him. "Who are you? What do you want?"

Swag's question went unanswered. The man shot him with a tranquilizer and knocked him out. Josie screamed at the top of her lungs. She thought Swag was dead, and she attempted to get out of the car. No such luck. The other masked man took her arm and poked it with a needle. She was out too.

Within seventy-two hours, they woke up to a new nightmare.

Chapter 49

Motherland

Swag finally woke up, feeling like he was in a sweatbox. He was hungry, and he smelled like shit. After gaining his composure, he realized he was in a room that looked like a dungeon with dimmed lighting. He also saw that his hands were chained, and his body was dangling. He tried to wiggle himself out of the chains, but couldn't. He looked around and saw that he wasn't alone. Josie was tied up on a bed. He then turned around and saw Santana and Tyler. Their hands were chained up next to him.

"What . . . What the hell is this?" Swag questioned.

"How the hell should I know?" Tyler was still trying to get loose.

"Ewww, shit, this place is hot and nasty," Santana whined, thinking he was too pretty for this shit.

"Swag, help meeee!" Josie screamed.

He saw that she was only in her bra and panties. "I'm trying, baby, but where in the hell are we?"

"Welcome to Africa!" a man with a deep, sexy voice said. He had a thick Spanish accent.

Everyone looked around and tried to figure out whose voice that was and where it was coming from.

"Who are you?" Swag shouted. "What do you want from us?"

A bright light came on that almost blinded everyone in the room. Swag did a double-take as he saw the big man with dark shades covering his eyes. Everyone else saw him too. They realized it was Blood. He laughed and removed his shades.

"What up, bitches?" he shouted.

Swag couldn't believe it. "Blood, what the hell is this?"

"Shhhh. Please have respect for the royal family."

Everyone appeared confused. They saw a handsome Cuban man and a stunning chocolate woman dressed to the nines in all white. The couple looked like they could've been in *People* magazine for Hollywood's hottest couple. Blood cleared his throat.

"Let me introduce you all to the original bosses and ringleaders who really run shit. Mr. Zeus and Mrs. Lewa Santiago."

They smiled at everyone and sat in chairs that looked like thrones. Everyone felt like they were in a hellish version of *The Twilight Zone*.

"Blake! Blake! Blake! What is this? What the hell is going on?" Santana felt betrayed by his partner.

Blood laughed and put his finger over his lips. "Shh. Santana, you will also address my wife first."

Everyone turned and looked at his *wife*. Things went from boiling hot to cold as ice when they saw the last person they wanted to see—King.

She fiercely strutted in the room and looked at her latest victims, chained. Her long, blond hair was full of thick curls, her makeup was flawless, and she wore a vintage Christian Dior sequined feather dress and black Dior heels.

"It can't be," Tyler said with his mouth wide open.

"What? No! You're dead!" Santana hollered.

King laughed and looked at them like the feline she was. "What's the matter, bitches? Cat got your tongues?"

"I can't believe you're alive." Swag thought this was a nightmare he couldn't wake up from.

King snapped her fingers in the air. "Well, believe it, baby. It's me, in the flesh."

"What the hell is this, Swag?" asked another female voice.

Swag's attention turned to the other person.

"Oh, I forgot about our special guest," King said. "Bring her closer, boys."

Two big bodyguards brought in Zaria. Her face was puffy from all the crying she'd done. Like Josie, she wore only a bra and panties. Zaria was trying to get out of the guards' grip but couldn't.

"Where am I?" she shouted and kicked one of the guards. "Where are my sons?"

Swag was shocked to see his ex here. He didn't know the purpose of all of this. When Zaria mentioned the boys, he was furious. He looked over at King.

"Bitch, where the fuck are my kids?"

King laughed at his remark. Blood, on the other hand, walked over to him and punched the dog shit out of him. He had wanted to fuck Swag's pretty ass up, especially for making his woman lose her way. He continued to punch Swag in his stomach and made him vomit.

"Blood! That's enough!" King shouted.

He stopped and looked at the weak piece of shit in front of him. "Bitch!" he spat.

Swag coughed and gasped for air. Josie and Zaria cried at the sight of what was going on. King hated weak females. She shook her head and went over to Zaria to slap her. "Shut up, bitch!"

Zaria muffled her cries. She was frightened as hell. "What is this?" she asked. "What did *I* do to deserve this shit?"

King laughed and rubbed Zaria's cheek, who turned her head, but King gripped her head, forcing her to look at her.

"Such a pretty little brown girl. You had so much promise. At first, I was going to spare you. I was going to make you one of my newest escorts, but that's not going to be possible. Because every time I would look at you, it would remind me of your bitch of a baby daddy."

Zaria breathed deeply as she looked at King, then back at Swag. "Do something! Help me, please!"

King shook her head. "What a waste." She pulled out her switchblade and sliced Zaria's throat.

"Noooo!" Swag cried out. He felt helpless that he couldn't save the mother of his children.

The guards let Zaria fall. She hit the floor, and her blood flowed on the concrete.

Swag cried out with fire in his eyes. He looked like a raging bull. "Why the fuck you kill Zaria? My kids' mother! Why? She didn't have shit to do with this."

King licked Zaria's blood off the switchblade. Everybody was grossed out, even Blood.

"Mmm, good," she said. "I had to kill her because she was someone you loved. I made a promise that I was going to destroy everything you cared about."

Those words scared the shit out of Swag. There was no telling what she'd done with his sons. "Where are my sons? What have you done with them?"

Tears streamed down his face. King didn't respond. She loved torturing him, and seeing the sorrow on all of their faces made her feel good.

Swag lifted his head. "Please, tell me. Where are my sons you—"

Before Swag could finish his sentence, Zeus spoke up. "Don't worry about your boys. They will live a wonderful life. And in time, they will call *me* father."

Swag was dead-ass shocked. He didn't know who this Al Pacino, *Scarface* wannabe fool thought he was, but he wasn't having this shit. No one was taking his sons away from him.

"What the fuck are you talking about, you fake-ass mobster?"

Blood pulled out a Taser and shot bolts of electricity through Swag's body.

"Have some respect for the original king!" he shouted.

"Blake, my friend, it's cool." Zeus got up and patted him on his back. "I got this."

Blood stepped back, and Zeus looked at Swag, smiling.

Swag was direct with Zeus. "You ain't taking my sons away from me. If you fuck with them in any way, you're—"

Zeus cut him off with laughter. "Your sons are Mrs. Santiago's and my sons now." He waved for Lewa to come over. She stood next to her husband. Zeus kissed her and looked back at Swag. "You better be lucky that King spared your children. She planned to sell the oldest boy into slavery in East Africa, and for the baby, she wanted to boil him alive in oil. So, you should be thanking Mrs. Santiago, who loves children." Zeus looked at his wife. "And whatever Mrs. Santiago wants, she gets." He kissed her again.

King looked at Zeus and Lewa. She gave them the side-eye for not letting her have her way with Swag's children. But she had to respect the ones responsible for her freedom. So she remained silent . . . for now.

"Mr. Carter, I always wanted a big family," Lewa said in a calm voice. "When I saw your beautiful sons, I wanted them. So Mr. Santiago and I are their parents now. You and that baby mama are about to be worm and rat food."

Swag wiggled around like a fish and tried to get loose again. He wanted to slap the shit out her. She looked at Zeus.

"Darling, I'm tired. I want to be with our sons."

"As you wish, Mrs. Santiago." Zeus faced King and Blood. "King! Blood! Come here."

The two immediately came their way.

"Mrs. Santiago and I are about to leave. Have fun with your guests."

Lewa kissed King and Blood on their cheeks. Zeus kissed King, and that made her heart melt. He patted Blood on his shoulder. "Congrats, man." He also whispered in his ear. "If you need any more help, just call us."

Blood nodded. King could read lips, and his words put a sly smile on her face. She knew Blood had some kind of contact info on the Santiagos. She planned to find them and meet them again soon.

Once the Santiagos were gone, King and Blood focused on their guests of honor.

"Back to business, ladies and gentlemen." King looked down at Zaria's lifeless body. "Or should I say, lady." She looked at Santana, who had just pissed in his pants.

She shook her head at her half brother.

"Damn, half of my bone and flesh," she said. "I cannot believe you would do some fucked-up shit like this to me. But then again, I can." She paced back and forth while keeping her eyes on Santana. "You're just as crooked as your father."

Santana's eyes widened. "My father?"

"Hmm," King grabbed his face and whispered, "And here's my little secret. I. Killed. Your. Father."

Santana had finally learned the truth about his dad. He was furious. He tried to break out of the chains and wanted to attack King. She knew he wasn't going to get free. It was a weight lifted off her shoulders that she'd finally told him the truth. Ivy was trying to protect him all these years.

Santana breathed heavily, still in disbelief. All his life, he had put in his head that his father had run off, thanks to King. He tried to process that his father was murdered at the hands of his own sister. To him, that was on a whole other level.

"You wicked, evil bitch!" Santana shouted. "I—"

Before Santana could get another word in, King scratched his face with her long nails. Santana's head was to the side, but she pulled it toward her.

"Don't forget that this 'evil bitch' was the one who gave you a life of luxury, mainly because of Ivy. You were living like the fresh gay prince of San José at *my* expense!" King was silent for a moment. "How could you do this to me? Why?"

Santana twisted his face up. "I just wanted a little bit more than the fake-ass crumbs you gave me." He looked over at Blood, who maintained a straight face. He then looked back at King. "And another thing, why isn't that bastard Blood chained up with the rest of us? *He* was the main one who set your dumb ass up anyway. All I wanted was the Palace and the money. He was the one who set you up with the drugs and the kidnapping charges. He also was the one who contacted your father to talk Swag into a confession."

"And like the bitch he is, he took it!" Tyler added.

Swag couldn't believe that at a time like this, Tyler was still hating. King shook her head.

"You are such a liar, Santana. Why are you so disrespectful to my hubby?"

"King! King!" Tyler shouted.

King shifted her eyes to him. "What, faggot?"

"King, your brother is telling you the truth. Blood *did* set you up. A few months back, he and Santana met in a gay bar to discuss bringing you down. Mainly Blood. I have nothing to lose, so it's time to tell the truth!"

"Amen to that. I told you, sis," Santana said sarcastically.

"Who's the snitch bitch now?" Swag said, looking over at Tyler.

"Fuck you, bitch! Again, it's your fault I'm in this shit!"

King watched them argue like two old ladies. And as they continued, she shouted, "Shut up!"

Silence filled the room, and all eyes were on her.

King strutted over to Tyler. "You, boy, you, I liked. You could do some hair. And you could've had a future, but you chose to be a fudge backer with the enemy." King looked over at Santana. "Santana, have you ever had a broken heart?"

Santana pursed his lips. "What?"

Without warning, King took her switchblade and stabbed Tyler deep in his chest.

"Aaaah!" Tyler shouted as blood dripped from his mouth.

"Nooo!" Santana dropped his head and cried. He couldn't bear to watch the one person he loved besides his mother die.

As Tyler's life was fading, he saw his whole life flash before his eyes. With the last bit of life he had in him, he looked over at Swag with tears leaking down. He didn't want to leave this earth before speaking his last words to Swag.

"Swag, I forgive . . . love—"

Tyler's eyes closed. He was no longer in this world.

The word "love" was a shocker to Swag. He didn't expect Tyler to utter those last words to him. It showed that Tyler still valued their friendship and loved him like a brother. Swag was speechless.

Santana, however, continued to cry like a baby. He thought about the lavish life they were living back in Jamaica while all the scandal was happening in Costa Rica. He gave Tyler so much, from clothes to all the cocaine he wanted. Santana lifted his head and looked at Tyler's dead body, hanging. King pulled the switchblade from Tyler's chest and licked his blood. "Salty but tasty."

She walked over to Santana and held the switchblade up to his face with Tyler's blood on it. He looked at her fearless.

"What are you waiting for? Go ahead and kill me!"

King lowered the switchblade and laughed sinisterly. "You'd like that, wouldn't you? Death is too easy for you, dickhead! I want you to suffer, and you still owe me a debt. Plus, now that your loverboy is gone, the debt just doubled."

"What are you going to do to me? And what about Mother? Can I at least say goodbye?"

"Don't worry about Ivy. I'll continue to send monthly allowances to her in Miami. And you better pray she lives for a long time. 'Cause when that bitch dies, you die!"

Santana continued to cry, not knowing where his future was headed.

King needed some different scenery, so she walked over to Josie, who was shaken and in disbelief.

So many thoughts went through Josie's head. *How did she find me? How did she survive the fire in prison?* She thought about getting Swag from prison and regretted doing that. She thought about how happy she had been in Paris.

King sat on the side of the bed and looked at her. "And you, my child. I raised you, fed you, and paid for the best dancing trainers in the world to get your craft just right."

She rubbed Josie's sweaty head, but she turned it, not wanting King to touch any part of her. That angered King. She had hoped to work out something with Josie, but she knew in her gut that was a lie. She no longer saw Josie as her child and future heiress to her empire. All she saw now was a thieving gutter rat. Her plans for her were to fuck her face up and break her legs so she could never dance again. But Josie was way too valuable, and her talents could be used in other ways. "You owe me a debt too, bitch! But first." King snapped her fingers. "Come in."

PJ Hernandez entered the room dressed in his best suit with two bodyguards and Manny. King looked at Josie.

"Luckily for you, PJ paid your debt. But unfortunately, you're *his* property now."

Josie looked away and swallowed hard. Swag couldn't believe it, and he was as helpless as ever.

King clapped her hands to make sure she had Swag's attention. "Congrats! I sold your bitch to PJ. Welcome to the world of sex trafficking."

"No!" Josie cried. "No, Swag, please, help me!" Josie tried to shake herself off the bed.

"Leave her alone! Take me instead! Let her go!" Swag hollered.

"Nigger! I don't *want* you!" PJ barked.

King hollered back at Swag. "Oh, don't worry. I have *big* plans for your ass. Just be sure to look at your whore for one last time before she gets used up."

PJ laughed. Manny gave King a suitcase with $50 million inside. She took it and was ready to hand Josie over to PJ.

"You cost me a lot," PJ said to Josie. "So, that means you're going to be my big moneymaker in my new location."

Josie shook her head. "No! No! No!"

"Yes, you will." PJ looked at his guards. "Shoot her up with some heroin, and let's be out." He looked back at King. "Thank you for considering my offer, King. Josephine, I mean, Cattleya, now, will fit right in."

The men poisoned Josie's body with heroin and welcomed her to the world of sex and drug addiction.

Swag hated to be helpless. He still tried to get out of the chains, with no luck.

"Leave her alone! You muthafuckas better hope I never get loose! I'ma kill everybody! Watch!"

King laughed so hard that she almost peed on herself. She couldn't believe he was so broken up over Josie, and it angered her even more.

PJ planned to take Josie to his new location in California. With all the sex she'd had with Swag, he now considered her damaged goods. King thought about the new fucked life Josie would be living. She glanced at her one last time and wished her well.

Now that Josie was gone, she turned her attention back to Swag. "I even thought about killing you too, Sol, I mean, Swag, but like Santana, death would be too easy for you."

"What you goin' to do to me? Send me to military school, bitch?" Swag chuckled. He didn't give a shit anymore.

King shook her head. If only he hadn't betrayed her, Swag would've been on her arm instead of her rock, Blood.

"No, motherfucker! First thing is you're a snitch, and snitches always get stitches. And second, I'm going to send a message to Bruno Bello for even thinking he could keep me down."

King stepped back to look at her surroundings. One dead woman on the ground, one dead man hanging, Santana whose mind was just gone, and Josie, who'd turned into a zombie, was being whisked away with PJ.

"Blood!" King shouted while looking at him.

He walked up and eased his arm around her waist. "Yes, my love?"

"I'm ready to go. Let's go home!"

Blood smiled. "As you wish."

They kissed passionately.

Swag rolled his eyes and closed them.

Santana still was at a loss for words. He couldn't believe Blood had fed him to the wolves.

King and Blood held each other's hands as they exited the building. All they heard behind them were screams of pain and misery. They got inside a white limo, and the driver took off.

King fell back on the seat, crossed her legs, and looked at Blood. "I can't believe that shit! Revenge is so sweet."

Blood laughed. "Did you love your wedding present?"

"I loved it. Thank you again."

"Now, remember our deal. You stay cool, and I'll take over the operation. Just relax and let your man take care of you—your hero."

King didn't like to sit back. She was used to being the one who ruled shit. But she did owe Blood, so she gave in.

"I promise. And thank you."

She kissed him on his cheek. Blood loved that he had King all to himself. She sat there thinking about the wild ride she'd been on for almost a year. And after she got revenge on her enemies, she felt more powerful than ever. Even though she was dead to the world, she felt like a phoenix who rose from the ashes. She closed her eyes and reminisced about the moments that led her from getting out of jail time to being a phoenix.

Chapter 50

Rise of a Phoenix

After King's big trial and her life sentence behind the prison walls, she asked her lawyers to appeal, but they told her it would be too risky. All they could tell her was that she was a boss and to create a new empire in prison.

King took it to heart and started to make many requests before entering the prison. First, with all the drama in her life, she finally had a private service for Madam Lourd. She had her attorney spread her ashes around the Palace so that her essence would always be around. Also, in prison, she wanted a private cell. Even though the Feds froze some of her accounts, she still had secret accounts. Neither Blood nor Ivy knew about them because they were under different names. She figured if she had to spend the rest of her days in a hellhole, it was going to be a classy one.

She didn't have to eat the nasty food the prison served, either. She continued to eat like the king she was. She even got to take private showers anytime, had private yard time, and used the lounge room on her own to look at what was going on in the world. While in prison, she gained respect from the inmates who asked her to be part of their gangs or lead them, but she declined. She didn't even mind wearing the light brown prison jump-suit. It made the guards wonder how she could make it look so expensive. She'd kept her hair in a French roll that was braided back.

While in prison, she spent most of her days working out because she had to keep her body right at all times. She read magazines like her personal favorite, Vogue. *That was how she found the article about Desiree, now going under Desiree St. Clair, talking about the scandal at the Palace and more about her upcoming book. King also read* People *magazine. She read about all the famous people's lives she'd fucked up, thanks to Desiree. Some celebrities were ignoring it, still trying to save their good names, while others were getting divorced. King loved the article more than the show* Love & Hip-Hop.

With all her free time, she still thought about getting revenge on those who did her wrong. She couldn't get over how Swag and Josie fucked her over royally. King couldn't believe they took her kindness and hospitality for weakness. If anyone should've been loyal to her, it should have been Josie. She gave Josie more than she gave herself at times. King couldn't believe she was going to give the Leopard Clit to her deceitful ass. And Swag, she thought he would be eating out of the palm of her hand. She was always the type of woman that got what she wanted. King was so blinded by Swag's good looks and smooth attitude that she didn't see that he didn't want anything to do with her. King couldn't understand why she'd fallen so hard for a man. She knew damn well that wasn't her style. She was the type that took control and sent her play toys on their merry way. She hadn't felt that way about someone since the Santiagos.

Even though she hadn't seen them in a while, the Santiagos still made her moist and hot. King thought she could re-create that moment with Swag and Josie. She didn't know how she let something as weak as love cause her to slip up so badly. And the part that messed her mind over was, not only did Josie and Swag sleep together, but they also slept in the room next to hers. In King's mind, if they were going to do that shit, they, at least, could've gone to a cheap motel. Just thinking about those two bouncing up and down made her wish she could've chopped up their bodies before the Feds came.

She even thought about how the Feds found out about Swag's kids. The only thing that tripped her out was how drugs got into her place. She never allowed drugs in her palace, and it made her think of Santana's ass. She was pissed off since she couldn't contact him or Blood. But one of her spies found Ivy. Ivy was living a lavish life in Miami Beach, Florida. She lived in a big condo and drove a Mercedes-Benz. She still had her boy toys, was getting a weekly allowance, and going on daily shopping sprees.

King wasn't surprised that her mother hadn't been checking in on her own child because when Madam Lourd died, everything went to shit. She thought of Madam Lourd's last dying words, "Stay hardhearted." And from now on, that was the way she was going to be.

While in prison, she remained strong and hardhearted by doing her time and not letting her time do her. She also kept in mind that if it took her until eternity, she was going to fuck up the lives of those who made her suffer.

One night in prison, as everyone was sleeping, King was in her private cell drinking a glass of red wine, reading The Godfather *by Mario Puzo. She hoped to get some ideas to build a new empire and to get tips about the mob. While reading the novel, she thought that, sometimes, she hated her Italian side. Soon, she heard a deafening boom that made the building shake. It felt like an earthquake.*

Masked men rushed in, shooting up everything in sight. The prison guards weren't ready for the attack. They hit the panic button. Finally, King's cell door was opened by one of the female guards, who was then shot in the head and fell to the ground. King leaned against the wall, not knowing what to do. The two big, masked men came in her cell and looked her up and down. King was only in her bra and panties. Her hair was damp from taking a shower earlier. Even though she didn't have a weapon on her, her claws were ready if either of those men put their hands on her. One walked up to her, and she was prepared to charge at him.

He laughed at her and took off his mask. King was stunned by who she saw.

"I'm here to take you home," said the man.

King was still in disbelief. "Home?"

He shot her with a sleeping tranquilizer. Before she hit the ground, the man caught her and tossed her over his shoulders. Just when he was about to walk out of the cell, he looked at the other masked man.

"Cut that dead bitch on the ground real good and burn her so no one can identify her ass."

"Yes, Mr. Blake, sir."

Blake Fernandez, aka Blood, smiled ear-to-ear while walking out of the cell and carrying King like he was King Kong, and he was her hero. And, hopefully, be the only hero she would ever need.

Forty-eight hours later, King woke up in a comfortable king-sized bed with Egyptian cotton sheets covering her up. She looked around the room, noticing it was a crème color with luxurious Victorian furniture. She thought she'd died and gone to heaven. But while lying on the bed, she thought about the arrest, Swag, the scandal, and wondered if prison were just a bad dream. She thought that her life was back to normal. She got up and saw she was wearing a pink, baby doll nightie. She looked at herself in a full-length mirror. Her hair was straightened and hanging down her back. "Beautiful."

She went on the balcony to look at her kingdom of San José. King noticed a few things. One, it was beautiful and sunny but not hotter than her kingdom. Second, she figured out the building and structure of the downtown area. She knew she wasn't in her beloved Costa Rica anymore.

What the hell! *King thought as she went back inside.* "Where am I?"

The door opened, and Blood walked in, wearing blue jean shorts and sandals. He was carrying a breakfast tray. She turned her head, looking at him.

Blood smiled. "Oh, Sleeping Beauty, you're awake." *He placed the tray in the middle of the bed.* "I brought you some breakfast."

On the tray was a glass of orange juice, toast, a fruit bowl, koko (fermented corn porridge) with bofrot (doughnuts), and a garden egg. King looked at the food with disgust and looked at Blood with so much anger.

"Where the hell am I?"

"Relax. We're in Accra, Ghana."

"Africa?"

"No, the moon." *Blood laughed.*

King wasn't in a laughing mood. She got up from the bed and punched Blood in his chest.

"Where in the hell were you when I was in that shithole? I tried calling you, Ivy, and Santana. You all dissed me when I needed my family the most." *Tears formed in her eyes.*

Blood let her hit him as he looked down at her face, loving that she was finally showing emotion. It was something Blood hadn't seen from her since she was a child. Soon, he'd had enough of her hitting him, so he took his strong arms and wrapped them around her. King broke down crying and let herself surrender to Blood.

She's mine, *thought Blood, loving this moment.*

"Shhh, it's okay. Your Blood is here now." He released her.

"Why didn't you reach out or return my calls? And one more thing, out of all the hiding spots, why Africa? Why not the French Rivera?"

Blood laughed. "Eat your food, take a shower, and your clothes are in the wardrobe." He pointed. "All will be explained downstairs in an hour and a half."

Blood headed to the door, and King thanked him before he left. He smiled as he walked down the hallway and hoped she was ready for the Big Reveal.

King sat on the bed and ate. Even though the food didn't look appealing, it was good. After breakfast, she took a long, hot shower, oiled herself down real good, and went into the closet to find something to wear. The closet looked like a mall. All types of designer label clothes were hung, as well as shoes and expensive jewelry. Her mouth dropped with so many options. She was overwhelmed. She looked around until she found the perfect outfit. It was a red pantsuit. She also picked out some red pumps and gold jewelry. Once her hair dried, she curled it and put on her makeup. She felt completely transformed, and as she looked in the mirror, she couldn't help but think that King was back.

King headed downstairs and admired the beautiful home.

"Ma'am," said an elderly male. King looked and realized it was Cleo.

"Cleo? Mr. Cleo? Is that really you?" King hugged him. She was glad to see him. She had been afraid she would never see him again. Out of all the men in her life, next to Zeus Santiago, she respected Cleo. Finally, she stopped hugging him.

"How are you?"

"I'm fine, Ms. King. Please come. You're expected in the parlor, so follow me."

They arrived at the parlor. It was a huge room with a bar and bartender who was ready to make drinks. The room was painted an eggshell color with urban-style furniture. Crystal chandeliers hung from the ceiling, and glass mirrors surrounded the room.

King saw Blood, sitting on a sofa. He held his hand out. "Come sit down."

Blood wasn't dressed in his signature suits. He had on the same shorts, sandals, and the white T-shirt he'd had on earlier. He looked so different than the right-hand man she'd known all these years.

"Blood, what in the hell is going on? What the hell is all this?"

"King, please sit down. I promise you that all will be revealed soon, so please have a seat."

King hated all the suspense and games. She wanted to attack, but she couldn't, knowing Blood had always been loyal to her. She kept all her questions to herself and sat next to him.

The room was dead silent, which drove her crazy. She looked over at Blood and shouted, "You bastard!"

Blood looked at her as if she were crazy. "Excuse me?"

"You didn't contact me or visit me when I was in that shithole. I couldn't give Madam Lourd the proper memorial that she deserved. I just had my lawyer spread her ashes around the Palace, which was hard from all the drugs and scandal going on. What kind of shit *is that? I knew my bitch of a mother and half brother wasn't shit. But you? I—"*

"King," Blood said, cutting her off. "First off, I never left your side. But with the trial, scandal, and Desiree coming out with that little book of hers, my associates thought it best if I broke contact with you until all this shit was over."

King hissed at him. "Associates? When was the last time you gave a shit about what someone says? We followed no one's rules but our own. What's up with these associates? Who the fuck are these bitches?"

Blood laughed his head off, knowing the real truth.

The laughing pissed King off. "What the hell is so funny?"

"Those bitches were the reason I had the resources to get you out of the shithole you put yourself in."

King was stunned as she folded her arms. "Come again."

Blood looked at the doorway. King did too, and she couldn't believe her eyes. It had been years since she had last seen her special guests—the Santiagos.

In King's eyes, they were the two most beautiful people she'd ever seen. They hadn't aged a day. Zeus Santiago looked handsome in a floral, short sleeve, button-down shirt, tan khaki slacks, and sandals. His mustache and beard were trimmed to perfection. His short, black hair was slicked back.

Lewa Santiago was stunning, as always. She wore a tan, khaki dress that showed off her smooth, chocolate skin. Her heels matched, and her long, black hair hung down her back like an Indian's. The Santiagos came into the room, holding hands. They smiled at King. She was so shocked that she believed they were two ghosts.

"Hello, King," Zeus said in his smooth, suave, Cuban accent.

King almost melted on the sofa. She quickly got up and rushed into their arms. "I missed you two so much."

Even though the Santiagos were her past mentors-foster parents, they were also her lovers.

"Please, sit down, baby," Lewa said.

They all sat on love seats, across from one another. So many memories flooded King's mind. She remembered how close they were back in the day. King didn't realize her mouth was open. Blood tapped her shoulder, breaking her focus.

"What, fool?"

"Stop drooling and close your mouth. No telling what shit here will fly in it."

The Santiagos chuckled. King snatched the napkin from Blood and wiped the sides of her mouth. She hated to be embarrassed, especially in front of the Santiagos.

"Hello, King, my beautiful King," Lewa said with a lovely, beauty pageant smile that displayed her perfect, pearly white teeth.

"Welcome to Ghana and our home. One of our many homes around the world," Zeus said.

King blushed.

"King, dear, would you like something to drink?" Lewa asked.

One of many homes, *King thought and lost focus of what Lewa said. She just shook her head. "No. I'm good."*

Lewa asked the bartender to make her an apple martini.

"Mr. and Mrs. Santiago, for all these years, I always wondered if you were dead or alive. Why did you leave me? I missed you both so much."

King realized what Blood meant about the "associates" that rescued her from prison. She slapped Blood's head. "And you! Why didn't you just tell me you knew where they were?"

Before Blood could speak, Zeus cleared his throat. Everyone focused on him.

"King, the reason Mrs. Santiago and I left you behind was that the Feds were on our family hard. So, all the Santiagos fled Cuba and went to parts unknown. We were still able to make money. I knew Blake would look after you. We told him that if you ever ran into serious trouble, to call us, and we'd come through for you."

King couldn't believe what she was hearing. "Why didn't you tell me where you were? I loved you both."

"Honey, you were still very young and starting off as a boss. And running away with us would've only messed up your hustle. Plus, you still didn't know what love was. We hoped you would find it one day," Lewa said.

"Love, shit. You see where fallin' hard for someone got me." King sucked her teeth. "Love is for the weak, no offense, Mr. and Mrs. Santiago."

They both laughed, not offended at all. They knew their love was no ordinary love.

"And she still can't see love when it's right in front of her!" Blood shouted.

All eyes shifted to him.

"Excuse me?" King looked at Blood as if he were nuts.

He wanted to shake her and wake her up. He did everything he could to prove his love to her. Hell, he broke her out of prison and faked her death. In his mind, if that wasn't love, he didn't know what was. With all that, he still loved King and only wanted to be with her.

"Don't you see a real man looking at you? Look what I did for you. If I didn't love you, I wouldn't have called the Santiagos. I could've let your ass rot in that cell you tried to make into a five-star suite, but I didn't." Blood got up and kneeled on one knee. He took King's hands. "King Kia Costello, I love you more than life itself. I have

*loved you since you were a child. You're all I think about.
I jack off to you every night."*

He kissed her hand.

I hope he washed his hands, *thought King, while
keeping a straight face. She was a tiny bit disgusted by
his little love speech.*

*Blood reached into his pocket and pulled out a black
box.*

What the . . .? *King thought.*

*Blood opened the box. Inside was a 12.65-carat
Octagon Halo Diamond Engagement Ring in 18K white
gold. The Santiagos were excited about the love Blood
had for her. They couldn't see her with anyone else.*

*"King Kia Costello, will you do me the honor of being
my wife? Let me be your hero for a change."*

*King couldn't believe that her right-hand man asked
for her hand in marriage. She thought Blood should
have known how she'd felt about love, especially with
her experiences with the Santiagos, Swag, and Josie.
But in the end, she started to feel her heart softening.
After all, Blood did save her and make the world think
she was dead, how could she reject him? King wanted to
start a new life. She knew that before she could do that,
she had to let go of some things in the past. King smiled
seductively and crossed her legs. "Blood, if I agree to be
your wife, I want two powerful wedding presents from
you."*

*"What is it? A bigger diamond or a honeymoon in
Greece? Whatever you want, I got you."*

"Anything?" King said, purring.

Blood nodded.

*"Okay, before I can move forward with you, I have to
take out the trash. I want revenge on those who fucked
over the King. I want Solomon, Santana, and Josephine
found and brought to me ASAP. I want them all to suffer,*

*and to make things fun, let's make it a family affair.
Find Tyler and bring Solomon's family along for the
ride, as well."*

Blood's eyes widened. Damn, she's nuts, *he thought.
But he put the thoughts aside, knowing he'd come too far
to lose her now. He smiled.* "Done."

*"Also, call PJ in his new location in Las Vegas. I have a
little something he's been wanting for a while."*

"Done." Blood nodded. "Second gift?"

"I want my palace back!"

Both Blood and the Santiagos were in utter shock by
her request. They thought she was nuts, especially since
everyone thought she was dead.

*"King, I don't think that's wise. With the building being
condemned, the escorts are all over the island. And
Desiree, with that tell-all book . . . It's too risky to go
back home right now," he said.*

*"Blood," King touched his face, "you must forget I'm a
savage. And Costa Rica is always going to be my home.
I don't want to build another empire. But I can make
the Palace into another business like a fancy hotel and
a home for us as well. Come on, baby, please." She gave
him the puppy dog eyes.*

He couldn't resist them. "Okay. For our future business and our home."

King smiled. "Okay. Yes, I will be your wife then."

Blood put on the biggest Kool-Aid smile and slid the
ring on her finger. Mrs. Blake Fernandez, *he thought as
he kissed her hand. The Santiagos clapped. Zeus got up
and patted Blood's shoulders.*

"Congrats, man."

Blood was on cloud nine. He was the happiest man in
the world. But for King to love him back, he had to lay
down some laws.

"And, King, once I'm your husband, and I give you the presents you want, I want you to promise me something."

King looked at the ring, admiring it. "What's that?"

"Firstly, I want you to be mine and mine alone. No more sex partners and secret lovers. I want your mind, body, and soul—all for me."

King kept a straight face, but on the inside, thought he was out of his mind. She didn't want dick all the time and needed some fish every once in a while. She smiled and nodded. "Okay."

"Secondly, no more drinking blood. It's just nasty, and you don't know what folks have these days. And lastly, I want to take care of you. Us. I want you to step down from being the boss bitch and be my wife. I want to take care of you and be your Superman. Let me be that for you."

King smiled, but at the same time, wanted to slap the shit out of Blood with a hammer. But until she could come up with a good plan to get out of this shit, she was going to play the good wifey.

"Done, Blood."

"Oh, one more request. It's Blake, not Blood."

King chuckled. "Okay, Blo—I mean, Blake."

He stood, and they hugged each other. "I love you, Mrs. Blake Fernandez."

"I love you too, Blakey." She licked the side of his neck, then lay her head against his chest.

Blake giggled, but on the inside, he was thinking to himself that he finally got the woman of his dreams. He knew that her time in prison would change and humble her real fast. And now she had no one to turn to but him.

If only Blood saw the scowl on King's face. She'd already worked out a plan in her head. It was only a *matter of time before she gave Blake's ass something he could really feel.*

Smiling, she faced him, thinking of all her bloody dreams coming true. But until then, King was going to play the role of the good wife.

Epilogue

Swag . . .

Swag woke after weeks of being in a coma. He thought he was in the next life, which, in his case, was hell. The last thing he remembered was being in Africa in the sweatbox tied up. Then the day King popped up after thinking she was dead. He tried to look around but realized he only could see out of one eye. He felt the eye that wasn't working and realized an eye patch was on it.

Damn, he thought, remembering one of King's goon's cut his eye out.

He breathed heavily, thinking of all the shit he'd been through. A beeping noise was driving him crazy. He looked around with his eye and realized he was in a white, brightly lit room. Monitors were everywhere, so he realized he could be in a hospital.

"About time you came back to the Land of the Living," said a polite male voice.

Swag turned his head around and saw Bruno Bello standing there with a big smile on his face.

"Where am I?" asked Swag.

"All you need to know is I have you in a secret location with the best doctors, nurses, and therapists looking out for you."

Swag's eye widened. "How—"

"Well, my crazy-ass child sent you special delivery in a wooden crate to my house, along with some dead chick with her throat cut." He walked back and forth, looking at Swag's bandaged up broken legs. "Thank God, my wife and kids opened that shit. Then I took care of you."

Swag looked at Bruno, remembering the dead woman was Zaria. "Zaria? What happened to her body?"

"Don't worry about her anymore. We sent her corpse to her family," said Bruno going to Swag's nightstand to get a mirror. "You need to worry about yourself." He showed Swag his reflection. Both of his arms were broken.

Swag looked disgusted at himself. Not only did he lose his eye, but also King's boys did a number on his face. He had black marks, bruises, and stab wounds. And the biggie was that he was missing some teeth too. Swag closed his eyes with tears coming down. "Take the mirror away. Take it away."

Bruno put the mirror down.

Swag cried, realizing he was no longer the pretty boy. Then his mind went back to the warehouse, remembering what Blood said to him after one of King's goons finished beating and breaking bones in his body. *"King did this to you!"*

Swag also thought about Tyler's death, Josie's screams, and his boys. "Josie! Josie! Where is Josie? Where's Li'l Swag and Namond?"

"Who the hell is Josie, Li'l Swag, and Namond?" asked Bruno, folding his arms and not giving a shit.

"That's my girl and my sons. PJ Hernandez took her, and some people named Santiago took my boys. I need to get them all back."

"My friend, first off, you're a cripple now. And like I said before, you need to worry about yourself."

Swag continued to cry, remembering the promise that Bruno made to him back in Brazil. "What about my $500K and erasing my criminal charges here?"

Bruno raised his eyebrow, surprised that Swag remembered that. But he knew if it's one thing that eggplants will remember, it's money. He chuckled. "Okay, as I promised, I cleared your criminal charges back in the States. You're no longer a convicted felon."

That put a smile on Swag's face.

"But that 500 grand, it's spent on this remote location and these folks helping you. So, my debt is paid. Once you get back on your feet, I wish you luck in whatever you're going to do."

Then Bruno walked away.

Swag was disgusted with his life right now, but he focused on getting better and finding Josie and his sons. His primary focus was to get revenge on King's evil ass.

Josie . . .

Josie was living in a big mansion in Beverly Hills, California. She was now the main girl/personal sex slave to Paco "PJ" Hernandez Sr. since she cost him a lot of money. She was able to shop and was driven around, but PJ's bodyguards guarded her constantly.

Her first night at her new home, she tried to escape, not knowing where she was going. She went to a police officer on his beat nearby to get help, only to have him take her right back to the mansion. On her return, PJ didn't beat her. He just punched her in her stomach once, drugged her with more heroin, and raped her to the point where her walls bled.

When alone in the mansion, she continued to dance, thinking about Swag, hoping he was okay. Occasionally, she looked out the window and gave up hope for freedom and living her dreams. One day, she got very sick . . . only to find out she was now pregnant with PJ's child, which made her feel so damaged.

King and Blood . . .

Back in Costa Rica, King, now a married woman, went by a new name, King Fernandez. They returned to the

Palace in San José, buying it and making it a legit high-class hotel that King operated. And she went almost a year playing the good wife in the background. Blake handled the business of the Leopard Clit. He loved the fact that he could be the man of the relationship and that he had gotten King, or should he say, King as his girl. Sometimes he even laughed at the thought that he set her up to get her, but that was something he was going to take to his grave.

Even though King played wifey, that didn't stop her from having her twisted way of fun. For example, she had Santana tied in the closet and pimped him out to dirty old men for pennies and nickels, knowing Santana stole $5 million from her. After mocking her brother for his downfall, she told him, "Only $4,999,900 to go." Or tell him, "Hope you repay my money before Ivy dies." She laughed at him.

But now it was time to fry bigger fish . . . and that was Blake for what happened.

For the last few days, Blake was on a business trip, which left King to having some more fun of her own. She was so tired of Blake's dick inside of her. She needed her assorted variety of men and women—and the perfect way to get back at Blake.

Once Blake got back in town, Cleo texted her to let her know he had returned. King got everything ready for her husband.

Blake came to the hotel, went to the elevator, and took it up to King's and his penthouse on the top floor. Once there, he went to their suite and opened the bedroom door. He came in and saw King in a bra and thong sitting on the bed, looking like the king she was.

Blake paused when he saw a half-naked man get out of his bed. King knew shit was going to really hit the fan. She lived for moments like this.

Blake was so heated that he was sweating bullets. "Hold on! What the hell is this? Another one again?" He knew that when he went out of town, she had her lovers but never addressed it.

King smiled and didn't say a word.

"What the fuck is wrong with you? You made me a promise! I was going to be your one and only!"

King laughed and stood up. "First off, I didn't promise you shit. *I'm* a king, and *I* do whatever the hell *I* want."

Blake was furious. "You ungrateful bitch." He felt stupid for getting her out of prison. He should've known King was never going to change from being the hard-hearted bitch she was. "I should've left your ass in that prison to rot!"

"You should have, especially since *you* were the one who set me up!"

Blake tried to play it cool. "What are you talking about?"

"Oh, don't play stupid with me. Don't think I don't know about your little meetings with the police chief, my father, and the president of Costa Rica. And especially the meeting with Santana and Tyler at the gay club. Are you that stupid to think I didn't have my guys spying for me in the clubs? Also, I know you talked to the police in St. Louis about the missing boys. And the list goes on." King waved for the half-naked man who had all the evidence in his hands. He went over to Blake and gave the evidence to him.

Blake looked at all the photos of him in St. Louis, at the gay club, and the hotel meetings. "You bitch!" He threw the pictures down. "How?"

"Like I said, I have spies everywhere."

Blake was outdone. "So, now what? Kill me?"

"Of course."

Blake turned into a bloodthirsty animal and tried to ram King, but someone suddenly shot him in his chest. He stopped, looking down at his bloody chest, feeling his life quickly ebbing away from him. He looked back at King. "Why? I had to stop you. You were getting out of control. And—"

King strutted over to him, and to shut him up, she sliced his throat with her switchblade.

Blood grabbed his neck and looked at her with wide eyes. "Shut up! I don't take orders from no one. This kingdom is mine, *not* yours. This is *my* throne." With that, she licked his blood off the blade.

"Bit . . . ch," Blake said his final words as he fell to the floor and was no longer a part of the living. King looked at Cleo, who was the one who shot Blood in his chest.

"Will there being anything else, Ms. King?" Cleo asked.

King loved a good kill, and she wanted more. "Yes, have one of my spies go to Miami Beach and kill that whore of a mother of mine. I'm so tired of looking at Santana's ass."

Cleo nodded. "Done."

"Now, excuse me. I'm about to take a shower before I plan my flight to see the Santiagos in their new location in Luxembourg, according to Blood's notes. I need some alone time with them."

"As you wish, Ms. King."

Cleo left. The half-naked man started to leave the room, but King shouted at him, "Where are you going?"

He halted his steps, not knowing what she was going to do to him.

"After all this, I need some dick in my life, so come here."

The man's shaft was as hard as a rock. Despite the bloody corpse in the room, he wanted to feel some King. She sat back on the bed with her legs wide open like Sharon Stone in *Basic Instinct*. She was ready for the man to eat. As he ate her kitty-kat, King Kia Costello closed her eyes and thought about her new life. She was still hardhearted, and one day, she was going to show the world why it's better to be feared than loved.